Praise ~~for the novels~~
of the Elemental Masters:

"Lackey's fantastical world of Elementals, plus her delightful Nan and Sarah, create an amusing contrast for Arthur Conan Doyle's Sherlock Holmes and John Watson.... The mix of humor, history, fantasy and mystery is balanced in a way that any reader could pick up the book and thoroughly enjoy it from beginning to end." —RT Reviews

"This is Lackey at her best, mixing whimsy and magic with a fast-paced plot." —*Publishers Weekly*

"Richly detailed historical backgrounds add flavor and richness to an already strong series that belongs in most fantasy collections. Highly recommended."
—*Library Journal* (starred)

"Fans of light fantasy will be thrilled by Lackey's clever fairy-tale adventure." —*Booklist*

"I find Ms. Lackey's Elemental Masters series a true frolic into fantasy." —Fantasy Book Spot

"The [Elemental Masters] novels are beautiful, romantic adult fairy tales. Master magician Mercedes Lackey writes a charming fantasy." —Worlds of Wonder

"This version of Victorian London is fascinating and magical, in both senses of the word. I hope we have plenty of return visits to look forward to!" —Reading Reality

"All in fine fairy-tale tradition ... with some nice historical detail, and just a hint of romance to help lighten things."
—*Locus*

THE SILVER BULLETS OF ANNIE OAKLEY

The Elemental Masters,
Book Sixteen

Mercedes Lackey

DAW

1

THE broom felt as if it was made of iron, not wood and straw. Annie was tired, mortal tired. Then again, she was always tired. There was always too much work to be done in a day and not enough hours to finish it. So it wasn't surprising that the broom she wielded chattered a bit on the puncheon floor—and the uneven surface of the split logs didn't help.

"*Small* strokes with the broom, you lazy little tramp! You're sending dirt everywhere!" The woman at the stove turned and glared, her hand hovering over the stout cane switch she always had at her side, tied to her apron string. Annie thought of her as "She-Wolf," regardless of her real name, because she was as cruel and vicious as a rabid wolf. So was her husband "He-Wolf," though his cruelty manifested itself in other ways than just the beatings Annie was accustomed to get from his spouse. Hard words, punishments like being deprived of meals, being sent into the cold, dark root cellar for an hour among the black beetles, and long lectures on her inadequacies, while he watched her with a gleam in his eyes that made her shiver, though she didn't know why.

Annie Moses winced and ducked her head, murmuring "Yes'm," and tried to make the strokes of the broom smaller. It was hard, though, because she was small for her age, the broom was taller than she was at a mere ten years old, and she was already exhausted from an entire day of tending the baby, cleaning, helping to prepare food, chopping wood, and pumping water. Pumping water outside in the winter cold was brutal, and her red hands and feet were covered in aching chilblains. By her reckoning, Annie did most of the work in this household; all the She-Wolf ever did was stir a pot now and again, rock and feed the baby, and beat Annie.

And the moment she turned her back on her employer, she heard the quick steps on the wood floor, and braced herself for the blow of the switch. Inevitable and unavoidable, the blows came, raining down on her back and shoulders until she dropped to her knees. She was holding her breath to keep from sobbing, as She-Wolf scolded her for being impertinent.

The She-Wolf yanked the broom out of her hands and flung a tiny whisk broom and dustpan at her head. The dustpan caught her in the cheek hard enough that she knew there would be a bruise and maybe a cut, the pain bringing more tears to her eyes. "There!" the woman spat. "*Now* finish the sweeping!"

On hands and knees, shivering with cold in the thin calico dress and apron that were all she had to wear, Annie went back to sweeping the kitchen floor with the whisk broom. Every time she gathered a dustpan full, she got to her feet and carefully emptied it into the pail she'd be expected to take outside when *it* was full. Her hands and feet were numb with cold, but she wouldn't be allowed near the stove until after He-Wolf and She-Wolf went to bed, and by then it would have been banked for the night and barely warm.

All the time she swept, the She-Wolf kept up a running commentary about how useless she was, how when they had hired her, she was supposed to be able to cook, pump water, and tend the baby (just now, thankfully, asleep in his cradle) like a good strong woman, how she was useless at all these things, and how she should be thanking her lucky stars that the She-Wolf was keeping her on despite how she was nothing but a drag on the household and not worth the money it took to keep her fed.

She'd have broken down in tears if she hadn't been so used to it by now.

It was an old song, one Annie knew the words to by heart. And most of it was a lie.

She'd been "bound out" to the Wolves on the promise of fifty cents a week for a *little light* housekeeping and tending the baby. Her widowed Mama couldn't afford to keep all her children, and at ten, Annie was the most likely to get any kind of employment, so she'd been sent to the Darke County Infirmary—which was the official name of the county poorhouse—and from there she'd been bound out as the Wolves' servant with her Mama's consent. And Annie herself had thought it a fine plan; she knew how much of a difference that fifty cents a week would make to the little household, and it made her proud and happy to be able to help. And there had been the promise of school, too; the Wolves had pledged to the people in charge of the Infirmary, Mr. and Mrs. Edington, that there was a school within easy walking distance, and she'd be going every day. Since there was no school near the Moses home, that had seemed like a dream about to come true.

She'd thought she was prepared for the work. She wasn't afraid of hard work, after all. She'd done more than enough of the housework at home to know she could do a lot of things, and do them well, and she'd helped tend Baby Hulda, so she knew she was competent with an infant. What's more, she knew she could take up a rifle or snares and easily add to the Wolves' larder with her uncanny hunting skills—most of the Moses' meat came straight from her hunting efforts. And she'd have been happy if she'd been treated fairly. She could easily understand how a new mother, perhaps weakened by the birth of her first child, would need some help, and if there were no relatives nearby to lend a girl, obviously they'd have to hire someone. Annie's own mother was often paid to come be a midwife, and afterward to cook and clean for a few days while the new mother recovered.

But Annie was effectively doing *all* the chorework, a great deal of the housework, most of the baby-tending, almost all of the water-pumping and wood-chopping, and a goodly share of the cooking. She was supposed to be going to school during the day, not slaving from dawn to dusk.

As for the She-Wolf taking an adult woman's share of the work, well, mostly the She-Wolf sat in her rocking chair by the stove and glared at her, or retired to the bedroom to nap.

When this all began, she used to cry herself to sleep every night, wake up still crying, and have to hide her tears during the day. Now, all she felt was numb, and a dull, resigned fear. She was too tired for anything else.

She'd written to her mother several times, asking when she would be able to come home again, and pointing out that between her trapping and shooting she was probably able to supply more than enough meat to make up for that lost fifty cents a week, but what had come back had been short replies, not even enough to cover one side of a very small piece of paper, admonishing her that she was to be grateful for what the Wolves were doing for her, that she was to do everything exactly as the She-Wolf told her to do it, and not complain. All these "letters" sounded strangely alike, and none of them sounded like Mama. At least not to Annie.

As for the promise of school, it had been a lie from beginning to end. The school was so far away it took most of the morning to walk there, and most of the afternoon to walk back, and that was in good weather. And of course He-Wolf was not in the least interested in driving her over in the cart. Now that it was winter, it was impossible, so she hadn't been more than a handful of days in the autumn before the Wolves started piling work on her. It had begun to dawn on her that the Wolves lied a lot. Were they lying about those letters being from her mother? Had they written those replies themselves?

Had they even sent on the letters *she* had written?

The chores she got set were often more difficult than they needed to be, and wouldn't have been nearly so bad if the She-Wolf had just lent a hand. It wasn't just that she was only ten, it was that she was small for her age—probably because for most of her life she'd never really gotten enough food. Things in the Moses household had gone plummeting downhill with the death of her father, and had never really recovered. Back home, food was scant, a lot of it came from the children foraging and Annie hunting, and her mother was out working as often as she could get jobs. Wood was free for the chopping, thanks be to God, but everything else cost money the Moses family just didn't have.

But as hard as life had been back home, things were worse here. She got up at four o'clock in the morning, made breakfast, milked the cows, fed the calves and the pigs, pumped water for the cattle, fed the chickens, cleaned, rocked the baby to sleep, weeded the garden when it wasn't winter, picked wild berries in summer, made supper after digging the potatoes and vegetables or getting them from the root cellar in winter—and then was expected to go hunting and trapping if there was any daylight left. And if there wasn't, of course, she was expected to do other chores, like washing and mending clothing.

Finally the floor was cleaned to the She-Wolf's satisfaction. But there was no respite. A basket full of stockings was thrust into her arms with a grunt. "Put your lazy hands to work mending," the She-Wolf ordered. Well, at least she would be able to sit down while darning the stockings. She moved as near to the stove as she dared and began.

The She-Wolf settled back into her chair by the stove, and smiled; she seemed to take pleasure in making Annie's life as hard as possible, though Annie could not imagine why. Was it her size? How could she help being smaller than the She-Wolf had expected? It was her husband who had chosen Annie, after all. If she didn't like Annie's size, she should blame *him*. It wasn't *Annie's* fault. And it wasn't as if there was anything she could do about her height, or lack of it. So why blame her for not being a strapping, muscular woman, when they *knew* when they talked to the Infirmary that they were only getting a ten-year-old girl, and when the Wolf himself had interviewed her?

But they'd have to pay a big woman more than fifty cents a week, I bet. And that's why they came looking for a girl. But they could've sent me back and asked for another. . . . But maybe they'd known there wasn't anyone but her to be had. Most of the inmates of the Darke County Infirmary were either old people too feeble to tend to themselves, with no kin to tend them, or children younger than she was, either orphans or from families too poor to support them all.

Finally warm, and finally sitting down for the first time since dawn, she found her eyes drifting shut. Several times she caught herself just as she was nodding off, but eventually sleep ambushed her and her eyes drifted shut, the stocking, darning egg, and yarn-threaded needle falling from her hands into the basket in her lap—

For less than a minute.

And then She-Wolf was on her, digging the claws of one hand into Annie's shoulder while she slapped at Annie's face with the other, shrieking like a steamboat whistle the whole time. She-Wolf had beaten her before, but this was different. This was incoherent rage, and as the blows rained down on her, only the pain kept her on her feet. She found herself stumbling toward the front door, and only terror at what She-Wolf might do if she stopped kept her moving. This wasn't a mere slapping, such as the woman did when she was displeased, nor a whipping with the willow-switch. This was a *beating,* and the pain and fear were unbearable.

Step by step, Annie sobbed and apologized and begged forgiveness, all to no avail, as She-Wolf drove her across the room. She-Wolf kept on screaming incoherently, pulling Annie's hair until hanks tore loose, slapping Annie's face so hard her eyes began to swell and her face felt on fire. Behind her the baby howled with what sounded more like startled anger than pain.

She-Wolf snatched the switch from her belt and beat Annie with it until it broke, then retreated only long enough to seize the broomstick to use it on Annie instead. By this point, Annie was past thinking; like a whipped dog, all she had in her head was to try to escape the pain. Then, as they both reached the door, She-Wolf snatched it open and drove Annie out into the dark and snow outside, slamming it behind her as she stumbled and fell to her knees into a small drift beside the door.

Then there was nothing but silence and darkness, except for a single square of yellow light falling on the snow from the window beside the door, which was covered in greased parchment instead of glass, making it impossible to see what was going on inside.

She tried to get up; crawled to the door and pulled herself to her feet to pound on it feebly. "Let me in!" she sobbed. "Please! It were an accident! Let me in!"

More silence was her answer, and she fell against the door, and slid down it until she huddled against the rough wood, openly sobbing, as she had not cried in months. Her hands were so swollen she could scarcely bend her fingers, but the cold gave a very brief respite from the pain—

But not for long. Within a minute or two, she curled in on herself, shivering uncontrollably, as the cold easily penetrated her thin clothing. Her tears froze on her cheeks and her teeth chattered so badly she had to clench her jaw to keep from biting her tongue.

She could not help herself; all she could think about was that this was how her father had died when she was small. Alone, in the cold and the dark—

He had been on his way home with the wagon full of bags of flour made from the grain he'd taken to the mill, when a blizzard had blown up out of nowhere. She remembered it like it was yesterday: how the horse had managed to find its way through the blinding snow sometime after midnight, with her father perched up on the wagon seat with the reins around his neck to keep from dropping them, so still and snow-covered her mother had thought he was already frozen to death. She'd helped her mother get him down and into the house, while her older siblings tended to the poor exhausted horse and got the supplies inside.

He hadn't frozen to death, but the cold had gotten into his lungs, and he had died soon after of pneumonia, never leaving the bed he'd been carried to.

She tried to open her eyes, but the tears on her eyelashes had frozen them shut. Clumsily, with swollen fingers like frozen sausages, she rubbed the ice off, and tried thumping on the door again.

"Please?" she faltered. "Please?" It was all she could manage. And at that moment she realized that the She-Wolf, who had *never* liked her from the moment the woman had set eyes on her, intended her to freeze to death out here.

She sobbed helplessly and shut her eyes again. Despair as black as the She-Wolf's heart settled over her. She was going to die out here, alone, in the cold. Already a strange feeling of warmth was creeping over her, and she thought, from the stories she'd heard, that this was a sign that she was already dying.

But I don't want to die! She clasped her hands together as best she could and tried to pray, but words wouldn't come. Desperately, she managed to force her eyes open, thinking to look up at the stars for some kind of inspiration—

But what she saw was not stars. It was a tiny, faintly glowing woman hovering just inches from her nose, a woman no bigger than a doll, with butterfly wings, as naked as Eve. She stared at the vision, incredulous, and certain in that moment that she must be having fever-dreams, because—well—what was a fairy doing hovering in front of her nose in the middle of Ohio?

The little thing was either supremely unconscious of her immodesty, or supremely indifferent to it. In either case she hovered closer to Annie's face, close enough that Annie felt like her eyes were crossing as she tried to look at the fairy. There was a frown on the tiny face. What could the fairy possibly be frowning about?

She closed her eyes again; this was surely some sort of dying vision. And she didn't want to die, but the She-Wolf most certainly *did* want her dead, or she wouldn't still be out here. And it was too hard to think. Lethargy enveloped her, as did a perverse feeling of warmth that settled over her like a blanket. With a sigh, she surrendered to it, and let her mind drift.

After a while she was warmer and cozier than she had ever been in any bed in her life—except maybe on those balmy summer nights when everything was perfect and it was neither too hot to sleep, nor were the quilts inadequate against chills. She thought she felt something move against her cheek and cracked her right eye open, turning her head slightly to look at herself—but she closed it again, because what she saw was nothing but sheer madness. Her entire exposed body seemed to be enveloped by the glowing, multi-colored wings of dozens of fairies, all of them clinging to her dress with their wings spread out, like the most beautiful quilt in the entire universe. If *one* fairy was madness, what was a congregation of dozens? Impossible.

She kept expecting to see the "dark tunnel with light at the end" or the "open door into Paradise" that people had sometimes described within her hearing when they talked about being near death, but there was nothing. Well—actually, that wasn't true. She wasn't drifting off into "eternal sleep." In fact, she was drowsy, but otherwise awake, and she was deliciously warm. It felt exactly like lying in a sunny meadow on a perfect summer day. And the pain from her bruises was gone. She couldn't even feel the places where the She-Wolf had torn out her hair, nor the cut on her cheek from the thrown dustpan. The only thing keeping her awake, now that she was warm and mostly pain-free, was that she was powerfully hungry. The Wolves fed her about as well as they housed and clothed her, which was to say, not very well. And the She-Wolf watched over every scrap and drop, so the only time she was ever full was if something got burned and she could eat her fill of the burned mess after the She-Wolf salvaged what she could. But that only ever happened when the She-Wolf was doing the cooking; if Annie had allowed something even to overcook, there'd be a beating.

With no warning, she heard heavy footsteps coming up the path to the house, and suddenly the icy winds whipped at her, startling her eyes open.

The fairies had vanished as if they had never been. And He-Wolf came clumping heavily into view. Before she could think of anything to tell him—for surely he would blame her for being out here, and not in there, helping his wife—he spotted her.

He gave an angry growl and reached down to grab her by the shoulder and haul her to her feet, wrenching the door open with his other hand as her shoulder ached with the hard grip of his hand. "What's the meaning of this?"

he shouted, shoving Annie roughly across the threshold so that she stumbled and fell to her hands and knees in the middle of the room. The She-Wolf turned from the soup pot, the wooden spoon raised like a weapon.

"She—" She-Wolf began.

He-Wolf silenced her with a roar. "Shut up, you stupid bitch! *I* say what goes around here! What the *hell* did you think you were doing, shoving her out to freeze like that? She's *not* some damn orphan that nobody cares about! If she dies, *there'll be questions!* People coming around! Maybe even the sheriff!"

"She just fell asleep instead of doing the chores!" She-Wolf countered in a shrill voice just short of a scream.

Evidently He-Wolf didn't think that was justification for putting Annie put into the cold to freeze, since he stamped toward her, fist raised, shouting incoherently. She-Wolf threw the spoon into the soup pot with a splash and prepared to meet him.

Annie scrambled out of the way on hands and knees, hiding in the shadows beside the stove as best she could.

As they screamed in each other's faces and she cringed in the corner, the words became more and more incoherent—and then the impossible happened.

Their faces changed.

Thick hair sprouted from their skin. Noses lengthened, drawing the mouths along with them, until the two no longer had human facial features, but abbreviated muzzles. They were less than half human now—the hands the Wolves waved in the air in pure fury had become elongated paws sporting lethal claws. And it wasn't words they were throwing at each other, it was something bestial, part snarl, part growl, part howl.

Annie shook her head hard, squinching her eyes up tightly, sure that when she opened them again, there would be two humans there, not two monsters. But no; and at the realization that this was *real,* and actually happening, terror paralyzed her. Either the Wolves *were* monsters, or she had gone mad. Either prospect was terrible.

But only one carried with it the implication that she might be torn to pieces at any minute.

Finally, the male monster struck a back-handed blow at his mate, a hit that sent her tumbling across the room to land beside the cradle. The baby, who had been eerily quiet through all of this, whimpered softly.

The She-Wolf grabbed her face with one paw, and Annie was sure that after a blow like that, there must be bones broken. But all she did was stare up at her mate, and snarl—something. Something about He-Wolf claiming "her" for his pack, but the She-Wolf didn't want "her" there. "Her" had to be Annie, but what was the rest of that about?

He-Wolf's face writhed and Annie had to look away, because it sickened her. "Damn right I claim her for my pack, my *bitch*. What's the matter? Afraid she'll challenge you when she grows up? My pack! My rules!"

The She-Wolf's reply was just a snarl that sounded like canvas tearing. But she crouched down, head bowed to the floor in submission, her hair tumbling about her face and the back of her neck exposed.

He-Wolf glanced around the room until he spotted Annie. Unable to move, she shook in every limb as he grabbed her shoulder again and hauled her out of her hiding place. He shoved her against the wall, then he smacked his free paw over her stomach as she whimpered like the baby. She wanted to beg him not to hurt her, but she couldn't get the words out.

He looked over his shoulder at his wife. "Be clear about this. I claim her for my pack. She is *mine*."

The She-Wolf lifted her head, her face human again and a trickle of blood dribbling out of the corner of her mouth. "Until someone stronger and smarter than you comes along and takes her!"

Annie expected him to erupt in a rage, but he just threw his head back and laughed.

"Laugh all you want!" his wife cried. "But you haven't brought her *into* the pack, and until you do, she's anyone's for the taking!"

"Little fool, you think you can goad me into trying to change her while she's too young to breed? Do you think I don't *know* that if I did that, she'd be a pup for the rest of her life and useless to me?" He spat at her. "You're as transparent as your sire, and as stupid as your dam. Besides, I don't have to do that to mark her as claimed."

He turned to Annie, his hand still on her stomach, pinning her to the wall. Then he said—

—something. But what?

It was incomprehensible, and not because of his vulpine face. It was words, but she didn't understand any of them. But underneath his hand, her stomach got warm, then hot, then so painful she thought she was being burned up from inside, and she whimpered again, tears rolling down her cheeks. What was happening to her?

Then it felt as if something had struck her in the stomach, knocking the breath out of her for an instant. The heat vanished, he pulled his hand back, and she dropped to her hands and knees on the wooden floor.

"Satisfied now?" he shouted. "I have claimed her for mine own, and there'll be no whelps from her that are not of my get!"

An inarticulate shriek erupted from his mate, as he threw back his head and laughed maniacally.

Annie broke into uncontrollable sobbing.

And woke, still sobbing, in the arms of her husband.

"There now, there now," he was saying, murmuring the words into her hair as he held her trembling body close to his. "Wake up, Annie, it's only a dream."

She got herself under control, gulped back her tears, and whispered, "I'm awake."

"That's my little fairy," Frank replied. "You want I should light a candle?"

She shook her head, knowing he could feel the motion.

She didn't need a candle, not as she had in the years before she'd met him. All she needed was him. That was enough.

Slowly she took stock of her surroundings. The rosemary that the hotel here in Strasburg used to scent the sheets reminded her that she was, in fact, in Germany, in Strasburg, and not ten years old and back in Ohio, nor in the Wild West Show railcar fitted up as an apartment, nor in some other bed in some other city. But her heart raced, and she trembled in every limb, and she focused as hard as she could on her husband's soothing words, as well as his comforting arms. This was by far not the first time she'd had this nightmare, and probably it would not be the last, and Frank always brought her through.

She had told him . . . *almost* everything about that nightmarish night. Not quite everything. Not about the fairies, nor how both Wolves had warped into monsters, nor He-Wolf's strange words. He would have told her those were only nightmare illusions and not her real memory. And to tell the truth, more than half the time she was sure he was right. You could dream things so real you were sure they had happened, only to find that in fact your mind had made them up in the night.

"Talk on, Annie," Frank prodded her. "Let's get it out and over with. That cad Wolf sent you to bed after the She-Wolf near froze you to death. That night you determined—"

She pulled herself closer to him, and let him guide her through the familiar paths that always brought her through the lingering fear and to the other side. "I determined I was going to run away that spring. And the She-Wolf stopped beating me as much; she only did it when she thought *he* wouldn't notice."

"And what happened that spring?"

"They were a-welcoming a new bride and her husband . . ."

Was he gonna bring them into his pack? Was that why they were there? She wrenched her mind away from that train of thought; it was crazy, and she did herself no good speculating on craziness.

". . . and they took the horse and cart and the baby to show the guests around their property and the rest of the town, and left me alone." It had been the first time she'd been left alone since she'd arrived! She still didn't know *why* they had left her by herself, though both the Wolves had seemed charmed, even enchanted by the handsome newlyweds. Maybe they figured that after so many months of beatings, Annie was sufficiently cowed to be left alone. Maybe they were just distracted. "The She-Wolf left me with a big old list of chores, but I saw my chance, and I took it. I walked all the way to the train station, and I got on a train for Greeneville."

She heard, as well as felt, Frank's chuckle, a rumble in his chest. "Bold as brass without a ticket!" he replied.

"It was a long way to Greeneville, and I couldn't hardly walk it," she pointed out. "But when I got aboard, there was a nice old man what noticed me get on, and he nodded at me friendly-like and patted the seat beside him, and . . . I just trusted him, I don't know why." To this day she still didn't know. It was as if he had been surrounded by a kind of halo, an aura, as if he was a safe haven. "He asked me what I was doing alone on the train, and I told him the truth." The words had just poured out of her, although she had spoken them in a near-whisper. Again, she did not know why. "And he just sat there and listened; he frowned, but not like he didn't believe me. And when I finished, that was when the conductor came up and asked for my ticket, and scowled at me like he was sure I didn't have one."

"And then what?"

"Then that man said, 'I'll take care of this, good man.' And he looked back down at me and asked, 'It's Greeneville, isn't it?' And I said yes, but I was pretty surprised, since I'd only said the town once, and that meant he really had been listening. 'One ticket to Greeneville for the lady, if you please. And send the lady with the sandwich basket to us as well,' he said. And he paid for my ticket right there, then he got me some food to eat and made sure I et it all, and then when we got to Greeneville he made sure I was safe on the station platform, and I told him I knew the way from there, because I did, and he stood on the little stair between the cars and waved goodbye until the train was out of sight. And then I walked home, but Mama wasn't there, so I went to the Shaws, who were neighbors. Mama had to send me back to the Infirmary, but the Edingtons were good folks, and when the Wolf turned up again, Mr. Edington gave him a piece of his mind and threatened to thrash him, and he went away and I never heard of them again."

"And the name of the man that helped you?" Frank prompted. He knew, of course. She'd told him the story twenty times or more. But the name was a talisman; when she spoke it, it meant *safe harbor,* somehow.

She smiled. "Oakley," she said, and felt all of the fear and remembered pain fall away, feeling the last of the nightmare fall away into the darkness. And then she relaxed into Frank's arms and fell asleep, this time to dream of nothing at all.

2

THE rosemary scent reminded Annie of where she was, even before she was quite awake. *Das Edel Gasthaus.* Not one of the multistory tower hotels in the more modern part of the city, but a much humbler establishment. It was tucked into one of the older sections of Strasburg, and was a place that had been in the business of tending to travelers longer than the United States had been a country. Surrounded by other buildings, which had been converted into shops and offices, with rooming houses within easy walking distance, it still served its original purpose as a center of local hospitality. This was in part because it supplied hungry bachelor officemen and shop-girls with meals they did not get with their rooms, and, as a guesthouse, provided rooms to be rented for any visitors they might have. The establishment might not have a modern bathroom, nor electricity, nor even gas, but then, there were plenty of places Frank and Annie had lived or stayed in back home that didn't have those amenities either. And it more than made up for those deficiencies with the comfort of feather beds, feather pillows, and feather comforters, servants who cheerfully met even Annie's high standards of cleanliness, and an affable host who was extremely happy to have two of the stars of the Wild West spending the winter on his premises.

And while it wasn't a first-class hotel like they'd lived in during the first overseas tour of the Wild West to England, nor her special railcar back home, it wasn't a tent either. And if she hadn't been the show star, they *could* be sleeping in their tent, pitched under the greater canvas of the arena ring. That was where the Indians and a lot of the general cowboys were. Truth to be told, it was her own frugality that had them here instead of more modern lodging. The Wild West hadn't gone home when winter came on this jaunt to the Old World; Buffalo Bill had decreed they'd make winter quarters here in Germany and continue on as soon as the weather was good enough to perform. No one had objected, remembering the rough winter crossing they'd had when they went back home after the first tour. It proved to be a pretty good decision for another reason—it was December, and the people of Strasburg were in a festive enough mood and hardened to the cold enough that the Wild West was able to put on a twice-weekly, abbreviated show, which was paying for all that grub the company chowed down on three times a day. The cowboys weren't complaining; normally when the show went into winter quarters, they were expected to find their own lodging in town, and pay for their own grub, too. Only the few animal hands that needed to stay on got winter pay; they were there to tend the horses, the buffalo, the cattle, and the odds and ends like Jerry the Moose. As for the Indians, camping in their teepees under the shelter of the big canvas was better than camping on the open plains. And since, for a very modest fee, the Germans were allowed during daylight hours to come tour the Indian and cowboy camps and gawk at the animals and the troupe practicing, things worked out well for everyone.

If this wasn't a big, modern, first-class hotel, that didn't mean it was a ramshackle boarding house either. Stout walls framed by big wooden beams and plastered inside and outside kept the weather well at bay. If the furnishings looked as if they might have served knights of old— well, it meant they were well built, and the bed was big enough to have held the Butlers and half of Annie's family. Their host was extremely anxious about their comfort, sending a servant up to poke up and feed the fire in the porcelain stove before they were awake, and making sure the water in the drinking pitcher and washing pitcher was clean, and there was a kettle full of more wash water warming on the stove itself. The rosemary-scented sheets were supplemented by the featherbed beneath them and the down comforter over them, as well as woolen blankets, which kept them more than cozy even when the fire in the stove was banked. The stove was a beautiful thing, about the size of a cast-iron pot-belly stove at home, but square, and covered in beautiful green tiles, with an isinglass door so you could see the fire burning.

She opened her eyes to see that Frank had already gotten dressed, and was pulling his suspenders over his shoulders with his back to her. It was just like him, to let her sleep in after a bad night. How many men would do that? Not many, by her reckoning; likely most men would have ignored her nightmares last night, and expected her to be up to lay out their clothing for them, and set up the washbasin and all their shaving equipment before they got out of this warm and exceedingly comfortable bed. Her eyes stung a little as she thanked God once again for sending her this good man, who adored her as much as she loved him. For a moment, her chest went tight and she found it hard to breathe, her emotion was so intense.

"Morning," she said, as he began to turn around.

"Mornin', angel. I reckoned I'd let you sleep. Better?" he asked. She nodded. No need to ask, "Better from what?"

"Figured I'd better let you wake on your own. The Colonel sent up his card, but I reckoned he can wait. He is down in the dining room waiting for us."

By "the Colonel," Frank meant, of course, Colonel William "Buffalo Bill" Cody; in the Wild West Show, there was only one "Colonel."

That got her out of bed in a hurry, and she rushed into her clothing after a fast wash, choosing one of her ordinary gowns rather than anything that would identify her as a member of the Wild West—because there weren't that many women in the show, and anyone who saw her done up like a Western girl would probably guess who she was, and she wanted breakfast without being gawked at. "I wonder what he wants?"

Frank shook his head, and shrugged on his coat. "Just sent up his card. Nothing on the back." He offered her his arm, and she took it, reflecting for the millionth time on how much she adored this man. And how many men would put up with playing second fiddle to a show star like she was? *Only the one, that I know of.*

They went down the back stair nearest their room, which took them directly into the dining room of the *Gasthaus.*

The Colonel was indeed waiting for them in the dining room, his long blond hair marking him, even from the rear, as a rare bird among the earnest, short-cropped German men of business and clerks who hurried here for their breakfasts before going on to their offices. The dining room was more crowded than usual, and as the sober fellows munching away on their bread and cold meats and cheese cast covert glances at Buffalo Bill, she had a shrewd guess why. The show was wildly popular in Germany and she had no idea what the reason was for such a torrent of enthusiasm. It seemed the Germans were quite mad for cowboys and especially Indians, and most likely these fellows were not able to get time off to see the abbreviated shows, had got wind of the fact that

Annie and Frank were staying here, and hoped to catch a glimpse of them.

Well, it was clear by the way that their eyes slid over the couple that they did not recognize short-haired Frank nor (especially!) demurely clad Annie for who they were, but Buffalo Bill positively reveled in attention. As far as she was aware, he literally did not possess an article of clothing that did not have some "Western" aspect to it, be it beading, fringes, bolo ties, or the cut of the garments, and he did love to peacock about in them. So he sat in the middle of the busy dining room, nursing what looked like a good cup of coffee, and probably soaking in all the covert glances. With just a touch of exasperation, she found herself wondering how many frauleins of negotiable virtue he had on a string here in Strasburg. *Probably more than I imagine.*

Then she dismissed those thoughts as he turned slightly, caught sight of them, and beckoned them to join him.

Their host had already spotted them, and before they took their seats at the table with Buffalo Bill, one of his serving girls was hurrying toward them with big plates of farmers' rolls, sliced ham, a white cheese she had learned was called "Gouda," hard-boiled eggs, butter, marmalade, and cups of coffee. This, evidently, was a standard German breakfast, and although it wasn't much like the beans, eggs, and bacon the show cooks served up, it was delicious and Annie looked forward to it. The serving girl reached them before the Colonel could say anything and efficiently got them served and whisked herself out of the way before Bill could attempt a flirtation. The Colonel looked disappointed; Annie hid a smile. That girl, she happened to know, was the host's young cousin, and Buffalo Bill would have more luck wrestling Jerry the Moose to the ground with one hand than getting past the fearsome dragon their host could be when it came to supervising his female kin here at the *Gasthaus*.

With Bill's attention back on them, Annie tried to read his intentions from his expression as she silently layered ham and cheese on her warm buttered roll and took a sip of coffee. *He wouldn't have come this far out of his way for anything trivial.* The spot where the Wild West Show and camp was laid out was about halfway between this part of town and the part of Strasburg where the best modern hotels were. And it wasn't to "see how they were getting on," either. They'd all been rehearsing together yesterday; he already knew they were getting on just fine in their own version of winter quarters.

He made small talk with Frank while she ate, but when she caught him glancing at her, he quickly looked away. That told her generally what this must be about. *He wants to do something, probably about the show and our act, and he thinks I'm not going to like it.*

"Spit it out, Colonel," Frank said with a smile. "And you might as well help yourself to the ham you've been eyeing on my plate."

Buffalo Bill didn't hesitate when it came to taking half a roll and some ham, but he did when it came to just coming out with what had brought him here. He was clearly stalling for time, eating slowly rather than stuffing the whole thing in his mouth like he did when eating with his show folks. But finally the roll and another from Annie's plate were eaten and there were no more excuses. He took a gulp of coffee, cleared his throat, and began. Awkwardly.

"You know I've added the Rough Riders of the World to the show," he began.

Annie tried not to be impatient. This was scarcely news.

"I got a chance to pick up an act that fits with that part of the show," he continued. "I'm gonna audition the act this morning. I'd like Annie to pass her eye over this act."

Annie jumped to the immediate and logical conclusion, given Bill's reticence in saying what the act was, the fact that he wanted Annie to watch, and the fact that he had very carefully referred to "the act" and "it" without mentioning a performer.

She felt a very slow burn of anger building in her. She was about to snap her answer, when Frank obviously came to the same conclusion she had, and began to speak. "You mean, you're lookin' at another female sharpshooter," he stated.

"No one can replace Annie!" Bill blurted, and turned to her. "Now, missy, you know I've got no intentions of— of trying to upstage you. But from what I've heard, this act is good, and she *does* fit with the Rough Riders."

Annie stewed. *She* had not forgotten when Bill had brought in another female sharpshooter for the first tour—Lillian Smith, who had done everything she could to upstage and challenge Annie at every turn. Smith was everything Annie was not—a braggart, a boaster, rude and crude, a flashy dresser who delighted in wearing short skirts of showy material, and who flirted with every male in the show, even Frank! She took every opportunity presented to her to irritate Annie. It had taken every bit of Annie's self-control to keep her composure as long as Smith was with the show. Why, it had been Smith who started the story that Annie was so penny-pinching that she lived on the free lemonade Bill provided his performers.

"How *is* 'Princess Wenona'?" she asked between gritted teeth. Failing at upstaging Annie, when they'd gotten back home, Smith had either quit or been fired— Annie wasn't quite sure which—and had assumed the phony persona of an "Indian Princess," calling herself "Princess Wenona, the Sioux Huntress" as she toured with Pawnee Bill's rival show.

"Don't know. Don't care," Bill said, and pulled at his mustache, looking at her pleadingly. "Missy, I learnt my lesson. That's why I want you to look this gal over. I want to know if she's cheatin', and I want to be sure she ain't gonna be another Lillian Smith. She's only stayin' with us for this tour; when we go home, she stays here. But I ain't a-gonna hire her unless I get your say-so."

"Why another sharpshooter?" Annie asked, a bit more sharply than she had intended.

"Cause the little gal's German. Belongs to some bunch called the *Bruderschaft von Jaegermeistern,* whatever that means." Annie had gotten enough of an ear for the language to know the poor Colonel had mangled the name terribly, but she didn't say anything. And he didn't explain what it meant, if he even knew, so it didn't actually matter much. "She says she does some tricks you *don't,* so it'll be a good change-up, and it'll be good publicity for the show to have her along. What do you say?"

She wanted to retort that she didn't want to have this woman "along" in any capacity—

But that would look mean-spirited, and it certainly wasn't Christian. She could almost hear her Mama saying, "Now Annie, what if she's a good woman, and you're standing between her and an honest job of work?"

And she knew how hard it was for a woman to be taken seriously in a situation like this. Men assumed that all women in shows were wicked (*Well,* said a little voice in the back of her mind, *Lillian was no better than she should have been. . . .*) and that they were only there to show their legs and look pretty. But the Colonel, for all his faults, knew better than to advocate for someone like that, especially after Lillian. So she thinned up her lips, gritted her teeth, and reluctantly agreed to "at least see the act."

Maybe I can catch her cheating, said that bad little voice in her head.

Hush, now, she told it.

But she wasn't going to rush through her breakfast just to please Buffalo Bill's whim. So she took her time, finished up with a satisfying cup of coffee (the Germans made *excellent* coffee, which was more than could be said for the English), and finally rose, signaling the other two that she was ready to go.

They walked as a trio out into a ridiculously beautiful winter's day. Brilliant sun beamed down on a street swept so clean of snow and horse dung that it practically shone. Icicles hung from the eaves of the picturesque black-beamed buildings, which ranged between three and five stories tall, and a frosting of snow coated their roofs. There were evergreen garlands and wreaths everywhere. Of course, this was *nothing* compared to the *Christkindlmarkt* held in the center of the Old City, where everything was hung with decorations, and tempting smells of baked goods, mulled wine, and sputtering sausages filled the air. Stalls filled with every sort of Christmas present one could ask for crowded the square, and Annie was quite glad they were not going in that direction, since the many dazzling temptations were quite enough to overwhelm even *her* legendary frugality. All it took, really, was for her to gaze at the hundreds of toys, the ornament-bedecked trees, and remember all the Christmases of her own childhood when the Moses family was lucky to have something she'd shot for supper and toys were not even dreamed of. That was more than enough to loosen her purse strings, telling herself that it was all right because she was buying presents for her mother and "baby" Hulda, her favorite sister. Already a huge box had begun the long journey to Ohio, stuffed with neat little fur hoods and muffs and matching mittens for both Hulda and her mother, lengths of beautiful woolen fabric, and sundry other delightful things. And there had been a lovely doll in there too, one that Frank had insisted on buying. And he had kindly made no comment at all when Annie had tried every one of the pretty little articles of clothing on the doll "to make sure they fit."

Annie walked between Frank and Bill, dwarfed by the two of them, but utterly eclipsed by Bill, who tipped his wide-brimmed hat and uttered cheerful *"Morgen!"*s to people who gaped at the presence of a cowboy on the street.

They collected a little tail of young boys, all of them curious about where they were going, and likely wondering if this was who they hoped and prayed it could be. From time to time Bill glanced over his shoulder and grinned and winked at them, sending them all into paroxysms of giggles.

Of course, once they reached the edge of the space where the Wild West had set up, the boys *knew* that this was the one and only Buffalo Bill, and the sound of their rejoicing likely warmed Bill's heart even though he couldn't understand a word they said.

There had been a light snow last night and the great tent had a dusting of snow on it. "Tent" was something of a misnomer: the Wild West traveling arena was a compilation of an entire village worth of tents.

The arena itself was a vast rectangle of canvas, with the middle open to the sky—pure logic there, since anything covering the arena itself would soon be riddled with bullet holes and useless, and having the arena covered would have meant the animals, wagons, and performers would have to dodge around a forest of tent poles. People were funneled into the entrance of this structure by canvas walls that featured the big oil-on-canvas paintings of the show's attractions. Hidden behind these canvas barriers was the stable-tent, and along one side were the mess-tents where all the cooking and eating was done. The buffalo were corralled next to that. They had no problem with the German winter; then again, they endured worse on the Plains. Cowboy and Indian camps would normally have been next to that, but instead, some of the seating had been taken down and the camps were under the canvas that normally protected the grandstands at the far end of the arena. At the very rear there was no seating, just a huge painted canvas backdrop. At another venue all these various tents would have been spread out over considerably more distance;

here they huddled around the big arena tent as if for warmth and shelter. And back home in the US, there would have been a midway under canvas as well; the closest thing the show got to a midway here was that the Colonel had invited some of the same people who had stalls in the *Christkindlmarkt* to set up in front of the arena tent as an incentive to make people linger, and perhaps part with their money to take a tour of the camp. And meanwhile, no one would be grumbling that there was nothing to eat and no way to warm up. There was plenty of mulled wine, sausages, and other treats on offer, and a few enterprising toymakers had created buffalo, cow-ponies, and entire stagecoaches on wheels, cast-lead armies of cowboys and Indians, and one stall even had dolls of Indian maidens and cowgirls.

As this was not a show day, there were only a few people milling about the entrance, seeing what they could see for free. As one, Bill and Frank turned and angled toward the cook tent in order to avoid them.

One of the cowboys, Fred Gibbs, lifted up the canvas at the back of the arena-tent to let them inside. "Thet li'l sharpshooter gal's here, a-waitin' for you in the arena, Colonel," he said. "She come early," he added with approval.

Annie schooled her face into an expression of neutrality. Everyone in the show knew how things had gone around Lillian. And certainly Fred did not hold any ill will toward Annie. So—maybe the fact that he seemed to approve of the girl meant she was *not* another Lillian?

Or maybe she's just good at hiding it. After all, she needs to make a good impression to be hired. After that she can show her true colors. Lillian had been antagonistic from the beginning—but then, Lillian had been convinced that she was going to displace Annie because she was younger and thought herself to be prettier, and spent every moment of her time trying to convince everyone else too.

Sure enough, there was a couple waiting in the arena,

in the end where the bandstand was, with a table that had guns laid out on it. For a moment, Annie thought that the man with the woman was one of their own cowboys, until she got closer and realized that she didn't recognize him.

But the woman was a very different proposition altogether.

She was *very* blond, and had extremely long hair, made up into a plait on either side of her head, plaits which had been looped several times over her ears and fastened in place. Above this extraordinary hairdo was a jaunty little peaked cap with a short brim in an odd color of dark green, which had a badge on the right side with a little plume of feathers sticking over the top. She wore a closely fitted coat of the same color that appeared to be wool, with silver buttons and a second badge like the first, worn like a brooch. And she had a divided skirt of the same wool, shortened to just above the ankle, and black riding boots. She was holding a rifle properly: pointed down and broken at the breech so there was no chance of accidentally firing it.

She also was not a "girl." She was certainly older than Annie, middle-aged at least, even though she had the figure of someone much, much younger. It was not so much that she looked "aged" as that she looked experienced. The man with her was likely about her age, though the sun-weathered look of most cowboys made it impossible to guess their real ages once they were past their teens.

The two spotted the trio of Frank, Annie, and Bill and the woman put the gun down on the table before the couple headed in their direction.

The man stuck out his hand as soon as they were in reach. "Cap'n Jackson Cate, at your service."

Annie could not have been more astonished had he spoken in Russian. Accent, demeanor, and all said this was the genuine article, a cowboy from home.

Bill grinned and took the hand. "Colonel William Cody at yours. It seems you're from America."

"We share more than being from America. I was top roper and shootist for a little 'cowboy and Indian' show over here for a piece, afore a no-good German as was supposed to take care of us run off with all our money. But you ain't here to listen to old sad stories. You're here to see what my wife can do. Gentlemen, miss, this here is Frida Cate, my wife, who's top shootist for a local lot called the Brotherhood of the Foresters hereabouts."

"Right pleased to meet you," the woman said, with a sunny smile, as she held out her hand in turn, first to Bill, then to Annie. Annie took her hand, trying not to show how dubious she was about all this. But the woman seemed to pick up on it anyway, and gave her a friendly little wink, before extending her hand to Frank.

"I was not expecting you to palaver in English, ma'am," Bill said, with the admiration he always had for a pretty woman. "Nor to bring your husband along."

"Well, *if* you hire us, Jack is my assistant and can certainly pass as one of those hussars you hired. He is a trick shootist as well, and he and I do a very German horse act." The young woman had a distinct but not unpleasant accent, her voice a musical soprano. "There are other things we can do, but I was under the impression that you wished a distinctly German tone to our act, and such other things are not German as such."

Annie glanced over at the table and saw that among the guns was something that looked like a child's bow mounted on a gunstock. Frida followed her glance, and smiled again. "That is a crossbow. A very old, and very German, weapon. That is for the conclusion of my act."

"Well, speakin' of your act, we're here to see it," Bill declared, and motioned to Annie and Frank to join him at the arena wall.

Frida offered the usual assortment of trick shots, but had some that Annie did not do. She drove a nail into a board with a bullet, for instance—or rather several nails, so that the driven nails formed a star pattern in the otherwise pristine pine plank. She put out a candle flame with a bullet. Jackson hoisted up a bag of billiard balls overhead as a target and she "called her shots" by the color of the ball, disintegrating them one by one while sparing the rest in the bag, ending with the black 8-ball. And she split a bullet on a sword, just as Annie herself could split one on an axe blade.

On the one hand, Annie was full of admiration. On the other . . . *yes, yes, I am jealous. But . . . there is something odd here.* She couldn't get over the notion that Frida was . . . cheating, somehow. Annie couldn't see *how,* but something inside her was saying that there was more going on here than she could see.

Annie stared so hard at Frida's targets that she began to develop a headache. And still she couldn't make out why she thought the German woman was cheating. But the more she stared, the stranger she felt, because that feeling came and went. With some shots, she was certain that there was no way Frida could have made it without help. Then in the next shot, she would be just as certain that Frida had hit the mark honestly.

Then came the conclusion of the act. Jackson brought out—a kite.

"Whoa-up there, son," the Colonel said. "You don't mean to tell me you intend to fly that there thing every show?"

"It'll be fine, Colonel," Jackson said. "Just watch."

He went to the middle of the arena, kite in hand, gave a little run, and suddenly the kite all but leapt out of his hands, as if it was alive and flying without the aid of any wind, heading skyward. The tail of the kite was a string to which bright red bows had been attached. While Jackson held the kite string tight, Frida took up the crossbow, held it to her shoulder, aimed—and shot.

The arrow was a lot easier to track than a bullet. Annie shaded her eyes with both hands and stared as hard as she could. Meanwhile the kite danced and jigged at the end of the string, its tail lashing merrily. An impossible shot, for how could you know where the kite was going to be in the next second?

And in fact, she was certain that the arrow was about to pass through the air well below the kite.

But at the last possible second, the path of the string of the kite's tail intersected that of the arrow. The broad head sliced through the twine.

And for a moment, Annie could have sworn there was a tiny, winged creature no bigger than a crow guiding the string so that the arrowhead sliced it.

And one of the red bows came fluttering down to land in the arena, as the arrow arced immediately back down and buried itself in the arena sand.

That's not possible! The creature was gone, if it had been there at all. But that had been an impossible shot.

A shot that Frida repeated five more times, as cool and calm as you please, while Annie watched incredulously as little winged creatures flashed in and out of existence, keeping the kite aloft, and grabbing the kite tail and making sure the arrow cut it just above the bow.

Until the last bow fluttered down to the ground, and the kite, now without any tail to stabilize it, abandoned by the fairies, spiraled down after it.

Jackson ran down into the arena to collect kite, bows, and arrows, as Frida turned toward the Colonel with a little smile on her face. "So?" she asked, tilting her head to one side. "How do you like my act?"

The Colonel had taken his hat off by this time, and Frank was staring with his jaw slack. Annie felt a surge of jealousy and one of slow-burning anger at the cheat— but also of uncertainty. Because surely she could not have seen what she *thought* she had seen—the fairies that had appeared that night so long ago when She-Wolf had cast her out into the dark. The fairies that had kept her warm and safe until He-Wolf returned—but that she had never seen again.

Until now.

When they were helping that German woman cheat.

"Well, Miz Cate, I'd say I reckon to hire you," said Bill, clearly without thinking. Then he glanced down at Annie, with a guilty look, belatedly remembering he was supposed to be asking for her opinion before making a decision.

But before he could say anything, the German set her crossbow down on the table, as her husband returned with the kite, bows, and a handful of arrows. "Reckon I'll be palaverin' with you about terms and hire, then," said Jackson Cate. "Reckon Frida wants to have a chat with Mrs. Butler."

"Indeed I do," said the German. And before Annie could react to this, Frida had come up to her, taken her gloved hand in her own, and tucked it into the crook of her arm. "Let's go to my wagon, where it will be quiet and warm," she said and tilted her head at Frank. "Please to come with us, Mr. Butler?"

By this point, Annie was such a welter of emotions and confusion she just let herself be drawn along, across the arena and into the Cowboy Camp where, at the very end of the row of tents, there was a wagon parked with two stocky, coal-black horses picketed beside it, and Fred Gibbs waiting. "Thank you for watching the horses, Herr Gibbs," Frida called. "It seems we are hired, and they can move to the stable-tent."

Gibbs tugged at the brim of his hat, untied the horses' reins from the wagon, and led them away.

As for the wagon—well, Annie knew enough about gypsies from reading to recognize it as a gypsy wagon, with its rounded top and glass windows, but this one was painted in simple brown with green trim, not with the flamboyant floral designs she had read about and seen on the roads in England. There was a green door with a glass window in it at the front, and a glass bow window at the rear. Frida let go of her hand as they reached this remarkable contraption, went up the three stairs to the pretty door set into the front, and gestured for them to follow her inside.

The first thing that struck Annie was how neat and cozy it was inside, like a perfectly planned miniature cottage. There was a real cast-iron cooking stove along one wall and a coffee pot on the stove, which had been stoked and was emitting a most welcome warmth. The wagon was stoutly built; the roof seemed to be tin over a wooden frame, and the rest was made of golden-brown wood the same color as the crust of a loaf of bread. There was a curtained, platform bed under the window at the rear, with a storage cupboard underneath and red velvet curtains that had been drawn back to either side. On the right wall was a chest of drawers, and a bench seat with a cushion on top of it and more storage beneath, with a second chest of drawers at a normal height next to it. On the left wall was a fold-down table with shelves above, and a stool, and a bit of storage beneath. There was a cupboard above the stove, and many things hung on the wall below the cupboard.

Frida gestured toward the bench seat, and Annie and Frank took their places on it. "Coffee?" she asked brightly, and without waiting for their reply, poured two cups, offering sugar lumps from a little bag that she hung back up on the wall behind the stove, along with many other oddments and cooking equipment. She took a cup herself, then got a pottery jar of what must have been cream from outside. Which made sense; it was winter, after all, and keeping cream and milk outside was a smart idea. She offered them cream, took some herself, and settled on the stool across from them.

"Well," she said. "Your good husband doesn't know I cheated, but *you* do, don't you, Mrs. Butler?"

Annie felt her jaw go slack. Frank, who had had the good manners to take off his hat inside as if this was a real house, shook his head vigorously. "Ain't no way, nohow, you could've cheated, ma'am!" he exclaimed. "I know every cheat in the business when it comes to trick shooting and—"

"And you don't know mine," the woman interrupted him. "Not unless you have come across an Air Master before, and I very much doubt you have. I beg your pardon for a little imposition," she continued, and leaned forward to touch Frank lightly but firmly between the eyebrows. She removed her finger before he could pull back. "But now you will see my cheat."

She gave a little whistle. And a half a dozen tiny doll-like heads poked around the bed curtains. *"Versammeln, meine lieblinge,"* she said, and six little fairies whisked around the curtains and flew to hover between her and the Butlers, looking from her to Annie expectantly.

They were just as Annie remembered them. About a foot tall, with the wings of butterflies, moths, and a bird, clothed in nothing but ankle-length hair of various colors, some of them not the natural colors of hair. She gasped, every emotion in her brought to a complete standstill with the shock of seeing them.

So did Frank.

She glanced at him; his mouth was open, his eyes wide, and his expression one of pure astonishment.

"You *see* them?" she asked, almost as surprised at that as she was at the fairies.

"If what you're a-seeing is six naked little fairies—" he barely managed.

"Sylphs," Frida corrected him, gently. "The smallest and most helpful of the Air Elementals. They make sure that when I shoot, I hit the mark every time—and they make sure no bullet nor crossbow bolt will ever go astray and endanger anyone. This is why I only use a crossbow or a rifle; there is too much discharged from a shotgun shell to be certain every pellet goes somewhere safe."

"But—*how?*" Annie almost wailed.

"I am an Air Master, a Master of the Elemental Magic

of Air," she said, which—well, they were words, and they had come out of Frida's mouth, but they made no sense at all to Annie. But Frida could obviously see that from Annie's distressed and befuddled expression, and she added, with a smile, "And now I will explain."

3

ANNIE'S head spun.

By the time Frida had finished her explanation—with several pauses as Annie interrupted with questions—the coffee pot had been emptied and refilled twice. The homely scent of coffee lingered in the air, along with the faint scent of gun oil and beeswax. Frida had been quite matter-of-fact and detailed in her answers, and seemingly had held back nothing.

And it still all seemed completely impossible to Annie. Never mind her own memories. Never mind that she had been vindicated. This was madness.

Yet there were those six little fairies—or "sylphs" as Frida called them—now disporting themselves about the confines of the otherwise perfectly ordinary wagon. A wagon that was as solid and real as could be. The embroidered canvas of the bench cushion she sat on had a familiar, soft feel to it. Her Ma had flat cushions like this one on some of her chairs. And yet the little "home" was full of fairies.

One of the sylphs had gotten hold of the last foot of

one of Frida's plaits and unbraided it as far as she could, and now three of them were plaiting and unplaiting it again, giggling the entire time. Frida seemed used to this. One sat on the edge of Frida's cup-hand, inhaling the scent of the coffee with a blissful look on her face. One seemed to be flirting with Frank, who honestly was blushing and clearly did not know where to look. The last one sat on Frida's shoulder, watching Annie with great intensity.

She wanted, with an urgency that was definitely desperate, to go back to this morning, before she had ever heard of any of these things! Magic, fantastical creatures, all of that—she didn't *want* to know about them.

Because that just makes what you saw with the Wolves that night real, doesn't it?

. . . yes. And that was what made it horrible.

And because if what you saw the Wolves turn into was real . . . what else is out there?

Was *every* nightmare creature from fairy tales real?

She felt like a poor little mouse trapped in the bottom of a bucket, running around and around and unable to escape no matter how fast she ran.

Frida just sat there and watched her with those knowing blue eyes, as if she was reading Annie's thoughts. And Frank was too preoccupied with the flirtatious fairy to notice her thinly cloaked distress.

"Something magical, and horrid, happened to you in your past, didn't it, Annie?" Frida said quietly. "Something that terrified you. Something you have never told anyone about, not even your husband."

The statement made her start. Who and what *was* this woman, that she could conjure up Annie's innermost thoughts so easily?

"Do you want to tell me?" the German asked gently.

No! No, she certainly did *not* want to tell the shootist about it! And yet—her mouth opened, and the words came tumbling out.

The words came just as she would talk out her nightmares with Frank, and maybe her tongue had loosened because of all that practice. Once she started, she couldn't stop.

Frida didn't interrupt her, although Frank finally realized how distressed she was, shooed off his little flirt, and anxiously took one of her hands in both of his. The words came out like a flood, and she was very much afraid that she sounded like a madwoman, or at least incoherent, because she told it all exactly as she would tell it to Frank—with no explanation of who the Wolves were, or what their real name was, or how she had come to be in their household in the first place.

But finally she came to the parts she had never told Frank about. Nearly freezing to death. The fairies covering her like a blanket. The Wolves fighting over her—and transforming.

Now she stuttered and choked, tears burning down her cheeks, as the story fought to come out. Frank put his arm around her, and started to say something—even though she could tell that all of this shocked and disturbed him deeply—but Frida shushed him, and nodded at her encouragingly.

She got to the part about He-Wolf pinning her against the wall, slapping his paw on her stomach, and saying things she didn't understand. And she broke down entirely, throwing herself into Frank's arms, sobbing as uncontrollably as she had that night. She felt exactly like the little girl she had been that night: terrified, confused, unsure, and utterly helpless.

She found herself presented with two handkerchiefs that were thrust into her hands—Frank's big square of plain white linen, and a second, just as sturdy, but smaller, with a border of black and red cross-stitching. She needed both of them.

"Allow her to weep," she heard Frida say. "She has been holding this terror inside for a very, very long time."

"But—all that—" Frank stammered. "People turning into wolves—"

"Was *quite* real, I promise you," Frida said grimly, as Annie sobbed and sobbed, feeling at once terrified and helpless and yet—a profound relief in finally letting the secret go. And an even more profound relief, caused by the words *"Was quite real . . ."*

It was real. It was *real.* She hadn't gone mad, or made it up in her head. It was real. It had happened. And here was another person in the world who *knew* about these things and could verify that.

Finally when she had reduced the two handkerchiefs to soggy wads of fabric, and Frida had provided her with a third one out of her dresser drawer; when she was exhausted and parched and unable to cry another tear, the German shootist reached out, patted her on the shoulder, and said, not unkindly, "There now. The story is out of you. Now you can hear the truth about it. How did you come to be with those awful people?"

Frank answered for her, as she struggled to regain control of herself, simultaneously embarrassed, exhausted, and relieved. "Her Pa died, and her Ma couldn't keep all the young'uns, so she sent Annie to the Infirmary."

"Would that be like a workhouse?" Frida guessed. "An almshouse? A poor farm?"

Anne felt Frank nodding. "It would. The folks there were kind 'nough, from all Annie's told me, but the feller she calls 'He-Wolf' turned up one day saying he was looking for a girl to help his wife with her new baby. He offered money, room and board, and promised she'd go to school." Annie felt Frank shrug. "Reckon you've already figgered she got none of that."

"It would have surprised me greatly if she had." Frida uttered a humorless laugh. "These . . . creatures are by their very nature cruel and utterly self-centered, so much so that it never seems to occur to them that if they were *kind* to their victims, they wouldn't be exposed for what they are nearly so often. Annie," she added, this time with some force in her voice. "What would you do if He-Wolf were to appear before you this minute?"

That jolted her out of the welter of emotions she was wallowing in, and she *did* sit up, wipe her eyes, and look straight into Frida's. "I'd shoot that varmint right between his eyes," she said firmly.

Frida grinned fiercely. "So you would. And so you *should,* if ever you encounter him again. Now, hear me. He chose you deliberately the moment he saw you. He was a magician himself, as he showed when he tried to bind you to him—there are other magical paths besides Elemental Magic, and some of them are purely evil. He recognized the power in you, and even though what he *needed* for his servant was a much bigger and stronger girl than you were, you *represented* something much more attractive to him: someone with a power he himself could not command, whom he could have under his control. That was probably why his wife was so angry with him, and with you. She wanted a strong slave, and she got you instead, all because of his magical ambitions. And I think she was jealous, too, fearing you would supplant her position in his pack."

Frida whispered something to one of the sylphs, who took Frank's soggy handkerchief, whisked out a window Frida cracked slightly open, and came back with it full of snow. Frida handed it to Annie, who put the cold-pack against her eyes. It felt good. "That there makes sense," Annie agreed. "I never could figure out why he picked me instead of Sarah or Meg."

"Since you were young and small, he probably counted on breaking you thoroughly, then binding you to himself so that you simply would find yourself unable to disobey him," Frida told her. But there was something about the way Frida said that . . . there was a flicker of expression over her face that made Annie certain Frida knew more about all of this than she was telling.

But I am not sure how much more I can bear right now. . . .

And then, a question blossomed in her head. "How did you know?" she blurted. "How did you know I could see the fairies? How did you—"

"You are an Air Magician. Possibly, like me, an Air Master. Any other Air Master could see your power, and you—well, you have been showing yourself off in public in England, every day, sometimes twice a day, for weeks. Months!" came the unexpected answer.

Annie pulled the now-dripping handkerchief away from her eyes to see that Frida was smiling at her.

"We talk, we Elemental Masters. We have groups that seek out and destroy monsters like the Wolves, and we talk often, and we can do so instantly, as easily as someone goes to a telegraph office. Young Lord Whitlesford recognized you for what you were, by the aura of power, and his sylphs confirmed it. Several others did the same, over the course of all of your performances in the tour of England, and now this one on the continent. You were quite the subject of conversation! It was determined that you were unaware of your gifts and did not use them. Which meant one of us needed to approach you, inform you, and—" Frida paused. "Well, when the Hunt Masters all conferred, it seemed that I was the logical one to do that, since your schedule put you here in winter quarters, and Jackson and I had a natural means of approaching you by answering the advertisement for the German corps in the Rough Riders of the World. I did not expect to be able to get you alone quite so soon, but I seized my moment when it was presented to me." She shrugged. "Besides, there are a few areas of suspicion in and around the city that no one has been able to get to, and we all thought I could probably slay two birds with a single bullet."

It seemed to Annie that there was an awful lot that Frida was not telling her. On the other hand, just at the moment, her head was swimming with all the revelations she *had* gotten, and she was not at all sure that she wanted to know anything more at this point.

Frida held out her hand for the handkerchief. Annie gave it to her, and she wrung it out outside. "You and I will need to have several more talks, but I think by now, your head is full of things you need to think about. *Nicht wahr?*"

Annie nodded, but before Frida could say anything, there was a triple knock at the door, and Captain Jackson Cate opened it, poking his head cautiously inside. "Ev'thing all right here?" he asked.

"Better I should ask you!" Frida replied, before Annie could say anything.

"Well," Jackson replied, grinning, as he squeezed himself into the wagon. "I'm a right smart bargainer. We're makin' a nice profit, an' some of it's comin' in Henry rifles."

"Ausgezeichnet," said Frida. "Unlike Mrs. Butler, no one has been lining up to gift me their best craftsmanship." She winked at Annie and smiled. "When do we start?"

"Friday. It bein' so close to Christmas and all, from Friday to Christmas Eve, we're doin' a show a day, Christmas Eve an' Christmas Day off." He tilted his hat forward to scratch the back of his head. "Reckon the vaqueros would just about start another Revolution iffen the Colonel asked 'em to do a show over Christmas. They take Christmas serious."

"They probably would not be the only ones," Frank Butler put in. "With the addition of the Rough Riders of the World, there are a lot of the company that would revolt over being asked to put a show on during Christmas. The Injuns don't care, of course, and truth to be told, neither do some of the cowboys, any more than Jerry the Moose does. And there's them fellers from Turkey and China who wouldn't care neither. But them Germans? And the vaqueros? And the Cubans? And the Frenchies?" He shook his head. "I reckon not even bringing in a preacher and a priest to do services here in the arena would be enough to keep them from stagin' a revolt."

"Well, Prussians prolly don't give a yankee-doodle, but Bavarians do, an' so do a lot of Austrians—so I reckon you're right," Jackson agreed. "The kind of folks you got here ain't generally expectin' to be the ones doin' the entertainin' over Christmas."

"I'll just get our music over to the bandleader before everyone breaks up for dinner," said Frida, standing up, opening the top of the bench she had been sitting on, and extracting a solid block of paper. Jackson Cate backed up so she could leave, then turned back to the Butlers.

"Make yourselves at home, friends," he said, without a flicker of irony. "We gotta go make arrangements with the show-master to figger out where we fit our acts in, but it's cozy an' warm in here, and no point in you movin' on 'less you got somethin' to do."

He turned to go, when Annie put out her hand to stop him. "Wait," she said, and he turned back, closing the door that he had opened a crack. "What do you know about magic?"

"Not as much as Frida, an' mine ain't in the same Element, but I got a bit." He snapped his fingers and a flame appeared atop his thumb; he waved his hand over the flame, and it vanished. "She's Air, I'm Fire. So I never got no advantage in shootin', but it comes in handy other ways. I can see other Elementals, even if they don't talk to me."

The flirtatious little sprite that had been teasing Frank left him like the minx she was, flew up to hover in front of Jackson's face, and blew kisses at him. He shook his finger at her. "Don't you pertend to go all sweet on me, missy. _I_ know who was a-pullin' the blankets off my feet last night."

The sylph giggled, and whisked away to hide behind the bed curtains, peeking out roguishly.

"You jest stay here as long as you like," Jackson repeated, then pulled at the brim of his hat, and left.

"Well." That was all Frank had to say aloud, but his hands, both of them still holding one of Annie's, told her all she needed to hear. *I love you,* said those hands. *I'll stand by you. This is all strange and unsettling, but we'll figure things out together.*

She held to those hands and tried not to stare at the little winged creature that had taken up a perch on the plate-rail that ran along the top of the wall. The rest had vanished somewhere. "They wouldn't have joined the show if there wasn't more to this than just tellin' me I got this power," she said, thinking out loud. "They could'a just told me and gone."

"That's a fact," Frank agreed.

"So I guess we got to wait to see what else they want." She licked dry lips. She was rattled, and knew it, and didn't like it. It took a lot to shake her confidence now that she was all growed up. She wasn't that scared little mite of a girl anymore. She'd told the truth: if the Wolves ever showed their faces around her again, she *would* put bullets between their eyes . . .

. . . as long as I could get away with it. Don't fancy finding myself in prison.

But—magic! It was . . . unsettling. Nothing in what she'd been brought up to believe gave house-room to magic.

Her gaze went to the little fairy. What had Frida called it? *A sylph.* Well, it was real enough. So it followed that what she believed was going to have to open up to include such things.

There was no sense in pretending all this didn't exist. And if it existed, it followed it could be a force for good and the Light. And since *she* had it, it also followed that she needed to use it as a force for good and the Light. Well, she could just ignore it, or ask Frida if it could be taken from her, but wouldn't that be as foolish as asking for her foot to be chopped off?

The more she thought, the more she felt . . . settled. Among many, many other things, Frida herself had said the sylphs were why she never needed to worry about an arrow or a bullet going astray. That would be invaluable in the show.

"I have to say, darlin'," Frank said slowly. "I'd be a mite easier in my mind if you could get these little critters to make sure the only things that get shot are the ones you intend to shoot." He smiled slowly. "'Specially when you go shootin' cigarettes outa my mouth."

"We surely do think alike," she agreed. "I don't cotton to usin' 'em to cheat, but makin' sure a bullet don't go astray is something I could stand behind."

But there has to be more that they want from me.

"There's gotta be more that they want, though," Frank mused, echoing her thoughts. "Why else would they have gone to all the trouble of gettin' a job with the show?"

"They need the money?" Annie hazarded, then shook her head. "No, that can't be the reason. Mrs. Cate's gown. . . ." She'd been too shaken at the time, but in recollection—and with a deep knowledge of fabrics and the craft of the seamstress, polished to an art by making all her own costumes and many of her own gowns—she recognized it in retrospect as being new, quite up to the latest mode, and of an extremely fine wool.

"Worth a lot, was it?" Frank replied absently, since he had the usual male indifference to clothing. "Maybe they just missed bein' in a show."

"Well. . . ." Annie sighed. It was her own lifelong dream to settle down for once, in a house of her very own. But. Multiple trials had only proven that she was terrible at keeping a home, and her particularness about things, honed by being tended to by good hotels, drove off servants and cooks. "They seemed mighty concerned that I didn't know anything about all this magicstuff." She hardly dared say what she was thinking, but Frank said it for her.

"You reckon they mean to teach you 'bout it?" He

rubbed the back of his neck. "Seems to me it's a darn sight better that someone that knows it all teaches you, than you go on about it on your lonesome. You ain't little Annie Moses pickin' up her Pa's gun this time." He squeezed her hands to take the sting out of the words.

"No . . . I ain't," she agreed, reminding herself that Frank meant no harm, only good practical advice. And back when she'd picked up her Pa's gun—

Well, she *had* trailed after her Pa, and more or less knew how to use the dang thing.

And maybe, just maybe, the reason nothing had gone horribly wrong, and she hadn't hurt herself or somebody else—could it be these little sylphs had been guiding her hand and her bullets until she mastered shooting?

She looked directly at the sylph still visible, and the little thing looked fearlessly back at her. "When I was a little mite—" she said aloud. "When I first picked up my Pa's gun and started a-feedin' the family—were you little things helpin'?"

The sylph blinked her pretty violet eyes, the same color as a pansy, as if she was thinking. *"Maybe?"* she said aloud, making Frank *and* Annie jump. *"It sounds like something we do. But you are from over the great water, and we don't know any of our kind from that far away."*

She sighed, exasperated with herself. There had been no reason to assume that creatures on *this* side of the ocean would know what creatures on the *other* side of the ocean had done decades ago.

An irritation came over her at the thought that she'd had *help* and hadn't done it all herself. But it was irrational, and she knew it, and Frank was right. She should be grateful if that was what had happened.

"You lot still helping me?" she asked, throttling down that annoyance.

Because if they were still "helping"—cheating!—she was going to be—

The sylph laughed. *"You need no help. Nor does the*

Jaegermeister, *not really. We just make things safe. Then people laugh and applaud and it feels good.*"

"Don't get your hackles up, angel," Frank said with a little smile. "If they *was* helping, how's that bad? It let you feed your family. And you heard the little fairy, it's all your own doing now."

Well. . . .

Shots that hit meant no wasted bullets, and we couldn't afford to waste even one lead slug or round of powder. Shots that hit meant a rabbit for the pot or a bird to sell, and we needed every penny. And if it had been, say, an angel helping, would I be so nettled? No.

"Well. That's pure truth." She let out her breath in a sigh. "Do I look like I been weeping?"

"Naw. You reckon we could get some practice in, since we're here?" Frank replied, easily.

"That, and I'm partial to seeing what else this lady and her husband can do, and then there's dinner," she replied, standing up. "Let's go have a look-see."

As it happened, they arrived just in time to see the two with their pair of stocky black horses, dismounted and talking to the bandleader. Only about half the band was there at the moment, and they were all looking over sheets of music paper. The woman was beating time with her index finger in her hand, obviously telling the bandleader what tempo she wanted the band to play in. He nodded along as she talked, and Annie could tell that Frida wasn't irritating him, which was a relief. The bandleader gave one more decisive nod as she finished talking, and motioned to the two of them to go to the entrance where the curtains were pulled back out of the way to start their act. Annie and Frank went to lean together on the arena wall to watch.

The pair mounted up on their horses, which had the sort of saddle the English preferred. *Not* the sort of thing you could use for trick riding, so she wondered just what it was they were going to do. She got her answer a moment later, when the band gave a brief fanfare, then started a march tune she did not recognize, in a tempo slightly slower than she was used to hearing a march played in.

Side by side, they entered the ring, the horses performing a peculiar—and very pretty—high-stepping trot-gait in absolute and perfect synchronicity. For a moment, Annie enjoyed what she thought was pure accident. And then she blinked, as she realized that this was no accident. The horses really were moving, deliberately, together, just as perfectly as if they were trained chorus dancers.

They reached the middle of the arena, turned the horses to face the "head" end, the music paused, and they reached up with an exaggerated motion and took off their hats. Jackson Cate was wearing a handsome bowler, and Frida wore that little conical thing with a small brim that was like no hat Annie was familiar with, but which matched her dark green coat and divided skirt.

She could tell it was a divided skirt because Frida was riding astride, not sidesaddle, and it gave her a little shock, even though she had seen such anomalies before.

The music struck up again, and the Cates resumed the act.

Annie was fascinated. She'd never seen horses do anything like this, not this—mannered. *They're dancing!* was all she could think. Even the seasoned hands stopped to watch.

Then they took turns doing the most amazing tricks—first rearing to half-height, something Annie knew from experience was harder for a horse to do than rearing at full height—then rising a little more and hopping forward three times. Then jumping from a standing start so high they would easily have been able to jump over Annie, if she'd been silly enough to stand in front of them. Then repeating the same jump, but then lashing out with their hind feet at the top of the leap.

The Cates ended the remarkable performance as

they had begun it: riding side by side to the center of the arena, stopping, slowly and gracefully removing, then replacing, their hats, and riding out again.

They dismounted at the entrance to the applause of the rest of the cast. Annie and Frank made their way over, just in time to hear Frida say, ". . . both ten years old, and a breed called the 'Lippizan.' They're from Vienna in Austria. There is a very famous riding academy that teaches both horses and riders how to perform like this. Most of the horses are born black or brown and turn white over the course of the first four years. White is the preferred color. We . . . have friends in the Austrian Court who persuaded the school to part with these two because they are *not* the preferred color, and until we got them, they were not . . . the best pupils."

"I'm purt good with horses," Jackson put in. "They'll work for us when they won't work for anyone else."

Now, given what she knew about these two, Annie was certain that there was a lot more to this story, but right now was not the time to ask questions.

"Will that do for an act to give the others more time to prepare?" Frida asked the Colonel, who, of course, had been auditioning the whole thing. "It is both very Germanic, and something normally only the members of the Austrian Court may see."

"Reckon that'll be a fine turn to put right before the hussars do theirs," Bill said, with a grin. "Give people a chance to settle down, then rile 'em up again."

"I can surely make a big thing of these hosses and their tricks only being shown to the Emperor's Court," Frank Richmond, the show's announcer, said thoughtfully.

"Only don't, as you value your life, call the performance 'tricks,'" Frida cautioned immediately. "This is *Hoch Schule,* the pinnacle of the training of horse and rider—"

"Hey!" someone in the crowd said suddenly. "These saddles ain't got no stirrups!"

"They shore don't," Jackson Cate agreed with a grin that showed a set of fine teeth behind that magnificent mustache he sported. "That's how they ride these boys there at the Spanish Riding School. If you cain't stick on their backs without stirrups, you got no call to be there and they'll kindly show you the door."

"We're holding up everyone else who needs to practice," Frida interrupted before Jackson could wax eloquent, which it certainly looked as if he was about to do. "Time to take the boys back to the stable-tent. Master Richmond, before we perform, you and I must get together. You tell me what you want to say about our acts, and I'll give you a German translation written out as it *sounds.*"

"Wait a minute," said one of the cowboys, holding out his hand to stop them. "Is they stallions?" He eyed the two horses as if he expected them to attack him, or more likely, each other.

Frida broke into a full-throated laugh. "Oh, don't worry about the others in the tent. Lippizan stallions . . . have manners. They won't be starting fights. They know that the stable is for manners, the arena is for manners, and even being turned loose in a field with other stallions they know is for manners. And the boys are very good friends." As if to prove her point, her horse reached over and nuzzled the other's neck.

No one got a chance to ask anything else of either of the two newcomers, as Frida made an impatient motion, and she and Jackson led their horses out of the way.

"I think that's our cue to get practicin', darlin'," said Frank.

After a full morning of running through her repertoire of tricks and some general target practice, Annie was more than ready for the daily dinner laid out by the cooks. The cooks had adapted some of their ways to what was available in the Strasburg markets in winter, and instead of the usual beef, white bread, and beans served in the States, the cooks had been presenting sausages, the rough black and brown bread usually found here in Germany, and potatoes. And cooked cabbage, although there were not many takers for this among the cowboys, Indians, and Mexican vaqueros. Annie liked it, though; it made her think of home, since many had been the days when cabbage was all there was to eat in the Moses household. *You'd think I would hate it. But when you are awful hungry, cabbage tastes pretty good.* There was plenty of coffee, though; there was no lack of coffee in Germany, nor coffeehouses to drink it in. And Strasburg supplied some of the best butter and cheese she had ever eaten in her life.

She and Frank got seats at the same table the Cates were sitting at. They already seemed to have made friends among the cowboys. As she cast her ears in their direction, it was clear why.

They were talking horses. There was nothing that a cowboy loved to talk about more than his horse, except perhaps his girl.

". . . two names," Frida was saying, as Jackson took a moment to inhale some sausage. "The first name is their foundation stallion, and the second is their dam. So our two are Maestoso Eidelweisse and Pluto Astarte."

"Hoo! Ain't that jest a mouthful!" said Frank Gibbs.

"Which is why we call my feller 'Dell' an' Frida's feller 'Arte.'" That was Jackson Cate, giving his wife a chance to snatch a few mouthfuls. "Only the mares get their own names. The fellers get stuck with hand-me-downs."

Headshakes all around the table, and various opinions about the "peculiarities" of "furriners," and of course, no one rendering an opinion thought even a little bit about the fact that *they* were actually the foreigners here, which Annie found rather amusing. The details of *Hoch Schule* training were fascinating, but even more fascinating was the way the Cates took turns talking so both of them could eat. It reminded her of how Frank would step in whenever she was getting tired of questions and smoothly direct the questioners to something *he* could talk about.

I was absolutely prepared to despise her this morning, thinking she was another Lillian Smith. And now I am thinking I should have been ashamed of myself for thinking that. We are more alike than I could have dreamed.

Including, apparently, in having magic powers.

4

THIS afternoon wasn't one in which they were holding a show, but *was* one in which tours of the camps were being held, so while the arena remained closed off for practice, Annie and Frank went to Annie's tent in the cowboy camp and prepared to hold court. It wasn't the most pleasant of situations in the cold, but they had a good fire at the front of the tent, Annie had a charcoal-filled foot warmer at her feet, there was a pot of hot coffee at the fire, and she was bundled in a buffalo-hide robe. In warmer weather she would have worked on one of her costumes to pass the time between visitors, but not in this cold; she kept her hands inside the warm robe unless she actually had to use them. Frank was the one who drank most of the coffee, since he didn't have the benefit of the fur robe. Fortunately, today the visitors spaced themselves out. Unfortunately, there seemed to be a paucity of translators—

That is, until Frida showed up.

"Jackson is demonstrating what else he can do to help

fill in acts," Frida explained, as she turned up at the tent. "So I thought perhaps you could use a translator."

"Ma'am, you are a welcome sight," Frank said with relief, before Annie could accept the offer of help. "We'd be mighty obliged."

Thereafter, for the rest of the afternoon, Frida served as the interpreter for the curious who crowded around Annie's tent—and it seemed that having such a fluent linguist inadvertently caused people to linger, since before long, the crowd was so dense around Annie's tent that other showmen came up to gently "move some of them along." Frank seemed perfectly prepared to play the part of the spear-carrier, where he would silently bring out a weapon or medals or royal gifts for closer inspection by the visitors.

Of course, Annie was used to the tedium of answering the same questions over and over again. It was exceedingly rare when someone asked something different. She thought for certain that Frida would tire of it too, but instead, the German turned it to their advantage.

"Well, this is the question about what guns you use, so I'll answer it and you can think about this while I do," Frida finally said, after about an hour of the parade of gawkers, when Annie's nose was quite thoroughly cold and she had resorted to a cup of coffee to warm it. "Do you want to learn how to use your magic, or do you want me to get rid of it for you?"

As Annie was taking in that very pertinent question, Frida turned politely to the questioner and answered him in rapid-fire German and with such detail that he completely forgot Annie herself hadn't said anything. When Frida was through, he began to ask something else, but with a charming smile and a little tilt of her head she interrupted him with a brief phrase, and turned to someone else, a little girl all wrapped up in so many layers of shawls she looked like a woolen ball.

"This little girl wants to know about your shooting game for grocers. I told the other fellow that he really should allow others their turn. Now, have you got an answer for me?" Nothing about Frida's tone suggested she was doing anything other than translating. Annie was amazed; she really was an excellent actress.

"You can take the magic from me?" she asked instead. "Is that really possible?"

Frida turned to the little girl and spoke at some length, then took another question from the crowd.

"I suspect that if I had a silver *thaler* for every time you've been asked about Queen Victoria's presents and the medals she gave you, I would be a rich woman," Frida said, and gestured to Frank to bring them up in their display frames so the crowd could ogle them. "It isn't exactly 'take it away,' it's more like putting a shell around you so nothing gets in and nothing gets out, and no one, not even you, would ever know you have that power."

Then she turned back to the crowd and answered the question as Frank held the frames so everyone could see them.

By this time Annie had had a chance to think a little more. "What would you do if you were in my place?" she asked.

"The Good God gives us gifts, expecting us to use them to help others," Frida said with a shrug. "That is what *I* believe, but I cannot say what *you* believe, and I will not judge you, whichever answer you make."

Annie had to marvel a bit at the conversation they were having, surrounded by a crowd, in the open daylight. Madness. Anyone who understood what they were saying would probably be certain they were both insane.

And yet, of course, they were perfectly safe, unless someone came along who understood English, and looking at this crowd of children, housewives, and their earnest spouses, well, that wasn't likely.

"Are you really willing to teach me?" she asked.

"Why do you think I made a point of joining the Wild West?" Frida countered, and answered another question. "Both of you, actually. Your Frank has power too, more than Jackson does. Water, I suspect, which may be why he's not aware of it. I don't imagine either of you have had much to do with bodies of water, other than crossing them."

And another question.

"Oh, you'll like this, someone original. This young lady wants to know if you make your own costumes and where you get the very pretty patterns that are embroidered on them."

Annie smiled at that, despite her cold nose. She was rather proud of her needlework. "Yes, I do, with some help from the Mexican ladies who make most of the other costumes. The patterns come from ladies' magazines in the United States. I do all the fancywork myself."

The young lady, who, if she also made her own clothing, was certainly a fine seamstress and tailor, looked a little sad at that last. And Annie added impulsively, "Add that if she will come here to this tent tomorrow just after breakfast I will trade her some duplicates I made for some German designs."

The girl brightened at that and thanked her. Annie gave her a pass for the Cowboy Camp tour so she could get in without paying—one with a hole punched in it, to show that it had been given to her by one of the show people. For her part, Annie was exceptionally pleased with the bargain.

This went on for the rest of the afternoon, Annie asking what must be extremely elementary questions about magic, Frida pretending to translate while rattling back the answers to the unsuspecting tourists. Finally, as the sky went scarlet in the west, sending red light through the canvas on the west side of the tent, and shadows stretched out over the snow, some of the cowboys came through the camp to clear the last of the stragglers out, and the encampment was once again closed to outsiders for the evening.

Annie unwrapped herself from her buffalo robe and stood up. "I wish we could speak more over supper," she said wistfully, when Frida interrupted her.

"Of course we can," the German said. "Just not here. Jackson will be along presently as soon as he makes sure Dell and Arte are good for the night, and we plan to take you and Frank to a tavern we know. I'm sure you are a bit tired of camp cooking by now."

"It sounds ungrateful to say so, especially when I went hungry so often as a child, but . . . yes," Annie admitted reluctantly. "But what is so special about this tavern?"

"For one thing, I can get a private room where we can speak freely. For another, it is run by another member of the *Bruderschaft von Jaegermeistern,* so we can be sure of discretion. And lastly, the cook is a genius when it comes to good German cooking. Convinced?" Frida laughed.

Annie nodded, chuckling to herself. "More than convinced."

When everyone had collected, it was already dark, and Frank borrowed a lantern from Annie's tent to show their path so no one would stumble over frozen ruts and lumps in the snow. Jackson offered to trot on ahead to make the arrangements, and did not wait for an answer before heading off toward the lights of Strasburg. Frida shook her head and chuckled. "He hates waiting," she explained.

"We got that in common," offered Frank.

Annie had long decided that if she had to winter away from home—and away from her friends and relations and all their holiday celebrations—Strasburg was an excellent city in which to find herself. While England certainly did Christmas revelry very well, the English seemed to cherish the cold and damp, and even some of their best hotels were cold in the winter. And their cavernous "stately manors" and castles, where they were often invited to visit? She had to wear layer after layer and still felt cold. She had never managed to warm up to the French and Italians—well, nothing seemed further from home than France and Italy.

But the Germans were another matter. Except for the language and some—not all—of the food, they were not unlike the folks back in Ohio. The Germans loved cold weather, but only as long as it stayed outside of their homes and buildings. Everywhere you looked you found those excellent little porcelain stoves, merrily radiating a welcome heat. Strasburg was much, much cleaner than London, without all the soot and fog. And, she had to admit, it was much prettier than any American city she had ever seen, with its quaint timber buildings and the cathedral soaring above them all. Of course, now that it was dark, you couldn't see most of that, but the warm light thrown out of windows gave enough illumination to create a rather pleasant scene as people hurried by, often carrying intriguing parcels, and good smells hung in the cold, still air. And the sky was still just light enough, even with the stars beginning to come out, that the silhouette of the skyline with the cathedral looked like a picture postcard.

Still . . . she'd been sitting all afternoon in the cold, and even that buffalo robe hadn't been quite enough. *My nose is colder than ever. And so are my feet.* She was going to be very glad to get inside.

Fortunately, this tavern, or inn, or whatever it was, was not far from the field where the Wild West was camped. And it looked every bit as old as the *Gasthaus* where Frank and Annie were staying, but in a different style, all carved dark wood on the outside, like lace turned into wood. Jackson was waiting for them at the door, and ushered them in and across the main room so quickly Annie didn't have much time to take it all in. She did get the impression that this must be one of the enormous *bierstubes* she had heard of, and unlike pubs and beer halls in England, this place was airy and bright. It was more than adequately lit by the biggest lanterns she had ever seen, hung up by chains that went through decorated holes in the ceiling, bright as Maxim's in Paris when all the chandeliers were lit. Between the long tables, the big, four-sided pillars that held up the ceiling and supported the walls flared out at the top, creating the impression of many arches, not unlike a cathedral ceiling. The high ceiling itself, painted cream, displayed stenciled decorations all over it, in wildly different styles. Geometric patterns, stylized animals and birds, plants—in the brief amount of time in which Annie was able to take it all in, she got the impression from the faint hints of color beneath the paint that whenever parts grew too faded to make out, the owners just whitewashed them over and had someone else come paint something new.

The private dining room was just big enough for a table for eight, and by the doors along the back wall was one of six or eight identical rooms. The lady showing them to it opened the door for them, and they all filed in, Annie first. She took a moment to look about as the rest made their way in. Wooden wainscoting came to about Annie's rib-cage, with cream-painted plaster above that, and one of those little porcelain stoves provided plenty of heat in the corner. Light came from a brass-and-frosted-glass lantern overhead. There was already a pair of pitchers of beer on the table, place settings and glass steins all around, and a shelf with those enormous pottery beer steins the Germans loved running along the back.

There was much taking off of coats to be hung on a coat-tree in one corner, and settling of where everyone would sit—and meanwhile Frida was talking to the server who had followed them in, a cheery round-faced girl in the ubiquitous dirndl (this one in dark green), a spotless white apron, and a white blouse with green ribbon drawstrings at the neck and wrist-cuffs.

The girl left, and Frida at last took her seat across from Annie. "I assumed you are weary of sausages by now," she said. "And I have noticed that Americans do not much care for sauerkraut or any of our sour dishes, either warm or cold. So I took the liberty of ordering good roast pork all around, with roasted potatoes and carrots, and *apfelkuchen* to finish."

Before Annie could respond—though absolutely anything would have suited her at this point, she was so hungry—the girl bustled back in with a big basket of dark brown bread, another of crusty hard rolls, and pots of butter, and bustled back out again.

Although she wasn't much used to drinking beer, and didn't much care for it, Annie held out her stein to Frank, who was about to pour the pitcher he'd picked up. "Jest a second, pard," said Jack. "That's cider, in case you was thinking it's beer. The beer's t'other pitcher."

"Is it?" Frank said, pleased. "Hard or sweet?"

"Just a touch hard, not as hard as them Limeys like it, more like a sweet wine. They call it *apfelwein,* in fact."

"Obliged," Frank replied, and Annie was relieved on tasting the cider that it wasn't terribly strong, and was extremely pleasant, and had been warmed with spices. Much better, in her opinion, than beer. It went beautifully with the hard rolls, which were warm, and when the butter melted into them, they were so good she could have made a meal on them alone.

The food came soon after that, and when the server had left, Frida held up a finger to get their attention, as the murmur of voices outside the room grew slightly in volume, signaling that the evening crowd had begun. "Supper first, questions after," she said firmly. "My Papa always says that you should never use your head and your stomach at the same time."

Annie and Frank both laughed at that, but they had to nod in agreement, and indeed, although technically "simple" fare, the food was absolutely delicious and *nothing* like what the Wild West cooks presented, though it was not at all unlike the best roast pork Annie had ever eaten in American restaurants. For a place that apparently existed to serve vast quantities of beer and the simple sausages that the Germans seemed to require along with their beer, this cook was very good indeed.

Annie had assumed that *apfelkuchen* was an apple pie, but no. It was a cake with paper-thin apple slices baked into it, and lots of spices. She resolved to ask their hosts at the *Gasthaus* if *apfelkuchen* could be had for breakfast, because it would be a very lovely thing to have in the winter. At the moment they were just eating what their host served them, due to the lack of a common language.

Coffee with lots of cream accompanied the cake, and more coffee was poured after the cake and the last of the plates were cleared away.

"And now we can relax and speak at length," Frida said, when the server had left with the last of the dishes. "Jackson asked the owner of this place to come join us as soon as he is able—which might take a little while, until the serious eating has ended out there and the serious drinking begins. We are not far from the university, and where there are students, there will be drinking." She sat back in her chair with her coffee cup in both hands, smiling. "This is why, when we magicians meet somewhere other than another's house here in Strasburg, we meet here. Drunken students are likely to see just about anything, and think nothing of it. In fact, the drunker they are, the more likely they are to see plenty of things they don't talk about afterward. A few *haus-alfen* and sylphs? Much preferable to devils and serpents."

Annie had to laugh at that, and Frank cracked a smile.

"Now, Mrs. Butler—"

"I think you can call me Annie, by this time," Annie interrupted.

"Annie, then—the way that Elemental Magic works is this. You have your own, personal store of power that can be used in mostly small ways—because it is very tiring to use that magic, and usually you can do what you want much more easily just as an ordinary person would do it. But you can also use it to ask—or coerce— Elementals of your Element to do things for you. Coercion is considered to be . . . how to put this . . ." She stared up at the ceiling a moment. ". . . less than a crime but more than being impolite. It makes Elementals grumpy to be coerced, at the very best, as indeed it would anyone. At the worst, it leaves them with a grudge against magicians, and believe me, that's not good for anyone. Even the little ones can make their displeasure felt with pranks, and as for the Greater Elementals— they are very nearly gods in power and they are not to be trifled with."

"You mean there are more than just the fairies?" Frank asked.

"There are four Elements, four kinds of Elemental power, and Elementals for each. The weakest and most common of Air Elementals are the sylphs, or as you call them, fairies, who are winged, along with pixies, though I do not see a great many pixies in our empire. Pixies are generally clothed and look like children; that is how you tell them from the sylphs. Then there are the zephyrs, at least hereabouts, and the Winds, and lastly, the Great Elementals, the Storms, and the Tempests." Frida took a sip of her coffee. "But that is only here, in Europe. Elementals can take very different forms in other lands. So when you return home to America, you may see the Elementals that came to the New World with settlers, like the sylphs—or you may see the ones that have lived there all along, the ones that the Indians know. These will generally take the form of birds, animals, and fish, though not always."

"Well, if what you mostly do is to ask Elementals to do things for you, what *can* they do?" Frank asked, before Annie could beat him to it. His coffee cup sat forgotten on the table in front of him as he leaned forward intently.

"It depends on their own size and strength, or the strength of several of them all together. It can be something simple—as you saw today, when one of them brought me a handkerchief full of snow, or directed my spent bullets and arrows to the ground. Or . . ." She paused. "They can move air. If they felt kindly toward you, they could keep the air out of the lungs of someone or something that threatened you."

Annie blinked, as the implications of that set in. "You mean they could kill a man?" she asked.

Frida nodded. "Or you can learn how to use your power and do the same thing. I have a personal code that if I am forced to kill or injure something, I do it myself, rather than asking something else to do it for me. If I can. If I can't—" she shrugged "—if my life or the life of another is at risk, I will do what is required to save that life."

Annie sat back, a little stunned. This had gone from "shooting tricks" to "killing" in a couple of sentences. Now she was having second and third thoughts.

This wasn't a fairy tale. Or was it? Now that she thought about it, there was a lot of death and killing and maiming in fairy tales. And a great many of them had as the moral, "Be careful what you ask for." So if she asked to be taught how to use this—what would she, in turn, be asked to do with it?

But the Wolves. . . .

Frank blinked thoughtfully. "So, here you are talkin' about killin' things. So I reckon you've had call to do that?"

"Everyone in the *Bruderschaft* has. We have police for common criminals. But uncommon ones? The *Wolves* of the world?" replied Frida, echoing Annie's thoughts. "How would one bring them to justice? What jury would convict a man one claimed was able to turn into a wolf, or a bear, or to set fire to people from afar? That is what we do; we take care of those things that are themselves living nightmares. And yes, I am a *Jaegermeister,* that is, a Hunt

Master, and have over a dozen kills on my own. I have been a Hunt Master from the time I was fifteen, and tracked and killed a renegade Fire Master on my own." She cocked an eyebrow at her guests. "An Air Master is the proper response to a rogue Fire Master. Fire cannot burn without air."

"So, if you were to train me," Annie began, then paused. "How long would it take?"

Frida laughed out loud. "I have no idea! It will mostly depend on how quickly you grasp the principles. Then it's a matter of practice. But you must either be trained or muffled up, as I described to you, because now that you know of the power, and that you have it, that will always be in the back of your thoughts, and if you are startled or frightened you might accidentally do harm with it." She tapped the table with her fingers, thinking. "It is like a gun on a hair-trigger. If you know this gun, and know that it has a hair-trigger, you are safe with it. But if the gun is new to you, and you do *not* know how sensitive the trigger is, you can be hurt by it, or harm someone else."

Annie mulled that over, the cup of coffee feeling comforting in her hands—solid, reliable, and real, and not a part of this new world of magic and spirits.

But just as she thought that, she glanced up at the lantern overhead and realized there were fairies hanging and perched all over it, watching and listening to the proceedings of the humans with great interest.

And just at that moment, there was a polite tap at the door of the dining room, and someone let himself in.

If Annie had been asked to describe "a German tavernkeeper," the description would have matched this man. He had a healthy head of graying blond hair and a ruddy face with a blond, comic-opera mustache; he was going a little to fat, and wore a nearly ankle-length white apron over a pair of embroidered leather pants that reached to the knee, with suspenders with a peculiar sort of embroidered leather plaque between them, and a leather-collared white linen shirt with the sleeves rolled up. Tall stockings and heavy shoes completed his outfit. "Thunder and lightning!" he said in heavily-accented English, taking out a massive handkerchief from a back pocket and wiping his head with it. "The students are in force tonight!"

"Could be worse, pard," Jack said, speaking for the first time tonight. "They could be fightin'."

"*Himmel!* Or they could be Prussians and dueling! Good evening, my guests," he said, turning to Annie and Frank. "I am Karl Mittelsmann, and I have the honor of hosting many meetings of the Strasburg Hunting Lodge." He held out his hand for them to shake, which they both did. He had a nice, dry, firm handshake. "I am a mere magician, not a Master, and not a *Jaegermeister.* Has Frau Frida told you the difference yet?"

"I was just about to get to that, Karl. There is still beer in the beer pitcher. Our new friends prefer your *apfelwein.*" Nothing loath, the tavern master took one of the highly decorated steins from the shelf across the back of the room and helped himself to beer before sitting down.

Frida resumed her—well, it seemed to Annie to be a lecture of sorts. The sort that she would gladly have paid to hear. "Now, mere magicians—that would be like you, Karl, and Jack, and Frank, no offense meant—can only see the Elementals of their own Element, unless a Master puts the spell on them to be able to see other Elementals, or the Elementals themselves want badly to be seen. That is what I did for Frank this afternoon so he too could see the sylphs. A magician's power is very limited as well."

"How limited?" Frank wanted to know.

"Iffen I was a Fire Master, I could have this entire building a-roarin' in fifteen minutes," Jack said easily. "And I'd have the entire block in flames in half an hour.

But by myself, best I can do is start a fire with wet wood. And I ain't powerful enough to get the attention of a dragon, nor strong enough to force a salamander to do somethin' like set a buildin' afire, though I could arsk a salamander to start my home fire, an' he would."

"Wait—" Frank said, a dazed look coming over his face, "There's dragons?"

"Under the right circumstances, friend Jack, even what you have is not a power to take lightly!" Karl put in.

"Dragons?" Frank repeated.

"That only Masters ever see," Jack reminded him.

"Hold your questions for a moment, because I asked Karl here to help me, and it concerns you, Herr Butler," Frida interrupted. "I can tell you have some allotment of power, but not what kind. It is definitely not Air. Jack says it is not Fire. Karl—?"

"He is not Earth, that I can promise you," the tavern-keeper said.

"That leaves Water. Now I know what I am dealing with." Frida nodded her head decisively. "Good, good. That settles that. Now you may ask more questions."

"There's dragons?" Frank repeated for the third time.

"They are Greater Fire Elementals, and even Masters deal with them with great respect," said Frida, as casually as if she was talking about the human emperor. "They are not something you trifle with, and attempting to coerce them never ends well."

Annie licked her lips thoughtfully. "If we should accept your offer to train us . . . is this magic . . . Christian?"

"As Christian as a gun or a plow, or any other useful thing," Frida said immediately. "As Christian as a dog, or a tiger, or any other thing of Nature. It *is*. It falls to us to make it a thing of good or evil. And it has no affiliation with any religion, although in the old, pagan days it most certainly *did*, and Masters were often priests of the old gods."

Annie was mostly silent then, listening as Frank asked questions this time. After all, she'd had her chance as Frida had pretended to translate for her. Now it was Frank's turn.

To be honest, she wasn't entirely certain now *which* way she was going to pick. She had very much liked her life before she had heard about all this magic. And now at last she had a real answer to most of the questions that her life with the Wolves had raised—and the answer was not that she was mad, or had made things up in her childish mind. But did *she* want this new power—and new responsibility? Because she had no doubt that with this power came the responsibility not only to use it properly but to help others. Just as she used the money she and Frank made to help others—not only her own family, but through many charitable donations—she would have to use magic to help others. Frida's attitude had made that very plain. It wasn't a choice, really, it was an obligation. Was it one she was willing to take on?

Frank, however, was deep into the minutia of what being a Water Magician meant, and it was clear to her that he was actually quite happy to hear what even minor power would enable him to do, and was eager to be trained. *Well, fine, but being able to purify water or gather it out of the air at will, or predict rain—those are useful to be sure, but they don't carry the same weight of obligation.* No more than being a trick shot, really.

But this is likely to turn my entire life upside down.

At just that moment, Frida gave her a penetrating look, and into a lull in conversation, said without prompting, "Annie, if you are thinking that if you accept to be trained, your life will undergo profound change . . . well, you are correct. It will. And once you walk through that door, there will be no turning back. So if I were you, I would think about this very carefully."

"That was what I was just about to say," Annie replied, after a long pause, a pause punctuated by the kind of loud talking and louder laughter one would expect from a crowded place where quite a few people were getting happily drunk.

Frida nodded with satisfaction. "It is one thing to know from a young age what this sort of life entails, and thus, to be comfortable accepting it. It is quite another thing to have it thrust upon one out of nowhere, as we have done to you."

Jack leaned back, balancing his chair on two legs, and rubbed the back of his neck with one hand. "Miss Annie, we didn't come here to force anything on you. But you got two choices here, and both of 'em have good and bad parts to 'em. Now, iffen you decide you want no part of magic, Frida here'll bundle it up an' tuck it away so it cain't bother you no more, an' we'll stick around with the show to make sure it don't get a mind of its own and come out again. We ain't gonna just go 'howdy, thanks, goodbye' and leave you until we *know* it's all buttoned up and ain't gonna get loose."

Annie heaved a sigh of relief at that.

"And by the same token, if you decide you want it, we'll not leave the show until we are certain of your training," added Frida.

"I b'lieve I need to think this over some, like you said," Annie told them at last. Frida nodded, as if this was what she had expected, although Karl looked concerned.

"Don't get your apron in a knot, Karl," Frida advised him, after a sideways glance. "This is not something to be rushed into."

"I know that, Frau Cate, but—"

"There is no 'but' about this, Karl," she cautioned. "Frau Butler will take the time she needs to consider this in a thoughtful manner. Mountains will not crumble, nor seas dry, because she does."

"I'm powerfully curious about one thing that's got nothin' to do with magic," Frank put in, cutting short whatever objection the tavernkeeper was going to make.

"Jack, how in hell did a cowpoke like you make it over here all on his lonesome?"

"Just about when I was a-gonna muster out, couple of fellers what called thesselves 'professors' showed up with some Indian Bureau bigwigs, an' wanted to hire thesselves some Injuns fer a travelin' exposition over here," Jack replied, taking a cigar out of his vest pocket, examining it critically, then putting it back unlit. "They offered me a nice pay packet t' act as a translator, do a few rope tricks an' some shootin'. I was tired of getting' shot at, and tireder still of life on the trail, so I said yes."

"It wasn't anything big," Frida added. "Half a dozen Indians and Jack doing shooting and rope tricks and telling tall tales. It was supposed to be a series of educational lectures, but if either of those men were actual professors, I am the Queen of Norway. I met them in Stuttgart, which was where the showman ran off with all the money."

"An' she jest about saved our lives. Redhorse was 'bout to throw hisself off a building when he thought we weren't gonna be able to get him back home." Jack beamed at his wife, who blushed.

"All I did was what any Elemental Magician would do, which was help out a fellow in trouble. It was no problem. To make a very long story as short as possible, we found the Indians some *real* academics who were happy to continue the lectures until there was enough money to go home again, and back they all went. My big surprise was that Jackson turned up again on my doorstep asking if my Hunting Lodge could use a Fire Magician." She was blushing quite prettily now, and Annie smiled slyly to herself, thinking that there was definitely a great deal more to this story.

"Shoot, I had money fer a ticket back, no place I needed to be, I like this country, an' the purdiest gal I had ever seen was over *here,* not over *there.*" He laughed. "I asked her once she agreed to get hitched if she'd prefer to live here or there, but 'parently a tent on the plains ain't no match even for a *vardo*—that's what they call that wagon we got. An' mostly we're in *gasthausen* or *Bruderschaft* lodges, so life is a lot more comfortable than in a tent or some ramshackle bunkhouse."

"I can attest to the truth of that," Annie said ruefully. "I like your wagon. It would not fit in with the Cowboy Camp, though, so I am afraid my tent will have to do."

The tavernkeeper took his leave of them, then, after realizing that there was not going to be any more talk of magic, and his customers needed his eye upon them. But he assured them that they could stay as long as they liked and had another round of *apfelwein* sent in, so they passed some more time with Jack and Frank spinning yarns while Annie and Frida listened and laughed.

The truth was, Annie did so much talking during the day that it was restful, indeed, something of a treat, to *not* be the one making jaw-music.

Finally, Frank pulled his watch out of his vest pocket and allowed that they should probably be getting back to their room. "You ain't planning on walking, are you?" Jack interjected. "That ain't the best idea. I'll come out with you and show you how to get a taxi."

Annie was about to object to the expense—but then it occurred to her that heretofore they had always walked back to the *Gasthaus* after supper, when it was still fairly light, and when all the stalls in the Christmas Market were still doing a roaring business. This late . . . she nodded at Frank, who looked a little relieved, and the two men went out while Annie and Frida put on their coats in a more leisurely fashion. "This is the prettiest wool," Annie observed, as Frida donned her coat.

"It's a special color, called *loden,* that hunters in Germany like to use," Frida told her. "Ordinary hunters too, not just my sort. I can show you where to buy some if you take a fancy to it."

Annie's thanks were interrupted by Jack's return. "Frank knows all the tricks of getting a cab here now," Jack chuckled. "Now, let's go do the driver a bad turn by making him think for a moment he's got to squeeze four people into his two-person rig."

"Jack, that is very mean of you!" Frida exclaimed, laughing, but put her hand through her husband's arm, and her other through Annie's. They made their way out between tables that had been pushed together to form much larger ones, full of young men in casual suits, all wearing the same sort of flat cap. And all of them drinking steins of beer that were so large it made Annie a little sick to think of drinking that much. They paid no attention to the trio, as all of them were deeply involved in a dozen shouted conversations—which, from the earnest (if tipsy) demeanors of the participants, surely involved weighty subjects about the fate of the world.

The shock of the cold and relatively quiet air on the other side of the exit door woke Annie up out of the pleasant partial stupor the food and warmth had put her in. "What were they talking about with such force?" she asked Frida, as the cab driver did his best to conceal his dismay at being presented with two couples instead of one. "The students, I mean. They sounded as if they were deciding the fate of the world."

"Anything. Everything. They're students," Frida replied dismissively. "Everything is equally important to them." She turned from Annie for a moment to address the driver, who did not conceal his relief at what she said. "We will see you tomorrow at practice."

Frank was holding out his hand to her to help her into the cab, so she just said, "Thank you, and sleep well!" before feeling her way into her seat. The last thing she saw of the odd couple was as the cabman turned his horses to head in the direction of their lodgings. Jack and Frida were arm in arm, marching at a brisk pace back toward the show, cheerfully singing something that sounded as if it must be a drinking song.

5

BY the time Friday came, and with it the week of daily shows the Wild West would put on until Christmas Eve, Annie still had not made up her mind what she was going to do about this magic. Part of her wanted it; wanted it more each time she caught a glimpse of a little sylph, or one of the curious little creatures that inhabited the *Gasthaus,* tiny men about a foot tall, dressed in rough, homespun clothing. On Frida's suggestion she had taken to leaving a saucer with a cake in it underneath that pretty porcelain stove for the latter, and a bit of lint with some of her Eau de Cologne on it where she often saw the sylph perching. It seemed to be the right thing to do; the cake was always gone in the morning, there was never even a hint of a mouse or an insect, their clothing was always cleaned and pressed and left neatly hanging in the wardrobe or folded on the chair, all their toiletries were cleaned and precisely arranged on the dressing table, and even Frank's razor never needed stropping anymore.

But part of her kept reminding her that she was *not*

the heroine of a dime novel. That she was *not*, in fact, what she pretended to be in the Wild West Show. She certainly wasn't someone who ran about stopping bandits and marauders. She was not even a cowgirl. Given the choice, she would *never* live in the West. She hated Texas. The show seldom traveled west of the Mississippi and that was how she liked it. She was a girl from Ohio farm country, nothing like the Great Plains. She hadn't become a markswoman because she was fighting bandits or savages—she'd become one to put food on her family's table. She remained one because it was the best money she could imagine, and it had bought her mother a house of her own at last, it continued to help keep her entire family in small luxuries, and it allowed her and Frank to put money aside for their old age.

I'm not the sheriff. I'm not the marshal. I'm not the cavalry.

Other children daydreamed about such things, she knew that for a fact simply because of all the toys sold here at the show. But she had been too busy trying to help keep the family fed to daydream, or to play. Play! *As if I ever had time to do such a thing.* Her earliest memories were of working.

But that was not the point. The point was, gallivanting about "protecting" folks was not something she had ever done, nor dreamed of doing. Except, maybe, for keeping the proverbial wolf from the door.

But if I could have done something about the Wolves... would I have? If I had the chance ... would I now?

She shook her head—mentally at least. Because if she accepted training in magic, that was surely what she would become. Someone who went gallivanting about the countryside like an ancient knight. And to be honest, she just could not see herself in that role.

But Frida and Jack seemed in no great hurry to hear her answer on the question. They both practiced diligently, every day, both their own acts and the ones they had joined, like the Prussian hussars. They ate happily with the company, camped among the other bunking-wagons with their *vardo,* and volunteered to translate from the German whenever and wherever it was need-ful. The Colonel beamed on them with proprietary sat-isfaction every time he saw them; it was clear he was attributing their presence in the show to his own genius at recruiting talent. Granted, he *was* a genius at spotting talent and acquiring it, but . . . well, Annie just had to smile a little whenever she saw him acting as if he and he alone was responsible for them being here. If only he knew!

Because they were quartered so far from the show—and not the least because it was so cold!—Annie and Frank hadn't been socializing as much with their fellows as they usually did when rehearsals were over. The main Cowboy Camp campfire was always a good place when the weather was fine; there were so many people in the show that there were plenty of new stories to hear and tell, and the bandsmen all seemed to enjoy sitting around making music even when they weren't getting paid for it. But no one wanted to huddle around a fire that was warming only the coffee, especially not in the dark, and by the time the cooks finished serving supper it was dark. But Frida and Jack had gotten Annie and Frank into the habit of going back to the Butlers' lodg-ings after supper, settling into a quiet corner of the *Gasthaus,* which was *not* overrun with students after supper, and chatting or playing cards.

It was an extremely pleasant place to socialize. In fact, when all the office-men and shop-lads were gone—the ones whose lodgings did not offer supper along with a room—the dining room was practically deserted. So the four of them would take a table by the fire, order hot, spiced *apfelwein* and perhaps a pastry, and talk un-til nine or even ten. Magic was only alluded to in care-fully coded phrases, but there was plenty else to talk about.

Frida and Jack were not at all reticent about their

personal histories. Frida's parents, it seemed, were magicians themselves, and lived on the estate of a Master magician outside Munich. Her father was a gamekeeper, her mother a highly skilled craftswoman employed solely in the production of embroideries and laces for the nobleman and his family.

But it seemed that the possession of a powerful gift of magic—at least among the circles of those who were, themselves, magicians—superseded any secular rank. From what Annie understood, Frida was considered an equal to anyone short of a princess within those circles. "Which is very amusing," Frida allowed, the Thursday night before their next performance, "since we Bavarians are very conservative that way. I've rubbed elbows with several hundred people I ought not have been allowed anywhere near. It's a bit like your fame with the Wild West. You're not considered an actress, which would make you 'fast,' so you are acceptable in polite society. On top of that, your reputation is shining and untarnished, but you are exceedingly famous, and because of that, it's quite permissible for the titled to know you, want to know you, and be proud of hosting you and inviting you anywhere."

"Money talks louder than titles in the US," Frank said, as Jack nodded sagely and refilled his cup. "The older the money, the better. But we get your meaning. There's uncrowned kings and queens in New York society who think they're just as high and mighty as the real thing."

"Well, that's partly because their money is making it possible to marry into English titles," Annie pointed out. "All those American heiresses in London! It's a wonder there's a single wealthy girl over the age of fifteen left in New York!"

"We Bavarians are not as egalitarian as you Yankees," Frida replied, "but you probably would not guess that in a social gathering of those belonging to a Hunting Lodge." She left it at that, although Annie was already quite curious about those Hunting Lodges—the term, she had learned, meant the *group of magicians,* and not a physical building, although many of the Lodges were ... well, lodges in the American sense, large communal halls where magicians lived and worked, and from which they sallied forth, like the old knights, to protect the countryside and the people in it.

The more that Annie heard about the magicians and their lives, the more curious she became. But the more she heard, the more concerned she was that, should she accept this training, she wouldn't be able to conduct her *real* life, the one that put money in the bank and food on the table. She and Frank talked this over every night before they finally slept; if she didn't bring it up, he would. Of course Frank had his jobs that were not part of the Wild West Show—he was the representative for the Union Metallic Cartridge Company, as well as the Remington Arms Company, and he had several other lucrative endorsements, as did Annie. But it was not to be argued that the bulk of their income came from the Wild West, and how were they to do that *and* do—well, whatever it was that these magicians did? Moreover, if they stopped performing and competing, the endorsements would eventually dry up as well, going to shootists who were still in the public eye.

Like Lillian Smith. . . . The very idea grated.

So she went to bed the night just before the start of their series of Christmas show days, as she did nearly every night since she had met Frida and Jack, wondering. Wondering if she would be a fool to pass this opportunity up—or a fool to take it up.

But the next day she didn't have much leisure to wonder about anything. They would be doing two performances, one in the afternoon and one in the evening. For the first time since they'd gone into winter quarters, there was going to be an evening performance, which meant that the big electric generators that ran the special spotlights would be fired up. The fellows that tended these creatures—who had very little to do with the rest of the show folk in the ordinary course of things—had been fussing and tinkering with them for the last three days. Although these electric lights were becoming commonplace in theaters and even taking the place of gaslights in homes and streets, Buffalo Bill's show was one of the first to have them on the road. The Ringling Brothers were said to have them as well. There was an obvious advantage for any show that was held under canvas. Having lights like this meant you could do evening performances, like regular theaters could, and in towns where attendance was good, that was doubling your profit. Annie wondered what the two magicians would make of such things.

But right now, her concentration, and Frank's, was going to be on doing the first performance in a week, which always made her a little anxious. She reminded herself, as she got into her costume in the blessed warmth of the Cates' *vardo*, of what she was. She was not, after all, "Annie Oakley, magician." She was "Annie Oakley, the champion marksman." "Champion of the World," as Bill liked to tout her. There was nothing in that description about magic.

But having seen the fairies again, can I bear to never see them again? And what about all the other wonders out there?

She did feel sorry for the other performers, who were changing inside the dubious shelter of tents. Frida had offered the use of the *vardo* for changing last night, pointing out that she and Jack were not exactly going to take all day getting into their rigs, and that Annie and Frank were welcome to use the wagon too. Annie was very grateful, although the fact that she was wearing two sets of woolen underwear would have saved her from *too* much cold. Her show costumes, made as they were of a soft canvas that looked like buckskin, were not well suited to shows being held in the snow just before Christmas.

The Cates must have already headed to the show tent when Annie and Frank reached the *vardo*. She was immensely grateful to find her costumes had already been laid out for her on the bench seat, and wasted no time getting into the one for the entrance parade.

The Cates were already in place, on their horses, when she and Frank hurried up to the line. They were far, far back in the procession, just ahead of the Prussian hussars, whereas Annie was in the front with Bill, and Frank didn't ride in the procession at all. This was the first time that Annie had seen their show costumes—

I thought they were just going to use their Hunter garb, she noted as she waved to them, heading for her horse at the start of the line.

But they weren't. They were wearing something that looked like the hussars' military uniform. Except instead of the big bearskin hats, they had bicorn hats, and instead of being gray, their outfits were a light blue and white. Once again, Frida was wearing a divided skirt and riding astride.

That was all Annie got to see as she hurried to her mount. Bill gave her an enormous grin as she hoisted herself into the saddle beside him. "Well, missy," he said, using his pet name for her, "seems you're getting along just fine with the new act."

"The Cates are fine people," was all she had a chance to say before the fanfare announcing the Grand Entry sounded.

After that, it was the usual controlled chaos of a show, although Annie did have a chance to look in on the Cates' acts in between getting ready for her own. The first act, the trick-shot act with the kite, went beautifully. Frida had added something in rehearsals to take the place of one of her tricks that duplicated one of Annie's—she fired her hand-crossbow, hitting the bullseye with ease, then tossed the crossbow to Jack, snatched up a rifle, and split the arrow with a bullet. The crowd sounded appreciative to Annie, though it soothed her soul to note that the applause for her own act had been a little louder.

The second act, the dancing horses as Annie thought of them, was something she was actually a little concerned about. After all the wild riding and shooting and all, would the crowd really give two hoots about a couple of horses trotting to music around the ring? *She* could see the artistry, and the difficulty, but would they?

But to her surprise, the moment the couple rode side by side into the ring, the crowd erupted in cheers. And it seemed they hung on every precise maneuver just as avidly as they had the trick roping or the War Dance, and when the horses performed what Frida called the "Airs above the ground," the crowd exploded with applause. So she allowed herself to relax, and to concentrate on her own acts and not worry about the Cates.

When the Final Procession was over, she rushed back to her tent at the Cowboy Camp only to find Frida was already there, had gotten some coals into the foot warmer, and had the buffalo robe ready for her. She was still in that trim blue uniform, which looked a lot more comfortable up close than it had at a distance. It was also clearly wool, a beautiful, fine, but heavy wool, and Annie greatly envied her.

"Well, that was fun," Frida said as she helped Annie bundle herself into the robe. "The roar of the crowd is quite as intoxicating as brandy!"

"Why *did* they cheer so loudly when you and Jack rode into the arena?" she asked curiously.

Frida laughed. "Oh, you noticed that, did you? We are wearing something very like the original Bavarian military uniform. It was taken away from us not that long ago by the emperor, who ordered our forces must now wear the uniform of the empire. Everything has gone to the worse since they forced our dear King Ludwig from the throne and put another in his place." She shook her head. "Never mind. But I am sure you can understand that the sight of the old uniform makes Bavarians happy, and there are many who consider themselves Bavarian allies in Alsace-Lorraine."

Annie nodded, although this was all a mystery to her.

"We'll wear our *Jaeger* outfits when we are north of Bavaria," she continued. "They should serve just as well."

It was Frida's turn, it seemed, to get questions today, now that people had seen the Cates do their acts. Annie could always tell when the question was for Frida; she smiled a little more broadly, and if it was a child that asked, stooped down a little to get on the child's level.

With Frida taking some questions, Annie had a chance to relax and watch the German woman at work. She was a stark contrast to some of the Germans Annie had met in the earlier part of the German tour, who had been stiff, formal, and either ignored people they considered "below" them, or else were uncomfortable with them. Frida was quite egalitarian. Almost American.

In fact, in general, the people in the north were the stiff ones, and the people in the south are much more open and welcoming.

Before they had started this tour, she had had the vague—and now, she knew, naïve—impression that England, France, and Germany were sort of monolithic, and all the people within their respective borders were much alike except as to wealth and class. Now she knew better; that, for instance, the folk of Berlin were no more like the folk of Munich than the people of Boston were like the people of Memphis, Tennessee. On the whole, she much preferred these southerners. She didn't much care for the look in the eyes of some of the "great and powerful" she had been introduced to in the north. Particularly the emperor and his chancellor.

Kaiser Wilhelm wants to rule all of Germany, Austria, and Hungary. Perhaps all of Europe. Bismarck wants to rule the world through Wilhelm.

Those touring the camps were shooed out so the cast could snatch something to eat before the second show. This one would be performed with the assistance of the electric lights, which Annie both abhorred and adored. She loved them because of how dramatic they made things look, at times making it possible to forget they were all performers in an arena. She hated them because they made every trick of hers harder to perform. The light was very harsh, and the shadows cast within it were harsher. Things could be visible—then the light would turn a little and they would be invisible in the darkness.

It's all very well for Frida, she thought, as she took her place on her horse for the Grand Procession. *She has all those sylphs to make sure nothing goes amiss. All I have is my eyes and hands.*

And of course, that brought up the inevitable afterthought. *But if I accepted being trained in magic, I could have those sylphs too. . . .*

The second show went, if anything, even better than the first. Fortified by good suppers and plenty of beer, and unencumbered by offspring, the people of Strasburg were prepared to enjoy a Christmas present given to themselves. For the first time, Annie was seeing the faces and figures of the fashionable at their show, not just the stout middle-class burghers and the working-class folk. The prime seats were full, and there was even the glitter of ornaments in the darkness, and the hint of rich fabrics and feathers.

The end only came when the arena lights were snapped off to the sound of tumultuous applause, and the lanterns at the exit lit up. The crowd had no choice but to leave, since the option was sitting in the cold and dark. But the babble of German sounded happy and fulfilled, as Annie and Frank handed over their horses to one of the handlers and left the staging area.

She and Frank retired to Frida and Jack's wagon to change back into their street clothing, and the moment she entered the warm space, she thought that the one thing she really wanted to do was lie down here and not get up until morning.

"It's gonna be a long walk to our bed," Frank groaned, "an' I wisht we had a wagon like this one."

A tap at the door warned them someone was coming in, and Jack stuck his head in. "I hired a couple locals to come take everyone what's got lodgings in town back to their bunks," he said. "Stir your stumps, they ain't a-gonna wait for long!"

"That's extraordinarily kind—" Annie began, but Jack cut her off with a laugh.

"Ain't gonna lie; I want you two to sign up with the *Bruderschaft,* so I'm makin' sure you can see we take care of our own," he retorted, and closed the door.

And sure enough, there were a couple of drays of the sort that carted beer barrels waiting at the show entrance. Not the comfort of a taxi, nor the elegance of a carriage, but right now it had all the attraction of both, since it meant they would not have to walk. It was not just Annie and Frank who hopped in; there were quite a few people who preferred hot water and warm beds to the cold camp, and even the Colonel was not amiss to catching a ride in a beer wagon if it meant he didn't have to walk all the way into town to hail a taxi to take him to his fine hotel.

All the work—and the work of staying warm in the cold—had taken their toll. Annie was asleep as soon as she got between the sheets, and Frank was already in dreamland ahead of her.

Friday and Saturday were matinee and evening shows, but shows were frowned on during Sundays in very Catholic Strasburg, so they all got Sunday off.

But the Christmas Market was still in full swing. It appeared that "shows" might be prohibited, but unlike in America, commerce on Sunday was encouraged.

Frida took Annie under her wing that day, and took

her on a personal tour of the Christmas Market, with special attention to things that Annie wanted to bring or send home as presents.

"I love these markets," Frida said happily, as they wandered the square between rows of stalls full of color and glitter, interspersed with stalls selling hot mulled wine, hot chocolate, the ubiquitous sausages, enormous pretzels, and pastries. "The village Jack and I live in is a small one outside of Munich, and it's so tedious to get into Munich over Christmas that I rarely get to go to the market there."

"Snow?" Annie ventured as a guess.

"Deep and frequent, and that's not all," Frida confirmed. "Because everyone else in the region wants to be there for the market too, *and* of course there are families who want to reunite over Christmas, so although ordinarily we have several lodging options, finding someplace to lay our heads is a chancy operation unless we make arrangements well in advance. And just for shopping? It generally makes no sense."

"Well, I can see that, but it seems sad, somehow. Oh, look!" her attention was distracted by a display of finely carved little multi-storied carousel-type things, all powered by candles at the base. The heat from the candle moved a sort of horizontal "windmill" blade at the top, and made the entire thing turn. As it turned around and around, there were processions of wise men and camels, flocks of sheep, and other Nativity-themed displays passing by their eyes. The carving was superb, and not all of the mobile-structures were Christmas themed.

"Sadly, those would never survive a voyage across the Atlantic," Frida pointed out reluctantly. "To be honest, most of them have trouble surviving being packed up after Christmas and unpacked the next year, that's why there's a steady market for them. They're very fragile; they have to be kept lightweight, or the candles couldn't propel them."

Annie sighed. She could imagine Ma's delight at seeing such a thing, and the little ones crowing at the moving shadows the displays cast.

But alas. They would not survive in any condition fit to show.

Neither would the ornaments that seemed somehow to be made of mere wood shavings. Nor the beautiful blown-glass pieces, meant to be hung on Christmas trees in the German fashion.

"Ah, but look here—" said Frida, pointing out some tiny perfume bottles of colored and cut glass, like gorgeous, glittering gems. "Small, and surprisingly strong. Look, here are even bottles you can wear as a necklace!"

Somehow Frida managed to spot things even Annie's avid gaze missed, and they took their treasures back to the *Gasthaus,* where Frank and Jack were enjoying beer and cigars in exclusively male company. Annie was pleased; Frank wasn't a teetotaler, but his normally abstemious nature meant he didn't have as many male friends in the show as a person would think. But Jack seemed to be of a similar cut to Frank; neither of them liked to be showy—certainly nothing like the Colonel—they enjoyed drink and tobacco in moderation, and neither of them cared for cutting up and getting into trouble. They liked to play cards, but not for money. In short, they were new best friends.

"Christmas shopping done?" Jack asked with a grin as they came back down from the guest room unburdened.

"I think so, actually," Annie replied, mentally going through the list of people back home she wanted presents for. "Frida is very good at finding things."

"Frida has been scouting the market for days on your behalf," Jack pointed out. "If there's one thing she enjoys, it's helping spend someone else's money."

Frida took off her hat and hit him with it, before settling down next to him. "Are you two done smoking those filthy things?" she asked. "If you are not, I am going to take Annie out again. And this time we *might* come back burdened with hats and shoes and lace!"

"No, we're done," Frank replied before Jack could answer. "Although . . . lace don't take up much space. Ain't this place supposed to be purt famous for it?"

"Alsace lace, yes," Frida agreed. "The best of it isn't at the Christmas market, though. If it won't disappoint Annie not to go out again immediately, I'll take her to some shops after Christmas."

"It won't disappoint me none," Annie replied. "'Specially if we can get us some bargains on account of Christmas is over."

Frank laughed, and so did Frida. "And silk floss for embroidery," Frida added. "Now, that is a skill you possess that makes me mightily jealous. No amount of magic can make the threads do anything other than tangle into knots in my hands."

Then she sobered. "I do not know if you are aware of it, but tonight is a . . . difficult date, magically speaking. It is the winter solstice, and tonight is when . . . bad things can break through. So I would advise you to be within doors by sunset, and not leave before morning. You, Annie, are particularly vulnerable, because you are now aware of your power, but untrained. As you were as a child, you are now a desirable object to those who crave power they can steal."

Annie and Frank sobered immediately. "Well, we can stay right here, all right, and I'm right glad that we ain't gonna have to do a show," Frank said, finally. "But what'll you be doing?"

"Hunting," Jack said, with a gleam in his eye. "Same as every winter solstice, every *Walpurgisnacht*, every All Hallows Evenin'. When dark things come out, they find the *Bruderschaft* waitin' for them."

"Surely not in a big city like Strasburg," Frank objected.

"Where better?" Frida replied. "Big cities are full of people who will not be missed. So the *Bruderschaft* emerges from our forests and mountains and come into the cities to hunt the hunters."

Annie glanced over at Frank. She could see it in his eyes. It wasn't often that Frank Butler got riled, and determined to do something drastic, but she could see what he wanted to do.

And truth to tell . . . so did she.

"Can we help?" she asked.

Frida and Jack exchanged an unreadable look. "May be prowlin' the streets until dawn and not find nothin'." Jack cautioned.

"It is true that you do not need any magic at all against many of the creatures of the dark," Frida mused. "Just courage, and skill, which I know you both have, and some special arms and ammunition. Just the right bullets."

"We want t'help," Frank said firmly.

Frida nodded. "All right, then. In fact . . . this would be a very good opportunity for you to see exactly what we of the *Bruderschaft* do without committing to learning magic. You may decide that instead of embracing magic, you wish to run as far and fast as you can in the other direction."

"Fine, then. What do we do and where do we go?" Frank asked.

"You meet us before sunset at the Castle—that's that big beer hall, *Der Schloss*—where we took you to eat," said Jack, getting to his feet. "Dress warm, in somethin' that ain't gonna show blood. Boots, not shoes. Handguns, not rifles. We'll supply the rest." Frida nodded.

"We'll see you there," vowed Frank, as he, too, got to his feet. "I reckon a nap might be in order if we're gonna be out all night."

"See you there," Frida agreed, and the couple moved toward the door—not running, but moving without any suggestion of leisure.

"Wear somethin' that won't show blood," mused Frank. "Well, *that* ain't ominous."

6

FRANK and Annie were dressed somberly, and just on the genteel side of shabby, as they approached *Der Schloss* with the light beginning to fade in the overcast sky. It was already colder, with a hint that it might start snowing again. They were wearing old outfits, too good to make into rags, not good enough that Annie reckoned they were going to pack them up for the trip home, and if they were ruined by the end of the night, Annie wouldn't be sorry. The only loss was that it was a nice, warm outfit: a thick woolen walking skirt, shortened to just above her ankle like all her skirts were, a cotton flannel shirtwaist, and over that a jacket that matched the skirt and her waterproof—hopefully blood-proof—winter cape. Beneath it all she wore two sets of long underwear, a flannel petticoat, and flannel leggings. The problem? Every one of those garments had multiple careful darns, mended seams, and even a patch or two.

The only thing she was wearing that wasn't shabby were her boots.

Frank was similarly clad, insofar as warmth and number

of patches and darns were concerned. And unlike many men Annie knew, who clung to shabby old favorite garments until they looked like scarecrows, Frank took great pride in his appearance, and wouldn't mourn the loss of his clothing either, if it came to that.

The beer hall seemed unusually quiet, with a couple of families going inside, rather than carousing students. Annie was puzzled, but then remembered that it was still Sunday. Those students that weren't nursing big heads from a Saturday-night, pre-Christmas carousal were probably still sleeping that carousal off. As they pushed open the doors and were met by one of the waiters, Annie cast a glance around the room and noted only half the tables were full, and there was none of the singing and toasting going on that there had been the last time they were here. Instead, it looked like a number of families were having a pre-Christmas treat of a meal here. Or perhaps, many *hausfraus* had had the same notion tonight: after working to prepare Christmas treats *and* Sunday supper, they deserved to be taken out of the kitchen for a few hours.

The waiter led them not to one of the rear, private dining rooms, but up to the next floor and a much bigger room. Like the *bierstube* downstairs, this room was done with light wood wainscoting halfway up, then plastered walls with paintings on them, and furnished with simple wooden tables and trestle stools. Karl was there, and so were Frida and Jack, dressed, like all the others with them, in dark green wool hunting suits, and stout boots made for walking.

They joined the others, who were gathered around the table nearest the stove.

"And this is the last of our group for tonight. We will speak English for the convenience of our guests," said Karl, standing up and gesturing at the folk who were already seated. "Tonight, as you know, is the Winter Solstice Hunt. This is half of the Hunting Lodge of Strasburg; the rest of us are meeting on the other side of town tonight. Frida and Jack have experience, but you, American friends, do not, so I will explain what is to happen tonight."

Annie wondered why Frida, who was supposed to be a Hunt *Master,* and who was an Elemental Master rather than just a magician, was not in charge. But then it occurred to her that Frida and Jack were strangers here and this was not their "hunting grounds," so to speak. Karl must be a Hunt Master as well—and he was the native here. Certainly everyone else seemed to accept Karl as the leader without question.

He has probably been doing this every Solstice for years.

"We will be issuing you cartridges for your revolvers. Do not worry about the quality of the powder. I assure you, it is the very best. There will be three kinds of loads. One will be silver shot. One will be blessed lead from old church roof repairs. The third will be blessed rock-salt loaded as shot."

Annie couldn't help it, she probably looked very puzzled at those instructions. Karl glanced at her and responded.

"Silver is fatal to some kinds of supernatural creatures. Lead is only fatal if it is consecrated. Salt ordinarily would not even penetrate clothing, but certain supernatural beings find it deadly, and doubly so if consecrated. Father Gerhardt has personally blessed all of our ammunition, and will be Hunting with me. Frau and Herr Butler, you are not to shoot unless Jack or Frida shoot first, or direct you to shoot. They know how to tell a supernatural threat from something that is not. We do not want to frighten innocents, and we don't even want to hurt common footpads—who should, in all honesty, take one look at our groups and decide to find victims elsewhere."

Annie and Frank nodded their agreement. It was only sensible, Karl was right. But then . . . robbers were not always thinking before they attacked. "And if the footpads are particularly stupid?" she asked.

"We'll try not to hurt them too much," smirked Frida.

"We will divide into four parties, quartering our part of Strasburg. We need not include the Wild West Show; that stretch of common ground has never been known for attracting or spawning troublesome creatures, and the vigilance of their usual night guards will probably discourage anything from wandering within their bounds."

Well, that's good, I suppose, even though I don't know what it means. Well, other than the fact that he is fairly sure the show is well-protected enough.

Which, except for supernatural threats, it certainly was, with an armed night guard at all times—and with most cowboys sleeping with their weapons near at hand.

Karl proved to be a man of few words, for he was finishing up. "Salt for ghosts, blessed lead for witches and anything that looks mortal, silver shot for anything that does not, and if you cannot tell, then use all three. If you think your attacker is just a human, then salt—chances are that merely being shot at will make him run away, and the salt will do no harm to something merely mortal. For the uncanny, shoot to kill, and Butlers, please follow Frau Cate's orders."

Again they nodded, and came to get their ammunition. Fortunately there was plenty of the right caliber for all four of their revolvers; Annie and Frank loaded the right-hand ones with alternating lead and silver, and the left-hand ones with salt. She sighed at the thought of the salt. Salt did not do good things for the inside of a gun, and even though the salt was enclosed in a lead-foil packet, she didn't like the idea that so much as a grain of it could touch the pristine metal of the barrel. *I shall have to clean this gun within an inch of its life after I unload it.* But it wasn't to be helped; this was what was needed, so this was what she would load. Karl gave them each additional ammunition pouches to sling over their shoulders: leather for the silver and lead, and cloth for the salt, to help keep them from getting the cartridges confused in the dark.

Frida and Jack looked them both over like a pair of military commanders on inspection, and signaled their satisfaction. "We're farthest, so we will begin our trek to our section now, Karl," Frida called over her shoulder, then motioned to Annie and Frank to follow her. Annie noticed then that Frida had a third weapon; her crossbow was strapped to her back, and there was a quiver of arrows for it at the rear of her belt. Jack had an additional piece of equipment too, a lasso.

They left without anyone taking any notice of them—which seemed odd. Annie would have thought that a woman with a crossbow on her back would have garnered *some* sort of attention. But they left the warmth and delectable aromas of the *bierstube* with some regret on Annie's part. Although, on the one hand, she was anxious to help Frida and Jack, on the other, it was hard to leave that pleasant spot for the darkness and the cold.

The Christmas Market was still in full roar when they passed through it. "Where are we patrolling?" Annie asked Frida, as the woman cut through the crowd as effortlessly as a draft horse through a flock of sheep.

"The poorest part of the entire city," Frida replied. "Just as well that it is winter, too, because otherwise there are many bad smells. It is a place of despair, and thus, the most likely to see evil come to prey on that despair." Frida glanced aside at her. "That is in part what the evil things of the magical world feed on—despair, anger, fear, misery, sorrow. And here we are, on the longest, coldest night of the year, near to Christmas—but for the poor, Christmas is a day in which others get good things and they do not, others may rest but they may not, and all those emotions are very close to the surface of their thoughts tonight. It is said that the barrier between the world where evil things dwell and our own is very thin on the longest night, and they can scent what they crave before they even try to cross."

Annie felt apprehension grip her gut, and not just for the evil spirits they might meet, but for what *else* was going to be prowling the slum streets tonight. For all that the Moses family had been poor, it had not been the kind of poverty of an urban slum. Neighbors had helped one another, not fought tooth and nail over scraps. The worst she had ever seen, aside from the Wolves, was drunks. And from the time she became a performer she'd been insulated from "the bad parts" of the cities she'd been in. The closest she came to true poverty was orphanage visits.

But despite Karl saying that it was unlikely that thieves and robbers would bother a group that looked like theirs . . . that despair and hopelessness Frida had just now spoken of had driven folk to desperate measures before this. There was always the chance of that tonight.

The change from "respectable neighborhood" to "poor" to "dangerous" was marked not by presence, but by absence. An absence of street lights. An absence of police. An actual absence of lights in the windows. Perhaps one window in a dozen had a hint of flickering light at it, showing through whatever the inhabitants had put up to close off drafts.

Already her feet, nose, and the tips of her fingers were cold. She wished that it was possible to shoot accurately in mittens, because mittens would be warmer than the thin leather shooting gloves she was wearing.

She stumbled over a frozen lump of snow, and jostled Frida. "I'm sorry!" she said immediately.

"Stop for a moment," said Frida. All four of them paused for a moment in the middle of the street. Annie heard her muttering a few words, then out of nowhere, a glowing ball of light appeared, floating about chest-high. She jumped.

"It's just a mage-light," Frida said, amused.

"But won't someone see?" Annie asked, shivering as a gust of wind kicked around a corner and up her coat. "I thought—"

"In this part of town, I want anyone thinking about setting on us to see it," Frida replied. "Seeing this thing should make even the most hardened gang of footpads think twice about attacking us."

"Is that likely?" Frank asked.

Jack shrugged. "We got guns," he pointed out. "They'll have knives, at best. Blessed lead bullets work just the same as regular lead. I'd use the salt, though; at distance, they'll be startled by the *bang* and the muzzle flash, and at point-blank range it'll hurt somethin' fierce."

"Hmm. We hope," said Frida dryly. "Still, we don't make good targets; armed, and four of us. That's why I want us to be seen clearly. So it's clear we are not to be trifled with."

"But what about—things that aren't human?" Annie asked, as they resumed walking, keeping to the center of the uneven street, mage-light being pushed through the air over their heads by a little sylph with night-black bird wings. "Won't they see us too?"

"I'm counting on it," Frida replied. "The stupid ones will attack us. The smart ones will flee. Either way we keep them from harming innocents."

Annie saw nothing to find fault with in that statement, but she couldn't help wondering . . .

"This isn't all an elaborate joke on us, is it?" she asked, finally.

Frida snorted. "If it was, it isn't something I'd be playing at. *Why* would I tramp about the dangerous parts of Strasburg in the dark, in the cold, until nearly dawn, just for the sake of a joke?"

Put that way. . . . "What did Karl mean by 'witches'?" she continued, since Frida seemed inclined to talk. "We aren't Hunting a lot of old ladies, are we?"

Frida shook her head. "The kind of witch we are Hunting isn't human," she said decisively. "They are a kind of malevolent place-spirit. That is, they are bound to a particular spot and can't leave it. They are more dangerous than a ghost, because they have a fully solid body. And they have rather startling powers of movement, so be prepared for that."

Annie kept talking, in no small part because hearing someone's friendly voice in this place was comforting. She was grateful that it was the dead of winter even though she was so cold at the moment—these narrow streets smelled bad enough even though it was freezing. They smelled of ingrained filth, stale urine and feces, cabbage, and—despair. She knew that last smell. The desperation of the poor and hungry.

You didn't smell any rotting garbage here because no food remained long enough to become garbage, and no food item was so spoiled or mold-covered that it would not be salvaged for eating.

And all this just brought back sad memories of her own. How many times had she and Ma scrubbed the mold off something so they could cook it? How many times had they sifted weevils out of flour before they made bread with it?

Poverty is a curse. And anyone who thinks the poor are only poor because they are lazy or they bring it on them- selves is a monster as bad as the ones we are hunting.

"Witches are . . . creatures of the dark woods and haunted pools," Frida went on. "Are you familiar with the story of Hansel and Gretel?"

Even she had heard that story. "You mean, that was real?" she gasped.

"Not real in the sense that the witch had a cottage made of cakes," Frida admonished, as she stopped to peer down a dark crack of an alley. "But in the sense that these are creatures that use illusion to snare victims and devour them. In the city, parents that can't afford to feed their children sometimes sell them, or hire them out to anyone who will give them money for services. In the country—parents sometimes take children into the woods and abandon them there. And that is how the witches get them."

"But how do they end up in the city, then?" Frank asked logically. "Witches, I mean."

"As I said, they are rooted to a place, so when their place gets enveloped by the city, they remain, use their illusions to hide themselves, and go on hunting. They're probably more successful when they're consumed by the city than when their lairs were hidden in the forest," Frida added. "There are more potential victims here."

"How is that?" Annie asked. "Wouldn't it be easier in a forest? Besides those poor children you talked about, people get lost in forests all the time."

Frida snorted. "People disappear in these streets daily," she said. "Particularly children. And no one cares. The poor have no one to look for them when they vanish. Even if a parent dearly loves a child, who are they to turn to for help? They can't abandon whatever work they have to look for it, and the police will not go knocking door to door looking for a child of the poor."

That statement, so very true, struck Annie to her core. If she had completely vanished, if the Wolves had hidden or even killed her, who would have done anything about it? Who could have? How would Ma even have known until it was long past too late? It would have been months, or a year or more, before her Ma decided it had been too long, took her courage in her hands, and made any inquiries, and if the Wolves said she'd run away, how could her Ma have proved any differently?

"Well," added Jack, "when it comes to uncanny critters, we're the ones that take care'a the poor. Get 'em revenge, if nothin' else. But mostly, we take the things down before they get a chance to hurt someone."

They were speaking in near whispers, for the streets were nearly as silent as a graveyard, with few lights showing in the windows—perhaps one light for every two or three buildings. This didn't surprise Annie at all. The poor couldn't afford light any more than the poor could afford heat. On this longest night of the year, it was most likely that every soul in every room or apartment was huddled together beneath every scrap they had that could serve as a cover, with the luckiest being the youngest, who would be at the center of the human pile.

She could remember huddling in one bed with her siblings on cold nights such as this, too cold to sleep well, too tired to try to do anything else, and longing for daylight when she could go out and hunt for something to eat.

But she was not given any time to think about Jack's statement, because both Jack and Frida stopped dead in their tracks. And a moment later, Annie saw why.

The little mage-light over their heads showed it all clearly. The crossroads ahead of them gushed clouds of smoke or steam, as if there was a hole there, right in the middle of the crossing, serving as a chimney to some subterranean furnace. The clouds even glowed at the base with a dim, reddish light. The sylphs flying with them vanished, leaving the magic light hanging motionless in midair. And in the next moment, Annie got a breath of sulfur that made her nose burn.

Sulfur! *Demon?* she wanted to ask, but Frida held out a hand to keep them from moving forward (needlessly!) and growled, *"Krampus."*

A gust of wind blew the sulfurous clouds away from them, dissipating the stink, and Jack made a gesture that made the mage-light glow as brightly as a good lamp, giving all of them a good look at the thing that had apparently materialized right in the middle of the crossroads, like an unholy traffic conductor.

It was taller than Frank or Jack; seven feet tall, in fact, at least. And if this *"Krampus"* wasn't a demon— well, Annie didn't know what else it *could* be. Goat horns, literally fiery eyes in a slate-gray face stuck in a rictus-grin of false mirth, shaggy black pelt, goat legs, and a long, tufted tail. It could have been funny-looking, if it weren't for the three-inch fangs it sported, the madness in its eyes—

—and the *tongue* that lolled out of its mouth so far that it curled on the ground.

—and the *smell*. Like a filthy billy-goat that had been rolling in something unspeakable.

It had a pair of those fancy suspenders that German men wore with their *lederhosen,* but no other clothing of any kind. It had a wicker basket on its back, fastened to those suspenders, chains on its wrists and ankles that apparently didn't bother it any more than if they'd been made of sewing thread, and a bundle of switches in one hand, as if it was going to beat a naughty child.

Strangely, she didn't feel frightened. She felt electrified. It was almost as if this, and not the sylphs, was the *real* confirmation that there actually were uncanny horrors roaming the world.

"Ha!" it shouted, spotting them. *"Fang mich, Sterbliche!"* And it leapt high into the air, sailed over their heads, and landed on the road behind them. They whirled to face it, and it brandished the bundle of switches at them. *"Ihr wart schlechte Kinder! Der Krampus wird dich schlagen!"*

And then it shot out its tongue like a frog trying to catch a fly. Except *they* were the flies.

"Did he say *schlagen* or *essen?*" Jack bleated, leaping out of the way as the tongue lashed out at him like a whip.

"It won't matter if he gets that tongue around you," his wife countered, jumping the other direction.

But Annie and Frank had both reacted—after the initial shock and out of sheer panic—by drawing and firing, one round each. She was pretty sure her round was silver and Frank's was lead; they'd coordinated their loads when they'd collected the ammunition.

Annie had aimed for the center of the creature, which stumbled back a moment, although it didn't seem to take any actual damage from the shots even though the bullets were hitting it. But now it was definitely angry.

The light in its eyes blazed up, and the tongue, that horrible, wet, black tongue, shot at Annie, who evaded it, but only just. It made an awful sound as it slapped on the pavement beside her.

"Don't shoot the basket!" Frida cried frantically. "There might be a child in there!"

A child? In the basket? No time to ask any questions right now. She balanced lightly on her toes, ready to move in whatever direction was safest, and holstered her right-hand gun since the lead and silver weren't doing any good.

She pulled the revolver loaded with salt and aimed again, letting off another shot.

This time she sent a round into its thigh, thinking perhaps to cripple it, this time the rock salt. *That* seemed to have an effect. It staggered back again, this time with a bleat of pain. Jack let off a shot of his own at the same time.

"Salt!" Jack yelled at the same moment that she shot. "Salt works! Keep him busy!"

Keep him busy? What kind of instruction is that? But the thing jumped right at Annie and this time she had to duck under its lashing tongue, drop to the ground, roll out of the way and onto her feet again before she could fire a third time. A roar from Frank's revolver followed by one from Jack's distracted the creature so Annie could get into the dubious cover of a recessed doorway.

That was when Jack's lariat whipped out of the darkness, *glowing,* and settled around the *Krampus*'s shoulders. Annie jumped out of hiding, shot the thing in the face, and jumped out of range of that tongue before it could lash at her.

Frank unloaded another round, while Jack whipped another loop of the rope around the *Krampus*'s shoulders, pinning its arms down.

Annie sent her third round of salt into the *Krampus*'s face; Frank evidently had another idea. He unloaded four rounds at nearly point-blank distance into the thing's tongue.

The howl of rage, agony, and mindless bestiality the *Krampus* let out at that moment dropped her to her knees, the revolver still clutched in one fist, her hands covering her ears to absolutely no avail. The sound was so raw, so piercing, that it brought tears of pain to her eyes, and for a moment she couldn't see.

When she blinked the blurring out of her vision, it was to see Jack casting a third loop of his lasso around the demon, and Frida taking careful aim with her crossbow.

The first bolt pierced the *Krampus* in the right eye. The second took out his left.

And with a final shriek and an explosion of sulfurous smoke he vanished, leaving behind the wicker basket and his bundle of switches.

Annie scrambled to her feet and raced to the basket and ripped the top right off, fearing to find a child—or worse, a dead child—huddled in the bottom. But it was empty.

She dropped the top, and let go of the basket so that it fell over sideways, and staggered to Frank's side, feeling her energy draining right out of her.

"What . . . was . . . that?" Frank asked slowly.

"That was the *Krampus*. Or rather, *a Krampus*," said Frida, walking over to the artifacts and prodding the basket with a toe.

"I thought it was a demon," Annie gulped, holstering her revolver and staring at the basket, halfway expecting the thing to materialize again.

"He's—well, some say he is a demon, and some say that he isn't," Frida explained. "This is the only night he can appear on earth in the entire year. He punishes wicked children in the same way that Saint Nicholas rewards them. Some think he's one of the saint's 'helpers' in that way." She picked up the bundle of switches and dropped it in the basket, shoving the lid in on top of it. "There are legends about Saint Nicholas defeating him in a fierce battle and forcing him to serve the saint's purposes, but *I* think those are all old priests' tales. Naughty children get a beating with the bundle of switches. Bad ones get beaten by the chains. Wicked ones, so they say, end up in the basket, and literally no one knows what happens to them, only that they are never seen again."

"They'd have t'be purt wicked afore that'd happen though, don't you think?" Jack observed. "I expect it do happen now and again, or it wouldn't be in the legends, but I cain't recall a single story—story, like direct from the source, not a legend—that anyone in the *Bruderschaft* has ever told 'bout kids goin' completely missing. Kids scared out of their minds, but never ones gone missing."

Frida snorted and waved her hand at the street around them—a street which, despite the howls and the shooting and the clouds of sulfurous smoke, *no one* was in except themselves. No one was looking out of windows—or at least, if they were, they were doing so furtively. No one had come out of any of the doors.

"Look around you! Do you think anyone here dares go to a constable to say their child was missing? They'd be accused of doing away with or selling the little one themselves!" Then she deflated. "Of course, Jack is right about one thing. A child would have to be very wicked—murderous, even—before the *Krampus* would take it away in its basket." She shook her head. "Or perhaps—pah. Let us dispose of these things so *this one* at least cannot manifest for a year."

Jack closed his hand into a fist, and opened it to reveal a bright flame, which he bent down and put to the side of the wicker basket. The basket flared up as if it had been soaked in oil, and in moments was gone.

Annie checked her revolvers and reloaded them, breathing slowly and deeply to steady her nerves. Frank and Jack were doing the same. "Wait," she said, remembering something. "You said *this one* cannot manifest for a year—"

"I did," Frida acknowledged. "This was the Strasburg *Krampus*, but there are many, many more. I've never heard of more than one of them materializing at a time in a city or town, but they will be manifesting all over Germany, Switzerland, and Austria tonight, and there will be Hunting Parties waiting for them. I'm just glad we got this one before he hurt any children."

Annie wondered why on earth the parents of beaten children didn't have a few things to say about such an outrage—

"But wait—if children are terrified and beaten in the morning, wouldn't that be evidence to people that *Krampus* is real?" she blurted.

"The children the beast beats are healed completely in the morning," Frida sighed. "So, of course, no one believes them but us magicians."

"If you don't think it's a demon, then what is it?" Frank asked.

Frida kicked at the ashes of the basket, scattering them. "You know there are Elementals, both good and bad. *Krampus* is an Earth Elemental, one of the bad ones. And perhaps he used to be one of the truly powerful ones. I think he deliberately heals the children he beats, not to spare them any more pain, but to provoke emotional pain, when their own parents will not believe what the children know is real, and even the children are left confused when the evidence vanishes from their very bodies."

Annie felt herself shudder with sympathy for the poor children, bruised and battered and probably frightened within an inch of their lives, huddling in their beds until morning, paralyzed with pain and fear—and then having their wounds vanish with the rising sun. And then, of course, with no proof, they would be laughed at, at best, and beaten again at worst, for lying.

"Frida, what did you shoot it with, and why did our cartridges have little effect?" she asked, as Jack coiled up his lariat again, and the little sylphs reappeared cautiously, flitting overhead like bats.

"Crossbow bolts made from last year's Christmas trees," Frida replied, with a crooked smile. "I've got those, I've got holly, and I've got sacred oak rubbed with mistletoe juice. As for your ammunition, the blessed salt worked, because *Krampus* is closer to being a spirit than anything else. But it didn't work *well* because Elementals are not spirits. Now that I think about it, that's an argument against it being a demon—the consecrated lead should have worked, and the blessed salt would have worked better than it actually did."

"Went a sight faster than last year with you two along," Jack put in, slapping Frank on the shoulder.

"Wait, you did this last year, too?" Annie gasped, aghast.

"Not here. We did a horseback patrol of the villages in our part of Bavaria, a little village called Schwandorf." Jack rubbed the back of his head with his gloved hand. "We do that every year. No other way we could cover all the ground we needed to, but it's hard on the horses, even with mage-lights to see by."

"Dell and Arte are the best boys we've ever had for Hunting, though," Frida added. "Rock steady. Not even *Krampus* made them bolt."

Annie was still feeling a lot of distress, thinking about the poor children that were the *Krampus*'s victims. "*Why?*" she asked angrily. "Why does this . . . *thing* come out, year after year? Why don't you do anything permanent about it?"

"Don't you think we've tried?" Frida replied, in a much more reasonable tone than Annie was using. "For centuries now, we've tried. Some of the more scholarly among us think that the *Krampus* is more than an Earth Elemental, that he is a degraded old god, no longer worshiped, only given enough power of belief to manifest for a single night, unable to claim any sacrifices but children—and even then, he doesn't get to *sacrifice* many of them, which limits his power even more. They think the reason he beats children and leaves them with nightmares for the rest of their lives is *exactly* because that's the only way he keeps the story and the belief going, so he can keep manifesting. How do you defeat a god?"

Annie opened her mouth—but could find no words.

And that was when a new horror jumped down off the roof of the building next to them to land atop Jack's shoulders and drive him to the ground with a dull thud.

"Jack!" Frida cried, as the thing leapt off him and away, to stand there in the middle of the street, cackling and staring at them.

It looked vaguely human . . . but its arms and legs were too long, and too spindly; its torso was too short, and it seemed to have next to no neck, just a hunched-over back with a head jutting from the top of it, a head covered with an unruly shock of straw-like hair. The more Annie stared at it, the more inhuman it looked, as if everything about it was wrong in some way. It didn't move right; the joints bent in unnatural places. It made her a little sick to look at, and her skin began to crawl.

It was dressed in black rags, and when it turned sideways for a moment, she saw it had a face that was like the caricature of an evil witch in a child's book, all nose and chin, with glowing green eyes.

It was the eyes that made her feel truly horrid, although she could not have said why. The eyes were the least human thing about it. There was a malevolence there that she could not even begin to measure.

No one moved.

Jack groaned, and stirred. *He's not dead! At least, not yet—*

She didn't even think about pulling her lead-and-silver-loaded revolver, she just did it, and so did Frank and Frida. The guns roared, and a hail of bullets riddled the thing, which staggered back, and back, and back, jerking in an obscene parody of a dance, until it collapsed against the wall of a building and slid down it to end up in a tangle of rags and spidery limbs in the dirty snow.

Frida ran to Jack's side; Jack gasped in a huge breath of air, levered himself up to his knees with her help, then got to his feet. "Good thing them witches don't scarcely weigh nothing," he said, wheezing as he got his breath back. "She was like to break my back."

"Is she going to stay dead?" Annie asked, as Frank went over to the thing to poke at it with his toe.

"Blessed lead from a church roof will ensure that. Frank, would you drag her into the center of the road?" Frida asked. "I need to make certain Jack hasn't broken anything."

"Wisht I had. It'd hurt less," Jack groaned, as Frida felt all his limbs for damage and Frank obliged by dragging the creature to the place where they'd burned the wicker basket.

"Why am I doing this?" Frank asked, although it was clear from the lack of effort he put into the task that Jack had spoken the plain truth—the witch didn't weigh anything to speak of.

Frida took a flask out of a pocket and sprinkled the corpse with the contents. Annie picked up the scent of lamp oil. Jack spat on the thing, then made a tossing motion with his hand; a tiny fireball appeared in his hand as he "threw," and it landed on the witch's body.

If anything it burned more briskly than the wicker basket had.

Frida gestured, and the mage-light brightened until the street where they stood was illuminated almost as brightly as if it were noon. She bent and retrieved something, while Jack sat down hard on the pavement and made stretching motions with his shoulders and neck. She repeated the motion until she straightened with a handful of—

—*oh, of course. She picked up all the lead and silver bullets. I expect lead from a church roof is not easy to come by. And each one of the other bullets probably has half a silver thaler in it.*

Frida tucked the bullets away in a pocket. Jack made sure he still had his weapons, and rubbed the back of his head, wincing.

"Good thing my head's harder than this pavement," he joked, and pulled on his coat to straighten it. "Right. Reckon we've cleared out this block, on to the next."

On . . . to the next. For a moment Annie was aghast. But then she felt something inside herself straighten up as Jack had . . .

"On to the next," she agreed. "But first, we all really need to reload."

7

THE rest of the night was relatively uneventful. The things they ran across in their hunt through the worst parts of Strasburg were mostly purely mortal dangers, and the show of guns certainly made the threats go skittering off into the darkness, looking for easier prey.

As for supernatural threats—one was a giant raven, twice the size of the biggest eagle Annie had ever seen, that Frida spotted perched on a rooftop. Frida motioned them all to remain still and deliberately grazed it with a crossbow bolt, which sent it flying off into the darkness. One was an old woman with wild eyes, driving about in a little cart pulled by a black dog. She took one look at them and snarled, but said nothing, and drove the cart away so quickly the dog's legs were a blur.

When the clocks struck three in the morning, Frida declared it was safe to leave the streets to the merely mortal threats and go back to their beds. By this time Annie was half frozen despite all her preparations. Nose, feet, and hands were all freezing, and she huddled inside her coat wishing that the *Gasthaus* was a lot closer. The clocks were just striking four when they entered the *Gasthaus* and tiptoed up the stairs to their room. With a sigh of relief, they let themselves inside and began shedding clothing; whoever had left the stove stoked had done a good job of making sure the room would be warm when they arrived.

"Left word not to wake us unless we ain't up by two," said Frank, as Annie slid back the bedclothes and discovered to her joy that the maid had left a bed warmer in it—the kind that used hot bricks rather than coals. She pulled the long-handled pan out and left it beside the stove for the maid to find. Whatever else Frank said was lost to sleep and exhaustion, because as soon as her cold body slipped into the warm bed, she was sound asleep.

The staff didn't have to come wake them, but it was a very near thing, and it was dinner they had instead of breakfast before they headed to the show for the late afternoon performance. Annie could scarcely believe that Frida and Jack looked as if they'd done nothing at all but sleep last night, especially not after that witch had knocked Jack to the ground. She couldn't see a bit of sluggishness in their reactions, nor anything other than clear-eyed alertness in their faces. Was this an effect of their magic?

"Come walk the Christmas market with us," urged Frida after they had all finished eating supper after the show. She made the invitation to the entire table, but of course, only Annie and Frank took her up on it. The novelty of the market had worn off for most of the show folk, once they'd taken in the sights and made whatever purchases their pocketbooks would allow. Those who had family at home had probably found the *pfennigs* to send or bring something home, but they had done so within the first few days of the market opening.

There were a few families in the show, and it was to be expected that the children that were permitted to roam ended up at the market nearly every day. Annie's resources did not extend to buying presents for *every* member of the troupe—there were nearly a thousand of them, after all—but she loved the children with all her heart, and they loved her and would do anything for her. She'd paid special attention to what those young hearts were yearning over, and on Christmas morning, she had a very big surprise planned with the help of Jerry the Moose.

"Ah dunno what you ladies like so much about wanderin' around in the cold half the night, lookin' at gewgaws," teased one of the cowboys as they headed out.

"*Gluehwein,* brother," Frank cast over his shoulder, causing a general laugh. *Everyone* loved *gluehwein*—a staple at Christmas, she'd been told, red wine heated with spices, raisins, and oranges. Even the cowboys who professed a greater love for Strasburg's strong beer would not turn down a hot mug.

As Annie had expected, they did not head in the direction of the Christmas Market. Instead, just at the edge of the field where the show was, a dark, expensive-looking carriage pulled by four horses stood waiting. It was pretty clear that the carriage was waiting for them when Frida led them straight to it.

The driver helped them in without saying a single word, leapt up onto the box, and drove off briskly.

"We have been asked to give our reports in person at a Lodge gathering at the home of the Hunt Master of Strasburg Lodge," Frida explained, as the carriage lurched into motion. "There will probably be a fair amount of . . . well . . . fawning involved. You're quite famous, after all, and they've been rather jealous that I was chosen to interact with you. I presume after meeting so many crowned heads, a lot of German businessmen and a couple of minor nobles will be nothing to you."

"Not *nothing,*" Frank replied. "And if all these people have been Huntin' things like the ones we did last night, well, they're doing a gosh-darned sight more than *I've* been doin' with their lives."

Annie was a little relieved to hear Frank voice what had been in her own mind—that now that she'd seen what Elemental Magicians did, well, her life as a show person seemed awfully shallow.

But you're good at it, admonished her practical side. *Doesn't it make more sense to concentrate on what you're already good at, and use your money as you have been, to benefit the rest of society?*

It was a perfectly good argument. She just wasn't certain she believed it now. Especially not since it seemed that nasty things were rather thicker on the ground than the magicians that fought such things.

The carriage pulled up to a magnificent townhouse on the corner of the street they had just crossed. The bottom floor was stone; the remaining four stories up to the steeply slanted roof were dark wood, elaborately carved and ornamented, featuring big leaded glass windows that filled nearly half the wall space. It was evident that the attic beneath the roof was also in use, judging by the light coming from the windows set into the rooftop itself.

Probably where the servants sleep, Annie guessed, as they climbed out of the carriage and she stared up at the place. It was impressive even by the standards of the English "stately homes" she and Frank had stayed in. And it would certainly take a small army of servants to keep it running.

A footman or doorman in old-fashioned knee-breeches met them at the door, and they were passed off to a maidservant in a sober black uniform for guidance. It was apparent that the first floor was used for grand entertaining; it was dimly lit, and they were ushered quickly up a handsome staircase to the second floor, and from there, to what—in a comparable English house— would be the parlor.

Annie had been in too many grand houses now to be in awe of furnishings, though this room certainly gave off an air of effortless luxury. The dominant colors were brown, cream, and gold, and by the abundance of plushly upholstered pieces, the owner was the hospitable sort. *And* modern; he had abundant gaslight brightening the room, the fixtures fitted so elegantly into the walls that they might have been there when the building had been constructed. At one end was a fine, big fireplace with a beautifully carved mantle and a tiled hearth.

The room was currently full of a crowd of many gentlemen and three women, all dressed casually. But it was otherwise the most disparate crowd Annie had ever seen gathered for a "social" occasion, because there was very little to suggest that any of these people had anything at all in common.

Several were obviously common laborers: dressed in their best, but even with an hour of brushing and the best of intentions, moleskin trousers would never look like fine wool. And others were dressed as well as the wealthy of England. Some looked like shopkeepers, and some like prosperous men of business, the law, or professions. But they were all mingling, drinking together, workman with nobleman, quite as if the Gospel was being made manifest and there were no distinctions among them.

All three of the women were extraordinary, each in a different way. One had dressed as if this was a masquerade, in something like ruby-colored, medieval robes, wearing a heavy gold necklace and matching chatelaine belt that looked to be genuine gold and gems. One, with her hair cut short at chin-length, and wearing a plain and uncompromising gown without any ornamentation, could have been a suffragist. And one was a very old lady, with silver hair in a single braid down her back, dressed in pale gray lace, who would have looked like a ghost if her complexion had not been a healthy pink.

Annie's group was approached immediately by one of the men who looked wealthy, with the Germanic "look" as Annie had come to recognize it: blond hair, square chin, clean-shaven, athletic build. He wore an

evening suit with a sash across the front that held several
jeweled orders. He held out both hands and used them
to shake Frida and Jack's hands. To Annie's relief he
spoke in English. "My dear Frida and Jack! You are the
last of us to arrive. Let us commence this meeting now
that you are here, if you have no objections."

"Gladly; unlike you lot, we four all had to work today, Theodor, and we are perishing for lack of sleep,"
Frida replied, her voice pitched to carry over the murmur of conversation. "These, as of course you know, are
the Butlers: Annie Oakley and her husband Frank."

And with those words, the dance began. It was the
moment when the gathering stopped being a random
group gathered together for socialization, and became
centered on Annie and Frank.

The dance was very familiar to Annie now, after so
many visits to so many expensive drawing rooms in England. So many receptions, so many people who craved
meeting her. The ever-so-subtle shifts of posture so that
everyone in the room was angled to face her and Frank;
the hush of conversation, the careful glances out of
hooded eyes so that no one was actually *staring,* which
would have been impolite. The only thing that was different between this room and all those English parlors
and drawing rooms was the mix of classes in this room.

"Annie, Frank, this is Graf Theodor von Hirschberg,
the Lodge Leader and Grand Hunt Master for the Strasburg Hunting Lodge," Frida said, continuing the introductions. "Theo and I have been shooting and Hunting
partners since we were both no bigger than bear cubs,
but I am a better shot than he is."

"Yes, but you cheat," Theo said without rancor, then
actually clicked his heels and bowed slightly to Annie
and Frank, before shaking their hands. She stopped herself from giggling with an effort, since she had never
seen anyone do that outside of a comic opera or oper-
etta.

"And you don't?" Frida chuckled. "The Butlers do

not have the head for liquor that we do, so don't ply them with your brandy."

"Always seemed to me that the onlyest way to get a head for liquor is to drink too much of it," Frank said mildly. "Man that does that ain't going to stay a prize-winning shootist for long."

Theodor made a gesture that brought one of the servants mingling with the crowd to his side. A whisper in her ear, and the servant left the room, and a moment later, appeared with a pair of beaten silver mugs on her tray, which she offered to the Butlers. "Completely innocent and healthful freshly pressed, unfermented apple cider, treated as *gluehwein*," the Graf pronounced, as they took the mugs. "You are not the only of my guests tonight to prefer their wits un-addled." Then he raised his voice only a trifle, but of course, with everyone paying close attention to Annie and Frank, he didn't have to raise it much to be heard. "Comrades, in deference to our guests, we will be speaking English in our reports tonight. As you know, these are the Butlers, Frau Annie Oakley and Herr Frank Butler, from the Wild West Show, who participated in our Solstice Watch last night. Now if you will all take seats, we can begin."

Frida caught Annie's eye and motioned with her chin toward a pair of upholstered settees, which had the advantage of being very near the fireplace—which, rather than being an open fire, had one of those porcelain stoves set into the hearth. This one was really beautiful; it had been painted in muted, tasteful colors to look like a beer stein, except that instead of humans drinking and dancing and carrying on their lives, it portrayed what she could only assume were Elementals. Sylphs, and things she didn't know: dwarves and fiery lizards, girls dressed in gowns of water, tiny child-like creatures with the hindquarters of goats and miniature horns sticking up from their curly hair. Annie was enchanted. If there was one thing she would have liked to take home with her from Germany, it was that stove.

She and Frank took one settee, Frida and Jack took the other, as the others settled themselves in various seats about the parlor.

"Our first order of business. Which of you encountered the *Krampus*?" Theodor asked.

Jack and Frida raised their hands, and Frida stood. "Port du Rhin," she said. "Manifested right up in the middle in the crossroads if you please, as bold as a cockerel, right across from the *Old Sailor* tavern. It was shortly before midnight and right at the beginning of our patrol. Blessed salt hurt him when Frank had the presence of mind to blast it into that tongue of his, and evergreen crossbow bolts sent him packing."

"Prize of the night to the Cates' party!" Theodor said, as there was a soft patter of applause. "Anything else?"

"A *hexe* immediately ambushed us, and we killed her outright, good riddance to bad rubbish, and we convinced a *buschgrossmutter* and a *nachtkrapp* it was unhealthy to linger. We didn't see any spirits, but then—" she shrugged "—Jack and I never have, you know."

"That *hexe* escaped us last year in the same place," said the mannish-looking woman. "And she's *been* escaping us for years, if it's the same one, which it probably is. I'm glad someone put her down."

"Did anyone else spot the *buschgrossmutter* or the *nachtkrapp?*" Theodor asked. "Keep it in mind if you saw them. Next report then, please."

The litany of monsters spotted and either routed or destroyed altogether was interspersed with sightings of ghosts, which Theodor noted down in a little book. "Ghosts can't harm anyone, can they?" Annie whispered to Frida, under cover of someone else's report.

"No, but they don't belong bound to earth," Frida told her. "Solstice makes it possible for ordinary folk, or people who don't have the right sort of Sight, to see them. Theodor notes where they were seen, and that will allow Frau Schnee to track them down later and put them where they belong." Frida nodded at the silver-haired old woman, who was also making notes in a book.

"Schnee means 'snow,' doesn't it?" Annie asked. "Surely that isn't her real name. . . ."

"Ah-ah—" Frida waggled an admonishing finger. "We don't question what a person claims is their name. Some people in the Lodge don't use their real names for various reasons, some do, some have come to be known by a pet name for so long that it might as well be their real name."

Strange name after strange name came up as the litany of *things banished* was told, and Annie only wished she had some notion as to what those *things* were. There were more of the *nachtkrapp* spotted, or perhaps the same one, but it was merely chased away, in no small part because the Hunters were in districts where it would have been ill-advised to use a gun, and it was extremely good at avoiding arrows. In fact, one of the Hunters noted with chagrin that the *nachtkrapp* had quorked derisively at him, then snatched the arrow he shot at it out of the sky and flown off with it.

When the last of the Hunters had given his report, Theodor closed his book with a sigh that sounded relieved. "A good Solstice, for a change. It's clear now, after we dealt with Ernst Kaufler last summer, that he was at least the attractor, if not the actual cause, of all those horrors that have been showing up the last five years."

This meant nothing to Annie, of course, but the rest of the group nodded with evident relief. If this had been a *good* Solstice for the patrols, Annie was quite glad she hadn't been here for the bad ones!

"Have we anything the Lodge needs to be doing then at Christmas Eve?" asked one of the workmen.

"Only come to my party and enjoy yourselves. You as well, Frau and Herr Butler." He smiled. "My wife has her gathering of the rich and ranked downstairs. I have my gathering of the good and great up here. Sometimes there is even some mingling of the two groups."

"Great? That's a matter of opinion. Good? As good as we ever are, which with too much of your brandy, is not very," said the very old lady, with a silvery laugh. "You know, in my youth I was very scandalous indeed at the Hirschberg parties."

"I will never believe that," Theodor replied gallantly. "But now, if the Butlers do not mind staying a little longer, perhaps you can answer some of their questions about magic and the Lodges."

Annie had been thinking strongly of begging leave to go until the moment he said that. It had never occurred to her that *they* might be able to interrogate the others, rather than the reverse.

She and Frank exchanged a look and a nod. "I think that will be possible, for an hour or two," Frank said. "We've got a show tomorrow and the day after."

Shortly after that, the gathering began to resemble others like it, at which people clustered around Frank and Annie and asked them—mostly asked Annie—all manner of questions. But this was, of course, "polite society," so no matter how burning their curiosity was, no one asked anything too intrusive.

It turned out that all of them had been to at least one show, and all of them were fulsome in their praise of Annie's marksmanship, which made her relax, and glow a little with pride. After all, she *was* doing everything she did without the aid of magic, and it was clear that these folks marveled at such purely physical skill.

And they were quite polite about letting her have her turn—for every question she answered, there was a pause, and a quiet tilt of the head, inviting her to ask questions of her own.

And there was one she desperately wanted answered, but didn't know how to ask politely. At least, until one of the tradesman-types got done with wanting to know where all the glass balls she destroyed in the shows came from.

"We have our very own glassblower," she explained. "Just as we have our own electricity generators and their minders, and cooks, and even a doctor. I'm sure you noticed that I am not the only one that uses glass balls as targets. It is very showy, and impresses people more than clay pigeons."

"Ach! That never occurred to me! And here I was wondering how you kept a vast stock of glass balls from breaking during your journey between cities!" he said. "This is a logical solution to that problem, and also the one of depletion of your stock."

"If you don't mind my asking," she said, "what do you do when you are not chasing ghosts and bad magicians?"

"Me? Or all of us?" He evidently did not find her question impertinent, because his eyes crinkled up at the corners as he suppressed a smile.

"Yes," she said simply.

He laughed. "Well, Theo there doesn't have to work. He's not as rich as Croesus, but he has enough money that he can hire people to do just about anything he needs done, so he can concentrate on running this Lodge and on his magic. He's a Water Master. His wife *isn't* a magician, but she *is* from a family that produces about one a generation, so she grew up knowing all about it, which is about all he requires in a wife. Frau Schnee is her mother. She is very special; normally you only see magicians of the first four Elements, but she is of the fifth, the Spirit Masters."

"My ears are burning. You must be speaking about me, Gaspard, you naughty boy," said Frau Schnee, coming up behind him. "Are you telling them that old story about how I was caught in the butler's pantry with Lydia Martin, Cecelia Lavin, and a bottle of Theo's grandfather's best brandy, forging the signatures of the handsomest men at the dance on our cards so they would *have* to dance with us?"

"I would never dare, radiant one," said Gaspard. "She was just asking what we do for a living when we are not putting crossbow bolts through a *Krampus.*"

"Hmm! Hmm! Hmm! A very good question! Some of us have the good luck and poor taste to be ridiculously rich without actually working for it," the old woman said, sitting down beside the tradesman. "Gaspard here is in the China trade—cups and teapots, not opium and silk, and his wares come out of the Netherlands, not the Orient. Delftware, I believe it is called?"

Gaspard nodded. "You have all sorts here in Strasburg, and it's as much French as it is German. The Alsace-Lorraine has been traded or fought over back and forth since we all kicked the Romans out. We have the Rhine to do all our shipping, so we're as much a port as Hamburg."

Gaspard nattered on, and Annie quickly got two impressions. First, that this disparate and congenial group was *not* something you'd find anywhere but under the roof of an Elemental Master. And second, that even among Elemental Masters, Theodor von Hirschberg was exceedingly broadminded about the divisions between the classes. Or at least, he was within the privacy of his own four walls.

The mannish woman claimed Gaspard's place before the latter had gone on too long. She actually asked a question no one on this side of the ocean had asked Annie before. "Where, exactly, in the United States do you come from?" she asked. "Because, forgive me, I have an ear for accents, and neither you nor your husband sound like Jackson Cate."

Annie had to laugh at that one. "Well, tell the truth and shame the devil, I am *not* from the actual 'Wild West.' I am from Ohio, and nearer to Chicago than to Texas by several states."

"And I was born in Ireland and lived in New Jersey before I started traveling with my shootist act," Frank chuckled. "Hope that doesn't disappoint you."

"On the contrary, it satisfies me quite a bit that my ear had not deceived me." She nodded. "It doesn't matter a toss to me where you are from; skill is skill. Now, is there anything I can tell you?"

"What was a *bad* Solstice like?" Annie asked, though not without trepidation.

The young lady sobered, and told her; on the one hand, she was relieved that no one had died, because she had seriously been expecting to hear something of the sort. But on the other hand, there had been several serious injuries, and one creature of the night had very nearly occasioned a fatality.

"I had never seen a Nightmare before and I hope never to see it again," the young woman concluded with a shudder. "I thought all they did was give people bad dreams. But not on the Winter Solstice."

"Oh, that villain Kaufler must have conjured the thing," said Frau Schnee. "He called up a good many things that had no rights being here. The only mercy was that he wasn't a necromancer. That would have been very, very bad."

By this time the servants were circulating with trays full of bite-sized delicacies just as they did at the parties that had been held in England for Annie and Frank. There was quite a lot of sausage, ham, and cheese on the ones being presented to her now, but there was also pickled fish, radishes carved to look like roses, radishes carved like long, curled wood shavings, pickled eggs, and an amazing assortment of spreads on an amazing variety of breads. This certainly made up for missing breakfast!

But it had been a very long night, and not nearly as much sleep as Annie would have liked, because spending all that time in the cold was as physically exhausting as anything they had ever done, and she found herself eating and drinking just to keep herself awake.

Fortunately their host was keeping an eye on them, and eventually drifted over when a lull occurred in the questions.

"Shall I bring the carriage around?" he asked them. "I am loath to deprive myself and my guests of your company, but last night was your first Solstice Watch and it was a very active one. I should not like to be the cause of missed shots tomorrow."

"Yes, please," Frank said. And it was not much later that they found themselves being escorted by yet another servant down to the front door and out into the cold.

In fact, it was only the cold that kept Annie awake at that point. Once again she fell into bed—at a decent hour this time. And woke in the morning with relief that after all the hair-raising stories last night, her dreams were of nothing more sinister than chasing sylphs and other strange, flying creatures over a mountain meadow full of flowers.

An actual engraved invitation to the Graf's Christmas Eve party was delivered to the *Gasthaus* the very next day, although they didn't get to see it until after the show. Frida showed them hers at supper, though, and assured them that one had been delivered for them, so Annie had plenty of time to think about whether or not they were, in fact, going.

She also had plenty of encouragement from Frida and Jack. "The Graf's wife hosts the society party downstairs," Frida told them. "Theodor's party includes the children."

In the end, that was what decided her. When they arrived back at the *Gasthaus*, their host presented the invitation with ill-concealed glee (he felt that apparently some of the cachet of being invited to Graf Hirschberg's party rubbed off on him) and informed them that the

Graf's page would come for their reply in the morning. They left their affirmative reply in his hands.

"You're going, of course," were Frida's first words to her over dinner.

"Of course!" she replied. "But this is a Christmas party and I don't want to go empty-handed—"

Frida laughed. "Autographed pictures and souvenir bullets," she advised. "Perhaps reserve the bullets for the adults, as children are apt to lose small things."

On Christmas Eve, at precisely seven in the evening, the Graf's carriage arrived at the *Gasthaus*, and Annie and Frank got in to discover Frida and Jack were already there. "Do you have your presents?" Frida asked, once they had settled, and the carriage rolled off.

"As if I would forget!" Annie held up a hatbox, which was just sturdy enough to take the weight of the bullets.

"In Germany, we give presents to the children at midnight, and they are permitted to stay awake and attend the party until that time," Frida explained, as the horses trotted briskly down the newly cleaned street toward the Graf's mansion. "That allows the poor adults to sleep to a decent hour on Christmas, rather than being awakened by clamoring children at some unsanctified hour."

Annie could not help but think back on her own childhood, when Christmas was not celebrated because there was nothing to celebrate *with*. But then—there had been some lovely Christmases with her siblings' families, and . . . well, yes, the children *did* arise at an unholy hour to check their stockings and open their presents. Charming, but very hard on the parents who had stayed up past midnight to arrange the surprises.

"That seems very sensible to me," Frank agreed. "Now, is this non-society party just the family?"

"No, no, it's the Graf's children, and anyone in the Lodge that cares to come, and any of Strasburg's magicians who are *not* in the Lodge. Not everyone is, you know," Frida continued, although that was news to Annie. "Not everyone is suited to being Hunters. And we don't allow anyone as a Hunter until they are of age, or their parents are also Hunters and take them as a sort of squire."

That's more reasonable than I would have thought . . .

And it meant they wouldn't *have* to necessarily become Hunters in order to learn how to use magic. "How many people will be there, do you think?" she asked, while she mulled this over in her mind.

"About forty at any one time, but people will come and go," Jack said. "Some will come up from the ball downstairs. Some will be making rounds of Christmas parties, and spend no more than a half hour there. It's held in the parlor, the ladies' drawing room, and the music room, and I reckon Theodor has it in mind to set you up in one of those three rooms for you to hold court." He chuckled. "So, just like the Cowboy Camp, but warmer, an' there'll be servants askin' you what you want to eat or drink so often you might start to get annoyed."

At just that moment, the carriage rolled to a stop in front of the building, which had been decorated and illuminated inside and out, so that it looked like a gigantic Christmas present. Another carriage was just rolling away, and one was pulling up behind them as a footman handed out the ladies and directed them to the door.

Annie felt a smile lifting her lips as she murmured thanks to the doorman. She had the feeling this was going to be a wonderful night.

8

A MAID intercepted them at the foot of the stairs, which had been bedecked with wreaths and festoons of evergreen. Scents swirled in the air, somehow harmonious—fir and cinnamon, nutmeg and sandalwood, vanilla and coffee, chocolate and mint. The maid asked to see their invitations, as a footman on the other side of the stairs did the same with more newcomers: two couples, one middle-aged and one elderly, both ladies swathed in fox and sable cloaks, with bejeweled feathers in their hair. *They* were directed to the right, past the stairs, where Annie could only just get a glimpse of double doors, open wide, and people swirling about under brilliant light.

The maid sent the foursome up the stairs, where they were intercepted by maids who took their coats, and Annie and Frida finally got a chance to get a good look at each other's gowns. They'd talked about them, but apparently neither of them were very good at describing fashions, because Annie knew she was surprised, and Frida wore an amazed smile.

Annie was in a gown she had bought in Paris during the first part of the European tour. She had taken the advice of one of her English friends with extremely good taste, and visited the same fashion house that the lady did. Annie probably *could* have done what the wealthy young women of New York City did: visited a more famous house like Worth, and bought an entire wardrobe meant to be worn for a single season, or two at the most. But her advisor didn't believe in squandering money like that, and neither did Annie. It was, however, true that she had not had a gown that would measure up to the standards of fashion in London . . . and although most of the time she was perfectly contented with her home-sewn dresses and costumes, attending some of the events she had been invited to awakened a very feminine avarice in her heart. So she had gone to the atelier, chosen her fabric and style, and had never once, outside of the fitting room, gotten a chance to wear the result. It was a beautiful garnet velvet, trimmed in heavy garnet silk fringe—and frugal as always, Annie had a swatch of the original fabric with her whenever she went shopping, in order to match with other trims. She was, by heaven, going to get as much use out of this gown as she could, and as she well knew, changing just the trim could change the look of the entire gown!

With it, instead of a necklace, she wore heavy garnet satin sash starting at her left shoulder and ending at her right hip, on which she displayed some of the truly beautiful gold medals she had been given or won, just as women in England with titles often wore their jeweled orders. She had wavered on that idea for a few moments, because it could look like boasting . . . but then, if she wore *all* the medals she'd won, the sash wouldn't hold them, and people were always asking to see them.

She'd put up her hair herself, and pinned garnet velvet roses into it. With all the medals and the rich trim, she felt that was enough. And anyway, she didn't really have anything else with her for hair ornaments, since she rarely wore them. Hopefully this would do.

"Oh, that's clever," Frida said, when she saw the sash. "Very clever! Your medals will give shy people something to ask about."

Annie beamed at her. "That was my hope. But Frida, you look like someone from a fairy tale!"

She did, too. Her gown was that same loden green as her show costume—but it had been made in the Art Nouveau style, like medieval robes, with a high collar and a great deal of emerald and gold embroidery, and a heavy "chatelaine" belt. Instead of bejeweled hair ornaments, flowers, or a diadem, she wore her hair bundled inside a net bag made of gold beads.

"She allus looks like a fairy tale," Jack retorted with a grin.

"I hope you don't mean the one where one sister drowns the other in order to marry her prince," Frida teased. "I'm not sure which would be worse, to look like I'm drowned, or like a murderer!"

"You both look like fairy queens," Frank said firmly. "Hold on a moment, missy—" he added, stopping the maid from carrying off the hatbox with their coats. "Those are supposed to be presents for everyone. Do—"

The poor maid looked bewildered until Frida translated. Then she brightened and gave a reply, to which Frida assented. As she turned to go again, Frida explained, "She says the Graf has a special place for you, as I suspected. She's going to go put the box under the chair he has waiting for you. So when you are ready to hold court, find me, and I'll get you settled."

Since that sounded perfect, Annie and Frank followed Frida and Jack into the drawing room, which appeared to be the largest of the three. Someone was playing a harp in a second open room, and there was the sound of clinking glass from the room in which they had met the night after Solstice.

The biggest Christmas tree Annie had ever seen

soared to the ceiling of this two-story room; this was where the sweet smell of balsam had been coming from. The tree had been set in the middle of the bank of windows, which showed a lovely view of the city, lit up for Christmas. The tree itself was an absolute wonder, glittering with silver tinsel and hundreds of gold and silver ornaments and ornamental mirrors, miniature toys and full-sized toys, but there was one thing it lacked.

Candles. The Graf, or his wife, had substituted tin "candles" with diamond-shaped mirrors instead of flames for the real ones that were usually clipped to the ends of Christmas tree branches. And after a moment, Annie understood *why*.

What if a child endowed with the gift of Fire, like Jack has, got excited by the tree and started showing off? The result could be tragic, even fatal; there were enough fires every year around Christmas trees as it was, quite without the possibility of a child able to manipulate fire in the same room as the tree.

Certainly, with all the lights in this room, the chandeliers, the gaslights on the wall, the tree lacked nothing by not having "real" candles on it.

Better safe than sorry.

"Frau Butler! Herr Butler!" The sound of the Graf's voice woke her out of her contemplation of the stunning tree. She turned to find the Graf standing behind her with three children around him, two boys and one girl, she judged to be ten or eleven, seven or eight, and nearly thirteen. All three of them looked like miniatures of him: blond, blue-eyed, and quite handsome.

"Frau Butler, Herr Butler, may I present my children, Wolfgang, Ludwig, and Anneliese. Children, this is Annie Oakley from the Wild West Show, and her husband," he said, as the children practically glowed with excitement.

"Oh! Oh!" burst out of the little one, who clasped his hands together to keep from clapping them. His emotions overcame him at that point, and he was unable to utter a single word.

"Sir, you are a brave man, to be letting your wife shoot at you," said the older boy to Frank, who laughed out loud at the statement.

"Wolfgang!" the girl said, aghast, and before he could move, she boxed his ear. Then she made a sketch of a curtsy to them. "I ask pardon for my brother. Only of late have we let him in the house to live. Before, he slept in the kennel. Perhaps he should return there."

The little boy turned red, then shamefaced, as his father chuckled and ruffled both their heads. "Wolfgang, you must learn that some things are funny when a man says them, and impertinent when a boy does," the Graf said, chiding him a little. "That was impertinent. And also, it was wrong."

"I just meant—what if she is angry?" the child replied, making Annie hide a smile.

"I know what you meant. And that is why what you said was also wrong. Guns are not toys, Wolfgang," his father replied. "A gun is *just* like magic. You must treat it with the greatest of respect, at all times, because misuse or even accident can be deadly. Annie Oakley knows this."

"Indeed I do, Wolfgang," Annie told the child. "You must always be aware that you are handling something that can end a life, and act accordingly. It is never good to make a joke about guns or killing, because that makes killing into a joke, and it is never a joke, even when someone who deserves it dies."

She spoke quietly so as not to shame him too much, especially with all the adults around.

"Forgive me, Frau Oakley," the child replied, staring at his shoes. "I did not think."

"It's quite all right," she assured him. "I have to say the same thing to adults as well as children at home in the United States, and many of them grow up shooting and hunting."

Wolfgang raised his eyes then, and she smiled encouragingly at him. "If I were going to be here longer, I would like to teach you and your sister to shoot," she said. "But learning requires daylight, and I fear in these short days of winter, shooting lessons would interfere with your schoolwork."

"That would be all right!" He brightened at that, then narrowed his eyes, and glanced at his sister—then at Annie and over where Frida was talking with two other Elemental Magicians. She knew what he was thinking, of course. That girls didn't shoot, couldn't shoot, shouldn't shoot. But here he was, standing in front of the world's best female shooter—someone who, modesty aside, was as good as the best men, and maybe better. And over there was his father's friend, also a markswoman and a Hunter to boot.

"Maybe Anneliese would not like it," he said, finally. "The noise. . . ."

"Anneliese would very much like it," said his sister flatly. "That way I need not wait around for a *man* to rescue me."

Annie once again hid a smile. This was exactly the sort of thing she wanted, for exactly the reason Anneliese said. For all women and girls to be able to defend themselves, depending on no one but themselves, and no skills but their own.

"But it *would* interfere with your lessons," said their father. "You are both learning schoolwork and magic work, and there is not any daylight left for shooting lessons."

"But Frau Oakley—"

"Frau Oakley was not learning magic, so there was time for me to practice my shooting," Annie said gently. "And it was very important that I shoot well, because I was putting food on our table with my skill."

Oh, it would have been nice to be a child who had everything in life that she had not had—including the chance to *be* a child, and a proper education. It was the education she missed most of all.

Anneliese gave her brother a withering look. "Shooting must be practiced out in the snow. You never leave the fireside."

Wolfgang was clearly embarrassed by this revelation. He also didn't protest, so it was probably true.

Then the girl narrowed her eyes a bit, looked long and hard at Annie, and added, "I am seeing your power is Air, like Tante Frida. But you do not use your powers to shoot, as Tante Frida does."

"No, she don't," Frank put in, with pride. "She's just that good, she doesn't need the least little bit of help."

"Now that you have been properly introduced, you may go back to your friends," the Graf said, with a glance that told them this was an order, not a request. "You may ask Frau Butler and Herr Butler questions later, when they have gone to their place in the music room; for now let them do as they wish."

"Yes, *Vati*," said all three children together, and they slipped through the crowd to destinations unknown.

"They insisted on being introduced to you right away," the Graf said apologetically. "All the children have seen you and all are excited that you are here."

Annie laughed out loud. "So I am the children's entertainment tonight?"

"No, no, not at all!" the Graf said hastily. But Annie interrupted him.

"I love children, as Frank or the Colonel would tell you, and I will enjoy being their entertainment. How many are there?"

"Nine. My three, and six more who came with their parents. Not unmanageable, I hope?" The Graf seemed anxious when he asked that.

"Not unmanageable, since I know they will be on their best behavior, or they know Saint Nicholas won't bring them anything. Hmm?" she replied archly, and he laughed and nodded.

"I have a lovely settee for you and Herr Butler, when you are weary of standing," he told her. "It's right by the fireplace in the music room. If you wish to dance, you may certainly go down to my wife's party—"

"That—why do you have two parties?" Annie asked.

"My wife's job is managing our social calendar; she is in command of it, and—as long as the Lodge has no pressing cases—of me." He laughed, and Annie was relieved to see that it wasn't fake laughter. "But on Christmas Eve, on the one hand, in Strasburg one is expected in our social circles to have a ball. But on the other hand, there is the traditional gathering of family and friends, also expected. So she runs the ball, and I run the party of family and friends, and it all works out very well. It does not harm things that I have an exceedingly handsome cousin who is a cavalry officer and dances as well as he rides, who arrives in his dress uniform and plays host and escort at her side." He winked. "Meanwhile, the important people are in the ballroom, and the interesting people are up here. Sometimes important people who are also interesting find their way here. Sometimes, they don't go back down."

And before Annie could think of anything to say, he looked over her head—which was not difficult, being as she was so short—and his eyes lit up. "Ah!" he called. "Anzig! Come and meet my special guests!"

"With great pleasure!" boomed a voice behind her. Annie turned, and looked up, and up—

Frank was not small, but this man was astonishing. He looked quite as if someone had stuffed an ancient pagan god into a fine suit and left him to wander the streets of the city, bemused. Blond, as muscular as a strongman, and broad-shouldered, he would have looked more in place on a stage or in the wilderness with a spear in his hand than in a parlor. He even seemed to have a whiff of alpine herbs about his person.

"Herr and Frau Butler, this is Thor Anzig. He is a professor of English and American literature from the university. Anzig, this is—"

"No introductions needed!" the man boomed, took Annie's hand with surprising gentleness, and kissed it. "The incomparable markswoman! Little Sure Shot, adopted by the great medicine chief Sitting Bull! I am honored!" Then he turned to Frank and offered his hand. "And just as honored to meet you, Herr Frank Butler. It is a rare man that eclipses himself so that his wife may have the spotlight."

"Well now—" Frank rubbed the back of his head sheepishly. "I know when to step back and let the talent do the talking."

"Nonsense! But I will let you have your false modesty. Come, I will steal you both away—there is a group over there in the corner of university people *and*—" he coughed "—those who were about the city on the Solstice. They are perishing to meet you and vexed that Frida and Jack kept you to themselves."

"And I have more guests to greet," the Graf said, and somehow vanished into the crowd as Thor Anzig took Annie's elbow and steered her in the direction of the group he had mentioned.

"Does *everyone* speak English here?" Annie asked, as they reached the group.

"Not everyone, but all of us who do have conspired amongst ourselves to make sure that you have one of us at your side at all times. Gentlemen! I have braved the dragon of the household and emerged from battle victorious with the fair Western Princess and her Knight!"

She and Frank then spent a very enjoyable hour or so in the presence of several learned gentlemen professors from the university, all of whom were as giddy as schoolboys over being around her. They had some quite interesting questions to ask about Mark Twain's writing, and were very good about answering hers and Frank's concerning German customs and the differences among Bavarians, Austrians, and Prussians.

Then one of them took charge of her and Frank, and took them to another group of non-English speakers, who clearly were also dying to meet her. She thought briefly about instead asking Frank to take her downstairs for some dancing . . . but she was quite certain that *none* of the dances were the sort of thing *she* knew how to do, and she had a horror of looking foolish.

Besides, the people up here were charming, and amazingly varied, from the folks she had already met after the Solstice Hunt, to students and artists, musicians and merchants, and of course, the children. The children must have been told they were not to bother her until she was in the music room, because none of them ventured near while she was speaking with the adults.

And meanwhile, servants passed by with food and drink, and their interrogators did not ignore Frank but included him in their questions and conversations, so this was already a much more enjoyable outing than some of the ones she had attended in England.

Finally—and after dropping little hints that she and Frank had some general "Christmas trinkets" to bestow on everyone—the Butlers finally got into the music room.

The harp player chose that moment to take a break. The music stopped, and she stood up, a slim column of a woman in a white dress that seemed mostly draped about her, like a Grecian gown. She was nothing like what Annie had imagined, from listening to the ethereal strains from the other room. She was as muscular in her way as Thor Anzig, tall, with a sculptural but unreadable face, and a crown of dark brown braids. She nodded at Annie as she passed, and smiled faintly, but it was clear that she had some goal in mind and Annie was not going to keep her from it.

But if she has to move that harp about on her own, perhaps it's not surprising she is strong, Annie thought, as the woman slid her way through the crowds as easily as a fish slips around obstacles in a stream.

The spot the Graf had set up for her was, indeed, a lovely settee right beside the fireplace with its porcelain

stove insert. Under the settee was the hatbox, and sitting
on the seat was a beautifully made wooden lap-desk.
And when she raised the lid after sitting down, she discovered three Waterman fountain pens, already filled,
and a bottle of ink to refill them if they all ran dry. Well,
that solved how she was to autograph her pictures!

The children pounced immediately, arriving to sit on
the floor at her feet, waiting patiently for their pictures,
but not leaving once they had secured them. Instead, the
six new ones, who evidently had no English, peppered
her with questions which the Graf's three translated.

The adults, of course, though they might be just as
eager to fawn over her as the children, still had to retain
some semblance of dignity, and trailed into the room,
got their pictures and bullet-souvenirs, listened and occasionally asked a question themselves, then drifted out
again when the press around Annie grew too great.

Finally, everyone who wanted one had gotten their
gifts, and a servant brought Annie and Frank coffee and
cake and carried the hatbox away, leaving Annie shaking her hand to ease it of cramp while Frank examined
a bullet with a faint frown.

"We never had this done—did we?" he asked, turning
the bullet so it caught the light, and there on the brass
casing were the initials "A.O." engraved as prettily as
you please. "I sure don't remember havin' that engraved
before I put them bullets in the box."

She shook her head, baffled. "I'd have had it done if
I'd thought about it, but—no—"

Anneliese, who, with the other children, was still sitting at her feet, said, "Perhaps I can be of service?" and
politely held out her hand. Annie gave her the bullet.
Anneliese regarded it with a faint frown of concentration.

"The *Gasthaus*—it has a hearth in your room?" she
asked.

"Why, yes—"

"And when Frida told you of . . . our mysterious

friends . . . you began to leave milk or cakes on the hearth overnight?" Anneliese persisted, handing the bullet on to the other children to ooh and ah over. "And did you speak of the photographs and bullets while in the room? The box, it was left full, all alone, when you went out, yes?"

Well, Frida *had* suggested she start leaving out cake for some unnamed "house Elementals," so she had. The cakes were always gone in the morning, and she'd never heard mice, so she'd assumed *something* other than rodents was taking them. And yes, she and Frank had discussed the little gifts more than once.

"*Heinzelmaennchen.*" Anneliese spoke with authority. "You have favor with them for being kind to your sylphs, for being a Master, and for leaving them gifts. They are clever. Such a thing to them is nothing. They are such clever craftsmen, it would take no more than an hour."

"How do you—"

"I am Earth, as the *Heinzelmaennchen* are." Anneliese finally smiled. "Perhaps they will allow you to see them. You must ask aloud, politely."

"Thank you, Anneliese," Annie finally managed. She longed to ask the child other questions, but—well, she did have Frida for that, and it seemed cruel to interrogate a child at a party.

But one thing was immediately apparent. Having magic might bring with it a great many obligations, but it conferred as many advantages.

The music room had emptied out somewhat. One of the children whisked away their plates and cups, and a servant came by with something more substantial than cake—more of that spiced apple juice, and a selection of cheeses on tiny bread slices, which was left on a little table beside their couch. Frank undertook telling the audience stories *he* had heard from the cowboys, phrasing them as "I heard tell that—" and "A feller told me—" so that the stories almost sounded as if Frank himself had done them. Then, when Annie's voice had sufficiently recovered, she took her turn telling them about the Sioux with the show, and particularly Sitting Bull.

She was personally rather sad that Sitting Bull had not undertaken this part of the tour with them, but after England, he had wanted badly to go home again. She didn't know why—but she'd had a very uneasy feeling about that, and had told him so. But he would not be dissuaded.

The Sioux that remained had been quite frank about their reason for staying—the money. This was "easy money" by their standards; they were not being half-starved or abused by "Indian Agents," and a few of them viewed it as a way to get back from the white man some of what the white man had taken from them, by means of little cheats and tricks. Like cutting buttons off their shirts to sell to the gullible—buttons they'd bought by the quart right here in Strasburg and loosely sewed on just before a camp tour.

But she didn't tell any of that to the children and lingering adults. No, she kept to the stories they had told her—their legends and tales of monsters and heroes, what Sitting Bull himself had told her of the life in camp, in times of peace. That, in particular, utterly fascinated them.

Although they seemed to have the odd notion that all Indians lived in pueblos. Even she knew better than that.

She had just finished one of those stories when the sound of several clocks, inside and out, striking midnight, followed by that of a gong, signaled the fact that the Christmas presents were about to be distributed. The presents to the *children,* of course, not the adults, who had either brought presents for their host and left them discreetly in the hands of the servants, or had or would exchange gifts in the privacy of their homes.

The children swarmed out of the music room, and Annie and Frank took a moment to sort themselves out before following. The harpist returned as they were leaving, and they gave each other friendly nods in passing.

Soon more harp music came wafting out of the room, accompanied by squeals of delight from the nine children. Everyone got gifts, and their personalities certainly showed in what they did with those gifts. Wolfgang and his brother simply tore wildly into each one, as did one of the other boys, making an explosion of paper bits and discarded ribbon that was cleaned up by one of the long-suffering servants. Anneliese, two of the girls, and one of the other boys very carefully undid their parcels, smoothing and folding the paper and ribbons, and stowing them in the bottoms of the boxes they came from, probably for use later as doll-house wallpaper, doll sashes and hair ribbons, book covers, and other similar projects. And the rest of the children unwrapped their presents, wadded up the ribbon and paper, and gave the detritus to the servant to carry away.

It was the middle lot that Annie found easiest to relate to. Every scrap of anything pretty that had come into her hands as a child had always been saved and remade into something useful. Fabric too small to be made into a crazy quilt was saved and unraveled for the colored threads. Even bits of ribbon too short to use for anything else could be woven together into ribbon trim, or used in embroidery and applique.

As she contemplated the happy children, and took note of a couple of unique toys she thought the children of her brothers and sisters might enjoy, the Graf appeared noiselessly at her side.

"Frau Schnee wonders if you would spare her an hour before you go?" he said, making the statement into a question. "She is particularly eager to speak with you."

"What about?" Annie asked, surprised.

"I honestly do not know," the Graf confessed. "But she is a Spirit Master, and perhaps some spirits had something they wished you to hear."

Well, that sounded intriguing. Although Annie was

not entirely certain what to make of "Spirit Master" and "the spirits had something they wished you to know." Annie's Ma was a Quaker, and insofar as Annie had had much religious instruction, it had all been in that faith. And Quakers didn't believe in haunts or ghosts. . . .

Yes, but Friends don't believe in Elementals either, yet there they are.

Frau Schnee seemed like a . . . well, not exactly a "good" woman in the strictest sense, given her tales about certain youthful shenanigans, but certainly an honorable and kindly one. "Yes, of course," Annie said after a moment.

"Would now suit you?" Theodor asked diffidently.

Annie glanced at Frank. "Now is as good a time as any, and better than most," Frank said for her.

So the Graf conducted them to yet another room on this floor, which seemed to be his private study, as it was lined with books and featured a ponderous desk that was covered with papers and yet more books. Dimly lit, the mingled scents of pine, old leather, old books, and a hint of lavender met them as they opened the door.

But Frau Schnee—this time gowned in gray velvet with gray satin trim embroidered with white snowflakes, with her hair piled up and ornamented with a diadem of snowflake crystals—was waiting for them beside the fireplace.

"I'll just leave you alone," Theodor said, before Annie could say anything.

"Please come and sit, children," the Frau said, gesturing to a chocolate-colored tapestry couch across from her. Annie had not realized how very noisy the party had been until Theodor closed the door, leaving all of the hubbub outside. "I will not keep you long, but—I observed something about you when we first met that I believe I need to ask you about."

Now feeling a certain trepidation, Annie took her seat, followed by Frank. "If it has to do with magic, I'm not sure I can help you," she replied.

"It does have to do with magic, and that remains to be seen," Frau Schnee told her. She leaned forward earnestly, her hands loosely clasped together. "Tell me, did you have ever any contact with . . . well, I can only say, wolf-people? Perhaps when you were a child?"

That shocked Annie so much that she gasped, and Frank took her hand. "Did you speak with Frida?" she managed to stammer. Frida must have told the old woman about Annie's childhood, and the Wolves who had turned out to be, well, more wolflike than she had ever dreamed.

The Frau shook her head. "No, I have not. The opportunity did not present itself. I take it by your reaction that you have?"

"I—perhaps I should just begin at the beginning." Annie took a deep breath and began her explanation, starting from the death of her father and ending with getting off the train that Mr. Oakley had paid for. It was easier speaking about it the second time than it had been the first, although she held hard to Frank's hand the entire time she was talking about the sheer terror of seeing the Wolves transform before her eyes.

Frau Schnee nodded gravely the entire time. "Forgive me if I repeat something that Frida has already told you, but I come from a Hungarian family that has a tradition of hunting one sort of these creatures, and one sort only."

"You—actually hunt them?" Annie said. "But they're human, or part human. Doesn't that get you into trouble?"

Frau Schnee smiled thinly. "Parts of Hungary are very wild. Terrible things can happen to those who venture into the wilderness. The thing about the wolf-people is they rarely live in cities. But not all of them are bad."

Annie blinked, as the sound of laughter managed to penetrated into the study. "They aren't?"

The old woman nodded. "As we are taught, there are

three sorts of people that can transform into wolves. There are those that are born that way. They are our—my family's—allies. At their worst, they are no worse than people who like to fight for the fun of it, or get drunk a little too often. At their best—they are noble folk and brave allies to say the least." She smiled fondly. "I am great friends with several of them. But your 'Wolves'—and I can tell you that I know this for a fact—are not that sort of shape-changer."

"How do you know that?" Annie asked.

"Because of what the man did. Your 'He-Wolf.' Among the *verfarkas*-folk, what he did, taking in a vulnerable child, intending to terrify her into submission, and then forcing her into his pack, that would be anathema. They would never countenance such a thing." Frau Schnee pursed up her lips. "No, your 'Wolves' were never of the Nagy clan. So that disposes of the first sort of man-beast. Nor were that man and his wife of the third sort, the kind that are transformed against their will."

"You can do that?" Annie asked, aghast.

"Well, *I* most certainly cannot." Frau Schnee fell silent for a moment. "Truth to tell, the third sort, the ones transformed against their will, are never leaders. They are always completely subordinate to the ones that transformed them in the first place. So that eliminates the third sort as being your captors."

"Which leaves the second?" Annie prompted.

"Indeed. And neither of those sorts of *verfarkas* would have been able to do to you what that wicked man did. He cast an actual spell on you that night. Only the second sort would have that power."

"And what sort is that?" Frank asked.

"Magicians," the Frau said, darkly. "Not just Elemental Magicians, either, but the sort that get their power in other ways. Bloodletting, killing, the taking of drugs, the stealing of power from others—these are *bad* people, Frau Butler. Truly evil people."

"Do *all* bad magicians turn into wolf-creatures?" Frank asked, looking utterly bewildered now.

Frau Schnee laughed shakily. "No, no, child. There are several complicated spells that can do it, but they are all esoteric even for magic, and not every evil magician wants to go through with them. There are many other ways to accomplish the same goal—unless, of course, your actual goal is to merely to become an inhuman monster."

"What did they want with me?" Annie asked. "The Wolves, I mean. Besides to keep me as a slave? I mean, I suppose they were doing that, since they never paid Ma after the first couple of months. . . ."

Frau Schnee frowned fiercely. "The man wanted you for his pack. These magicians sometimes form packs, just like a wolf pack, except that the chief male is always the leader, never to be challenged." She reached across the space between them and briefly touched Annie's hand. "And . . . this is where what I have to tell you is distressing, and possibly painful, and certainly not fodder for Christmas. But I am old enough to know that there is *never* a good time to give someone bad news, so it is better to have it out and done with."

Annie stiffened all over, and tightened her grip on Frank's hand, because nothing, nothing good ever came when it was presaged by a sentence like that.

"My spirits tell me that he wanted to bind you to his pack and transform you. He wanted to make you one of them, and wanted to dominate you in every way. But if he had done that, transformed you while you were not yet grown, you would never—" she groped for words "—have become a woman. You would have remained a child all your life. And he wanted children from you, most desperately, to increase his pack *and* because they would likely have carried either your magic or the potential for it. This is what my spirits have told me."

Annie had thought that nothing much would ever

shock her anymore after the revelations that magic was real and she could, if she chose, become a magician. But it seemed that the universe was not finished with sending her life-shattering shocks.

"I suspect, although I do not know," the old woman continued, "that he also had no magic that would break your will. I suspect he may have been one of those magicians who got hold of someone's book of spells, and could do nothing that was not in that book."

She looked sharply at Annie as if to prompt her to recall that she had seen such a book. But Annie shook her head. "If he did, I never saw it. In fact, I never saw a single book in that house, not even a Bible." She sighed.

Frau Schnee tilted her head to the side as if Annie's statement amused her, but said nothing for a moment. "Well, here is my speculation. What he did was to count on the notion that he could break your will and your spirit with simple abuse. And instead of actually binding you to him, he bound your . . . fertility to himself. So that you will never have a child by anyone but him." Frau Schnee shook her head. "I do not know why he did that; perhaps it was because he didn't know how to do anything else. Perhaps because binding your fertility took less power than binding you. But the end result is—you cannot have a child, unless it is with him. I am so sorry."

Annie sat in benumbed silence. At first, all she could think was, *Well . . . that explains a great deal.*

After what seemed like an age, she dimly heard Frank say in tones of anger of the sort she had never heard from him before, "I'm going to find him. And I am going to kill him."

"That won't lift the spell," sighed Frau Schnee. "It's . . . it's poorly done magic, sloppy and full of errors, and strangely that makes it even stronger. I asked my spirits to read it for me while you were signing pictures this evening, and report to me on what it was. I couldn't even begin to unravel it. It's like a knotted snarl of what used to be a ball of yarn."

I should be crying, Annie thought, in a strange calm. *I should be upset. I should be angry.*

But the truth was, this revelation didn't actually change anything. Literally nothing about her life had changed, now that she knew this. Unlike the shock of being told she could be a magician, this made no difference at all.

Why? Well, Frank still loved her. She still loved Frank. There really was no urgent reason for him to *want* children, because he had them, by his previous wife. One of them was even a boy, that would carry on Frank's name.

And another truth was this—their life would have been a difficult one for a child. There were a handful of children among the show folk and life wasn't easy for them. If they had a child, they'd almost certainly have to settle somewhere, or else leave the child with her family for long stretches of time.

Not to mention how *complicated* life with a child would have been.

But the problem had been "solved" for them.

"It's all right," she said out loud. "We still got each other. Nothing's changed." She nodded at Frau Schnee. "Did the Wolves do anything else to me? Could you tell if they have?"

"He knows where you are," Frau Schnee said. *"Getting* to you is another proposition altogether. And he probably didn't realize until you crossed the ocean that you are *Annie Oakley.* He still may not."

"No, he wouldn't. He knew me as Annie Moses." She used her free hand to pat Frank's. "Unless he knows how good a shootist I turned out, there's no reason for him to put me and the name *Annie Oakley* together."

"So?" Frau Schnee prompted.

"So . . ." It all came back to learning magic, didn't it? Just because the Frau couldn't break the spell, that didn't mean it was impossible to break. But to do that, she'd have to *know* more magicians, or *be* a magician. Or both.

We've been saying we aren't staying with the Wild West forever. We have a lot of money put by safe. Frank can support us with his work for the powder and ammunition companies. I could take the time off for a child, now, that I couldn't have before now.

She took a very deep breath, patted Frank's hand one more time for reassurance for both of them, and said it, out loud.

"So . . . reckon Frank and me had better learn magic."

9

"Do you want to talk about it?" Frank asked, sitting on the side of the bed after he took off his coat and jacket, and giving her a long, considering look.

She sighed. *Did* she? Oh yes. She wanted to scream and cry, she wanted to gut the Wolves with a butter knife, she wanted—oh, so many things.

But she had learned long ago that *wanting* something didn't mean that it was good for you to have.

"Knowing doesn't change anything," she finally said. "And I am not minded to have a temper tantrum over it all like a baby. There is one thing that can change the situation, and I reckon I need to do that."

"You mean, to learn magic." He licked his lips carefully. "Well, then. I can see the fairies, and Miz Frida said I had magic too, so I reckon we need to learn it together."

She let out a breath she didn't even realize she had been holding in. She'd scarcely dared to hope for such a reaction. Oh, Frank was and always had been her rock in a troubled land, but he had put so much of his own

concerns and even his pride aside to support doing what
she wanted to do, that—

*It just wasn't right of me to ask him to get involved in
this, too. Not unless he wanted to.*

But he was actually smiling. "Well, they didn't know
quite what kind of magic I got. So it ain't Air, like yours.
Which means, whatever it is, it'll be different, and I
reckon I'd enjoy getting good at something different
from you."

She shook out her hair and put the velvet roses aside,
and turned to face him. "I was a-feared—"

He stood up and gathered her to him. "You don't got
to be a-feared of nothing. There's nothing we can't handle if we face it together. Reckon this curse what's on
you, and magic, and all, it's no different than bad man-
agers runnin' off with the till, or getting' sick or hurt, or
any other troubles. We'll face 'em down because we'll
face 'em together. Isn't that right?"

When he got emotional like this, the "Irish" came out
and he waxed poetical with a hint of the accent he'd
mostly lost. She buried her face in his shirt and nodded.

"Besides, so far, magic looks like fun," he observed.

"Fun?" She pulled her head away and looked up at
him. *"Fun?* With great big demon-things with six-foot-
long *tongues* a-chasin' us?"

"We made pretty short work of that *Krampus,*"
Frank observed. "And Jack's the one what got jumped
on by the witch."

"It could be you next time!" she cried.

He shook his head. "Not me, I don't reckon t'be
where a witch goes to jump."

She couldn't help it. She started to laugh. So did he.

"Now, we get to sleep as long as we want, an' there's
the Christmas party the Colonel's puttin' on for the
show-folks. So tomorrow'll be a good day, and the day
after there's no show, so that'll be a good day to round
up Frida and Jack and talk about how we go about get-

ting lessons. So, my little fairy, there's no reason to get to sleep straight away."

She smiled to herself. "No," she agreed. "There ain't."

"What we need," said Frida, as they all crowded into the *vardo,* "is a good place to meet together where we can teach you magic without interruption. Someplace *warm,*" she added with emphasis. "Nothing makes it harder to concentrate on magic than distractions, and nothing distracts me more than having a cold nose and cold toes."

She was the last in, and closed the door behind them all. As soon as the door was closed, the wagon began to warm up again. Annie and Frank took their usual spot on the padded bench seat; Frida and Jack climbed up into the cupboard bed. Frank poured everyone coffee and distributed cream and sugar, before nearly emptying his own cup.

"You call yourself a shootist!" Annie scoffed. "Why, a little thing like cold never stopped me! I've won contests in the rain, in a snowstorm, under a blazing sun, in wind so bad it was blowing the live pigeons into the next town—"

"And this is why I am not Annie Oakley," Frida retorted lazily from where she sat cross-legged on the bed next to Jack, who was lounging at full length behind her. "Well, I think I have a good idea. The Graf will certainly let us use his manor, and it is not very far. We can either all ride our own horses rather than going to all the trouble of hitching up a wagon, or Dell and Arte are quite used to taking two, and either of them will tolerate a good rider."

"We'd cause less talk on four horses," Annie observed, after a moment of thinking. "I don't think I've seen many people riding double since we arrived here. We don't want anyone looking too closely at us."

"And why's that, missy?" asked Jack.

"Because if anyone recognizes us as being from the Wild West, much less that *I* am Annie Oakley and Frida is the *'Bayrische Schuetzin,'* we'll gather a crowd." She smiled wryly. "People will positively materialize out of nothing if they think they can see something for free that they otherwise would have to pay for."

"That's true. Well, then. Annie, if you would just reach in the top drawer under your seat, there's paper and a pencil in there. I'll write a note to the Graf and one of the sylphs will take it to him." She waited as Annie fished out a square of paper and the pencil and handed it to her. "We'll see what he says, but I am all but certain the answer will be 'Yes, you certainly may.' That barn he calls a house was built for an extended family three times the size of his, and all the servants one would need to care for them. He can spare us a room."

"Did you have the paper cut to a size the sylphs can carry?" Annie asked, as Frida took a book from somewhere near Jack's head and began writing, using the book as a desk.

"Observant! Yes, I did," the mage replied. She finished the note, then folded it up into a tiny, intricate little package. "And this is something I need to teach you that's not magic," she continued, uttering a soft whistle and holding the packet out to the sylph that answered her. "It's called 'letterlocking' and it ensures that if anyone intercepts your note and tries to read it, even if he figures out how to unfold it, he'll never fold it back up again correctly." The sylph took the packet and whisked out the window Jack cracked open for her.

"That sounds useful. Well. In the meanwhile, is there any way you can tell what Element I got?" Frank asked.

"It's not Air and it's not Fire, or Jack and I would know immediately. It's not Earth or Spirit, or little Anneliese or Frau Schnee would have said so—Anneliese because she can't keep from blurting things like that out, and Frau Schnee because she likes things tidy and likes everyone to know precisely what is expected of them. She hates mysteries. So that leaves Water." Frida settled herself with her hands clasped loosely in her lap. "Has anything ever happened to make you think you have an affinity for Water?"

Frank scratched his head at that, but Annie was struck by a memory. "Do you remember the show's first trip to England?" she said slowly. "How the steamship hit a bad storm?"

"I do. All the Indians thought it was the end and started singing their death-songs." Frank shook his head. "Bet plenty folks were sure they'd die too. Or wished they would!"

"And everyone was sick except you and me," she reminded him.

"That's a good sign we're on the right track," Jack observed lazily. "Never met a Water Mage that got seasick."

"I never had much to do with water, 'cept for drinking and bathing in it," Frank said slowly, perhaps as he toiled over his memories, looking for more signs. "I was always too busy trying to make a nickel to go skylarking like some boys, off to ponds and rivers and all to play."

Annie patted his hand with sympathy; one of the reasons she had allowed herself to become attracted to him in the early days of his earnest courtship—even before he was formally divorced—was that he was *so* much like her. He understood her as no one else did, when it came to having a hard childhood, being focused on earning money, and even more focused on saving it. Like hers, his family had been poor. Like her, he had had to forgo having a childhood in order to help support his family. Truth to tell, that was what in part had won her very skeptical family over as well, that he was serious and very careful with money.

Poor Frank had had a very uphill climb in wooing both Annie and her family. They were hard-working, ordinary farmers. He was show-business. He had discovered quite young that he had a knack for show business, and was a natural marksman. He had begun with a dog act, and the dog he had been touring with at the time he had met Annie, his poodle George, was the remains of that act. George notoriously disliked women; so when Frank had invited Annie and her family to see his act after the shooting match he had lost to her, it had been to his shock and delight that George mirrored his own attraction to the "pretty little girl." Part of the act was to shoot an apple from George's head, with George catching one of the larger pieces that fell before it hit the ground. On *that* night George had snatched half the apple out of the air, jumped off the stage, and took it straight to Annie, laying it in her lap.

I miss George. If it hadn't been for George. . . .

She hadn't missed that Frank was interested in her; that would have been obvious to a blind man. But he hadn't pressed her—instead, he'd courted her through George, sending her cards and letters supposedly written and signed by the dog.

"George" won, of course. Meanwhile, Frank had won over her mother. His sober living and frugality—he was absolutely notorious for clean living and saving money among his fellow showmen on the shooting contest and vaudeville circuits—had worked greatly in his favor.

But a lack of a real childhood meant that when either of them wanted to do something simple, silly, childish, the other generally encouraged it. Because neither of them had had a chance to do most of those things when they had been actual children.

"Tell you what, there's a quick test I know of," Jack put in. "You two put your cups together so the rims touch. Frank, you just see if you can move the coffee out of one into the other."

"All right," Frank said agreeably, and Annie held her tin cup up against his. He tilted his cup, and she began to laugh.

"I'm not *pouring* it!" he objected over her laughter. "I'm just . . . kind of encouraging it."

"Oh, is *that* what you're calling it?" she giggled. "Well, be more *encouraging* the next time you get me a cup of that spiced apple cider!"

Jack, meanwhile, had been keeping an eye on the two cups. "Frank, whose cup had more in it when you all started?"

"Mine," Frank said promptly. "Before we even sat down, I pretty near drank everything, and refilled it. Annie's about half finished."

"Well, look now," prompted Jack.

Sure enough, it was Annie's cup that had more coffee than Frank's.

"I never—" said Frank, staring at the cup.

"Nothing happened until Annie told you to pour her more the next time we had spiced cider. I was watchin' real close. When she said that, and you were lookin' at her and not the cups, I saw the level risin' in Annie's." He grinned, and Frida rubbed her hands together gleefully. "I reckon it's settled. You got magic, and it's Water. Frida can teach Annie, so we need to get you a Water Master to teach you."

Frank continued to stare down at the cups. "I'll be," he said slowly. "When you all were talking about me having magic too, I didn't really believe it."

"You can believe it," said Frida. "That coffee did not move itself." There was a tapping at the window behind her, and she let a sylph in; it too was clutching a bit of folded paper.

Frida took it and carefully unfolded it. "The Graf says he would be pleased to play our host, and wants to know if there is any reason why you two should not be his guests until the show moves on instead of paying to live in a *Gasthaus*."

Annie looked to Frank. "It would save a lot of money," she pointed out. "And we could ride our horses to and from the show, since he has a stable and the *Gasthaus* does not."

"Are you certain he—" began Frank—because the

notion of saving money was always a good one in his opinion, and because the idea of *riding* to the show for rehearsals and performances was much more attractive than walking.

Frida quickly waved away his concerns with a flick of her hand. "Don't be silly. That monstrous pile he lives in is literally built to hold guests. His children already adore you. Two days and Anneliese will be worshiping you, Annie, if she doesn't already."

"What about his wife?" Frank asked dubiously. "Surely she has some say in this."

"If he has tendered an invitation, she's already had her say." Frida already had another little square of paper in her hand. "I'll just say, 'yes,' shall I?"

"Wait," Annie cautioned. "Surely he has a big New Year celebration planned?"

Frida paused. "Hmm. You're right. Shall I say 'yes' but after the New Year?"

"It only seems polite," Frank pointed out—tacitly agreeing to the whole idea.

The return message made it very clear that the Graf was more than agreeable to this. It was, in fact, a multi-part message, being several tiny pages written on both sides. He instructed the Butlers to let him handle their erstwhile landlord—*"I will make all well with him, and see to the removal of your goods"*—and also made it very clear that his wife was in favor of having them as visitors.

"Without even having met us!" Frank exclaimed.

"You were good enough for the Queen of England, surely you are good enough for the *Graefin*," Frida pointed out. "Well! What do you have planned for New Year's Eve?"

The Colonel had made a calculation that no one would be interested in the show on New Year's Eve when there was serious drinking to be done. New Year's Day, however, was a different proposition, and he reckoned they could do both a day and an evening show.

And the day after that, everyone was exhausted from doing two shows in the cold. Annie had decided that doing two shows in succession was even harder in the middle of winter than it was in the middle of summer.

So it was a very good thing indeed that the Graf had suggested that they wait until the fifth of the month before making the move. He evidently sent someone to speak with their landlord on the third, because they came back from the Saturday show to find him waiting for them.

"I will be very sad that you are leaving us," he told them, as he conducted them to a table himself. "But to be a guest of Von Hirschberg! It is a thing marvelous! And not to be saying *nein* to."

He didn't seem all that upset that they were leaving him, which was something of a relief to Annie, who had been torn between saving all the money they were paying in food and lodging and depriving a kind working man of that same money.

But Frida had a perfectly good explanation for why he was not upset that they had found other lodgings. "Oh," she said casually, when Annie mentioned it the next day. "Theodor will have sent gratuity to the landlord, and probably bought enough barrels of beer from him to make the man's temper sweet. So he is not as out of pocket by your leaving as you think. In fact, he may have made a tidy profit on the beer."

"It is good beer," Annie said tentatively.

"It's very good beer! And the Graf goes through a lot of beer. No one is coming off the worse here." Frida patted her head like a child. "Don't worry about it. Everything will be fine."

And so it was. In fact, it was all handled so smoothly it seemed to be a different sort of magic. They walked to the show rehearsal as usual in the morning, leaving every-

thing packed up but still in the room, and when the rehearsal was over, Frida and Jack joined them in riding
to the Graf's mansion rather than staying for supper.
There were two grooms waiting right at the front door
to take their horses. Aside from the fact that the street
was very quiet, the mansion looked as it had on Christmas Eve. But once they stepped inside the front door,
what a change from the night of the Christmas party!

The decorations had all been taken down, and some
hall furnishings that must have been taken away that
night were back. These were mostly tables with very
large and ornate vases on them; Annie thought they
looked fragile, and it had probably been a good idea to
get them out of the way for the party. They were not,
however, antiques. These were very modern glass and
porcelain in a style that had taken Paris by storm—even
the Metro had wrought iron-signs done in that style. In
America, that same style was often called "Tiffany
style," because the famous glassmaker and jeweler was
so prolific and so popular that when most Americans
saw this "Art Nouveau," or "New Art," Tiffany was
what they thought of.

There were two matching statues on either side of the
front door, also in that same style.

But she didn't have any time to contemplate the furnishings, because the Graf was waiting for them just
inside the door, and so was his wife.

"My good American friends, I am so happy to meet
you at last!" said a truly stunning blond woman dressed
in the same slightly eccentric and very modern style as
Frau Schnee—a sort of open-fronted sapphire velvet
coat or overdress with enormous sleeves and heavy embroidery down the front, worn over a lighter blue silk
dress with brocaded trim at the square neck, the cuffs of
the sleeves, and the bottom hem. Over the dresses was
a wide belt that featured alternating panels of the bro-
cade and the embroidery. She wore no jewelry at all except a wedding band and a magnificent sapphire ring.

She held out both hands to Frank, who took one and, somewhat to Annie's surprise, kissed it. The Graefin laughed—beautifully. It seemed she did everything beautifully.

"You are absorbing our manners, Herr Butler," she said playfully, and turned to Annie. "And you, my dear, are most welcome. The house becomes rather empty after New Year's Day, and I am most eager to have interesting guests and hear stories I have not already heard a thousand times."

She took Annie's hands in hers and squeezed them gently.

"It's mighty kind of you to have us," Annie began, not sure what else to say. The titled English had welcomed them, but not this effusively.

"Nonsense. It's our privilege. Theo will be dining out on tales of our famous American guests for the next year." She turned to Frida and embraced her, then allowed Jack to kiss her hand. "I am glad I tempted you to stay with us as well, my dear. We shall have a lovely little winter party of it."

"You're not staying in the wagon?" Annie asked.

Frida shook her head. "We'll leave it at the show, and lock it up when we leave the grounds. It will be a good thing to have it there to rest and warm up during rehearsals and shows, and to store all our costumes and guns, but Theo and Sophia have hot baths."

"Oh, we have more than hot baths, as you shall see," the Graefin said. "I have not had a chance to show off our improvements in far too long! As you can see, we installed gas lighting—" She waved her hands at the fixtures, which, by dint of clever craftsmanship, looked as if they had been there since the house had been built—and were of that same sinuous style that looked like living plants had been turned into brass. Now that there were not swarms of people everywhere, Annie got a good look at the entrance to the house. This foyer was all of the same dark, polished wood as the exterior of the building and the front doors. The grand staircase rose from the middle of it to the second floor, with the entrance to the ballroom behind it. All the large windows were clear leaded glass; the brocaded red curtains, patterned (again) in Nouveau style, were pulled all the way back from the windows, which brightened what would have otherwise been a very dark room. A great deal of the wood was carved in ornate, baroque patterns, which somehow harmonized with the Nouveau trappings. It made Annie's head spin to think how much work that must have been—and how much it must have cost!

"I'll show you all over, or Anneliese will, but later. I am sure you will want to see your suites first, and the working room for magic, and I am doubly sure you will want a nice hot bath," Sophia said merrily. She took Annie's hand in her left and Frida's in her right, and led them all up the staircase to the second floor, with the three men trailing silently behind. At the second floor, the staircase split, with each half going up the outside wall. Here things remained substantially the same— dark wood, leaded windows, elegant but sturdy furnishings, all ornately carved. In front of them were the doors to the rooms that had played host to Theodor's party, now currently all closed. Between the doors were small tables, this time in the Nouveau style, supporting more Nouveau vases, holding cut balsam branches and holly. "The house was built in 1512, and was renovated in 1700, which was when most of the carving you see and all of the glass windows were put in," Sophia continued. "Oh, I do love this house. So much nicer than my family's gloomy old stone pile. I think I married Theo just to get the house."

"Your family's gloomy old stone pile was meant to guard the Rhine and enforce tolls," said Theodor from behind them. "You can't do that if you are easily burned out." He chuckled. "You must never forget that my dear and lovely wife comes from a very long line of robber

barons. The kind of people who enforced their river
tolls by chopping off the hands or feet of the ones who
wouldn't pay. If she ever shows her teeth, run."

"Grr," said Sophia, showing her teeth. Theodor mock-
yelped and hid his face in his hands.

They went up the right-hand staircase to the third
floor. "These are all the family rooms, so we are not
there yet. I'm afraid you'll have a lot of stairs to climb."
They couldn't see much of what was in these rooms, except for the first one, which appeared to be a sort of
sitting room. "When Theo and I did the renovations, we
left the rooms on the first three floors the way they were,
laid out in the old style, with no hallways. *We* don't
mind; I was raised in a castle with rooms laid out in just
that fashion, and we don't mind parading through other
people's spaces to get to where we are going, but that
would be a little too much for our guests."

"We did most of the extensive renovations on the
fourth floor, where the guest suites are," Theo added.
"That spate of renovation was when we arranged for
proper, very modern bathrooms; full bathrooms on the
third, fourth, and fifth floors, and partial bathrooms on
the first. I am sure that my ancestors are howling about
my decadence, but frankly, I don't give a toss."

And up to the fourth floor they went, where they
were greeted by a landing, more stairs, and a hallway.
And the strong and pleasant scent of balsam from the
branches in Nouveau vases on tables between each door.
"I'm putting you both nearest the bathroom since we
have no other guests at the moment," Sophia chirped.
"That will be all the way down at the end of the hall."
She led the way, and threw open three doors: the one at
the end of the hall, and the two nearest that door.
"Frida, you'll have the Fire suite," she said, gesturing to
her right, "and Frau and Herr Butler, you will have the
Water suite." She turned to smile delightedly at all four
of them. "Your things are all in your rooms, and the
servants put them away for you. We've arranged gun-

cleaning stations in both rooms, and if you need any more cleaning supplies, just ring for a servant. Oh! And that reminds me, Theo, I looked into getting more of that gunpowder you say is so excellent, and our guests will be able to obtain as much as they need."

Annie could see from where she stood that the "Fire" suite was evidently decorated with red as its predominating color, and the "Water" suite was done in green.

Sophia beamed at them all as if she was their own personal fairy godmother. "When we are just a family party, as Frida knows, we do *not* dress formally for supper, we dress comfortably, and we eat in the family dining room on the family floor. When you hear the bell for supper, Frida can show you the way."

She turned to her husband. "If you'd like to stay with your guests, *liebchen,* I have a desk full of correspondence to deal with before supper."

"Go, *meine koenigin,* and I will attempt to be as good a host as you are a hostess," Theodor said gallantly, and kissed her hand. She sailed off down the hall, somehow managing to move very fast without appearing to do so, and Frida and Jack nodded their heads toward the Butlers.

"See? We're not guests, we're family. Told you everything would be hunky-dory," said Jack. He tugged on his hat, took Frida's elbow, and the two of them went into the Fire suite and shut the door.

"Well, then, I will continue the tour." Theodor first showed them the bathroom, which was as well equipped as anything in any modern hotel Annie had ever stayed in. It might have been thought odd to show *that* room off as part of a tour of a home . . . except that bathrooms with flushing facilities and hot water were still luxuries even at their most Spartan, and this bathroom certainly was not Spartan.

It had been tiled, floor to ceiling, but nothing like a simple pattern—oh no, these were all clearly handmade tiles of the sort that made up the fireplace surrounds.

The theme was a water-meadow; the floor tiles had been glazed with ripples, water-lilies, and fish, while the wall tiles portrayed a meadow full of long grasses, reeds, and birds in the sky. Even the ceiling had been painted with clouds. There were four enormous celadon-green lion-footed tubs along the right-hand wall, with little vanity desks between them loaded with anything an indulgent bather might want, four celadon sinks sculpted to look like giant leaves along the back wall, and four cubicles with beaten-copper doors showing acanthus lilies along the left-hand wall with water-flushing stools inside them. Theodor told them to let the servants know if they wanted a bath, and showed them where the bell-pull to summon a servant was. "I suspect you won't use it," he said, dryly. "But a great many of our friends would think it positively barbaric not to have a servant to help them with everything. You *will* want them to draw the bath for you, though. The water comes out extremely hot, and it really takes someone who knows how to use the system to draw a bath safely."

It really was the most decadent bathroom that Annie had ever seen. She could easily imagine herself in here after a day of double shows, immersed up to her neck in hot water, surrounded by all these pretty things, letting the entire universe go on without her for an hour or two.

Then he showed them the Water suite, and here is where the character of the renovations Sophia had spoken of shone forth like the rays of the sun.

Instead of wallpaper or the original wooden panels of the rooms downstairs, the walls of the suite were covered with murals of seaweed and fish in that new art style. It was clear that Sophia was extremely taken with Art Nouveau. And the huge, heavy, very old-fashioned furniture seemed to fit very well with it, as did the woodwork—although there was not nearly so much carving as there was downstairs, and the carving was more restrained. The first room was a sitting room, complete with fireplace and stove insert. The second room was the bedroom, also with a stove. And there were plain little third and fourth rooms, which were merely painted green and furnished with a single bed and dresser each.

"If you had brought a valet and a lady's maid, this is where they would have slept," said Theodor. "Some of our friends absolutely refuse to travel without their personal servants."

Annie giggled and snorted at the same time. "Can you imagine what the Colonel would think of us having a *valet* and a *maid* with us?" Even the Colonel didn't have personal servants along; he either did things for himself, relied on the show staff, or relied on hotel employees or casual laborers he hired for the job.

"He'd probably find some way to make them useful in the show," Frank observed.

"Which would affront them terribly, and they'd give notice within the week," Theodor said, quite seriously. "Valets and ladies' maids are superior servants, with a great deal of expertise in what they do. Telling them to take part in the show would be very much like expecting a skilled cabinet-maker to bang a kitchen vegetable box together. He would be very insulted, and would walk off in a huff."

Annie blinked. To be absolutely honest, she had been more often the "serving" than the "served" in her life. Of course she knew better than to tell a cook to make a bed, or a stablehand to help out in the kitchen. But the idea that there was such a thing as a "superior" servant came as a bit of a revelation.

"Sofi's maid will help you dress and arrange your hair if you prefer, or if you don't mind, one of the upstairs maids can help you," Theodor continued.

"I can—" she began. Then hesitated. Of course she could do all that for herself. But perhaps that wasn't the "done thing"?

Theodor smiled. "We employ enough servants that even when the house is full, they are not run off their feet, and now that it is empty, they have time for improving themselves, and for recreation, such as learning to do whatever interests them the most. But allowing an upstairs maid to assist you allows *her* to perfect the ladies' maid skills, and that puts her in line for a promotion, or she can be recommended to a lady of her mistress's acquaintance. And in either case, that means more money, and better position in the household."

"You know an awful lot more about your servants than rich men in America seem to," Frank said, a bit boldly.

But Theodor just nodded. "You will find that is the case with the majority of Elemental Magicians who are also of means. We find that . . ." He took a deep breath. "I am about to lecture."

"Lecture on," said Frank, crossing his arms and leaning against the very substantial desk in the sitting room. "I'm always good for learning something."

"As magicians, we are affected by those around us; the happier those around us are, the happier and more stable we are. You'll come to notice that too, as you grow into your power. And as magicians of means, we are faced with a choice: include the servants in what we are, and thus risk them saying something to someone they should not, or do not include them, and thus risk that they will find out and proceed to gossip in the high street."

"Right," Frank said, and Annie nodded.

"Most of us take the path of including them, which has often had the happy accident of finding people with the gift of magic among one's own staff. Now, if your servants trust you, and you treat them well and with kindness and consideration, as a magician your life is going to be much more pleasant. Their happiness increases your well-being. Being treated well means they are inclined to protect you, above and beyond their actual duties. So it's pure selfishness on our part: we make sure our servants are treated as *we* would like to be treated, were we servants. We don't overwork them, we pay them well, and we treat them as thinking adults, not as ignorant peasants or children, and explain to them when something we do magically may have an impact on them. We make sure when there are festivals and treats, they get a part. If, in the heat of the moment, tempers flare and words are said, you will find even Sofi or me tendering an apology to a 'mere servant.'" Now he smiled. "So, Frau and Herr Butler, you see why my household runs smoothly, and my Sofi goes about her own work smiling and singing. Because if something happens, we can absolutely count on every servant to leap to our aid. They are family as well as servants."

"That is about the wisest thing I ever heard," Frank said, slowly.

"It is as I was taught, and my father, and his father, and so on back. No one has ever left our service except for old age or illness, and in those cases, we see they are provided for." Theodor paused, possibly to let Frank or Annie make any comments they cared to. But Annie didn't have anything to say, and Frank seemed contented with this explanation.

Theodor then gestured to one corner of the room, where heavy cloths had been spread over the carpet, a heavy, battered table placed on it, and the gun cases that had been in the *Gasthaus* all stacked beside the table. "As you can see, we have put your gun cases in one corner where the cleaning station is, and spread hessian over the carpet to take care of any accidents. The servants put your clothing away, and put jewelry cases beside Annie's dressing table . . . because . . . apparently there were too many of them to put *on* your dressing table, my dear."

Annie giggled again. "That isn't even everything. I keep most of the stuff people ask about at the show, and they lock it all up in the pay-wagon at night. People will keep *giving* me things. . . ."

"Well, we are going to give you something, but it will

be something that cannot be lost, cannot be sold, and will be of immense value to you," the Graf said proudly. "Knowledge. The most valuable gift of all."

"I'd be inclined to agree with that," Frank told him.

"Now, I have a few things to attend to myself. Ring if you need anything. Ring if you want a bath. A bell will ring signaling supper. I am exceedingly happy to have you as my guests."

As soon as he was gone, Annie ran across the room and jumped into the enormous, curtained bed with a whoop of pleasure like a child. This . . . never got old. All of the cold beds, the thin blankets, the hard straw mattresses she had endured as a child made her eternally appreciative of a beautiful, soft, warm bed. "The Colonel is going to be so envious of us!" she crowed.

Frank just walked over and sat on the edge of the bed, chuckling. "Well," he said after a moment. "Looks like my fairy's finally in a proper palace."

10

ANNIE had been to many suppers in the homes of the rich and famous, but she had never enjoyed herself as much as she did with the Von Hirschbergs. Theodor sat at the head of the table and Sophia (still wearing the gown she had worn to greet them) sat at the foot, with the Butlers on the right-hand side with Anneliese next to Annie, and the Cates on the left-hand side with Wolfgang next to Jack. "Ludwig is too young for suppers with us," Anneliese said seriously to Annie as they took their seats. "He confuses the forks and spoons, then starts to cry because he got it wrong."

Personally, Annie was just glad she'd had coaching in the art of formal dining, and a lot of practice, or she probably would have come to grief over the many forks and spoons herself. Knives were not so much of a problem; their very different shapes gave clues as to what they were supposed to be used for.

"Poor Wolfgang!" Annie said sympathetically, drawing a faint smile from the footman ladling soup into her dish. "Thank you," she said as an aside to the footman (and noted that even the children thanked him after being served). "I'll tell you a secret," she continued, lowering her voice, so that Anneliese leaned closer. "If I hadn't had someone give me a whole three days of lessons two years ago, I would be crying over the spoons and forks too."

"Did you grow up in a log cabin?" the girl asked. "Did you eat with your hands like the Indians? Did you shoot all your suppers yourself?"

"I grew up in a very small and very poor house, but not a log cabin; there weren't many of those left in Ohio by the time I was born, because as soon as they could afford a house, most people built one and used their old cabins for sheds." Annie had never hidden her impoverished childhood from anyone—she had learned, though, that rich people tended to think of her more like a "noble frontier savage" than as "a poor girl who had to go to the workhouse." That made her "exotic" rather than "lower class." "We didn't eat with our hands, but we carved our own spoons and forks ourselves out of cow horn, bone, and wood, and we shared knives. We didn't have special spoons and forks for different foods. We ate everything using the same implements, then washed them quickly, and used them for the next meal. And I did not shoot *all* my suppers, but I was the only one of the family that was a good enough shot to put food on the table regularly, and the only one who wouldn't waste bullets on missed shots, so I went out as often as I could to hunt for meat."

"What did you shoot?" asked Wolfgang. After being inadvertently rude—or at least impertinent—he was on his best behavior tonight.

"Mostly rabbits, quail, squirrels, ducks, geese, and pheasant. Sometimes turkey. I didn't often shoot anything as large as a deer, because I was generally alone, and I had no way to bring the meat out of the forest."

Wolfgang looked at her with his head tilted, and giggled a little. "You would have been buried beneath a deer!" he said.

"Quite right. And the first law of the hunter is *Never kill anything you don't intend to eat.* So I shot for our table, and then I began shooting for the tables of good restaurants in the city, selling them what I killed. And they always bought it, and paid good money for it, because I always killed my target immediately, with a shot through the head." She held her head up a little, because she was extremely proud of the next part. "Before I was fifteen I had saved up enough money to pay off the mortgage on Ma's house, so my little mother never needed to worry about having a roof over her head again."

"A mortgage," Theodor said, before the children could ask about the word, which clearly puzzled them, "is a loan people take from a bank in order to buy a home. As you know, children, most people do not own their own homes. They rent houses or apartments; that is, they pay money to someone to be allowed to stay there, as one does at a *Gasthaus*, or they take a loan from a bank and do not own the house until that loan is repaid."

From Anneliese's expression, Annie was fairly sure that the children did *not* know this. At least, they had not until this very moment. But from the faintly approving expression on Theodor's face, he had judged it a good time to educate them.

"And you were only fifteen!" Anneliese exclaimed. It looked as if it was finally dawning on the little girl that Annie had been quite poor indeed. But she had the good manners not to say anything directly about it. "But of course, you were using your magic to help." She faltered as she looked at Annie. "Weren't you?"

"I didn't even know I had magic until Frida told me," Annie confessed. And it wasn't a lie, either; all this time she'd thought that the sylphs had been dying hallucinations of fairies.

"Everything that Frau Butler does in the show is pure

skill," Sophia told her children. "You see? It does not take magic to be able to do fantastic things."

Annie got the feeling this was one of the things Sophia said to the children a lot. Possibly because they were not permitted to use magic yet?

"Is Frida going to teach you?" Wolfgang asked.

"Frida is going to teach Annie, and Pierre Lyon is going to teach Frank," said Jack, giving everyone else a chance to finish their soup. "Your good Papa is letting us use his working room."

"Can we watch?" Wolfgang asked eagerly.

Sophia and Theodor exchanged a look.

"That will be for Annie and Frank to say," Sophia temporized.

"It will be baby teaching at first," warned Frida. "Exactly the same teaching that you are getting—and closer to the teaching Ludwig is getting. And you must be very quiet, and your own schoolwork and magic work must be completed first. And Annie and Frank and Pierre must say yes."

"I don't mind," said Annie.

"Me neither," Frank agreed.

With that settled, they were on to the next subject and the next course. Although Wolfgang took over, wanting to know all about the Lippizans, Dell and Arte. Frida and Jack were only too happy to tell them all about the horses, how they were trained, how they'd gotten hold of the stallions, with promises that the children would be allowed to ride them.

Sophia's expression said as clearly as words, *Is that wise?* But Frida was already prepared for that.

"Old horses train young riders at the Spanish School," Frida explained. "And by now our lads qualify as 'old' horses. I will put ordinary tack on them, and a single-bitted bridle, and they will know this is pleasure riding, and not show riding. No *levade*, much less *caprioles* or *croupades*; perhaps some elegant footwork, but that is because they both love dancing."

The rest of the meal was just as pleasant, although—as was usual at meals with the rich and ennobled—Annie couldn't have named the ingredients or the dishes of half the things she ate. The dining room was just big enough for this single table, which could seat twelve, and was comfortable for eight. Each new dish came up to the table from a dumbwaiter, so everything was hot and fresh, or cold and fresh—which was a marked difference from some meals Annie had had in England, where the dishes took so long to get to the table from the kitchen that they were barely tepid. Worst had been the supper with Queen Victoria. Etiquette said that when the Queen was finished with a dish, *everyone* was thus finished with the dish, and it was taken away. And since the Queen was served first, and there were almost a hundred people at the supper, that meant that if you were one of the unlucky ones to be served last, you might be able to snatch a mouthful or two before your plate was taken and replaced with something else.

That had almost made Annie lose her temper. Not because she was hungry, but because of the sheer waste of food, when there were thousands starving in the slums, with no way for them to go and hunt food as she had. But one just didn't leap up and go into a tirade about such things in the presence of the Queen of England and the Empress of the British Empire—

But it looked increasingly as if the Graf and his family could not be tarred with that same brush. Although the courses were many, the servings were all small, a mouthful or two. And in between courses, there was a lot of conversation, conversation in which the children were clearly encouraged to participate.

In this room, Sophia's hand was unmistakable. The china, the linens, the ornaments on the table, the pictures on the wall, the ornaments on the mantelpiece, and the fireplace surround were all in her favored style. The walls had been painted and stenciled in very pleasant colors of brown and gold with touches of red and green. Only the carved baseboards and crown molding remained of the original decorations.

"Do you remember what this room was like before we renovated?" Sophia said, as if she had noticed that Annie was taking in the décor.

Theodor closed his eyes and shuddered slightly. "It was very . . . German," he said, finally. "Suits of armor in each corner. Chimney smoked constantly, and the smoke had darkened all the wood in here until it was almost black, despite the best efforts of the servants to clean and polish it. But the worst thing had to be all those heads!"

"Heads?" said Frank, quizzically.

"Hung up on the walls. Deer. Chamois. Boar. Even a bear, which had pride of place over the fireplace. All staring down at you with glass eyes while you ate, as if accusing you of being a murderer." He shuddered again. "It almost made me a vegetarian. I often choked over venison. I didn't let Father know, of course; he had a trophy or two up there himself, and he was very proud of them."

"It could have been much worse," Annie said. "We were asked to supper by several people who did trophy hunting in Africa."

"Ghastly," Sophia said firmly. "That sort of thing is all very well for a trophy room, a billiard room, or even a library, but a bunch of taxidermied heads has no place in a dining room."

With every word that came from Sophia's mouth, Annie liked her better. She *certainly* liked what Sophia had done with the décor.

"This room is . . . just lovely," she said impulsively. "Everything about it is harmonious."

Sophia blushed prettily. "I enjoyed putting it all together. The renovations were going to happen anyway; Theo was tired of living like a medieval noble, and so was I, and his father was no longer with us to object, God rest his soul. There was enough that needed repairing that we could demolish what we needed to without any guilt that we were destroying something priceless and irreplaceable. It wasn't lack of funds that kept previous generations from rebuilding and repairing, as it often is with the English. It was just sheer neglect because of other pressing matters, so that the house always took third or fourth place in the family's considerations."

"Woodworm and carpenter beetles know nothing of class or wealth, and care less," Frida said with a shrug. "And I remember that those pretty carved panels . . . some of them were just sawdust held together with varnish. You could put a finger through them with no effort."

"That would be unfortunate," Anneliese piped up. "Wolfgang would probably have gotten into trouble for breaking them."

"Ach!" Wolfgang protested.

"You would. You are always throwing balls in the house. And you do other things that Mutti would not like if she knew about them," Anneliese added darkly.

"Dessert, I think," said Sophia, putting an end to the fight—and the tattling—before it began.

There had been a bitter cold snap after New Year's, so the Colonel had decreed there were to be no rehearsals and no weekend shows, to spare both the animals and his performers.

This only meant that now Frank and Annie could devote themselves completely to learning magic, and Frida could devote herself to teaching it. Annie was deeply grateful to Theodor—he was insistent that at this point they must call him "Theodor" or "Theo"—had made them his guests. They neither had to go out in weather so cold that it threatened frostbite once you had walked a single block, nor were they anything like bored.

"So this is the room where you do magic," Annie said aloud, casting a glance around the space. "It seems very sparse."

If there was any room in this house that *could* be called "Spartan," this was it. The walls, floor, and ceiling were plain wood, and there was no carving anywhere. There was a single table in the center, heavy enough that it was probably difficult to move. It had a thick sheet of marble as a top, and the remainder of the table was very thick wood. There were upholstered benches around the walls, and four matching chairs, one in each corner. Inlaid in the floor was a circle of what was *probably* steel—although, since this was Graf Theodor's house, it might be silver. There were eight plain wooden lantern hooks attached to the four walls. There was no fireplace, although there *was* a square of heavy ceramic tiles set into the wall at the same location as the fireplace in the other room. A rather clever way to get heat into the room without a fire, Annie thought. Warmth radiated from those tiles in a very pleasant way. The opposite wall held the room's only window, which was of frosted glass, rather than clear.

Hanging from the lantern hooks were eight peculiar lanterns: round, like glass balls, and not square or octagonal, and if there was a way to open them, Annie couldn't spot it. They had lit up by themselves when Frida had opened the door to the room. At least, it seemed to Annie that they had lit up by themselves, though perhaps Frida had done it, somehow.

Frida gestured to Annie to come join her on one of the benches, which was more comfortable than it looked. "Well," the magician said, "I was not joking when I said we would be doing baby magic. Right now, you are not able to do much of anything by yourself, because you cannot see the power you are working with. Today will hopefully change that."

"What are you going to do?" Annie asked, cautiously.

"I am going to do nothing. *You,* however, are going

to learn to see and feel in a new way." Frida paused. "Or to be more precise, you are going to *realize* you are seeing more than most people can. First lesson. Look at my hands." She held them up. "Just relax, don't tense up."

Annie followed her instructions, looking closely at the woman's hands. *Though I wish I had some idea of what I was supposed to be looking for. If I—*

—wait a moment—

There was a sort of shimmering around Frida's hands. And the more Annie concentrated on it, the clearer it became. It was as if there was a faint blue light coming from Frida's hands!

"Ah, you see it now, don't you!" Frida made that a statement, rather than a question. "That is the energy of Air Magic. As a Master, you'll eventually be able to see all five kinds of Elemental Magic, although it isn't likely you'll be able to do anything with the other four elements. Now look around you. The one enormous advantage that Air Magic has over the other four is that it is literally everywhere."

Annie didn't wrench her attention away from Frida's hands just yet. First she wanted to get things straight in her mind as to *how* she was seeing that blue glow. *And can I—un-see it?*

It took her a few moments of concentration before she figured out the trick that allowed her to not-see the power, then to see it again. She spent a little time switching from one state to the other, until she was certain she could do it easily. Only then did she look around her as Frida had instructed her.

Filling the entire room were sparkling drifts of cerulean. It was . . . lovely. Little skeins of blue glow floated everywhere, including in and out of the closed window. Now *this* was what magic should look like! It was like slow fireworks. She enjoyed taking it all in while Frida smiled slightly.

"Now look at the circle in the floor," Frida suggested.

She did, and there was more of that blue glow. This time it looked as if the glow emanated from the circle, as it did from Frida's hands, but it was more concentrated, and steady rather than drifting. "What is the circle for?" she asked.

"When someone needs to do something that might be dangerous, they do it inside a protective shell," Frida explained. "That circle is a permanent anchor and a supplier of energy for one of those shells; its presence makes it very easy to bring such a shell up around you, and it's already primed with quite a lot of energy stored in it. Most magicians know how to do this, even the ones that don't use Elemental Magic as we know it."

"Like the Indians?" she said after a moment.

"No, more like the people who know magic exists, don't have the ability to see it themselves, and use other means to take the power and force it to their own ends." Frida's expression was stony. "Like your tormentor, the He-Wolf, for instance. Magic is a force. Elemental Magicians are in tune with that force, and we don't control it so much as guide it. Magicians who cannot see it bludgeon it into doing what they want." She paused and thought for a moment. "I will say this; magicians who are not Elemental Magicians have extraordinary willpower, an incredible ability to visualize what they want, and the patience to go through interminable rituals to get it. The spells and rituals *work*, actually, and sometimes we use them as shortcuts. But we are far more accurate. To give you an analogy, we use a swatter to kill a spider. They burn down the entire house."

Annie had to laugh at that, not the least because she actually knew someone so terrified of spiders he nearly *did* burn down the house to get rid of one.

"So, clear your mind and your vision, and let's start again at the beginning," Frida ordered. Annie nodded, and did, although she did wonder a little why Frida was having her repeat something that appeared to be so basic. Shouldn't they be moving on to something more difficult than this, since she had clearly grasped this part of using magic?

But a quarter of an hour later, she wasn't wondering anymore, because her eyes ached as if she had been trying to read in bad light, and her head ached as well. She began to squint, which didn't help matters. And when Frida paused and looked at her quizzically, she confessed as much.

"Ah, I have been anticipating this, and I am actually surprised you managed as long as you did," Frida said. "This is why we do baby magic first. We will stop now, because you are going to hurt much more if we go on. You are using a kind of muscle you have never used before, so of course it is going to hurt, just as if you were learning to ride a horse for the first time. This would be much easier if you had been brought up in magic. Then, as soon as you were old enough to understand, or old enough that your Elementals made themselves known to you, you'd have been taught how to see your magic, and how to speak with your Elementals. You would— ah! I have it. Because you learned to shoot so young, you trained yourself with much less effort than it would have taken when you were older. The 'muscles' are more pliable, more flexible, heal quicker, and are more apt to respond to being used without the owner suffering pain afterward. It is the same in all such things. It is easier both mentally and physically to learn things when young. So if you had, for instance, begun learning at Ludwig's age, it would never have hurt you even after several hours of practice seeing magic and calling on Elementals."

"But you do not train them to actually use magic so young?" Annie asked. She could think of many things that could happen with a child knowing how to use magic, and very few of them had happy endings.

Frida shook her head. "It's a very fortunate thing that children are too weak to do such a thing. The temptation to use it for their own purposes would be overwhelming. No, it's thought that just learning to use what we call the Sight, and learning about the Lesser Elementals, is sufficient until they get to be roughly Anneliese's age, and have more self-control, and understand parental consequences, if not adult responsibilities. Anneliese has learned just enough that she could, if she chose, plague Wolfgang using magic, but she is old enough to know that if she did that, the consequences from her parents would be very unpleasant. So she refrains of her own will, out of caution, having learned the limits of what her parents will permit. Not that she refrains from plaguing Wolfgang! But she uses her tongue and her wit, not magic."

By now Annie's head was *really* aching, and so were her eyes. "Time to stop," Frida declared. "Go back to your room and ring the servants for a hot bath with cold cloths on your eyes. They'll know what you need. There is plenty of time before supper." She tilted her head and gave Annie a penetrating look. "On second thought, I will come with you to help."

At this point Annie was more than willing to allow just that, and she was very grateful that they were learning this magic *here* and staying here as well, where everyone knew about it, knew what was going to happen to her (and presumably Frank), and had a sympathetic attitude and practical solutions.

So the two of them left the workroom, but not before Annie noticed a furtive shimmer on the door before they closed it behind themselves. "Is the door enchanted?" she asked.

"Well spotted; the entire room is. When you are in there, you are invisible to the Sight, and so is the entire room." Frida cocked her head to one side. "We can't have our enemies knowing where we are and what we are doing when we are working, now, can we?"

About halfway up the stairs to the fourth floor, Annie felt as if she had been climbing all the way to the top of one of those New York "sky-scrapers." Frida noticed that as well. "Ah, you've exhausted yourself," she said, as Annie paused for a moment on the landing, obscurely ashamed of herself for being so tired. "Don't worry. The more you use your powers, the stronger you will become. But this is your first cautionary lesson: the power to use magic comes from within you. Elemental power is boundless; *yours,* however, is not. This is why we don't use magic for trivial things. We can learn to store magic, like a granary, but like a granary, there is a point at which there is no room for more."

"I just want to lie down at this point," Annie said, straightening, and regarding what now seemed like a very long hallway.

"I'm sure you do, but a hot bath will do you more good than merely lying down. Come along, I will help you," Frida said encouragingly.

Annie mustered up enough energy to get to the bathroom, but it was Frida who rang for the maidservant, and the two of them consulted as the servant cautiously and carefully manipulated faucets and drew the water for the bath, then left. As the tub filled, Annie slowly disrobed. She was now so used to changing clothing in front of her friend that she thought nothing of it, only how good that hot water was going to feel. Frida even helped her put up her hair—loosely—so that it wouldn't get wet.

With the tub full and the water at the just-bearable temperature that Annie preferred, and Annie eased into it, the servant returned with a little silver goblet on a tray. *"Trinken Sie, bitte,"* said the maid, handing the goblet to her, then rummaging in the array of things on the little tub-side table until she found what she wanted. She opened a jar of what looked to be mixed herbs and sprinkled them liberally over the surface. Immediately a sharp, fresh, pleasant scent arose, and seemed to clear Annie's head. She detected lavender, rosemary, and balsam, but the scent was far more complicated than just that.

"Danke schoen," Annie said, and drank what was in the goblet, which proved to be a lovely cherry cordial with something extra in it, and between the herbs floating on the water and the cordial, the pain in her eyes and head slowly eased. She leaned back against a headrest built into the tub with a sigh as the maid left.

"Clearly better," Frida said with approval. "Good." She took up a washcloth, wrung it out in the very cold water from the tap of one of the sinks, and put it over Annie's eyes. "I'll be back in a little. By the time I am, you should be all right again."

Annie heard her footsteps retreating, then the door opening and closing, leaving her alone.

Faint sounds from outside penetrated the frosted glass windows; a little noise of horses, some of people speaking down in the street. Equally faint sounds came from elsewhere in the house, mostly voices, mostly female. The pipes conducted sound surprisingly well; if she'd understood German, she probably would have learned all manner of things. She guessed that most of that was coming up from the kitchen. Sophia hadn't said anything about renovating the kitchen, but then, the kitchen wasn't the sort of room she'd take guests on a tour of, even though it was the beating heart of every house. It stood to reason, though, that the improvements in plumbing were only the beginning. Obviously more efficient porcelain stoves had replaced open fireplaces, gaslight had been brought in to light the entire building, and very probably whatever arrangements had been in that centuries-old kitchen had been replaced with a modern range, modern sinks, and the hot and cold running water. The boiler for the hot water was probably down in the kitchen, where someone could keep an eye on it at all times. Such contrivances were inclined to explode.

I should do that for Mama. Not that her mother ever complained . . . but what was the point of earning all the money she did if she didn't use it to make Mama's life easier?

Whatever was in that herbal brew she was soaking in was working near miracles. Or maybe it was the cordial? *Probably both.* But this was very nearly heaven, so far as Annie was concerned.

She didn't fall asleep—but she did empty her mind in a way she had never been able to do before this except when shooting. What filled her mind instead of thoughts running around like worried mice was sheer sensation: the soothing heat of the water, the equally soothing cold cloth on her eyes, the ebbing pain, the faint taste of the cordial still lingering on her tongue, the mingled scents of the herbs in the water. The door opened, she heard a little movement, and it closed again. She didn't trouble herself to look, not wanting to disturb this tranquility that had been conjured up out of something as simple as a hot bath.

There's more magic in the world than just Elemental Magic.

It was only when the water cooled to lukewarm and she was contemplating getting out of the tub that she heard the door open again, and removed the cloth from her eyes.

It was the servant, back, with a bathrobe big enough for two of her. Her clothing had vanished; the servant must have come back to fetch it, and probably give it a good brushing, while she was lost in her reverie. She found herself with no eye pain, little headache, and feeling much refreshed.

And finally remembered the servant's name.

"*Danke,* Matilde," she said, and the servant broke into a smile as she helped Annie out of the tub and enveloped her in the robe.

And just as they were leaving the bathroom, the tub draining, poor Frank stumbled in with a manservant at his elbow, looking just as weary and in pain as she had been about an hour ago.

"The bath works," Annie advised him. "You'll be fit in time for supper."

"Praise God," Frank said. "It ain't fair having a hangover when you never got a thing to drink aforehand."

Annie patted his shoulder sympathetically, and slipped back into her room. As accomplished a quick-change artist as she was, she was probably going to have time to read one of the books on magic that the Graf had loaned her before Frank returned and they went down to supper.

Then, perhaps, just a *little* more practice. At least, until the first signs of strain showed.

You can never practice too much.

11

IT only warmed up enough to snow, then the temperature plummeted again. The Colonel grumbled about the lost revenue, but it was clear that there were not going to be any more shows until the spring.

Fortunately, according to Fred Gibbs, the folks that hadn't yet found an alternative to spending the winter under canvas were hardy souls, and, he said, "A little cold ain't gonna make 'em nothin' but frisky." And the Sioux were used to colder winters than this one. Everyone moved all their tents closer together, out of the "camps" and under the canvas of the main tent. Most of the show-tents had been dismantled and put into the wagons, and the wagons themselves had been arranged around the remaining tent, making a very effective wind-break. With the wind (mostly) cut, and the snow kept off, and several roaring fires going at all times, it was tolerably comfortable. The canvas did a surprisingly good job of keeping the heat in, although the Colonel instituted a strict fire watch. Although they were keeping the fires well away from the canvas, everyone knew that if a spark so much as touched it, the waxed canvas would go up in no time at all. The Colonel directed that everything that could be burned be cleared away from the edge of the tent, and day and night patrols kept on a regular rotation. The one thing that everyone in a traveling show universally feared was fire.

Frida and Jack loaned their *vardo* to Ricardo and Esmeralda Sanchez, who had a very young child, barely a toddler, and moved all of their things temporarily to the Hirschberg mansion. Ricardo was one of the Mexican vaqueros; his wife was one of the women in charge of keeping the costumes in good repair.

And meanwhile, the Butlers continued their education in magic. When they could use the Sight for an entire day without any weariness or other issues, their instructors moved on to actually *using* magic.

The workroom was preternaturally silent; no sounds drifted here from other places in the house, and absolutely nothing came from the window. Of course, that wasn't too surprising; it had warmed enough for a thick snowfall, which was muffling everything out of doors. This morning, Annie and Frank had taken the children out for a romp in the snow after getting permission from their governess and two tutors. It had been great fun, but it was a lot more fun knowing that when they came back inside, there was hot chocolate and a nice hot dinner waiting for them.

And dry clothes warming in front of the fireplace to put on.

Afternoons were always for magic lessons, so although Annie would have been happy to drowse in front of the fire, she was in the workroom with Frida. Frank was in another, improvised workroom made out of one of the empty guest rooms.

"I found when I was first learning that it seems to

help, in gathering magic to absorb into yourself, to twirl your finger above the palm of your hand, and imagine the energy being pulled into the vortex, like water going down a drain. Except, of course, it is going into you, not down a drain." This was taking longer than Annie had expected, but Frida seemed as patient as a stone. Annie took a deep breath, and tried again. She probably wasn't the worst pupil Frida had ever had, but she very much doubted she was anywhere near the best.

This was simultaneously frustrating and oddly normalizing. *After all, I can't be good at everything.*

The "twirling" idea seemed as good as anything else she'd tried, so she stared at the palm of her hand, twirled her finger, and visualized all those floating skeins of power being drawn into the imaginary vortex she had created, then sinking into her hand. In the silence of the room, Annie could hear both of them breathing, and the occasional creak of ice at the window.

And finally, *finally,* after what seemed like hours of trying, the magic responded to her. Sluggishly at first, but then, as if she had broken a barrier, more and more of it whirled around her circling finger and into her hand, and from there, deep inside her, into an energized place that seemed to be somewhere between her navel and her spine. Frida had told her that this would happen, but until this moment, she'd had no conception of how it was going to feel.

It felt very strange. Not unpleasant, but not like anything else she'd ever experienced. She understood now why Frida had been unable to describe the sensations; even now, while she was experiencing them, she couldn't find the proper words. She just knew, at some point, that she had taken in all that she could, and stopped. Stopped pulling the energies in, stopped twirling her finger. The last little wisps of power floated off into the room again.

Annie looked up at Frida, who nodded her satisfaction and tucked a strand of hair behind her ear. "Well done so far," she said. "Are you feeling any effects? Bad ones, I mean."

She shook her head. "I feel fine. Just . . . full."

"Well, the only way to empty yourself again is to use the power. It is much like wine. It will do you no harm in the 'bottle,' that is, yourself, but the only way to get it out again is to use it." Frida gestured at the table in the middle of the room. There was a candle in a silver holder on it, which she got up to light. "Now, use the power in you to move the air to blow out the candle."

"Not use it to call sylphs to do that for me?" she asked.

"That would be cheating," Frida said, smiling. "You already know how to call sylphs and how to ask them to do things for you. Now you need to understand how to do these things for yourself. Use the Sight, but this time, pull a little on the power. You should see how all the air in this room moves when you do that."

She did as she was told, and much to her delight, the air seemed to thicken somehow, while still remaining clear—and she could, indeed, see how it moved. It looked rather like water in a way; she could see where there were eddies in all the corners where the air encountered two walls and curled around itself, how it rose around the candle in a wavering stream.

And she became aware that it had a sort of weight to it now. That it was, in fact, something she could move by concentrating on it. She made a little experiment first, and created a faint wash across her face, just to be sure she *could* do this thing.

Now convinced, she gave the air between herself and the candle a little shove.

The flame wavered, but did not go out.

The second time, she pushed harder, and without a sound, the flame blew out, leaving just a bit of smoke curling up from the burned wick.

"Now try something different," Frida said, getting up

to light the candle again. "This time put it out by taking the air *away*."

This . . . was trickier. It took her several tries before she got the hang of it, because the first few times more air just rushed in to feed the candle when she pushed air away.

"Ah!" Frida said, when she finally managed it. "Now, listen. This is something only an Air Master can do; you can literally pull the breath out of someone's body if you choose. And it doesn't matter how strong someone is, or how big, or even if he has you tied up and 'helpless.' You can render him unconscious doing this; you can kill him. So this is something you need to practice—on a candle, please!—until you can do it in your sleep. One day you may need it, and when you need it, it will be urgent that you get it right the first time."

Annie licked her lips uneasily. Once again had come the reminder that she might have to use her powers to kill, and not just some creature or monster that should have been mythical. "How many not-human things need to breathe?" she asked.

"Virtually anything but a *vampir* or a spirit. Even the *hexen*. Even trolls! You probably will not encounter trolls, however; they are very solitary and are never seen near cities." Frida cocked her head to the side. "Which reminds me—when we move in the spring, do we pack up everything in wagons and make a giant parade of it through the countryside?"

Annie shook her head. "That would take far too long. The Colonel always has us on a tight schedule. We load the wagons, put the wagons on a train, and take the train to the next town. We rarely stay more than two or three nights, and often stay for only one. The workmen are breaking down everything not under the canvas as the last show is being performed, and loading the front of the train. That includes the camps, all the props and costumes that are not currently in someone's hands, the chuck wagons and everything the cooks need—well, everything that isn't needed in the performance. As soon as the last member of the audience leaves, the big tent is struck, the animals that were in the last act of the show are loaded into their cars, the electrical generators are shut off and loaded, we all get on the train, and the field is checked to make sure nothing was forgotten. We go on to the next venue, the camps are unloaded and set up first so the performers can get some sleep, then the show-tents and barricades and signs are put up, the animals are unloaded into their proper corrals, the cooks make whatever preparations they need for making breakfast, like lighting stoves, the generators come out, and it all begins all over again. If we stay in one place longer than a couple of days, sometimes some of us get rooms rather than living in the camp—but as long as the weather is good, the camp can be quite pleasant, and Frank and I usually live in our tent."

Frida shook her head. "It sounds like a model of efficiency."

"It is," Annie said, and made a face. "It is so efficient, in fact, that Bismarck had some officers following us around during the first half of this German tour making notes on everything from how we pack things to how many people it takes to erect each structure."

Frida pulled on her lower lip. "I—am not sure what to think about that."

Well, she might as well put all of her cards on the table when it came to politics. "I do not trust him. *At all.* And I hope you will forgive me, but I also do not trust Kaiser Wilhelm." She hoped that Frida didn't feel insulted, but—Frida had said that it was very important for magicians to be honest with one another. That words were important, and that magicians needed to be careful lest their power make their words come true.

"Well, you won't hear it outside these walls, because Bismarck has ears everywhere, but there are plenty of people in the Empire who feel the same," Frida admitted. "And I certainly do, and so do Theo and Sofi. Bismarck and the Emperor have gotten a taste for power by consolidating all the German-speaking lands into their own hands. They managed to do most of it bloodlessly, but . . . perhaps not entirely." She paused. "There are those who suspect that our dear King Ludwig did *not* take his own life. There are those of us who *know* he was effectively pushed from power by the Emperor's machinations, and that if it had not been for those machinations, Bavaria might well still be independent."

Then she shook her head. "I have said too much, and to no real purpose. It's not likely that you, an American, are going to ever need to worry about the Kaiser's grasp."

Annie felt cold for a moment, and, moved by something she didn't quite understand, replied, "I would not be so sure of that. They have already made moves to take parts of Africa. I have no doubt that their ambitions are wider than that." She rubbed her thumb and forefinger together thoughtfully. "In London, he was visiting the Queen, and there was a royal party to see the show. He wanted me to shoot the ash from a cigarette in his mouth, as I do with Frank. His underlings insisted that I do this trick only with him holding the cigarette at arm's length . . . but since that moment, I have wondered if I would have done the world a great favor by missing the cigarette."

To her surprise, Frida smiled broadly. "I see you are a woman with a stomach as strong as mine. I should have known that after Solstice Night, but it is good to have confirmation."

"Of—?"

"That you can kill something if you have to." Frida nodded. "And that you can kill a fellow man if you have to."

Annie bit her lip. She still wasn't entirely certain about that. If the He-Wolf appeared in front of her looking like an ordinary man?

Would I freeze, or would I just see red and kill him in cold blood?

It was a valid question. If he was attacking her, that

was different. But if she just saw him walking down the street or standing in front of her? Did his past actions mean that she had the *right* to take the law into her own hands?

. . . no. No one has the right to take the law into their own hands. That's what separates the rest of us from the He-Wolves.

"So!" Frida said, interrupting her thoughts. "Let's practice this. And if you are still not feeling any ill effects, we will move to something with more force. As an Air Master, you are the bringer of tempests. Combined with a Water Magician like Frank, you two will unleash the fury of a cyclone."

"I would prefer that we never had to," she sighed.

"So would I," Frida agreed. "But you need to know that you can if you must."

That . . . seemed to sum up everything she had learned so far about magic.

It was clear to Annie when they all came down to supper that Theodor wanted to speak with them about something important once the children had been sent up to bed. This was not the easiest thing to accomplish; Anneliese had decided that Annie was the most fascinating person in the universe and always had dozens of questions for her, and Wolfgang had found a sympathetic listener in Frank, who would patiently wait while the boy chattered like the proverbial magpie, and poured out all his dreams and woes. Frank would listen—actually listen, not just pretend to listen—then offer a soupçon of advice if it seemed that advice was called for. Both children enjoyed trying out their English with the Butlers too, and they loved learning cowboy slang and the few bits of Sioux that Annie knew. And this evening in the very pleasant parlor on the "family floor," both children had a lot to chatter about.

When they had finally been taken up to bed by their
governess, Theo immediately turned to the other magicians. "The *nachtkrapp* has been seen again, and it is
said there is at least one missing child." He sighed. "I do
not know whether or not this is true, nor whether the
child was taken by the *nachtkrapp*—nor whether or not
there is more than one missing child, because, well—"

"The children were poor, may have run away from
jobs, and no one cares," Jack said bluntly.

"Exactly. The missing child was a chimney sweep,
and only his master has any interest in finding him." The
Graf frowned. "And the only reason why I know of this
myself is because he accosted the agent I sent to investi-
gate the *nachtkrapp* sighting."

"Hmm. It might have returned, but it is more likely
that it never left in the first place," said Frida. "There is a
plethora of hiding places among the roofs and chimneys
of Strasburg."

"It didn't seem all that impressed with us at Solstice,"
Frank observed.

"I have never yet seen a corvid, supernatural or mortal,
that was impressed with humans," Sofi said lightly. "But
certainly this one needs to be gotten rid of, especially if it
has taken a child."

This time Sophia had joined the group, listening quietly while she did some fancywork. Annie was glad to
see her there. Even though she wasn't a magician herself, it seemed unfair for her to be excluded from what
was going on.

They might have been any group of friends, seated
around the fire in a lovely room—once again, Sofi's hand
was evident in the peacock-feather wallpaper, the sinuous, sensuous ornaments, the porcelain stove also done
in Nouveau style, and the draperies that had clever peacock ornaments holding them open. Annie was just a
little jealous of Sofi's seemingly effortless ability to create a room that was both welcoming and beautiful. They
all held cups of hot chocolate or spiced cider, and no one

looking at them would ever guess what they were discussing.

"Do we need to assemble the Lodge?" Frida asked.

"For a *nachtkrapp?* I don't think so," Theo said thoughtfully. "They're only dangerous to children who are out at night alone. If it were summer, when children play outside long after dark, I would be more concerned. In fact, I'd rather not kill it, just send it back to where it belongs."

"I'd just as soon shoot it," Jack said firmly. "If the gol-dang thing is the one with no eyes and raggedy wings with holes in 'em, it's been spreadin' disease an' death every time some poor fool looks at it."

"No, the one on Solstice definitely had eyes," said Annie slowly, remembering how the thing had looked at her as if she was a bug. "And the wings were fine."

"Tonight?" Sofi asked, pursing her lips, as if she was going to object to them leaping up and going on a Hunting expedition right this moment.

"Not tonight. I wanted to discuss the situation with all of you first, and come up with a plan. In the first place, it's going to be very hard to catch. The fact that the wretched thing flies complicates matters." Theo sipped his drink, and looked at them as if he was hoping they had some ideas.

"You say you don't want to kill it?" Frank asked, out of the blue.

Theo nodded.

"And the thing hunts children?"

"Exclusively," Theo confirmed.

"Well, then. I might just have that idea you wanted," Frank said.

For once, Annie's small size was exactly what the situation needed.

She fit rather neatly into a ready-made dress and leggings intended for a girl of about ten or twelve, and with her face hidden in the hood of her short cloak and her hair flowing loosely, the way she usually wore it anyway, she looked just like a girl of about that age. The matter of a disguise had actually been pretty funny—Sofi had objected that her dressmakers couldn't possibly produce a girl's winter outfit on such short notice, and seemed unaware that it was perfectly possible to *buy* one out of a shop window. Annie had just said, "Don't worry, I'll take care of it," gone out to the part of town where working-class folks shopped, and found exactly what was needed in less than three hours, including a nice, warm, second-hand cloak with a hood, lined with sheepskin. Sofi's astonishment had been comical. Annie actually liked the skirt, jacket, and shirtwaist, and was already planning alterations that would turn it into another Show costume. And the cloak was generic enough it could be worn by an adult as well as a child.

This was probably the first time being as small as she was had turned out to be an advantage.

They were all back in the neighborhood they had patrolled on the Solstice. After the snowfall two days ago, the temperature had dropped again, which was in their favor, because the cold kept everyone indoors, reducing the potential for someone to accidentally wander into a scene of supernatural combat.

In fact, there was literally no one out on the street, just like on Solstice Night. Annie walked in the middle of the street, making soft sobbing sounds. She wasn't really crying, but she was doing her level best to come up with a convincing imitation of a child in despair.

All that, and avoid the frozen ruts. In the dark. No one had bothered to scrape or sweep *this* street clean once the snow had fallen, and traffic had turned the street into a never-ending series of potential spots for breaking an ankle.

At least it's not smooth and frozen into a skating pond.

It was a very good thing she was supposed to be crying in desperation, and thus, anyone watching her would not be expecting her to move very fast.

The others were all moving from shadow to shadow on either side of the road among the buildings, trying to stay out of sight. She was the bait in this trap; Theo was fairly certain that the *nachtkrapp* could not tell if someone was an actual child or an adult disguised as a child. This whole trap-and-ambush had been Frank's idea, but she embraced it with enthusiasm, even though she was taking the most risk.

What they needed was to get the Raven-creature down on street level. Trying to chase it across the rooftops was never going to work. Frank had an idea for what to do when they got it down here, too. And if that didn't work, Theo had an idea, and Frida had a third.

She moved as if so burdened with grief that she could barely get one foot in front of the other. She kept her head down, both to hide her face, and because that would (hopefully) keep the bird from noticing she wasn't a child at all.

Meanwhile she had to literally feel her way with her toes, or she risked breaking an ankle.

She heard the *nachtkrapp* before she saw it. It didn't make the usual *quork* of a normal raven, but the sound of its wings was like a huge piece of canvas flapping in the wind. She heard it following her above and to the left. *Flap-flap-flap* and then a pause. Another couple of flaps and another pause. Probably the flapping was as it was getting over an obstacle on the roof, or jumping from one roof to the next, then continuing to walk along the roof ridge. That sound couldn't be coming from "just another bird," that much was certain. The only birds that would be out at this time of night were owls, and owls flew silently.

What was going through the creature's mind? If it had been human, it probably would have been wondering why a young girl was wandering the street in this part of town on a night so cold and dark. It would have been asking itself why she was weeping. A human then would either tell himself this was none of his business and walk on, decide to help, or decide to take advantage of the situation.

The *nachtkrapp*, however, would probably see prey. The lore said that the *nachtkrapp* left its hiding place— wherever that was—only by night, and only to hunt. Its prey was children, but only if they saw it—presumably, like for so many of these creatures, the intention was to scare children to stay in their beds at night. Except, of course, that the children of the poor, like their parents, often worked well into the night. Some had jobs that kept them late, some worked as beggars, some as street peddlers like the "Little Match Girl" of the fairy tale, some were scavengers, hunting in the alleys and streets for anything useful that might have been dropped or lost. It was certainly no naughtiness or fault that kept *them* out so late.

As if the poor didn't suffer enough, they are not only the prey of the rich, they are the prey of things like the nachtkrapp. *It ought to be coming for spoiled, bad children, not the poor things trudging through the snow on a bitter winter night.*

But then, the Krampus *comes for spoiled, bad children. Perhaps the* nachtkrapp *doesn't want to compete with it.*

At any rate, the lore said that if a child *saw* the thing, and only if the child set eyes on it, the bird would carry the child to its nest, rip off its limbs and eat them, then pluck out the child's eyes and heart—although *some* legends stated that the bird would simply put the child in a bag and carry it away, though the legends didn't say *where* the raven would take it.

In a just world the bird would carry them off to a land of sweets and warm beds.

She was warned by the sound of wings in full flight that the *nachtkrapp* had decided to move. And she didn't have enough time to wonder if it had lost interest in her or had decided to make her its prey. A huge, black shadow passed closely over her head and the *nachtkrapp* landed in front of her.

She started back with a frightened cry that was not at all feigned; the bird was bigger than the biggest horse she had ever seen, and it looked fully capable of tearing her apart with very little effort.

But before fear overcame her, Theo unleashed a torrent of water on the bird, conjured literally out of thin air. So much water that it drove the *nachtkrapp* flat to the ground, wings outstretched. In the next moment, Frida blasted it with a wind so bitter that the water turned to ice instantly, pinning it in place.

The *nachtkrapp* uttered a single broken cry as Frank's plan came to glorious fruition, and Jack, Theo, and Frida all conjured up magical lights and joined Annie in the street.

"Kaempfe nicht," said Theo. *"Du machst alles nur noch schlimmer."*

The *nachtkrapp* immediately stopped struggling and glared at him. *"Was willst du?"* it asked.

But rather than answering the bird, Theo looked at Frida. "Air is the power of languages," he said. "Can you—"

"Of course," she replied, made some gestures that left glowing lines behind in the air, and said a few things Annie didn't understand.

"Much better," said Theo. Except—at the same time, more faintly, Annie heard him say *"Viel besser."* And it immediately dawned on her that this was some sort of translation spell!

The raven gave what sounded like a groan. *"I am in pain, mortal,"* it said. *"Tell me what you want, or destroy me."*

"Promise me you will not escape and will not attack us if we release you," Theo ordered.

The raven groaned again, and reluctantly said, *"I give you my word."*

This time Frida and Jack together made some gestures and words, and a wind as hot as anything coming out of the desert washed over all of them and the *nachtkrapp,* thawing the ice and freeing its wings.

It did not immediately pull its wings into its body as Annie had thought it surely would. Instead, it slowly drew its wings toward itself, then stretched them out one at a time, and finally shook itself all over, sending shards of ice and drops of water everywhere.

"What do you want?" the raven repeated, hackles raised.

"One of two things, and it is your choice which it is to be," Theo told it. "Either return to the spirit realm, or cease preying on children."

The raven pulled itself up to its full height, startled. *"That is a bold request,"* it said. *"And why should I do either of these things?"*

"Because this lady and gentleman have rifles loaded with bullets made of blessed salt, blessed lead from a church roof, and silver," Theo told it calmly, despite the fact that the raven could easily have taken off his head, he was standing so close to it. "And the lady never misses. But I have no war with creatures that elect to stop preying on humans. There are few enough of you. I prefer to preserve your lives."

The raven cocked its head to the side. *"I have heard of you, magician,"* it said. *"I have heard of your bargains. I will take it—on two conditions."*

Theo gestured to the bird to continue.

"I will become an 'angry raven,' and merely terrify children I find wandering at night. That is my first condition. The second is that you permit me to eat dead children. That is, children that I find dead, that have been killed by something other than me."

Theo thought about this for a moment. Annie hoped with all her heart that he had seen the loophole that the clever creature had built into its promise.

"Only if you also pledge not to partner with another

night creature or a mortal to kill children so that you may 'find' them dead," Theo said.

The bird's hackles rose, but its words were reluctantly admiring. *"You are clever, magician. All right. I give my word. I will become an Angry Nightraven. I will not harm children nor cause them to be harmed, but I claim any dead ones I find as my prey."*

Theo gave a deep bow to the thing, and to Annie's surprise it bowed back. "The pact is accepted," he said. "Go in peace. May we someday meet in friendship."

The *nachtkrapp* gave a derisive caw. *"Unlikely. And yet, not impossible. Go back to your warm nests, mortals, and be grateful I do not hold grudges for outwitting me."*

And with a thunder of wings that blew all their hair and clothing back and made them shade their eyes, the *nachtkrapp* was gone, flying over the rooftops with a sound like flapping sails.

12

BY the beginning of February, Annie and Frank were deep in their studies, and progressing well, even by Annie's exacting standards. It certainly did not hurt that they were staying with the Graf; there was no need to hide anything, nor go huddled in corners or the crowded *vardo* in order to talk to Frida or Jack. Even better, Theo had his "workroom," a dedicated space for practicing magic, something they did not have at either the show camp or the *Gasthaus*. That meant Annie and Frank could practice the real thing.

Once the daily magic lessons and practice were over, and Theo's children were finished with their own daily lessons, Annie made good on her word and taught both Anneliese and Wolfgang to shoot. That would not have been possible, except that the Graf arranged for a small, temporary shooting gallery to be set up in the basement of the mansion. It was *relatively* warm—at least it was out of the snow—and well lit, so it didn't matter if the sun had set by the time they got to practice.

The children used very light rifles, and Frank loaded

their shells with only half the powder Annie would have used. The distance to the target was just far enough to be a challenge, and with only half a charge, there wasn't much danger of damaging anything but the target. Mage-lights created near-daylight conditions, so the worst they had to contend with were cold noses and feet, since the cellars were utterly unheated.

The children put up with these hardships without complaint, and even Theo came down once in a while to put a few practice rounds into a target. He was good, as was to be expected, since his Hunting used as much in the way of mundane weapons as arcane. The children weren't—but they improved with every round.

Annie loved every minute of this. If there was one thing she enjoyed whole-heartedly, it was teaching women and girls to shoot. She never wanted any female to feel the helplessness *she* had at the He-Wolf's hands. Anneliese and Wolfgang actually set aside their sibling rivalry to help each other at target practice.

And Sofi took Annie aside to thank her for the peace and quiet the lessons had brought to the house. All she could think was, *Peace and quiet? Those floors must be thicker than I thought!*

Life settled into a comfortable routine. Annie wrote to her family about the new lodgings, though not the reason for taking up with the Graf. She knew that her "baby" sister, who was now in her twenties, would be especially interested in what she could tell about the mansion and Sofi. It took at least a month for a letter to reach Germany from Ohio and vice versa, so Annie and Frank didn't get them very often, and the first letter from home to reach them after they had moved into the Graf's mansion had been mailed from Ohio before New Year's Day and had been sent to the *Edel Gasthaus* instead. A messenger boy brought it over and it was delivered to Annie over breakfast.

She longed to read it, but to engross herself in a letter at the breakfast table, even one from her favorite sister

Hulda, would have been very rude. But Frida mentioned some specious "errand" she had to make just as they were getting up from the table, and Annie was able to run back to her room with her precious letter and read it to herself, and then a second time to Frank, in peace.

Everything was fine at home. Except . . . Hulda devoted an entire page to something quite out of the ordinary.

Some stranger was poking round here asking questions about you. Most people reckon he was one of those big newspaper reporters, but it seems strange to me that a reporter would be digging dirt around here in the middle of winter—and when the Wild West is in Germany. I kept him from Mama and gave him the cold shoulder, but I couldn't keep him from everyone. The questions he asked were odd too. He wanted to know everything about you when you were a child and the family was going through hard times. Everything, like about how you looked when you was little, and whether you'd been sent to the Darke County Infirmary or not. I just said the truth, that I was too young to remember, but with all the people he was asking, someone probably told him the answer. Or brother John might have; you know how jealous he is of you; he thinks it was just luck and not practice that lets you shoot so good, and that rightfully it should have been him that is the famous shootist. Anyway, the stranger's gone now. I just thought you ought to know in case Colonel Buffalo Bill needs to hear about it. All the things you sent at the end of November came in time, and your trunk of Christmas presents was much appreciated and everyone will give you their thank-you letters once you are home in the United States and the postage isn't so dear. My land! Seven whole cents for a little bitty letter!

Annie read that over to Frank twice, because something about that passage struck her as very odd indeed. The first thing that was odd was that Hulda had mentioned it at all. Reporters descended on the county all the time to ask about Annie, especially when she won a shooting contest or the Colonel issued a press release or advertisement about her and the show. Which he was doing quite frequently while they were overseas, reminding people that *"There is only one genuine Annie Oakley, and she is with Colonel Buffalo Bill's Wild West and Congress of Rough Riders touring Germany!"* She had her impersonators, after all, and the Colonel periodically made sure to put them on notice that they would be found out. And now, with things so quiet while they were in winter quarters, he felt the need to do so often enough that it was not completely out of the question that reporters would come to Ohio and seek out her family for a biographical piece to accompany the advertisement or to add to the press release. Still. All that information was out there already, with no need to travel in the dead of winter to rural Ohio to get it from her old neighbors.

"That doesn't sound quite right," was Frank's comment when Annie read that part of the letter to him. "I can't think of one reporter in a hundred who wants to know about you being in the Infirmary. It's a depressing story. Nobody wants to hear about poor little girls darning socks and making uniform dresses for even poorer little girls. They want to hear about how you shot game to pay off your Mama's mortgage before you were fifteen, and how you beat the pants off me."

"So . . . it seems odd to you, too?" Annie was more than a little relieved to hear that Frank felt the same as she did. She trusted his instincts when she didn't trust her own. And there was one horrible thought that sprang immediately to mind as she had read Hulda's words. "Could it—could it be the He-Wolf?"

The idea that the He-Wolf was still out there, and might be sniffing around her family, was horrifying. She didn't know *why* he would be doing that—it wasn't as if

he could ever get her back under his control—but truth
to tell, if she heard he was dead she would probably arrange to have his corpse dug up just to prove it was him.

Frank sat on the edge of the bed and scratched the
back of his head. "Could be. But why?"

"Maybe he finally figured out that Annie Moses is
Annie Oakley now," she offered. "Maybe he was just
trying to confirm that in his head." But why, why, why
would he need to know that? If it was him. But who else
would it be?

And she couldn't help it; she shivered at the thought
that the He-Wolf was looking for her. Or at least, looking into her present. She'd hoped, in the back of her
mind, that something bad, something fatal, had happened to him. Or at least that he had forgotten about
her. Instinctively she pressed her left hand to her stomach, which answered with a dull ache.

Frank put his hand over hers. "Ain't nothing to worry
about, sweetheart," he said, without an ounce of conde-
scension. "You're here. He's there. You think a low-
down varmint like him is going to be able to get the cost
of a steamship to Germany in his hands? Even traveling
in steerage? Why, I bet he can't even drum up train fare
to Chicago!"

"Yes, but . . . what if he starts . . . telling stories?" she
asked, her throat tightening and her eyes beginning to
sting. "What if he goes to the newspapers? I can't do
anything about that from here!" She had worked *so* hard
at preserving her reputation—being *so* careful that she
didn't do any of the unladylike stunts that the Lillian
Smiths did, like turning handsprings in the arena so her
skirts fell, and watching every single word she said in
public so no one ever said anything but what a lady she
was. . . .

"Stories about *what?* The little poor gal who ran
away from him? Half the county will tar and feather him
just for talking mean about you, and the other half will
beat him senseless for how he treated you. That ain't a

secret, you know. There's plenty in Darke County that know how his wife threw you out in the snow, how he never did pay you or your Mama, and how he lied to your Mama about how you were." She must have looked unconvinced, because he gathered her in his arms and held her head against his chest. "Even John ain't going to let him spread stories about his sister. And as for going to the papers—the papers already know about you escaping from him. It's so old it isn't even news anymore. And anything he says is just going to make him look bad, not you, because more reporters will come ask your neighbors about it, and you can bet the neighbors and your friends will set the record straight."

She put her arms around him and told herself that Frank was right. John might be jealous of her success, but a slur against her was one against the family, and even for jealousy he wouldn't put up with that. And Frank was right that a lot of people knew about how she'd been treated. Mama hadn't made it any kind of a secret, and word like that spread, about someone who was likely to take advantage of you. Especially because anyone who heard the tale wanted to make sure no poor relation of theirs fell in with someone who was going to cheat them out of their just wages.

"Lots of water between us and him," Frank repeated. "And if you're thinking he'd be coming here to stir up dirt among the show folks, that's never going to be! *Everyone* in the show knows that story about how he beat you and cheated you and you ran away. If he somehow *did* come up with the money and turned up here . . . just what do you think all your friends in the show would do to him when they figured out who he was?" She felt him take her chin and tilt up her head so she was looking into his eyes. "He'd get beat bloody, and that's if he was lucky. If he wasn't lucky, well, someone's likely to tie a rock to his feet and chuck him in the river, and eliminate the problem *and* what he'd got planned at the same time."

She felt a little shock then. "You don't think anybody

in the show would murder a fellow like that!" Her voice faltered at his hard expression. "Do you?"

"Well. . . ." He chose his words carefully. "I know they're our friends, but honey, plenty of the fellows in the show have got things in their past that don't bear too close an examination. Plenty of 'em are hot headed. Plenty more are inclined to fix a problem in the most direct way possible."

Half of her felt . . . protected. Half of her was appalled. "Oh."

"And, sweetheart, that don't even begin to get into what the Hunting Lodge here is likely to do with him! Why, just because Theo got all soft with that giant bird, it don't mean he's going to be that way with the He-Wolf! That blackguard will *wish* he was in the river with a rock around his ankles if the Hunt gets hold of him!" He patted her hair. "But he ain't coming. We've most of the year before we go home, and by that time he'll have figured out he can't lay a finger on you and give up."

"You're probably right," she sighed.

"It ain't *probably*. I *am* right. Now, just in case, when you write back to Hulda, you let her know you think this fellow asking questions is really the He-Wolf, and let her spread *that* story around. He'll get run out of town on a rail!" He chuckled, and so did she. "And that'll put an end to him thinking about you, I'll bet. So, what's Frida got planned for you today?"

"How to make air cold like she did with the *nachtkrapp*. What's Pierre teaching you?" she asked, finally feeling her nerves starting to settle. And she felt a little bit ashamed. Because she had been working *so hard* to get over her fear of the Wolves, and yet, there it was again. The moment it looked like it was even possible he'd try and get his hands on her, every bit of the old terror came roaring back and she was as helpless as a baby bunny seeing a hawk's talons heading for her.

"Pierre reckons to teach me water-scrying, which is

using water like a crystal ball to see things." He sounded like he was eager to try it.

"Like telling fortunes?" she hazarded.

"No, nothing like that. Seeing things at a distance that are happening now. Like—you could look in on the family and see how they all are faring. And you can talk to other magicians that can do scrying too. You can even talk to ones that aren't Water Magicians, as long as they can scry. It's like being in the same room. You scry them, they scry you, and you can talk."

"But I thought looking into crystal balls was about seeing the future?" she objected.

He chuckled. "That's a myth, I guess. Pierre says the future changes too quickly for anyone to be able to scry it accurately. But the *right now,* well, that's there for any-one with the magic to see it." There definitely was glee in his voice.

She had recovered enough of her self-confidence to tease him. "Are you going to become a riverboat card-sharp, Frank Butler? Look in your water glass to see what everyone else at the table is holding?"

"Well, you're the one that thought of *that,* not me, missy, so don't you go putting that on me!" He laughed. "Besides, I've got no hankering for that kind of life, nor to get shot, neither. A fellow that wins too reliably is like to find his waistcoat perforated. Or at the very least, his good looks rearranged."

That made her laugh, and she shook off her feelings of unease.

"And now it's time for my lesson." He kissed the top of her head and left, closing the door to their suite be-hind him. Since Pierre—who Annie still had not met!—was only available in the mornings, that was when Frank used the workroom.

Annie had plenty to do in the morning anyway. With four times the space of their little room in the *Gasthaus,* Annie had had all their costumes brought over from the show and was mending, re- trimming, and refurbishing the old ones, and making new ones. Since she had joined the Wild West, this was something she always did when the show was in winter quarters. Before that, she had taken the time to refresh her costumes whenever she had a big gap of time and she and Frank were staying in one place. Until this year, she had always done this at her Mama's home, or Hulda's, because Hulda loved to sew and help with the costumes, and Mama's door was always open to Annie and Frank. She had planned to make over the costumes one at a time while staying in the *Gasthaus,* but now with the extra space she could do them all at once.

Sofi wasn't sure what to make of this; in *her* world, a lady went to her seamstress for creating whole garments or extensive alterations, and relied on her personal lady's maid for everything else. The notion that a lady would undertake to refurbish her wardrobe herself was bemusing. On the other hand, she did fancywork, which was appropriate for a lady of her rank and stature, and she greatly admired Annie's embroidery, and she *was* cognizant of the differences in income between the two of them. And she understood how exacting Annie was when it came to her wardrobe. So although this was almost a foreign concept to her, she was beginning to come to terms with it.

Of course, Annie *could* have had a seamstress make her costumes, but aside from the fact that she saved a considerable amount of money making her own, there were two solid reasons why she should continue to make them personally. The first was that she enjoyed sewing, whether it be mending, plain sewing, fancy sewing, or embellishment. Unlike target shooting, which was always an ephemeral accomplishment, she could look at the work of her hands with satisfaction whenever she chose to, or whenever she wore it. And when she was home, Hulda loved helping her with her costumes; Hulda was, herself, a considerably talented seamstress. The second reason was that of all the folk in the show that used costumes, it was only the Colonel who got them specially made. Everyone else made their own, had a spouse or sister make them, or adapted ordinary clothing, and having a seamstress would set her even more apart from the rest of the folks in the show. There were other considerations, too. If she'd gone to a seamstress for her costumes, it was likely she'd have to do some remaking, because a seamstress was *not* used to creating clothing for someone as athletic as Annie was, nor for someone whose outfits would have to hold up to things like shooting while riding a bicycle at full speed.

True, she was the biggest "star" other than Bill. But she didn't like *acting* like it. And having someone else make her costumes would put her "above" the rest of the cast. Lillian Smith's parading about as if she was irreplaceable had made Annie physically ill, and she did not want to be like that.

Her current project was remaking the "child's" outfit she'd worn to play bait for the *nachtkrapp* so that it was suitable as the base for a show costume. That meant removing the cheap lace that adorned the hems of both the skirt and the leggings, removing the little bows down the front of the jacket, and doing some actual alterations so that it would fit her better than it did now. After that . . . she'd probably leave this one plain, since she had other outfits that were enhanced with buckskin fringe, embroidery, or both. She'd bought it with an eye to turning it into a costume anyway, so the brown moleskin of which it had been made looked similar enough to the materials her other costumes were made out of that once she got done with it, no one would ever know it had come from a little middle-class ready-made shop here in Strasburg.

The street outside must have been cleared, because today she definitely heard the sounds of hooves and wheels on pavement coming from outside the windows.

If there was anything more soothing than sewing next to a warm stove on a bitter, snow-bedecked winter's day, she didn't know what it was. The moleskin was soft and pliable under her fingers, and just about the only thing that would have given her more pleasure would have been if she was embroidering on silk.

Still, silk embroidery brought with it its own kind of anxiety; silk showed every little mistake, and you had to take great pains to set every single stitch perfectly. Silk was meant for people to see up close, and if you made any mistakes at all, you would know it the whole time you were wearing the garment. Annie knew that she, at least, would be so self-conscious of a mistake that it would spoil the pleasure of wearing a pretty gown. But this inexpensive moleskin was very forgiving; mistakes could be picked out and re-sewn without any worry that they'd show later.

A half a dozen little sylphs drifted in through the closed window to arrange themselves on the mantelpiece and the back of her chair, watching her. Lately she had noticed that they brought faint perfumes with them—balsam, hay, flowers—that blended into a harmonious bouquet that made her think of spring.

A knock at the door interrupted her reverie, and at her *"Kommen Sie herein"*—she had learned a few German phrases at least—Frida poked her head in the door. Today her abundant blond hair was done in a sort of crown of braids on the top of her head, while Annie's was as she usually wore it—loose, in a mane of unruly curls.

"Oh good! I was hoping you were at work. Shall we make a—sewing-together-event—of this morning?"

"Sewing bee," Annie corrected, laughing. "Yes, I should like that."

"Why is it called a *bee?*" Frida asked, coming in with two skirts draped over her arm and a sewing basket in the other, and a handful of sylphs of her own following in her wake.

"I—don't know!" Annie replied as Frida pulled another chair up to the fire, to sit opposite her. "No one ever explained it to me. Perhaps because when we are sewing together we are busy as bees?"

Frida shook her head. "English makes no sense sometimes."

"I don't think about it too hard," said Annie. "What are you working on?"

"Costumes for the warmer weather, when the show goes back touring. We will be doing nine more cities in Germany before going on to Belgium, and nothing I have now is sturdy enough for a costume and suited for warm weather. I am exceedingly grateful for my Hunting costume, but it is very heavy wool." She draped one skirt over the arm of her chair and took up the other. Both were the same loden green as the show costume—her Hunting costume, as she called it—that she currently wore in performances. "My Mutti back home is making the jackets, because I have no patience for gussets and darts and faradiddles and setting in lining, but I am making the skirts because she has no patience for long seams and hemming."

From where she sat, Annie could tell immediately that the skirt Frida was hemming was a very light wool, the same weight as a man's autumn suit, and the one over the arm of the chair was canvas, not unlike her own show costumes. "Does Sofi know that you make your own clothing?" she asked, curious now. "When she found out I make mine, she stared at me as if I had grown rabbit ears."

Frida laughed. "I don't think so. The subject never came up. Sofi lives in a very enchanted world, which is a nice place to visit, but I would not care to live in it all the time."

"Hmm." Annie thought about this for a moment. "She seems very pampered, and she has a great many servants, but I think it must take a lot of work to be Sofi. I mean . . . she does a lot during the day. She oversees every one of those servants, she knows them all by name and duties, and if something goes wrong in the household she is the first to know about it and handle it. She spends hours consulting with her housekeeper and cook, and more hours writing people because 'social' and 'political' seem to go hand in hand when you are a *Graefin*, and hours and hours and hours organizing social things. . . ."

"And charities. She does a lot of charities. And she checks with the children's tutors and governess every day about their lessons. . . ." Frida rolled her eyes. "All things I would hate. I really would rather not be responsible for anyone other than myself and Jack, I don't care for social gatherings, usually, and oh! I hate politics!"

"What *do* you like?" Annie asked curiously.

"Things like this—two friends sitting together on a horrid day beside a warm fire, with something nice to do, and the prospect of a dinner I don't have to make in front of me." Frida grinned. "Patrolling the forest. Shooting practice. The company of Elementals in a mountain meadow on a day when the only thing that is going to happen is absolutely nothing. And Jack. I definitely like Jack," she added with a laugh. "And I like you and Frank and Sofi and Theo."

"Those all sound lovely. Do you like being with the show?" That actually had Annie quite curious now, since all those things that Frida had mentioned (other than the people) appeared to be quite solitary pursuits.

"Hmm." Frida paused to thread a needle, and begin a hem. "Sometimes. I must admit the applause is very heady. I would rather not have to have all the people crowding about us in the camp, but you, my dear friend, need a translator, and I can overcome my aversion to crowds in order to help you."

"I think it was wonderful of you to come in the first place, and a very great favor to me that you stayed, especially in this weather," Annie said. "I really cannot thank you enough."

"I am a Hunt Master and some things are my duty, but helping you has turned out to be an unexpected pleasure." Frida looked up from her sewing and smiled. "It will be better in the spring. The *vardo* will be more comfortable in warmer weather. In the meantime I am *eternally* grateful to Theo for inviting us to stay." She paused, her hands still for a moment while she thought. "I enjoy being here enough because there is a task to be done—that is, educating you in magic—but it's not something I would do on my own. That is, I would not join the Wild West just because I *can,* if you had not been here."

Annie considered her words for a moment, as her hands moved busily and a sylph flew down, curious as a cat, to examine what she was doing. "I couldn't have imagined doing this, being in this enormous show, when I first met Frank, but now I can't imagine doing anything else. I suppose it will have to stop at some point. The Colonel will get tired of traveling, or—well, shows fail all the time, even ones as big as this one. But Frank and I will probably still travel when we are no longer with the Wild West, doing shooting exhibitions, or theater work, and shooting contests."

"Would you ever settle in one place?" Frida asked.

She had to laugh. "Well, I *think* that I want to, eventually. Frank and I have spoken about buying a house when we return to America. We have been staying with my relatives between show seasons, but you know what the Swedes say, *fish and visitors stink after three days.* Everyone in my family has a life of their own, after all. It's not fair of me to come blowing in irregularly and disrupting all their plans, no matter how many presents I bring, and I think it would be better if we had a place of our own."

"In the West?" Frida asked.

Annie laughed out loud at that. "Oh, good gracious, *no.* Somewhere near New York City, I think. We're thinking about New Jersey. There is a very pretty little town called Franklin Township that I like. You should ask the genuine cowboys from Texas, Oklahoma, and Kansas, though, and they'll tell you I'm an Easterner. West of the Mississippi is too rough for my taste."

"And everyone thinks you are a real Western girl!"
Frida laughed.

Annie shrugged. "The Colonel tells himself that he
is showing the 'real' Wild West, but in his heart he
knows very well all he is showing is the dime-novel version. The real Wild West is terribly dull, the work is
mind-numbing and grueling, and all that vaunted 'free-
dom' is not worth much when you are scratching out a
bare living on a homestead." She paused. "Lots of people in our area went out West to make a fortune. Most
of them came back with little more than the clothing
they stood up in. But no one wants to see that, *particularly* here. Despite Bill ballyhooing how educational the
show is, the reality is that more than half the time he
does so in order to avoid the taxes on entertainments."

Frida burst into a peal of laughter. "That's *nothing*
like what I expected! I appreciate the candor!"

"I don't suppose I can learn scrying, can I?" Annie
asked as she and Frida took over the workroom after
dinner.

"One thing at a time," Frida chuckled, closing the
door behind them. "I am putting my priority on teaching you what will be useful in a situation where you
might have to Hunt something. Or where you might be
attacked. So. I've introduced you to the zephyrs, which
are stronger than sylphs. Now I am going to introduce
you to the Winds, which are stronger than zephyrs."

With that out of the way—and the Winds acknowl-
edging that Annie was a Master and an ally—Frida
proceeded to give Annie methodical and detailed instructions on how to invoke them, how to dismiss them,
and then, how to get them to "steal" heat from just about
anything. "You saw how fast they can do that when you
tell them to," Frida reminded her. "The water on the
nachtkrapp's wings froze immediately. That's not *all*

they can do, but it's the thing that is immediately useful to you and Frank. He can manifest water out of the air and you can freeze it, like Theo and I did. We'll show you how to do that when we start on the two of you working together."

The zephyrs looked like ripples in the air that glowed with blue energy. The Winds looked like nearly featureless humans made of blue gauze, but their sheer power belied their fragile appearance. The one that Annie was working with today could easily have blown out a window without trying, and according to Frida, they could take down trees and rip off roofs. After that would come Tempests, and then the Storms. "But we'll wait until we are somewhere out in the open to introduce you to Tempests and Storms."

After three hours of work, Annie was exhausted. The Winds were a lot more difficult to work with than the sylphs and zephyrs, and demanded more of her. Frida called a halt in midafternoon when it was obvious that Annie's concentration had started to waver.

"Let's get some hot chocolate and pastries," Frida said, after instructing Annie how to dismiss the particular Wind she was working with.

"I have a headache I believe only sugar will cure," Annie admitted. "And I want to ask you about something."

"From the look in your eye, it's something best broached only in private." Frida paused with her hand on the door, about to close it. "Well, let's see if anyone has left sustenance in the parlor. If they have, we won't have to ring for anything."

Down they went to the second floor, where they did indeed find "sustenance" in the form of coffee rather than hot chocolate, a variety of pastries, and even some pedestrian bread and butter. Plates and cups in hand, they went to the fireplace, as the sylphs reappeared and drank in the scent of the coffee.

Wordlessly, Annie handed over the page of Hulda's

letter that described the "stranger" who had been poking around asking about Annie. Frida read it, took a thoughtful bite of *pain au chocolat,* and gave it back.

"You think this stranger might be your He-Wolf," Frida said flatly.

"Yes!" Annie replied. "And if it is—"

"Hmm." Frida sipped her coffee. "Drink, and get rid of that headache while I think about this."

Annie drank, but also kept talking. "I don't *think* he can do anything to anyone in my family—can he?"

"Not likely, not now that they are all grown and have many, many connections in your community. You can make a child from a poor family vanish. You just claim that they ran away and no one will think twice about it. It's a lot harder to make adults or children from the family of a famous person disappear," Frida pointed out. She started on a piece of brown bread and butter.

"Am I overreacting?" Annie asked—the thing she had not dared ask Frank, because, bless him, all he would do would be to try and reassure her.

"Given how much you *don't* know about him—no." Annie started a bit when Frida made that statement, and made it so emphatically. "You don't know what his power source is. You don't know if he's an Elemental Mage himself—some of them do go to the bad, after all. You don't know if he managed to put a pack together for himself. You don't know what he's been doing the past couple of decades. He could be quite powerful. He could command as many as a dozen other shifters. Or more, really, but once the total rises above that, there often commences to be inter-pack strife over leadership, and the pack leader spends as much time fighting his own pack members as he does getting anything else done—"

"How do you know so much about wolf-people?" Annie asked, blinking.

"I—" She hit her forehead with the heel of her hand. "I am an idiot. I haven't given you the book."

"What book?" Annie asked.

"It's a sort of guidebook for Elemental Masters, mostly those in the *Schwarzwald*, but everyone in the *Bruderschaft* gets one. I made a copy for you and I have managed to forget to give it to you. It describes the sort of creatures we are likely to encounter and need to eliminate, and there's an entire chapter on *werwolfen*." She paused for a drink of coffee, then put her plate and cup aside. "Stay here, I will run up and get it for you."

Before Annie could object, she jumped up and actually *ran* out, while Annie sat there feeling as if she had inadvertently done something—not wrong, precisely, but had triggered something she hadn't intended to.

Frida must have run the entire way, because before Annie could make up her mind what to do next, she was back, with a leather-bound book that looked like a personal journal, with a pair of thongs tying it closed. "Here you are," she said, handing it over to Annie. "Don't read it just before bedtime, it's rather nightmare-inducing. And don't let the children see it, they're not ready for it yet."

Annie opened it, to find that it looked as if it was entirely handwritten, with many illustrations, often gruesome. The handwriting changed from section to section, and didn't seem to be organized in any way.

"Here." Frida took the book from her, leafed through it, and laid the ribbon bookmark bound into the spine down in a section. She handed the book back. "That's the part about the *werwolfen*. Read up on them and you will have a better idea of what you are contending with."

Annie glanced at it again, then realized something odd. The book was in English.

"I thought you said that this was a book you hand out to the *Bruderschaft*," she said. "But it's not in German."

"That's because I translated it as I made a copy for you," Frida replied casually.

That—

"Magically, of course," Frida added.

But—

"You'll learn how, but it's not a priority."

Under ordinary circumstances, Annie would have gotten rather testy about someone else deciding what was a "priority" for her to know about—but these weren't ordinary circumstances. And Frida was clearly as much of an expert in magic as Annie was in marksmanship. *Would I take it well if someone tried to tell me how I should handle my weapons? No. So perhaps, Annie, this is the time to keep your mouth shut and do as you are asked to do.*

"Thank you," she said, instead of replying snappishly.

Frida handed her the plate of pastries. "You may not thank me once you begin reading it," she said.

"Nevertheless—" said Annie.

"Nevertheless, I think it's something you need, although it is definitely not something you want."

13

ANNIE'S coat was not enough against the damp cold, and her feet ached from standing on cobbles as well as the cold.

March is a terrible month, Annie thought, shivering.

First it had snowed. Then it had rained. Then it got cold and rained—not cold enough to create ice, but cold enough to make her very miserable.

And now, if you please, the four of them were huddled in the dubious shelter of an alley, keeping watch over the home of someone that Theo suspected of being a black magician. Theo would have been here himself, if it hadn't been for the fact that he'd kept watch all last night. He'd looked so miserable this morning that all four of them had volunteered to take over the job tonight.

During the course of that conversation, Frida had let slip the fact that the reason the Cates and the Hirschbergs spoke excellent English was because Frida had arranged for Jack to be "taught" German overnight by magic, and the other three to have English by the same means.

The subject had come up because little Anneliese had objected to having to learn English the hard way, and both her father and Frida had informed her that she was too young to be granted languages magically.

Annie's reaction had been mixed. Annoyed that she was still needing to rely on Frida for translations. Surprise that such a thing was even possible.

And she had decided to finally say something about it. After all, they were all stuck here until dawn unless something happened, and they might as well talk about *something.* "If you could give me German," Annie whispered, hoping the rain wasn't going to resume, "why didn't you?"

"Because you are supposed to be a simple American Western girl," Frida replied, making use of a pair of opera glasses to survey the windows of the house they were watching—windows that showed not a trace of light. "Where and how would a simple American Western girl have learned German?"

"I could pretend not to understand!" Annie objected, as Frank attempted to suppress a chuckle.

"And someone would say something, you would respond to it, and then everyone would know you understood. There would be no keeping that a secret. Then everyone would want to know how and where you learned German." Frida was not taking her eyes, or the glasses, off that house. "It's not all that important, now that we are all staying with Theo—yes, I know the servants don't understand English, but they're all quite intelligent and you've gotten along just fine with a bit of pantomime. Just pick up phrases as you are, naturally. It's not as if Jack and I are going to leave you and the show until you go back to England."

Annie started to say something, then stopped, at least three times. Frida was right, annoyingly so. But she could imagine the astonishment on people's faces if she answered them in good round German! It would be wonderful!

Except for the part when someone, perhaps with a newspaper, asked her how someone with her simple background, with almost no formal schooling, had learned German. . . .

There was one thing that she had begun to dread from the moment that she had begun to be a "big draw," and that was what could happen to her at the hands of the press turned malicious. The newspapers loved her *now,* but that horrible man Hearst made his money on yellow journalism, and his reporters would be quick to pick up on such a thing, even so minor a thing as suddenly being able to speak German. They would claim she was hiding something, or that she had completely made up her own life. They could say, "Oh, she's not Annie Moses from Ohio, she's really a German beer heiress from Milwaukee, run away to be in Buffalo Bill's show! And all those trick shots she does are as fake as her so-called impoverished background!" She could see the headlines now . . . *Annie Oakley, Fraud?* Or *She Lies!*

Or worse.

Mama used to say, "All a poor person has is their reputation, so be careful never to lose it." And once a reputation was gone, it was horribly difficult to claw it back. She went to great lengths to preserve hers, and all it would take would be one stupid little slip.

Like—suddenly being able to speak German.

Frida was right.

"You're not exactly losing anything by having me translate for you," Frida pointed out logically. "You *know* if someone says something rude, or unwelcome, I'm going to translate it anyway and shame him in public."

Well, that was true, it had happened a handful of times; Frida had repeated back the unflattering words, loudly, so that everyone in the vicinity could hear, then translated. Those who had gathered around immediately turned on the bully when Annie's face showed her dismay, but by that point he (or she; one of the bullies

had been a wealthy lady who thought she was witty and
had not liked having her bad manners called out in public) had turned and left. Usually quickly and to the
sound of jeers.

"Remember what I said about saving your energy for
important things," Frida went on. "Learning German
will take magical energy on your part, and frankly, it is
not that important."

Annie sighed. "I suppose—" she began, when Jack
hissed.

"Door!" he said, as the door to the building they were
watching cracked open a trifle and someone muffled up
to the eyes in a coat, scarf, and hat eased furtively out.
He looked up and down the street three times, peering
intently into the distance each time.

"What *is* he up to?" Frida murmured.

"Nothin' good, I'd bet," said Jack.

The figure hesitated on the threshold, then ventured
into the street. "Curse it," Frida said with feeling. "Why
can't he just be trying to sacrifice a virgin with excellent
lungs in his own house like any self-respecting blood
mage would? I did *not* wish to track quarry across half
of Strasburg in the middle of a cold, wet night."

"Me neither," Frank muttered. But it seemed that
they had no choice.

Well, thought Annie with resignation, *at least he
didn't wait until after midnight. It can't be much later
than ten o'clock.*

But then, without warning, something black and
wreathed in darkness leaped out of the shadows to land
atop their target's shoulders. It was about half the size
of the man, but seemed unnaturally heavy.

It knocked the man's hat off, and he staggered toward
them a few steps, grunting with pain and clawing fruit-
lessly at the thing—and whatever it was, Annie was having a hard time seeing anything but a vague human-shaped
form made of shadow.

And Annie could scarcely believe her eyes when whatever it was started *growing!*

She was sure the moonlight and shadows were playing tricks on her when it first happened, but within a few moments, it was clear that the thing was doubling in size with every moment. And that was when what something that she and Frank had been reading together this afternoon in the guidebook Frida had given her sprang into her mind.

"Aufhocker!" she exclaimed, as the man went to his knees with a grunt of pain and uttered a strangled wail.

Before anyone could react to that, the shadowy creature pulled its prey to the street, and with a sound that would haunt Annie's dreams for the next few nights, *tore out his throat.* She *heard* it, a wet, tearing sound, as the thing dragged the man's head back and put its face to his throat.

The man screamed, or tried to, but managed nothing more than a wet gurgle and other incoherent sounds of absolute distress. He beat at the thing with his fists, but with every passing second his struggles grew weaker and weaker, and finally all sound and all motion ended. His body jerked a few times, then lay quiet and still, and the distinct smell of blood reached Annie's nose as the *aufhocker* straightened and looked straight at them.

"Don't move," Frida hissed, as a pair of incandescent green eyes glared at them out of the moving shadows that were the *aufhocker.* "Don't run, don't move, don't do anything."

There hadn't been a great deal about the *aufhocker* in the guidebook. *Undefined shape* was one thing. *Tears out its victims throats* was another.

And most disturbing of all, *cannot be killed.*

Annie wracked her brain, all of them frozen while the *aufhocker* glared at them. Was it going to attack?

But then she remembered something else.

It is said that the aufhocker *appears when it needs to teach someone a . . . permanent lesson.*

They'd had their hands tied over their current quarry because they'd had no proof that he was engaging in black magic. Approaching him had obviously been out of the question, and Theo couldn't call a Hunt on someone without proof of wrongdoing. But perhaps the *aufhocker* had delivered the justice that they could not.

Shivering, Annie got to her feet. The *aufhocker*'s eyes fastened on her as she took a step toward it.

"Annie! What are you doing?" Frida hissed.

"Trying to keep us all with our throats intact," she replied in a normal tone of voice, as she took another step toward the *aufhocker*, then put her rifle down on the pavement and advanced toward it again, with her hands spread out. "Easy, friend," she said, trickling some of the same magic into her words that she used when communicating with the Elementals. "I believe we all have the same thing in mind when it comes to that fellow you just dispatched." Would it understand English? With the help of her magic, she hoped it would.

The *aufhocker* tilted its head to one side. Listening. Otherwise unmoving. So far, so good.

"He was a bad man, or so we had every reason to believe," she said steadily, stopping at what she hoped was something farther than jumping distance from the creature. "He needed to be stopped, and he deserved punishment. We were trying to get proof of his misdeeds, but it looks as if you took matters into your own hands."

The *aufhocker* tensed and crouched, as if to leap, but Annie held her hand up in a placating gesture. "Don't worry, friend," she continued, still in the calm voice, with no hint of accusation in it. "It looks to me as if you have done us a great favor. It's much appreciated. Truly."

The *aufhocker* relaxed. *"How, a favor, mortal?"* it said, the sound of its voice making her jump a little.

The voice was like nothing she had ever heard before. If creaking trees could have spoken, that was what it sounded like. And it was a cold voice, uninflected, that sent shivers down her spine. But it was a question that demanded an answer, and if all she had been reading and learning was true, she would have to be very careful in how she phrased things.

In fact, "Careful, my friend," Frida murmured, reminding her that she mustn't give the creature any grounds to demand anything of her. The icy drizzle started again, pattering against her face, but washing the blood scent out of the air.

"It's difficult to find mortal grounds to punish an evil-doer that uses magic," she said carefully. "And we mere mortals cannot just take the law into our own hands. There are laws and courts, even if some of the laws and courts are not the sort that deal with ordinary misdeeds. We cannot merely say 'he is a bad man' and stop him."

The *aufhocker* snorted. *"Foolish,"* it stated. *"Evil demands lessoning. Those who do evil must be punished."*

"Foolish it may be, but it is the rule by which mortals live, just as *delivering a lesson* is the rule by which you live," Frida said, standing up herself. "Rules are rules. For us, and for you."

"Rules are rules," the *aufhocker* agreed. At least, Annie thought it was agreeing. There was no mockery in that voice.

"So, I think we're all saying that the man needed to be punished. You actually have, by your very nature, everything you needed to judge and punish him for what he was doing, and if you hadn't, we would have caught him, proved his evil, and punished him ourselves. So we're happy with the solution that you delivered, and we'd like to go home, out of the rain, and drink some hot chocolate and sleep. If you are willing to let us do that," suggested Annie.

The outline of the *aufhocker* kept shifting, but she noticed that its lines were softening, going from angular to gentle curves, as if it was relaxing. *"Go home,"* echoed the *aufhocker*. *"Sleep."* It looked as if it was settling back on its haunches beside its victim, waiting to see what they would do next.

"Is it letting us go?" Frank murmured.

"Sounds like it," Jack replied, as the creature continued to crouch over the body of its victim, eyes still blazing at them out of shadow.

"Let's not turn our backs on it, shall we?" Frida suggested. "Jack, you and Frank move first. Annie, I think you can pick up your rifle and back away."

She stooped, never taking her eyes off the *aufhocker*, and picked up her gun. It continued to stare, but did not move, and the contours of it remained soft. Step by careful step, she backed away, eyes on the monster, feeling her way with her toes. When she struck a curb, she worked her way along it, step by backward step. Still the *aufhocker* remained where it was, unmoving, until finally she had worked her way around a corner to the point where there was a building between her and it.

She sensed the others near her in the darkness. "Do we run?" she whispered.

"Better not," Jack advised. "Some critters, running makes 'em come after you, even if they didn't originally have any intention of attacking. It's just in their nature. If you run, you're supper. Or guilty."

"Annie, if you want to be our rear scout, Frank, take her elbow and guide her backward until we get to an area with streetlights," Frida said, though the tentative tone of her voice made it clear this was her suggestion, not an order. "I think once we get that far, we'll be safe to move normally."

"I believe that is a good idea," she agreed, and felt Frank's hand on her elbow, steady and reassuring.

"Sooner we get somewhere safe, happier I'll be," he muttered, as he carefully steered her around places where she might stumble. It was slow going, and Annie was torn between chills and sweating the entire time. There was no sign of the *aufhocker*, and no sounds either. Had it left? Had it vanished into the spirit realm? Or was it still sitting there, waiting to see if they did something that made them lawful prey? Her heart raced, and she kept feeling as if she needed air.

It wasn't until they finally got to the intersection with a larger street, where there were gaslights, that she felt secure enough to turn around. It was hard to tell in the streetlights, but she thought the others looked as white and strained as she felt. And her knees were so weak that it was all she could do to stay on her feet. She stumbled a little into Frank; he caught her easily and steadied her.

"Are we safe now?" Frank asked.

"If we're not, there's nothing any of us can do about it," replied Frida. "An *aufhocker* can't be killed. But it hates the sound of church bells, so—I'll keep an eye out for steeples with bells in them; the zephyrs are strong enough to make them ring. It's also *supposed* to hate the sound of praying, so have something in mind just in case."

"If that's true, we're safe," Frank said, giving her a quick squeeze of reassurance. "I been praying this entire time."

"I wish it wasn't so far to Theo's house," Jack muttered, looking up and down the street as if he expected the *aufhocker* to leap out at them at any moment. "I declare, I'm ready to drop down right here in the street, and that's the honest truth." But then he shouted, startling all of them so much they all jumped. *"Hey! Taxi!"* he called, waving both hands wildly over his head, then putting his fingers in his mouth and uttering an ear-piercing whistle.

Annie turned to look in the direction Jack was looking, and sure enough, there was the incredibly welcome sight of a cab—a nice, big brougham, not one of the two-passenger hansoms, one that could hold all of them. The driver lightly slapped his horse's back with the reins when he spotted them, just as eager to get a fare as they were to get inside his cab.

"I got this," said Frank, reaching inside his coat, as the other three of them, Annie included, fumbled for money. Annie tucked her rifle down at her side, hoping the cab driver would not see it and think he was about to be robbed.

But as the cab rolled up next to them, all the driver had eyes for was the little packet of folded money Frank held over his head by way of assurance that they weren't planning anything nefarious, nor were they a lot of improvident drunks or jokers who would try to get away without paying.

Annie surreptitiously handed Jack her rifle as the cabby jumped down off his box and opened the door for the ladies, extending his hand to help them each inside. Somehow they all managed to get in without the cabby spotting their weapons; Jack stuck his head out of the window and gave the directions, and they were off.

"Oh, good gracious," Annie said, sagging into the seat and taking back her rifle from Jack. "Was that as close a call as it felt like? It felt like the thing was going to leap on us at any second, just to eliminate witnesses."

"I don't know," Frida confessed. "I've never seen an *aufhocker* before. I don't think many people have."

"Them as sees one, I 'spect don't get a chance to tell about it," Jack put in, taking off his hat and mopping his brow with a handkerchief he pulled from inside his coat. "Lawsy! I've seen a lot of things since me an' Frida been together, but I never seen *nothin'* that give me the shivers like that thing!"

"I think we should wake Theo up, if he isn't still up waiting for us, and let him know about this," Frida declared, as the carriage lurched around the corner and over the cobblestones of another street. "He probably knows more about those things than I do. He'll know if it's something we need to worry about expelling from the city."

How would we even do that if it can't be killed? Make all the church bells all over the city ring for hours?

It had seemed like a long way to walk when they'd set out this evening on foot to embark on their surveillance, but the cabby brought them smartly to the front door of Theo's mansion in a remarkably short period of time; much sooner than she had expected. But then again, there wasn't much traffic on the street, and the horse seemed fresh enough to trot briskly the entire time.

Or the poor horse is as cold as we are and he's trotting to warm up.

Under normal circumstances she would have objected to making the trip back by expensive taxi when they had had no problem walking to get to their destination in the first place, but right now—she couldn't get away from where they had left the *aufhocker* and its victim fast enough, and if it had cost her the price of a month at the *Gasthaus* she'd have gladly paid it.

They all piled out and Frank paid the cabby—tipping generously enough that the cabby touched his hat and said *"Vielen dank, mein Herr!"* with great feeling. Theo's footman was still waiting to let them in before locking up for the night, and the welcome warmth that washed over them was almost enough to bring tears of gratitude to Annie's eyes.

"Ist der Graf wach?" Frida asked, as the footman took her coat.

"Jawohl, Frau Cates," the footman said with respect. *"Er ist in seinem Arbeitszimmer."*

"Sehr gut, danke," she replied, as he divested the rest of them of their coats—and in Annie's case, rifle. The others had brought handguns rather than rifles, but Annie had wanted something that was more accurate over distance. She let him take it; this was an old routine by now. He'd make sure there was nothing in the chamber, clear it if there was, and take it upstairs and leave it lying next to the gun-cleaning stand. Theo's servants were extremely good around weapons, and she trusted every one of them to handle hers properly.

If she'd had the energy, she would have sprinted up

the stairs. As it was, her trembling legs barely got her up the three flights of stairs to the family floor and as far as Theo's study. Frida was ahead of her and held open the door. She staggered in a few feet before she collapsed into a chair.

The others weren't in much better shape than she was. Until this moment, she'd had no idea that fear could be as draining as any athletic endeavor she had ever experienced. The *nachtkrapp* had been frightening. But the *aufhocker?* Terrifying. And she was beginning to think that at least some, if not all, of the terror the thing had produced was due to the creature's inherent nature.

This being a magician is not *all pretty sylphs and being the guest of a count.* . . . But it was too late to say "I don't think I want to do this after all." She had committed to becoming a magician, and she was not going to go back on her word.

Theo looked at them all in astonishment from behind his massive mahogany desk, before ringing for a servant and ordering cakes and hot chocolate. As well he should; Annie wasn't the only one who had collapsed into a chair. Frida looked drained and a little gray, Frank and Jack absolutely boneless. "Don't talk—" he said when the servant had gone. "Wait until you have some fortification first."

And when the hot chocolate arrived, he went to a shelf of bottles, picked out the peppermint schnapps, and poured a generous dollop into each of their cups. Annie had to restrain herself to keep from gulping it all down in one go. It tasted like heaven. So did the pastry.

"Now," he said, when they were all settled, and they'd had a few bites to eat and sips to drink, "I assume since you are not apologizing or looking for reinforcements, it wasn't a disaster, but obviously it did not go according to plan. So, what exactly happened out there?"

"Aufhocker," Frida said succinctly. "It was waiting to ambush him as he left his house, and tore out his throat.

Annie recognized what it was before I did, and she somehow kept it calm and negotiated with it until we were out of its sight."

Theo sat up straighter. "An *aufhocker?* In Strasburg? I haven't heard nor sensed any such thing—"

"Wait a moment and I'll call one of my little tattletales," Frida interrupted. She sketched a sign in the air, and two sips later, a moth-winged sylph popped into existence just in front of her chair.

"Do you and your sisters know about the *aufhocker?*" she asked the pretty thing, which settled on her knee.

The sylph nodded. *"He has been here almost half a moon. Now he is gone. I think he will not come back. He seemed satisfied."*

Theo sucked in a breath. "Interesting." He knew, as they all did, there was no point in asking the sylph why the Air Elementals hadn't said anything about the creature before this. Elementals in general were very literal-minded. They didn't volunteer information, and had to be asked very specific questions. Which, to be fair, was just as well. Many of them would just chatter on about *everything* they'd seen, from a stray cat in the stables to a dragon on the top of Strasburg cathedral, otherwise. Some did anyway; there was a particular little redhead with dragonfly wings that was an inveterate gossip, and anything Annie wanted to know about her fellow sylphs got spilled out in excruciating detail.

And no point in asking the sylph *where* the *aufhocker* had gone. Creatures of that sort were very good at covering their tracks, even from their fellow magical beings. It might have gone back to some home in the forest. It might have gone back to the spirit realm. It might have gone to Hell, literally, for all Annie knew.

"Well," Theo said, as the sylph flew to sit on the edge of Frida's cup to inhale the fragrances of chocolate and peppermint. They sometimes tasted what the humans drank—or rarely, what the humans ate—but they seemed to prefer the scents of things. "Tell me what happened."

Frida waved a weary hand at Jack, who was not at all loath to give a succinct retelling of their blessedly brief encounter. No one had anything to add when he was done, and Theo clasped his hands, elbows on his desk, and rested his chin on them, thinking. Annie closed her eyes for the moment, feeling as if she would never move again, knowing she was safe within the shielded and warded walls of the mansion.

"I don't see any reason to pursue the *aufhocker*," he said, startling her out of her half-doze. "It's done us a favor, actually, just as you told it, Annie."

She sighed in relief. "I was hoping you would say that," she said, finishing her chocolate, as the sylph lost interest in what was going on, and drifted, hovering, around the library, sticking her nose curiously into anything that caught her fancy.

"Many of the creatures out there are neither good nor evil," he replied. "They answer to their own rules, and they abide by those rules—and it was clever of you to remind the *aufhocker* of that. Since it's gone, I don't think we need to concern ourselves about it for now. And since the sylph said that it wasn't a native to Strasburg, I think we can conclude that tonight's target must have done *something* so terrible within its territory that the *aufhocker* felt compelled to pursue it here."

"That could be the answer for why we didn't find any evidence of magical working of any kind, much less black," Frida mused. "He must have been doing his bad deeds out of town, and then coming back to enjoy the fruits of his labor once the deed was done."

Theo nodded. "Which means we never would have caught him, unless we followed him remorselessly for months. His house was warded and shielded, so scrying was not an option, and—I think I would have had to ask for someone from the *Bruderschaft* to come track him. We're stretched a bit thin, here."

"I cannot even imagine being able to help when we leave with the show for the next leg of our tour in April," put in Annie. "So you wouldn't have had our help at all in this endeavor."

"I wouldn't dream of asking you," Theo said, with a faint smile. "Once you go, all four of you, you must proceed as you think best. You are already doing quite enough while you are here. No one is demanding that you become a Huntsman; not all magicians are, and no one thinks less of them for it. All that we ask is that you Hunt occasionally, when we need more than the hands we have."

He appeared lost in thought for a moment, which gave Annie some time of her own to think. Tonight, they had been asked to spy, not on a magical creature, but a fellow human being. And what would she have done if that human being had detected them and attacked?

She had been raised, more or less, as a Quaker—although it was a misapprehension to think that Quakers did not own guns, nor shoot them. There was nothing in the Friends' creed that said anything about owning and using weapons. Like her family, people had to hunt for food, and protect livestock, and get rid of nuisance animals. Lots of Friends enjoyed target and trick shooting.

It was only when you were talking about using weapons against fellow humans that things got . . . complicated.

Some abjured any sort of violence altogether and were absolute pacifists. Others felt self-defense was perfectly in order. There was no consensus among the Friends because all sides felt quite passionate about their beliefs, and all sides were just as sure that the opposition would one day come to their senses.

And Annie had never thought about that, much. From the time when she left the Wolves to this moment, no one had ever raised a hand to her, or even really spoken to her in great anger.

So . . . here she was, where she *might* have needed to shoot someone. Where she *might* in the future. She had told Frank that she would shoot the He-Wolf right between the eyes if he came for her again. But would she? Could she?

And what about some of those magical creatures? Did *they* count as human? She hadn't thought about it when the witch had attacked Jack and she had completely unloaded her weapon into it.

But she hadn't had time to think then. When they had encountered the *nachtkrapp* and then the *aufhocker,* she had. Was that why she had hesitated, and used words instead of bullets?

As if he was reading her thoughts, Theo echoed them. "Well, there is one thing that is certainly interesting. That is twice now that you and Frank have managed to handle a situation without destroying the magical creature that is in the middle of that situation. First with the *nachtkrapp,* and tonight with the *aufhocker.* Given the reputation of Americans in general as rash and inclined to fighting, and those from the West in particular, I am somewhat bemused to find you solving problems peaceably."

"Neither of us are from the West," Annie pointed out. "Frank is from Ireland and then from New Jersey, and I am from Ohio. And anyway, any problem you can solve without shooting is worth solving that way." She skirted the fact that she was technically a Quaker. She wasn't entirely sure how much sense she was making with that sentence, but she was bone-weary, and really all she wanted was her bed, and she had no idea if the others would even know what she was talking about if she mentioned her religion.

But Theo laughed. "Well said. And on that note, I think you all need rest. I will be very interested to see what the morning brings."

"Grusel Auf Der Strasse!" screamed the headlines of the morning paper laid out at the breakfast table, with a

gruesome illustration of a man with his throat torn out bleeding all over the pavement. Annie and Frank were the first to see it lying there when they came down to breakfast, but Frida and Jack were not far behind them. Theo was already there, but she didn't need a translation; the picture spoke for itself.

And then Sophia entered.

"Theo, really!" exclaimed Sofi, as she caught sight of it. "Must we have penny-dreadful murders over *apfelkuchen*?"

"Sorry, *meine liebchen,* but I wanted our guests to see it," Theo temporized. But he folded the paper so the illustration and headline were hidden. "So the *aufhocker* did not devour or otherwise dispose of his prey, as you can see."

"I feel sorry for the police," Annie said. "I hope that they don't arrest some poor random soul just so they have someone to try for the crime."

"I wish I could say that doesn't happen, but alas. . . ." Theo shrugged. "However, given the descriptions of the death wound, it is fairly obvious no human with a knife did it. They'll probably be looking for a big, dangerous dog."

"Really, Theo," Sofi chided, knife poised above the bread she was about to butter. "This is not a conversation for the breakfast table."

Theo picked up the paper and held it toward them. Annie shook her head.

"I'm just as glad I can't read it," she murmured.

"See?" Frida pointed out. "I told you there were good reasons not to know German."

14

ANNIE smiled as Frida openly gaped with astonishment. "I cannot believe my eyes," Frida said, as she watched the swarm of workmen disassembling the show, putting it on wagons, and putting the wagons on flatbed train cars, while others loaded horses and other animals into cars meant for them. "It's like a magic act."

The four of them stood at the head of the third of the commissioned trains, just before the passenger cars, which had been put on first. Second came the stock cars; those animals who were not helping with the breakdown were already installed in their cars, including Frank and Annie's horses, Bill's horses, and Dell and Arte. In theory, Dell and Arte could have helped, as they were used to harness, but Bill proclaimed he didn't want to risk an accident to them. Annie thought that was pretty wise.

The last part of the train was made up of the last of the show wagons loaded onto flatcars and locked down in place with wheelstops and chains. Frida and Jack's *vardo* had been one of the first. And they could have ridden in that, instead of a passenger car, and had a few more creature comforts, but seasoned hands advised against doing so. "It'll sway like a boat in high seas, and you're likely to get seasick," Fred Gibbs had told them, and they decided to take his word for it.

And then the flatcars were loaded.

There was a long string of them stretching out behind the stock cars, and presumably anyone who was not familiar with this process would wonder how each wagon would be gotten onto its proper car, for there was a particular order they needed to be loaded in. The four friends were watching that now. Meanwhile the first two trains were being loaded with the all-important tents and support wagons; in order, the tent train would roll off first, then the train with the cook-shop, bleachers, and generators and anything else that needed to be up before the performers got there, and the miscellaneous wagons would go on the show folks' train.

Off in the far distance, barely visible, was the end of their train—without the caboose, which would be linked up later. And as they watched, there was some movement back there, which gradually resolved itself into a team of four of the largest horses the show had hauling a string of wagons along the tops of the flatcars, as calmly as if they were walking along a street. The movement of the cars under them didn't seem to bother them at all, but then, they had been doing this for years, both here and back home. When they got close to the last enclosed car, they stopped. They were unhitched, encouraged to jump down from the flatcar, then hitched up again by means of long straps to pull the cars the few feet it took to get them to where they needed to be locked down. Then the horses were led or ridden back to the end of the train to pick up the next set of wagons, while the men up here at the front made sure the wagons were properly positioned, chocked, and locked down. Meanwhile there was another string of wagons coming on up the flatcars behind them. The very last things that would be loaded were the electric generators—because this was usually done at the end of the last show of the stay, after dark, and those generators were necessary lights to see by. It was only because they were breaking up and moving from winter quarters that this could be done in the daylight.

Annie was used to it by now—she and Frank had been doing this for years at this point. But Frida was right, it was like a magic act.

Granted, much of the show was canvas. But much wasn't. And they were not just taking things down, packing them up, and putting them on wagons. They were cleaning up, too.

"We can't have these people saying we're worse than a herd of pigs," Bill had decreed. "They're gonna need this field for their May Fest next month. I want everything that's ours erased from here by the time we're gone!"

There wasn't much that could be done about the torn-up earth, but grass was resilient, it was spring, and it would be sprouting just as thickly as it had been when they had made winter quarters quite soon. The one big and most noisome problem had been dealt with before anyone started breaking anything down.

The hundreds of animals had piled up a small mountain of dung over the winter. But before Bill could look around for a solution, as soon as it was feasible to take the stuff away, the farmers of the area had descended with ample carts and hopeful looks in their eyes. It was . . . as has been said before . . . spring. It was time to fertilize the fields, dung them well, and plow the dung under. And a farmer can never have too much dung. They got every speck, and were disappointed that they would not be allowed to dig up the urine-soaked earth that had been under the livestock corrals and stables and cart it off as well.

Frida and Jack had packed their *vardo* tightly over the course of a couple of days; Annie had helped, while Frank had seen to their own tent and properties. Now they all stood respectfully far off to the side while workers swarmed like ants all over the site.

"They're rusty," Frank said critically, checking his watch. "Loadmaster is probably cursing the air blue with how slow they are. Well, they'll get the hang of it again soon enough."

There had been two final performances here in Strasburg; *full* performances, not the abbreviated ones they had been giving this winter. That had tempted more money out of the pockets of the good citizens, even though by this point most of them had seen the show at least once, if not several times. Now they were on their way to a city called Karlsruhe, a city, so Frida had told them, in the Grand Duchy of Baden. Their train would cross the Rhine, head north and east, and within twelve hours they would be at the new venue, where this entire spectacle would take place in reverse. And, if they made good time, in the comparative luxury of daylight.

"Why not take the show by boat?" Frida wondered aloud. "It's a direct route up the Rhine."

"Where would we find all the boats we'd need?" asked Frank with a chuckle. "Look at the length of that train! And there's two more of them! And where would we load from? The docks? We'd tie up the docks for hours and that wouldn't make us any friends. Not to mention there's no small chance of a slip, which is bad enough when you're loading on land, but on water? Someone's going to drown, and Heaven only knows how we'd fish one of those wagons out of the river. *And* water's slower than rail."

Frida's mouth actually dropped open as the very last of the canvas structures came down and workers immediately began disassembling it.

"Come on, we'd best get to the cars while there are still seats," Frank teased. Annie hit him with her hat.

"One of these days, your fooling is going to get someone in trouble," she teased back, putting her hat back on again. "We get a reserved compartment," she explained, as Frank pretended to cower. "You can share it with us."

"First-class coach," Frank added, leading the way toward the front of the puffing and hissing train. "'Course, the Colonel gets a car all to himself. We do, too, back home, and we generally stay in it instead of a hotel. Only so much we could fit in that steamship, so we left all the special railcars back home and we're using German ones. Or French ones, or English ones, you know. There's passenger cars for the crew on the other two trains, so by the time we get there our show should be mostly set up."

The show had its very own conductors, one of whom was watching for their arrival and sent them in the right direction. The compartment they found themselves in even had Annie and Frank's names on a little card in a holder beside the door. The private compartments in this car were all along one side, with a narrow corridor faced with windows on the other. Annie's critical eye discovered nothing to find fault with as they settled themselves on opposing, plush crimson seats. There was a window with fringed crimson curtains, and a table between the seats. Frida and Jack had automatically taken the backward-facing seats, which Annie thought was a nice gesture on their part.

Since the encounter with the *aufhocker,* there had been no more supernatural threats that required Annie and Frank's intervention in Strasburg. Frida and Jack had gone out several times on arcane errands for the Graf, sometimes with Frau Schnee, but none of those errands had required Annie and Frank's help.

It had been the closest thing to a vacation that either of them had experienced in a while. Back home, going into winter quarters didn't mean the end of money-earning possibilities; there was vaudeville, exhibitions, and shooting contests. Usually all they got was a few weeks with Annie's Ma or one of her siblings (usually Hulda), and then it was off to perform as a solo act. And the Graf's mansion was at once more luxurious and more private than any hotel or boarding house they had ever stayed in. Sometimes Annie felt guilty about remaining here when the Graf didn't actually need them—but Frida pointed out that they were also staying here in order to master their powers in the shortest time possible. So the two of them had applied themselves to their studies of magic, and Annie was beginning to think she was getting the hang of things.

Together she and Frank could freeze things solid, as Frida and Theo had done to the *nachtkrapp's* wings. Frank could now talk to all the lesser Elementals of Water that he or Theo had been able to summon: the nixies, the undines, the naiads, the kelpies, and the rather dangerous Rhine maidens, which were the German version of the sirens, of which the Lorelei was one. And she could call on the sylphs, the pixies, the zephyrs, and all four Winds. The only Air Elementals she had not yet been introduced to were the Storms and the Tempests. And Frank had not yet encountered the greater Water Elementals, which would actually require him being near the ocean.

They were far enough up in the train—quite near the engine—that there wasn't much to see of the loading. Frida craned her head backward against the window and tried to see anyway.

"I hope Arte and Dell are all right," she fretted. "They've never been taken anywhere by train before."

"You saw them safe in their car yourself," Frank reminded her. "They're not left to mill about like cattle; they're all in loose boxes so they can keep their balance when the train starts to move. They seemed fine when we left them."

"Yes, but . . ." She sighed. "I had it in my mind we'd all be moving in a kind of giant parade to get from town to town, since the distances are so short."

"It would take us all day to get there," said Frank. "The roads just aren't that good after the winter; they'd make ten miles an hour at best. It would be eight hours at least, if not more, since horses need to stop for water and some food. Whereas we'll be in Karlsruhe in two at most by train. We'll spend more time unloading and setting up than we took to travel. And we'd have had to do the breakdown and the wagon-loading either way."

"But a trip on the roads would be so pleasant!" Frida objected. "Sunshine, flowers, fresh breezes. . . ."

"Thunderstorms, mud pits, rutted roads, places where a horse can break a leg, wagons breaking down, farm carts that won't get out of the way, people complaining we're clogging up the road—" Frank countered. "Don't worry about your horses. They'll be fine. They're in the company of horses that have done this a hundred times and are prepared to do it a hundred more. You know how horses are, they take their cues from the lead mare, and the lead mare for all the trick horses is in there with them."

Since the lead mare for all the trick horses was Annie's own Brownie, Frida stopped trying to see what was going on behind them and let out another gusty sigh. "I don't like trains," she said.

Annie looked at her with utter astonishment. "You don't like trains! How is that even possible?"

"Because when I want to go somewhere I prefer to ride, or at worst, drive. I don't like my safety to be in the hands of someone other than myself. Or Jack." She folded and refolded a handkerchief in her lap. "And it is somewhat harder to do magic on a train."

"Why would you need to perform magic on a train?" Annie replied, still trying to understand why her friend didn't care for a mode of transportation that would get her to her destination in a fraction of the time of riding.

"I don't know. I just know it's harder on a train and I don't like that," she said obstinately.

"Well, it will be trains all the way to Antwerp," Annie told her. "Which . . . is where you'll leave us."

"Yes, but before we leave we'll have to see if one of the

Greater Water Powers will consent to meet Frank," Frida replied, brightening a little. "There's a Water Master in Antwerp who runs a shipping company. I've never seen one of the Great Water Powers. If we are lucky, it will be Nehallenia; she's the one most likely to look kindly on mere humans."

"And that reminds me," said Annie, glad for the opening to ask about *her* further education. "When will I get to see a Storm or a Tempest?"

"That . . . is a good question," Frida replied. "Traditionally, it's on a mountain. But you know, a cathedral is tall enough, and every single city we are going to visit has one. The trick will be getting private access to the spire."

Annie was about to ask why they would need *private* access to a cathedral spire, because virtually every cathedral she had visited here in Europe had allowed visitors up in their spires with no question—and even if there had been an obstacle, discovering that the person who wanted to see the city from the highest building in it was *Annie Oakley* generally cleared those obstacles away.

Fame does have its advantages.

But the moment she wondered, she had her own answer without asking. Because calling a Greater Elemental was not something you wanted to do with a potential audience. The Storms were temperamental at best.

Well, they were once gods. And they have not forgotten this.

"You know," Frida said thoughtfully. "We don't have to use a building, actually. There's the Mahlberg."

Annie already knew that *berg* meant *mountain,* and it seemed to her that they'd have their best chance at privacy on a mountain. "If we have time," she temporized. "We have nine cities to play between now and the beginning of May."

"We'll make time, somehow," Frida said firmly. "I'll look for other possibilities. If I have to—" Her voice trailed off. "Well, best not say what I'll do until I find out if I actually can accomplish what I want."

"We may have our hands full in Karlsruhe," Jack warned her. "'Member what Theo said about rumors."

"What rumors?" Frank asked sharply.

But at just that moment, the train gave a lurch, a shudder, and several more lurches, startling Frida into a squeal of surprise and driving everything else out of their minds. The train was on the move. The next leg of the Great European Tour had begun.

All during the week before the show was to arrive in Karlsruhe, Bill's ballyhoo men had been slapping up posters and placards wherever they were permitted (and very likely places they were not permitted as well), and for the last day or two Bill himself had been in place, staying at the finest hotel, giving interviews to reporters. Annie just hoped that the translator he had was as good as Frida was.

Not that the ease of translation seemed to matter much. Bill had multi-page pamphlets in German printed up and distributed to every journalist that seemed even remotely interested. *Those,* she knew—because Frida had read them over—were good pieces of work. And more often than not, the reporters were so delighted to have their work done for them that they mostly just re-printed what was in the pamphlet. Now, she and Frank could have been there in the advance group in Karlsruhe too; but the Colonel was a very vain man, and he never liked playing second fiddle to anything, man, woman, child, or beast. Annie loved him like a brother, and so did Frank, but this was a simple fact of life with the Wild West, and they allowed for it, making sure that when he started to get that slightly petulant look in his eyes over attention paid to Annie that Annie and Frank always found a reason to be somewhere else. Usually all it took was pleading the need to rehearse, or weariness from the show. Then Bill would have the spotlight again, and all would be smiles and sunshine.

So when the train pulled into their appointed siding, after a tranquil and easy trip of a mere two hours, with Frida now excited by train travel instead of apprehensive, there was an enormous crowd waiting to see the show go up. They did so under ideal weather, slightly cool, dry, and brilliant blue skies.

And up it went, in reverse order from how it had been pulled down. First off were the generators, whose position marked the heart of the show. The wagons came off the back of the train as needed, the draft horses came off, the big canvas structures went up, then the smaller ones, the cook-shop with its twenty-foot-long grills, the corrals and stable-tents went up, then the animals that were not being used to pull wagons began their process of unloading.

They had already gotten off the train and were watching when the last of the wagons—the *vardo*—came off the train. Frida got that look in her eyes that told Annie that she was going to do something. "Wait," Annie said, guessing that what that thing was had to do with her horses. "Check with the loadmaster first. Then check with Fred Gibbs."

Frida looked rebellious for a moment, but then nodded, and went trotting off to find the loadmaster. Fred was easy to find, whooping and hollering at the wranglers getting the cattle and buffalo off.

She came back wearing a smile, and stopped just long enough to interrupt Gibbs for a moment. He listened, nodded, and went on with his business, allowing her to open the trick-horse car, then, with the assistance of the others, drop the ramp and jump inside to get Dell and Arte.

It was an easy business; if they'd been spooked at all

by the moving train, it didn't show, and they looked around, relaxed, as they paused at the top of the ramp, before calmly making the descent down to the ground.

"Let's get them—" Frida began, when Annie held up a hand.

"Let's just get our horses and we can walk them around and let them eat some grass," she said. "I know you want to get your *vardo* in place so you can set it up to sleep in, but be patient. The lot has been planned out to a fine detail; your *vardo* will stand out like a sore thumb in any of the camps, so they'll be putting it on the back lot where it won't be seen. Look—see? They're moving it now."

Sure enough, one of the big wagon horses was being led to the *vardo* and hitched up. A moment later, and it was rolling along merrily through the grass as if it weighed nothing.

Frida deflated. "All right, but let's ride them instead of walking them. I'm fairly certain there are a lot of places between here and the lot where the animals have relieved themselves and I'd rather not spend an hour cleaning my boots."

And before Annie could say anything, Frida had put both hands on her horse's back and heaved herself up bareback. Jack got a mischievous look in his eyes, handed her the reins to his lad, took a running jump at the horse's rump, and vaulted himself into place, causing a spattering of applause from the onlookers. They didn't know *who* they were looking at, but they knew enough to know they'd just seen a trick.

Although Annie didn't *like* to ride bareback—she preferred a sidesaddle, to reinforce her ladylike persona—she could. She sighed, and Frank offered her his cupped, interlaced hands as a mounting block, and up she went.

Brownie could be trusted like a dog—and was certainly every bit as steady, if not as educated or showy, as Dell and Arte. She could, and did on occasion, ride her with only a halter. So the four of them ambled their way toward the show lot, allowing the horses to crop grass as they went.

For their parts, the horses were utterly delighted by this turn of events. Every blade of grass back in Strasburg had long ago been trampled into the earth or inhaled by a hungry horse. They welcomed the fresh, green grass showing under the dried brown left by the winter as a child welcomes candy-floss.

All the while, of course, Frida was keeping a close eye on the *vardo* and angling their course to roughly follow it. When they did find it, it had been tucked away out of sight with the tents and wagons of the kitchen area.

Frida looked dubious, but Jack opened his mouth first, sounding as pleased as punch. "Lookee there. Hot water for washin', close to the latrines, an' we'll be first to breakfast, bar the cooks. Wisht we'd had that spot back in Strasburg."

Frida raised an eyebrow, then nodded. "And away from the cowboy and military camps, we won't be listening to drunken serenades at night."

"I envy you," Annie replied, quite sincerely. "Warm spring nights will, alas, mean more serenades."

Frida laughed at that. "I think I would rather listen to wolves howl."

Annie and Frank left Frida and Jack to "unpacking" their *vardo,* which mostly meant they were untying all the ties and unstrapping all the straps that had kept things from moving during the transit. They headed for their tent in the Cowboy Camp.

The show was always laid out the same, whether it was the behemoth that traveled the rails at home, or this abbreviated version on tour in Europe. They went straight to their reserved spot in the Cowboy Camp, passed their horses over to one of the wranglers to take to the stabling tent, and began a real job of unpacking. The tent was significantly bigger than the tents of the cowboys around them (and had a rain-fly), but that was not only because they were a couple, but because when she wasn't performing, Annie was on show for people who paid extra for tours of the camps. So the front half of the tent was essentially a parlor. The whole thing was installed over a wooden platform with a porch extending out from the front. And right now that porch was loaded with all of their gear.

Annie and Frank looked at each other, sighed, and got to work.

It took about an hour, but they had done this hundreds of times already, so they moved like a choreographed pair of dancers. Down went the carpet. In went the wooden chairs, the cushions to make them more comfortable, and Annie's rocking chair. The bicycle she used for one of her trick-shot sets leaned in the front, against a wooden folding chair that also supported two of her rifles. Next to that went the embroidered saddlebag with the name "Oakley" stitched proudly at a slant across it, draped over the back of the folding chair. They unpacked a couple of trunks that were needed in the front of the tent, hanging up the costumes across the back of the "bedroom" of the tent. Then those trunks came out to become tables supporting pictures, a mirror, a display tray holding some of her medals, and various other gifts she had been given. And an oil lamp, carefully positioned on a crate of its own and out of the way of being accidentally tipped over.

In the back, or "bedroom," there was as much comfort as anyone could expect in a tent. An ingenious wooden bed that packed down to almost nothing—though it made up for that by being fiendishly hard to put together, even with two sets of hands. More trunks containing everything *except* most of the jewelry Annie had been given on the tour—that lived in the pay-wagon under the watchful eye of the paymaster, his dog, and his two hired wranglers who did nothing but guard it. Another oil lamp, and Annie's fancywork basket. Right now she was working on a needlepoint-and-beaded belt to wear with her costumes. Washbasin and pitcher, lots of blankets, but no stove. Not that she wouldn't have liked one, but not at the expense of being burned alive. Lots of cushions, and another fine carpet.

Bill had a similar tent, but he didn't live in his, unless he couldn't get a room at a nearby hotel. That hadn't happened here in Europe, but it did back home. So Bill's tent was all "parlor," with a cot he could set up if he was forced to rough it.

Knowing Bill, he wouldn't spend a night in that tent.

Next to their tent was the tent of another of the show's stars, Johnny Baker, a crack shot, a thrilling trick rider, and billed as "The Cowboy Kid." Annie had taught Johnny most of his tricks, and Bill sometimes created a rivalry on paper for the two of them, though in real life they were the best of friends. Johnny was a good neighbor to have; he seemed to take his cues from Frank, being quiet and sober, good-natured, and handy at just about anything. His tent had already been erected, and about the time the Butlers came out of the back of theirs, he was setting up the display area of his.

"Say, Annie!" he said in a teasing tone. "Haven't seen much of you since you fell in with them two Germans. Hope you haven't forgotten your old pal."

Frank snorted, and Annie laughed. "Not at all. We have a great many mutual friends, is all. Have you actually had time to meet them?"

Johnny scratched the back of his head sheepishly. "Well . . . nah. Jule's Pa found a snug little layup with all meals laid on in Strasburg. There was a room free for me too, and I . . . uh . . . well . . ."

"Spent all your time courting her," Annie laughed. "Good for you! I expect there to be a wedding announcement soon, or I'll be very disappointed in how the third handsomest man in the show failed to get his girl."

Johnny turned bright red. "Reckon I'd better get back to work!" he stammered, and ducked into his tent.

Frida and Jack turned up about a half an hour later, when the sun was westering. "Cooks are about ready to serve," Jack announced, and Johnny popped his head out at the sound of a strange voice.

"Oh! The clever Johnny Baker!" Frida exclaimed, making Johnny blush even harder. "Finally a proper meeting!"

And Jack just strode right up to the front of the tent, holding out his hand. "Jack Cates. Frida's my wife. Pleased ter meetcher."

Johnny shook his hand vigorously, then took Frida's and shook it more gently, after snatching off his hat. "Pleasure!" he said sincerely. "I thought you was both German."

"Bavarian," Frida corrected him with a smile. "Yes, I am, but Jack is American like you."

"Whew!" Johnny whistled, looking from one to the other of them. "Must be a story in how you got here."

"We can tell it to you tonight, over supper," Frida offered. "We're leaving the show at Antwerp, when the Colonel doesn't need us anymore to bring in the local folk. We actually just signed up for a lark when we saw an advertisement recruiting for the Council of Rough Riders; things were getting dull in our little village, and we had Dell and Arte and our own little act—"

"Oh, gosh, Miz Frida, them dancing horses of your'n—" Johnny sighed and looked almost as heartsick over the Lippizans as he was over Jule Keen. "—I swan, they're purdier than a prairie sunset, an' move like I ain't never seed!"

Frida pondered him a moment. "You know, I have seen your riding. You can stick on the back of anything, can't you?"

"I dunno 'bout *anything*," he temporized. "Ol' Humps, the buffalo, he'll put up with me for a bit. Still havin' trouble gettin' the elk to let me sit him. Couple of the longhorns, though, they're none so bad."

"Well, I want you to know that you can ride Dell or Arte any time you like," Frida said. "Even with stirrups, though they'll put their ears back at you in contempt if you use them. As far as they are concerned, only amateurs need stirrups."

Johnny burst out laughing, but allowed as how he wanted to take Jack and Frida up on that offer. But before he could say anything else, the horn blew for supper and they all joined the rush for the cook camp.

Johnny warmed right up to the two magicians, just as Annie had hoped he would. But she was a little apprehensive about him wanting to join them after supper—though she needn't have worried. Jule slipped away from her father, the show treasurer and paymaster, and Johnny's new friends were no kind of competition for his sweetheart.

So the four of them headed for the *vardo,* which, aside from the sounds of the cooks clearing up and cleaning, was *much* quieter than the Cowboy Camp.

"I never got a chance to ask you about those rumors you had mentioned," Annie said, once they were closed safely inside the wagon and no one could hear them.

"Rumors of wolves where we're a-goin'," Jack said succinctly. "They've mostly been killed off in Germany. You almost never hear of one. But all of a sudden, people *say* they've been seein' 'em."

That sent a cold chill down Annie's spine, and she clenched her fists as the memory of the He-Wolf transforming in front of her flashed across her mind. She barely felt Frank's hand take hers. "Could that be—"

"Under normal circumstances I would count this as hysteria," Frida said slowly. "But Theo said that quite respectable and sober people who can tell an Alsatian from a wolf very easily have made these reports. But there is no sign of dens. Which makes all of us turn our minds to the *werwolf.* And you have the mark of the *werwolf* on you, Annie. There might have been one near Strasburg that sniffed you out and told the others. They can find that mark if they use the right spells. Or if any of them have Elemental Magic, they can send their Elementals to look for you."

She paused, and then said, with great reluctance, "I do not think this is coincidence."

"Even if it is," Frank put in, "Even if it has nothing to do with us, if we run into these varmints, we need to do something about them. We took on four of your monsters already. What's a few more?"

"Least these things kin be killt by silver," Jack pointed out.

Frida smiled and nodded. "I was hoping you would say that."

But Annie remained silent, because she still had not answered one crucial question for herself. Yes, she could certainly kill monsters, just as she hunted for game. Monsters were not human. And she could and would certainly *try* to communicate with monsters and negotiate something that both sides could live with, as she and Frank had with the *nachtkrapp* and the *aufhocker*.

But these wolf-people were . . . people. People who could change their shape, but still people. And at least some of them, if the He-Wolf and She-Wolf were any example, could not be negotiated with.

So there remained the question. *Could* she kill a *werwolf*?

Maybe . . . but if it put on its human face . . .

Maybe not.

15

THREE hectic days in Karlsruhe with two shows a day, all sold out, meant that there was absolutely no chance to leave the show to go seek out any kind of high place to speak to the Storms or Tempests. Annie fretted a little, but only a little, because she was too busy to get much chance to *think*. Tours started going through the camps at about ten in the morning, meaning any rehearsing had to be done between rising and that time. Once she had, in the back of her mind, been just a *little* scornful of Frida relying on her sylphs to make a shot. Now she was incredibly grateful to her sylphs for making sure she didn't miss any. The first show was at noon—scheduled at the request of the local food vendors, so that people who rushed to get to the show would be inclined to skip dinner, become hungry, and buy. Shows lasted four hours; the second show was at five in the evening, and once again, the food vendors counted on that for a lot of income. Usually the Colonel only allowed candy-butchers and peanut-men to sell to the stands, but given those show times—and the fact that the vendors paid him for the privilege—he allowed sausage, pretzel, and cider sellers under the canvas during the show, as long as they didn't call their wares.

It was cold—not as cold as in February, but still cold—and the damp air didn't hold any real hint of spring yet. But the show was used to playing in any weather that was decent enough that people would come, and come they did, sitting in the bleachers, bundled up to the eyes in their winter coats, drinking hot cider and munching sausages.

By the end of the second show of the day, everyone was tired and just wanted a late supper from the cook tent, something of a wash-up, and into bed. And now Annie missed the *Gasthaus* and the Graf's tender treatment; the portable bed was good, but not as good as theirs had been. It took a long time to warm up enough to sleep, and the camp was a lot noisier, even with most people sleeping, than the Graf's guestroom or the room at the *Gasthaus*.

At least after the first night, when Frida noticed her yawning over fried eggs and ham in the cook tent, she learned there was a solution to the cold bed. When she explained why she was so sleepy, Frida tilted her head and said, "Give me five marks. I can at least fix the cold part."

She was as good as her word, because at supper that night she turned up with what Annie immediately recognized as the German version of a bed-warming pan. How Frida had arranged for such a thing when she had been in the show all day, Annie had no idea—but the most logical thing was that she had magic contacts in Karlsruhe who had gotten it for her and brought it to the show, where she paid for it with the money Annie had given her. Brass plated, with a wooden handle and a pierced cover, Annie knew exactly what to do with it, and did not leave the cook-tents until she had gotten the cooks to fill it with coals.

"You shoulda arsked me, Annie," Fred Gibbs chuckled as he spotted her loading it up. "Most of the cowboys got one, or share one. I coulda gotten you a loan."

"Thanks, Fred, but this is something I probably should have gotten a long time ago," she told him, because— well, it was. "I should really know better than to travel without one."

"Well, when we're home, ya got yer own railcar, with a stove an' all," Fred pointed out. "You ain't slept in that tent once till we came over here. An' it didn't get all that cold till we got t' Strasburg, an' then ya got a hotel, like Bill."

And at least that night she and Frank got into a nice *warm* bed.

But the show was back to its usual brisk pace of moving from city to city, after the long, leisurely "stroll" that had marked their stay in Strasburg. The second day meant that at eleven, one of the hands fetched the star performers food from the cook-tents while they were holding court in their camps, then while they were lining up for their first entrance for the second show, hands brought everyone sausages stuffed inside bread rolls and dipped out dippers full of water from a bucket to hold them over until a late supper.

And supper was cold ham and beef sandwiches, eaten while they were packing their tents, because the cook-tents and all the cooking apparatuses were down and being packed into wagons. Annie and Frank went straight for the passenger cars, where someone had helpfully added Frida and Jack's names to the placard on their compartment. Annie was already asleep before the train started moving to Mannheim. A two-hour nap in a warm car was nothing to sneeze at!

Mannheim was the same, except that they would do four show days, and that they arrived in the dark, and the grounds were some distance away. Not quite on the other side of the city, but certainly through the streets. No matter; even if they *didn't* have the train of wagons, animals, and other vehicles to follow, Bill's advance men had laid out a course of red lanterns along the streets. All they had to do was follow them. Annie and Frank just found a wagon and caught a ride on it. When they left, Frida and Jack were debating whether or not they wanted to extract Dell and Arte from the stable car and ride them over bareback again. It was *cold,* and Annie was just grateful that the cooks were willing to spare her coals when they arrived at their camp.

There was also no time in Mannheim to even see the city (except at a distance), much less do any magic. Once again, four days, two shows a day, meant that Annie was performing from the time she left the cook camp to the time she went to bed. Frank was too—but Annie was the star, and while Frank could slip off from time to time and not necessarily be missed, she couldn't.

However, since it was only a little more than an hour away by train, on May first, Darmstadt got a parade.

The third train left Mannheim in the very early morning, and pulled into Darmstadt before eight. Blue skies overhead and an unusually warm sun made it finally feel like spring, even if there was absolutely no sign of the season in the closed buds and leafless trees. Bill's advance men and ballyhoo men had primed the city for a parade, so the streets were lined with people. This time the order for getting off the train was altered, quite a bit, because here everyone had to wait for the tent-wagons to go on ahead. The dray horses all came off first, the tent wagons second, and they got hitched up and headed for the showground immediately. The wranglers got their horses tacked up and ready to herd the cattle and buffalo and show horses as they came out of the stock cars, and all the performers, from the Prussian hussars to the vaqueros, to the stars of the show, all got their primary horses, tacked them up, mounted, and lined up in parade order. Bill, Annie, and Johnny Baker rode at the head of the procession, followed by the Indians, who were what most German people seemed to want to see. Then came part of the band, playing an

American march. Frida, Jack, and Frank were somewhere behind her; Frank generally rode with the rest of
the solo and duo acts. Probably Frida and Jack were
there with him as well. If any miscellaneous wagons had
gotten off the train and hitched to their respective
horses, they would be in the mix; Bill liked to alternate
riding or walking people with the equipment wagons.
After the solo and duo acts came the Wells Fargo Stage-
coach, a wagon or two, the rest of the band playing a
different march, a wagon or two, then the cattle and
their wranglers, and a wagon, then general performing
cowhands (men *and* women), another couple of wagons,
then the small herd of buffalo, then—well, it depended
on what had gotten hitched, who had gotten mounted;
once the buffalo were in, there was no order, and people
just added themselves to the tail of the parade. The tent
wagons and the men to set them up would certainly arrive first; the cook camp would probably arrive last.
Once the performers were past, they generally tried to
intersperse the otherwise dull wagons with mounted or
walking members of the show, even if those members
didn't actually participate in the show itself. So far as
the parade was concerned, only the leading riders
needed to be in full costume. By the time you got past
the first third of the parade, most of the onlookers were
perfectly fine with just a Stetson hat as a "cowboy costume."

Even though they had moved that day, Annie knew
that there would be shows at noon and five. And as soon
as the camps were set up, she would be expected to go
to her tent, sit outside, and be available for the tours.
Bill made almost as much money on the tours as he did
on the shows.

They got within sight of the grassy field where the
show was being set up, and unlike when they made their
moves in the dark, there was nothing in place yet. The
grass was flat after being under snow all winter, but at
least here green showed through the brown. Of course,

that meant that Bill and whoever was inclined to do so
could put on a little impromptu show for the gathered
crowds, because Bill was a generous man as well as a
vain one, and he liked to give people a little something
for nothing, while also collecting the applause he craved.
Nothing fancy, and certainly no shooting, just some
trick riding and roping. The Indians didn't have to do
anything except stand there to make the onlookers very
happy; here in Germany, the Indians' very existence was
enough to please the crowd.

Bill was on his usual parade horse, a tall white fellow
called Charlie, who was every bit as much of a showman
as Bill himself. So while the grounds began to fill up
with show folk, and the tents began to go up, Bill put
Charlie through his paces with wild applause following
every little trick. When Bill wanted to give Charlie a
little breather, Johnny Baker stepped in with some trick
riding that was frankly better than Bill's but didn't quite
have Bill's showmanship. Then Annie would move in
and have her horse rear a time or two in order to give
the crowd something to gasp about; her Brownie could
and would rear almost straight up, and she was in a sidesaddle. She'd done this hundreds of times—including
posing for a photographer—but the onlookers didn't
know this, and there would always be gasps at the sight
of the little woman seemingly about to be thrown off the
back of her horse. Then Bill would take over again.

All this time there was a group of about twenty men
in the uniform of the Prussian Army—men that had
nothing to do with the show—that were lurking on the
sidelines. They were not where Bill and anyone else who
cared to perform was entertaining the crowd, but off to
the side, watching the show go up and not the shenanigans for the crowd. They were entirely sober and not to
be distracted, with narrowed eyes; they were also constantly taking notes into identical notebooks. They had
turned up in every German city the show had played to
before going into winter quarters, from Munich to Stras-

burg, and it appeared that now that the show was on the move again, they were determined to return to their old ways. There were roughly thirty of them, all told; the other ten were probably back at the railhead, taking notes there. They never appeared singly; never in groups of less than five, in fact. When they had first turned up in Munich, the entire show had been unnerved; the Kaiser had given every evidence of enjoying the show when he'd come to the first British tour, but his secret police had a bad reputation. Did he think there were political revolutionaries in the show? Was someone going to be arrested?

But as time went on and nothing happened except copious note-taking, everyone relaxed. It appeared that the Prussians, always worshipers of efficiency, were interested in how Bill could uproot a virtual town and have it spring up again like a mushroom in a different locale overnight.

No one—at least, no one who had spoken about these men to Annie and Frank—seemed to have the darker impression of this note-taking that Annie did. Because *why* would the Kaiser want to be able to move this quickly, unless he intended to use this knowledge with his army? And what else would the army do with that knowledge except go to war with it?

She stared at them, and the only thought that came to her was . . . *Someday am I going to regret that my aim was so good when I shot that cigarette out of his hand?*

Seeing them again left a bad taste in her mouth—but by this time, about half the camp had been set up, and leaving Bill, Johnny, and a half-dozen others keeping the crowd entertained, she went to the stabling area, which was where she and Frank always met after the parade.

She found him there, resplendent in a fine suit in the Western style, with Frida and Jack, both still in their Bavarian Army–inspired costumes. "They're back," she said, making a face. She knew Frank would know what she was talking about, but she was surprised when Frida responded.

"The Prussians? Ugh. They make me feel unclean," she said. "Always the writing, writing, sideways glances, and writing. What are they writing about? Do they think we are harboring dissidents?"

"Logistics, probably," said Frank. "We're a pretty efficient operation, and the Kaiser probably wants to apply that to the army."

"Does the Kaiser know about magic?" Annie asked, with a sudden feeling of dread.

"No!" Frida and Jack said together. "No," Frida repeated alone. "At least, we don't believe so, but really, there's no way to prove it one way or another. He *doesn't* know about the loose organization of Lodges, at least. He might have a self-taught mage or two in his employ, but no one in a Lodge. We're . . . very careful about that. If he knew how many of us there are—well, anything he can't control, he locks up or eliminates. No one wants either of those three fates."

"I never liked him before, I like him even less now," Annie said with feeling. "Frida, with the pace the show is setting, I don't think we're going to get a chance even to look for a high place, much less do whatever we need to do to get the attention of the Greater Air beings."

Frida made a face, then nodded. "I wasn't really aware of the frenetic pace you people set, or I would never have suggested it, and we would have done something back in Strasburg before we left. I am very sorry—"

"Don't be," Annie replied, and gazed off across the rapidly forming encampment. "If even the Kaiser was surprised by how fast we move, you should certainly not berate yourself for not thinking about it. And I should have said something when you first suggested Mannheim as the place to try it; I *know* we don't have a moment to spare when we are on the move, and I didn't even think of contradicting you."

Annie was distracted for a second by the speed at

which the camp was going up, as if she was seeing it with someone else's eyes. "It's quite a spectacle," Jack said, following her gaze. "A show all its own."

"Well, once the show is up, we're free. What can we do tonight?" Annie asked.

"Hmm. Contact Mathijs De Witt in Antwerp and see what he says about summoning Greater Elementals when we get there." Then Frida laughed. "Although 'summoning' is very much a misnomer. It isn't anything like a 'summoning,' it's more like a politely worded invitation. You do not want a Greater Elemental angry with you."

That thought zipped through her mind and triggered something else. "Frida . . . would a Great Elemental take exception to that . . . thing . . . that the He-Wolf did to me?"

That stopped *all* conversation. Jack and Frida looked at each other with sudden concern. "That . . . didn't occur to me. We need to do some research," Frida said finally. "Another good reason to talk to De Witt, and perhaps see if we can contact Theo and a few other Masters. Tonight would not be too soon."

Annie put one hand on her stomach, self-consciously. "No," she agreed. "It would not."

Once again, Annie found herself envying Frida and Jack their snug little *vardo*. Once the sun set, the temperature had dropped precipitously. The air was still damp, and she pitied people who would be sleeping on the ground, without the furs and buffalo skins the Indians used to keep the cold away. True, they were used to it, but that didn't make it any easier.

The *vardo* was beyond cozy, warm with the scent of spiced cider in the air. There were sylphs everywhere; they seemed to know whenever Annie or Frida was about to do magic, and swarmed around them when they did so. Not that Annie had done much magic up to this point—mostly to "feed" the sylphs, who seemed to "eat" it and whatever pleasant aromas were around.

They certainly enjoyed spiced cider and coffee.

"I've done all the warding," Frida said, as they climbed into the wagon. "Everything's in place except creating the vessel and contacting De Witt. He's expecting us; I sent a sylph to ask him to speak with us tonight, and he said he would—" she turned to Jack, who consulted his watch.

"In 'bout fifteen minutes," Jack said.

"Have you ever had any dealings with him before this?" Annie asked.

"Not personally, but I've scryed him before this quite a bit," Frida replied. "Especially when Theo wasn't available. Shall we?"

Annie sat opposite Frida, on the bench seat and stool next to the bed-cubby. The two of them put their hands up, palms facing each other. Still marveling at how naturally this had come to her, Annie drew power from the air and willed it into the space between their hands. Soon, a softly glowing, amorphous shape appeared there, the light in it growing stronger with every moment. A sharp scent mingled with the scent of spice—the same scent that came with a lightning strike. Frida nodded a little and the shape began to spin.

As it spun, it condensed into a sphere, and at a second nod from Frida, they both dropped their hands and the sphere cleared. For a moment, it looked as if there was a giant glass ball hanging in the air between them.

Then something appeared in it—it wasn't an image, it was more as if they were looking through a window into someone else's room. A ruddy-faced, white-haired man with a slightly bulbous nose above a neatly trimmed mustache and beard looked her straight in the eyes; he wore a shabby blue smoking jacket, and it appeared as if he was looking *down* at her. In fact, what he was looking at was the bowl of water that he was using to scry with.

And despite the fact that he was facing away from

Frida, and at an angle to Jack and Frank, she knew they would all be seeing the same thing, and it would be as if he was looking straight at *them*. That was how scrying worked.

What he saw—she had no idea. At no point had she and Frida ever scryed more than one person at a time.

"My dear Frida!" he exclaimed in English, his voice sounding very far away, as if he was speaking from the bottom of a well. "So, you have run away to join the circus, have you?"

"Something like that," she said dryly. "My friends and I will be coming with our circus to Antwerp in May, so you and I will finally meet in person."

"Excellent! I am looking forward to it! But I am sure you are not calling on me to let me know what you could have told me in a letter." His blue eyes twinkled shrewdly.

"Well, we have two things we want to ask of you, and a question. I don't know if you can answer the question, but you have done more research into Elementals than Theo, so perhaps you can." She waited for him to take this in.

"You flatter me, you naughty child. Well, tell me the question first. Then we will see about your requests." The image shimmered for a moment, then cleared, but Annie was used to this. The farther away you scryed, the less stable the image was.

"My American friend here has . . . well, I suppose if I were to call it anything, I would call it a magical brand upon her." Again, Frida waited.

"Really!" He peered closely at Annie, as if trying to see it. "What is it, and what caused it?"

"It's a claiming mark, and it was put on her as a child by a *werwolf*. It was done clumsily, but powerfully, and Frau Schnee could not break it."

"I hope you are not expecting *me* to break it," he said immediately. "Because I will tell you now, I cannot. Not something too strong for the good lady Schnee."

Frida shook her head. "Not at all. No, what we wanted to know was, would a Storm or a Tempest see it, and would they take offense at it?"

He didn't even hesitate. "See it? Almost certainly. Take offense? Almost certainly not. The Storms and Tempests are . . . decidedly amoral. Well, they are almost chaos creatures themselves. They don't recognize good or evil, only friend or foe. I assume, Madame—?" he waited for Annie to give her name.

"Butler," she said immediately. "Or Oakley, if you want my performing name."

"Madame Butler, I assume this happened in America, since it occurred when you were a child?" He made it into a question rather than a statement.

"It did."

He threw up his hands. "Then there is no problem. It is wildly unlikely that a Great One of the Air would recognize the handiwork of anyone from America, and it is equally unlikely that a Great One lingering in the vicinity of Antwerp will have ever had anything to do with a *werwolf* in the first place. By their very nature, the *werwolf* is a creature of wildernesses, and Belgium is . . . exceptionally tame. There will be neither foe nor ally to recognize in that mark. So that answers your question. What are your requests?"

"We wondered if you would call one of the Greater Water Elementals to recognize this man Frank Butler as a Master," she said.

"Well, well, well!" he said with evident surprise. "The youngsters of the New World continue to surprise! Yes, I will certainly do that. Nehallenia will do nicely, I think. Benign, kindly to humans, and native to these parts. What is the other request?"

"That you help me summon a Storm or a Tempest to do the same for Frau Butler."

"No," said De Witt. "I will not. I will help you summon Telwaz."

"*What?*" she exclaimed, so sharply that Annie jumped.

"A Storm or a Tempest is too chaotic in nature for this," he replied, not at all perturbed by her response. "Especially given the brand that is on her—Telwaz renders justice, and he is no friend to the renegade *werwolf* that has made himself by magic. No, it shall be Telwaz. I have something in my collection that will help. Is that all?"

For once, Frida was rendered speechless. Finally she stammered, "Y-yes. That is—more than enough."

"Good! Then while I have you, tell me all the gossip!" And he actually rubbed his hands together with glee.

Frida obviously knew more actual gossip about the other Elemental Masters that both she and De Witt knew, but Annie and Frank were able to tell about how they had negotiated a sort of peace with the *nachtkrapp* and the *aufhocker,* which made his eyebrows rise and got a satisfied chuckle out of him. But by the time he was ready to close the conversation, Annie was absolutely exhausted. To date, this was the largest work of magic she had ever participated in, and she was feeling the strain of it.

Frida fortified them both with a last round of cider and sent them off to their tent, and Annie was so tired that she stumbled. She realized with dismay that they had not charged the bed warmer with coals, and she was too exhausted to go after them.

But Jack unexpectedly came to their rescue, turning up at the tent just as they lit the oil lamp with a round, black iron pot suitable for making stew over a fire; it was full of coals. He and Frank got them transferred into the bed warmer, and Annie put it under the covers, moving it around to warm the whole bed.

"Frank!" she exclaimed, suddenly realizing something.

"What?" he replied, quickly removing his clothing so as to get into that warm bed as quickly as possible.

"Jack brought over that kettle *in his bare hands!*"

"He's a Fire Magician," Frank reminded her. "Seems there's benefits to that."

She sighed. "That beats being able to freeze water," she lamented, as she quickly got into bed too.

He laughed. "Bet you won't say that come summer, when we're broiling under the sun."

Mainz was next, for four shows, and the land just seemed to get flatter and flatter as they traveled, so Annie quite understood why Frida had elected to try their luck in Antwerp and with De Witt instead of attempting to find a place high enough and private enough to try a summoning. Not to mention that they had absolutely no free time, because the show was running at the same breakneck schedule it did in the US. Breakdown as soon as the halfway point in the last show was reached, travel in the dark, setup in the dark, and falling into bed. It was beautiful countryside too . . . but Mainz was where she began to get the uneasy feeling that something was watching her.

It happened right in the middle of the second performance of the fourth day, as she was waiting to stride out into the arena for her first turn, the one where she shot glass balls out of the air that Frank tossed. Glass balls were the preferred target for most trick shots; they were easy and cheap to make, showy, and shattered in a most satisfactory and spectacular manner when hit. And she suddenly felt her skin crawling. Exactly as if someone was staring right at her.

She swiftly looked around, but there was no one in the entrance area that shouldn't have been there, and no one peering through a gap in the curtains or under the canvas. And this wasn't a "friendly" feeling either, it was something with tinges of anger and greed.

It shook her enough that it was a good thing she was using shot instead of bullets. With shot, she didn't need to hit the ball squarely; a single pellet would do, and the spread was a lot wider than most people realized. This was why she had stuck with the old rifle after she had begun shooting game to sell rather than switching to a shotgun; no one wanted to eat a fine pheasant only to break a tooth on a piece of buckshot.

When she came off, she was still shaken, and still felt those staring eyes. So, impulsively, she did what Frida had taught her, and shielded herself from magic.

The horrid feeling vanished, as if it had never been.

But she was not experienced enough in magic to keep up shields forever; she could feel them draining her, as if she was running up a high hill that had no end in sight.

"What's wrong?" Frank asked her, as she finished the shields. "You were very off kilter out there."

"I felt something watching me," she told him, as they quickly moved to the changing area to get ready for the next turn. "It was *awful.* And awfully familiar."

"The He-Wolf?" he asked under his breath. She nodded, shivering, and not just from the damp chill.

"I think it might be. I think someone back home told him that *Annie Moses* is now *Annie Oakley,* and it's easy enough to figure out where we are from the papers. I shielded, but I don't think I can keep it up all night." She felt as if she was right on the edge of hysterics, and she *never* was that out of control!

"Calm down, calm down, little fairy," he said, not in a patronizing way, but with his eyes all soft and kind, and he put his arm around her shoulders to enforce that. "First off, ask your fairies for help. Second, as soon as this show is over, we'll be in the railcar, and I'll bet Frida can teach you a new trick to keep that cur off you."

That steadied her; she went through the rest of her routines feeling strained, but no longer about to break down—although it was a good thing that the sylphs had begun to gather at her call to lend her magic power, because she also needed them to help her make a couple of shots.

Frida and Jack were already in the railcar when they got there, and as soon as the door closed, she blurted out everything to them. Frida made a sour face.

"I really do not like working magic in a moving train," she reminded them.

"Train's not movin', sweetheart," Jack reminded *her*. And then added "Lookee, this might be a time for that thing where you make people invisible. Once it's up it keeps a-goin' without any extra push."

She hit herself in the forehead with the palm of her hand. "Of course! I'm—"

"Tired," he interrupted. "We're all tired. You and me, we ain't used to this breakneck pace of living. Annie's draining into her shields. Frank too, prolly. Let's do this before the train starts a-movin'."

"I'm glad I raided the cook-tent before they took everything away," Frida muttered, then straightened. "All right, this is probably going to need energy from all four of us—"

"Wait!" Annie wailed, unable to help herself from reacting. "You said it would make me invisible! I don't *want* to be invisible! How can I—"

"To magic," Jack interrupted her, and patted her hand. "Just invisible to magic."

"It's just a good thing I shielded and warded this compartment," Frida muttered, shaking her head. "I *never* get premonitions—"

"Well, maybe you got a whiff of the thing that sniffing for Annie and not a premonition," Jack told her. "Let's get on with this."

By the time the train lurched into movement, the spell was complete—and it was a spell, an actual, real spell, that required a few material components like a pinch of blessed salt, and the burning of a few herbs that fortunately didn't leave much odor except smoke. Annie felt quite faint by the end of it, but she had faithfully written it all down in her book so that she could do it herself later. They shared out the contents of Frida's basket, and settled in to rest for the long journey to Cologne, where they would spend five days, and almost half of May would be behind them. Annie was sure that she would never sleep, but the next thing she knew, Frank was shaking her awake.

It was certainly somewhere near midnight, and every-one was eager to get to the camp and into bed. This was rather worse, she thought, than going a full overnight and then making a parade in the morning to the camp. She felt utterly unsettled and a little sick, and really, really missed her wonderful sleeping car back home. Alas that such things couldn't be brought by steamship! But *that* would have cost more than even Bill would countenance, and he almost never omitted an extravagance for his be-loved Wild West. She wasn't sure how much the expenses were per week, but they had to be astronomical, what with hundreds of animals, hundreds of people, and all of them getting full meals every day. Even the cost to move the wagons with the gear was considerable; they were able to seat fourteen thousand people at once, after all.

Her brain was in such a fog that she didn't remember getting up onto the seat of one of the wagons, only that for a while the fog lifted, and she realized she was up next to one of the mule drivers, a fellow who was just full of stories about Calamity Jane, whom he allegedly knew. She let him chatter, holding to the seat with both hands, since it seemed to be swaying more than usual. She blanked out again, and then found herself being helped down by Frank.

But as great good luck would have it, a few yards brought her to the tent, already set up. The bed wasn't warmed, but she didn't care. She only half undressed, and fell into it, still in her petticoat, and didn't awaken until morning.

16

MAY thirteenth to the sixteenth: Dortmund. May seventeenth to the nineteenth: Duisburg. Then a long train day and a parade (since the train ride allowed them all to catch up on some rest) dropped them in Krefeld for the eight performances of the twentieth to the twenty-third. Then another train day and parade in Aachen, performing from the twenty-fourth to the twenty-seventh. Every performing day they worked from rising to falling into bed—but at least, by now, Annie and Frank didn't need the bed warmer, and, tired as they were, even the camp bed was as good as the one in the Graf's guest room. No sign of *werwolfen,* or even ordinary wolves. No real chance to do much magic, much less invoke the Greater Elementals, but every night, Annie faithfully checked, and when needed, renewed the "invisible to magic" spell Frida had taught her, and she never got that feeling of being watched again.

Of course, *if* it was linked to the He-Wolf, he knew by now she was "Annie Oakley," and any allies of his over here only needed to look at the posted schedules in the German and Belgian newspapers to know where she was.

And if it had been some other unfriendly party, well, the same things held.

So she was taking nothing for granted.

On the other hand, their frenetic schedule left no time when she was alone, or even off the show grounds.

She didn't get to see a lot of the country, but what she did see of the Rhineland was beautiful. Lots of hills, lots of trees, and as spring progressed into a breakneck run into summer, everything was in bloom or leaf, and Annie thought she had never seen country quite as pretty as this.

And then, in the night of the twenty-seventh, the three trains crossed into Belgium.

And it was . . . flat. Still pretty—but flat. And definitely not possessing anything like a "mountain" one could use to summon a Great Air Elemental.

Nothing like the part of Germany they had just been through, which had at least had hills, if not mountains. Even in the dark on the train, Annie could tell. No curving paths through the hills, and no sense that the train was climbing hills either. Just straights and gentle curves, and they all slept through the journey in their compartment, so used to it now that their bodies automatically assumed the right curves for sleeping as soon as the train was in motion.

But at last there was to be some relief. Two weeks in Brussels; two weeks in the same place, with a performance on the first of June that would include the King and Queen of Brussels in attendance. And after that, a very short ride to Antwerp and six days there.

By this time, of course, crowned heads of state had ceased to impress Annie; or at least, to impress her as much as they first had. It was harder to get excited over a mere King and Queen of a small country when you've had the Empress of the British Empire call you a "Very, very clever little girl" and give you a present of a medal.

Nor were Frida and Jack terribly excited about the Belgian monarchs. For them, this was nearly the end of their adventure with the Wild West. But for Annie, well . . . there were still nine more months to go before she saw home again.

But there was one thing that she was anxious about.

If she was going to have to face the He-Wolf at home, she wanted to do so with every weapon at her disposal. And that meant magic, very powerful magic. And *that* meant she needed the anticipated introduction to a Greater Elemental. Or, as she had come to understand from Frida . . . a former, ancient god.

Frida came flying at Annie as she dismounted in the wings after the blow-off parade and all the ovations from the fully packed stands at the King and Queen's performance. "Annie!" she crowed. "Have you heard?"

Annie of course had not heard a thing, since she was either performing, changing, had just finished performing, or was about to perform for most of the last four hours. "Not a thing," she said, dismounting from Brownie and handing the mare off to a wrangler.

"We have an afternoon off!" Frida said with glee.

Annie stared at her with astonishment. "Has the Colonel lost his mind?" she asked, quite seriously, because she could not imagine Bill canceling a sell-out performance for any reason short of going mad, or breaking his own back. As generous as the Colonel was, even if *she* broke her back he'd find a way for the show to go on.

"The Queen is absolutely smitten with Buffalo Bill, and has invited him to visit the Waterloo Monument with her tomorrow afternoon," Frida replied, linking her arm with Annie's and waving to Frank, who was just riding his own horse in from the arena. "At her request he's taking half the Indians. That means there won't be enough to do a show, and that means he's canceled to-morrow's afternoon show."

"Do tell," said Frank, dismounting and joining them, as another wrangler took his horse away. "Well, a sit-down dinner without cramming food in my mouth and pouring hot coffee straight from the pot down my gullet won't come amiss, that's for certain-sure."

"Poor Frank," Annie said, patting his arm. "It could be worse. I could be the cook."

"That means we can have a word with De Witt to-night to find out if there are any snags in his plan," Frida pointed out. "Shall we go do that?"

Annie and Frank exchanged a glance, and Frank nodded, and spoke for both of them. "I think that sounds like a good idea," he agreed. "'Many's the slip 'twixt the cup and the lip' and all that."

He linked arms with Annie on her other side and the three of them headed for the *vardo*, which had become their default location whenever they wanted privacy. As the weather had improved, and people had gotten used to the pace of travel again, Frida and Jack had been taking pains to become acquainted with more of their fellow showmen. Back in Strasburg, there had been no single place big enough and warm enough for more than a handful of people to sit and talk and enjoy each other's company—except the bigger beer-halls, but that meant trying to fumble through the few words in German any of them knew, and immediately identified them as Wild West performers, which brought with it a different, though usually pleasant, set of problems—the admiration of the other patrons, their insistence on "just one more round, on us," and being peppered nonstop with questions in very broken English. It certainly was not conducive to an evening with "just one's friends."

But now it was quite warm enough before and after the shows for people to meet and talk, gamble or play non-gambling games, build a campfire and gather around it to sing or swap yarns.

So with Annie's encouragement, Frida and Jack had been making friends themselves, starting with Johnny Baker, and including people down to the roustabouts who erected and collapsed the tents and did a hundred and one other jobs and repair work on the show. They were happy to give little language lessons to those who wanted to memorize a phrase or two to get by in the cities; and, of course, Jack made himself popular by offering to go out with them on their (necessarily short, given how packed their days were) errands and act as translator. He had proved to be unexpectedly invaluable in the cases where there had been breakdowns with the electrical generators and lighting rigs, and he and the clever fellow who tended these creatures like the exotic babies that they were had been able to find the right parts, make sure they would fit, and be back to the show in very good time. Poor Jack had expressed himself to be bewildered those two times—attempting to translate English jargon into German and reverse. "And not one word of either language did I understand!" he had said in mock despair, throwing up his hands.

But this had the effect of turning "What is keeping our Annie and Frank all closeted up with them foreigners all the time?" to "Oh, the Butlers and the Cates must be having a card game, or somethin'. Mebbe talkin' about books, they sure do read a lot."

There was the *vardo,* parked in the choice spot among the tents for the cooks, a pretty plot of green grass that was not trampled flat or eaten to the bare earth as so much of the camp was. The Cates had gotten a lot of good-natured ribbing about snagging such a good place for hot water, latrine access, and after-hours snacks.

Jack was waiting, sitting on the steps of the *vardo* in the twilight, smoking. He jumped up when he saw them. "I wrangled some of that new coffee out of the cooks," he said, opening the door for them. "And I flat-out stole some ginger snaps when they weren't lookin'."

"Shhhh!" Frida said with a chuckle. "They'll hear you!"

At just that moment, a sylph flew to Frida carrying a small, folded bit of paper. With a quick look around to make sure no one was close enough to notice that she was pulling paper notes out of thin air—because obviously no one could see the sylph but them, unless that person was also a magician—she took it and spun up a little morsel of magic for the sylph to eat.

I seem to have had a good influence on her, Annie thought with amusement. *Before, she never rewarded them. Now she does all the time. And now she has clouds of them looking to serve her whenever she needs them.*

"It says, *10 in the evening. De Witt,*" Frida read aloud.

"It's almost that now," said Jack, taking out his watch. "Them ginger snaps are gonna have to wait."

". . . what do you mean, it's not possible?" Frida demanded with a stormy expression.

De Witt spread his hands wide. "There is simply not enough time! You can thank that madman Buffalo Bill and the pace he sets for his show for that. Your last show in Antwerp is the evening of the seventeenth of June. I have checked with the docks. You are departing on the steamer *Lincoln* in the early hours of the eighteenth of June. If you are not *on* that steamer the evening of the seventeenth, there will be great consternation."

"They could catch up by another steamer—" Frida began.

"*No, they cannot.*" De Witt mopped his brow with a handkerchief. "There will be checks. Questions will be asked. You might be accused of kidnapping. Police could be involved. We cannot have this. Do you wish Kaiser Wilhelm to become aware of magic? This is how such revelations often begin!"

Annie uttered a low moan of disappointment, but she agreed. "He's right, Frida. We will be missed. They will be making a cabin check three times, once when the performers are supposed to board the ship, once when we are all supposed to be aboard, and once about an hour before the steamer leaves. Bill has never forgotten how on the first English tour he accidentally left Black Elk and a handful of Sioux behind in London and they almost starved to death."

"Each ritual—of the ones I know, at least—takes four hours. I cannot do them together. That means an hour to transport you to the place where I intend to conduct them, eight hours for the rituals, and an hour to transport you back. You will have, *perhaps,* four hours before people begin searching for the lost stars. It cannot be done. It cannot be humanly or inhumanly done." He looked utterly miserable, and Annie didn't blame him. "I am so sorry, my friends. I am so very sorry."

Frida muttered some guttural things that Annie supposed were probably curses.

"We must all simply let our little Elementals know that such a thing is wanted and needed," De Witt continued. "With luck, they will communicate that among themselves, and there will be Greater Elementals who will take it upon themselves to sponsor your Masteries. It has been done before," he added, hopefully. "There are at least two people within my acquaintance that Greater Elementals came to spontaneously. It is said, 'When the pupil is ready, the Master will appear,' and rightly so."

Frida rubbed her temples with both hands, and sighed with resignation. "All right, De Witt," she said. "I have to agree with you. Much as I hate to. Thank you for trying."

"I am devastated," he said sadly. "I wanted very badly to help you and it seems I cannot. You will come to stay with me in Antwerp for a few days, will you?"

"Of course. It's long past time we met face to face, and this is certainly not your fault. It's the fault of that madman who rushes his show down the road as if there are no obstacles to fulfilling his insane schedule. Farewell. We will meet in Antwerp."

He waved his hand at the same time Frida waved hers, and the ball and the image within it vanished. Frida looked as if she wanted to break something. "I am *very* vexed with the Colonel," she said crossly. "*Very.*"

"He has no idea that this is going on under his nose," Annie felt moved by justice to point out, even though she was vexed and disappointed as well. "But could we do this in England?"

"Well . . . I'm concerned that you will need the formal acknowledgement before that." Frida didn't have to say why; the reason was on everyone's mind. "You can access an entirely new level of power when you have been acknowledged, or sponsored, by a Greater Elemental," Frida said. "Yes, it is true that you can do many things without that acknowledgement, but once you have it, you can do more, and more freely. Even without your asking, once you are acknowledged, a Greater Elemental may elect to help you." She sighed again. "No help for it. And crying won't change anything."

"Then let's go find whatever campfire that feller Tony Esquival's at," Jack said. "I do like to hear that man sing, and we won't get many more chances."

"Let's," Annie agreed, and smiled at Frida. "Perhaps he will sing you a Spanish love song and sweeten your bad temper."

Annie realized, as a lump grew in her throat at the sight of the steamship *Lincoln,* moored at the docks and being loaded with packed wagons under an overcast sky, that this was not the kind of farewell she was used to. Until now, when she said goodbye to a friend, it was with the expectation that they would meet again.

But this was by no means certain with Frida and Jack. The show might never come back to Germany. If it did come back, the couple might not be able to pull themselves away from other duties to visit. Or Annie and Frank might not even be with the show at that point; De Witt had a point, the grueling schedule that Bill set was insane, and she and Frank were getting weary of it. She loved Bill; she wanted him to have everything he dreamed of—but not at the expense of breaking the two of them on the wheel of his ambitions. They had been talking for a while about leaving the show and retiring to do only competitions, exhibitions, and stage work. This tour just might put the last nails in that particular coffin.

So this might really be "Goodbye and Farewell." And suddenly Annie, who seldom cried, was very near to tears.

"This isn't goodbye forever," Frida suddenly blurted, as if she was reading Annie's mind. "We're *Masters!* We can always scry each other!"

Annie sniffed and wiped away a tear, and tried to smile, as Frank and Jack did all the hearty, "we're tough men," unemotional things that men do when they are truly feeling something deeply. "That's true, we can," she managed, then the two of them flung themselves on each other's necks and cried unashamedly.

They both got control of themselves at about the same time, and pulled apart, getting out their handkerchiefs and sorting themselves out. "What about—every Sunday night?" Annie asked at last. "Because—Frida, you are as good a sister as my Hulda is, and—" She stopped, choking up again.

"I never had a sister, so you're the nearest I've ever gotten," Frida responded, and resorted to her handkerchief again. "Yes! Every Sunday! I promise!"

The two cried for a bit more, and although Annie knew she had to get herself under control, she couldn't help but feel as if part of her was being ripped away. She and Frida had become closer in the last half year than she was with anyone but her sister Hulda—but Hulda was much younger than she was, and there were things that Annie would never be able to share with her. But she could—and had!—shared all those things and more with Frida. She liked to think Frida felt the same. It was the first time she had had such a close woman friend that was her own age. It was hard for her to make female friends in the show—the men accepted her as an equal, and perhaps that was the problem. Some women seemed unable to understand that a woman could be merely friends with a man. Others treated her as a rival. And still others were jealous of her fame. She actually had more friends among the wives of the vaqueros and the Sioux than she did among the other female performers in the show. And that was what had made Frida so special. As fearless as Annie without being reckless, absolutely without any ambition to take Annie's place, willing to play either mentor or pupil at any moment. And . . . Frida knew how to have fun. That was a much underestimated skill.

"I'm never going to find anyone like you again!" she sobbed aloud, letting herself blurt out what she was feeling, which she almost never did, except with Frank.

Frida did exactly the right thing; she hugged Annie fiercely, and said in her ear, "And we aren't losing each other! We are friends for *life!*"

"Friends for life!" Annie whispered back, while the men fastened their eyes on the steamship as if it was the most amazing thing they had ever seen.

Finally, they couldn't put it off anymore; the ship blew its whistle in the pattern that Annie had been told meant the passengers must board, and the crowd on the pier surged up the gangplank, some of them carrying bedrolls meant to soften the floor or the benches that were all they'd get to sleep on. The show took up every inch of space on this ship, and the poor bronco handlers and the lower ranks of the show folk had to make do with what comfort they brought aboard with them. Before the cook-tent had been closed down and broken

down, the cooks had even made everything available
into food packets wrapped in brown paper, so everyone
would be sure to have something to eat for breakfast,
dinner, and supper. Everyone—except the stars, who
had tiny staterooms and a dining room to eat in—went
through the line once, and when everyone had gotten
enough to sustain them for a day, people with bigger
appetites were allowed top pick up what was left. Cold
sausages were not the nicest things, but they were better
than nothing, and it was possible—probable, really—
that with all the ingenuity in this group, they'd figure out
a way to warm them. Cold boiled eggs and cold boiled
potatoes were actually rather nice with salt, and the potatoes were certainly filling.

The food packets were Bill's idea, Annie was certain
of it. Vain he might be, and boastful, and more than a
little inclined to embroider his own legend out of all re-
semblance to reality—he was a drunk, and a womanizer
(although to Annie's knowledge he never once ro-
manced a woman who had not come to him first). But he
took care of his people, from Annie and Johnny down
to the Indian wives and babies and the roustabouts who
put up and tore down the show. With the exception of
that one slipup with Black Elk, no one had anything to
complain about in Buffalo Bill's treatment.

"I wish you would stay," Annie said forlornly, as
Frank picked up their hand luggage and prepared to
head for the gangplank. "Just think of all the jolly fun
we could have!"

"Alas!" Frida sighed. "Who would drive off the *Krampus* in Swandorf this Christmas if we did?"

"Who would satisfy the *bergmoench* with stories?"
said Jack.

"Who would chase the *korneber* from the fields?"
Frida chimed in.

"Who would keep the *tatzelwurm* from stealing
girls?" Jack added.

"Who would—" Frida began, and Annie finally laughed through her tears.

"All right, all right!" she exclaimed. "I understand. Your land is *excessively* haunted with monsters of all sorts, and you can't be gallivanting about the globe with me."

"I think it's the age of our lands," Frida said, seriously. "There's layer upon layer upon layer of human history here, and each layer has its own set of things that only an Elemental Magician can deal with. You'll find your own nasties to banish, too, but outside of cities, I doubt you'll find them as thick on the ground as we do. Although I could be wrong; some terrible things live in our wildernesses, and your vast tracts of wilderness might well hold uncanny things with a hatred for mankind."

The steamship tooted another warning to the passengers to get aboard. "Time for you to go," said Frida. "And time for us to be leaving as well." And to keep Annie from prolonging the farewell again, she began walking backward towards the dock exit, waving as she went.

Annie did the same, carefully steered by Frank, so that the last sight they had of each other was not one of a retreating back.

The "stateroom" was barely big enough to hold the two bunks and a tiny sink, but it was much better than the floor or a bench, and afforded privacy, which was not something many people on this trip were going to get. But it would only be about a day, and, Annie thought, most people could put up with about anything for a day. It did have a small window, but there was nothing out there but darkness and the sea.

And just as she thought that, she heard a tapping on that window.

What? She got on tiptoe and looked out, to see a sylph frantically flying to keep up with the ship.

Quickly she opened the porthole, and the poor little thing flung itself inside, panting with exertion. And now she saw why it couldn't get in through the window; it was carrying a note.

Quickly, Annie spun up a little magic to feed the poor thing, which she drank greedily while Annie opened the note. As soon as the sylph had finished the magic, she went to perch in a corner of the upper bunk, where she curled, eyes closed in what looked like a sleep of sheer exhaustion.

I've never seen one sleep before!

She opened the note. In Frida's tiny handwriting it said, *We have managed something. Go to the stern and see if it worked. If nothing happens for an hour, just go to bed; there are no guarantees in magic.*

She showed it to Frank. "Well, that's pure curious," he said. "Let's put on our coats and take a walk."

There was no one else outside—well, why would there be? Everyone was tired, and those who had sea-legs and sea-stomachs were doing their best to get some sleep. They found themselves a place in the stern where no one was likely to see them and ask why they were out, and looked out at the darkness, hearing the churn of the screws in the water, but unable to see them. Annie breathed in the clean, salt-tinged sea air with pleasure. Clean as Antwerp had been, it was not possible to breathe this kind of air there. It was chilly out here at sea, but with her coat on, she didn't mind. And it was so peaceful here, poised between sea and sky in the clean darkness, sheltered from the wind of the ship's passage.

"I cain't see a thing," Frank said after a moment.

"Neither can I, and if either of us would, it would be—"

The sound of a lady clearing her throat interrupted what Annie was saying.

"Pardon me," she said, as they whirled to see who had crept up on them while they were staring at the darkness past the stern. "But I believe you were expecting me, Master Butler."

They didn't need any light to see her; she glowed with her own inner light. Her hair was arranged in braids in the form of a crown; she was dressed in the height of fashion, except that she had a peculiar short cloak, a little like a Mexican serape, except that it was longer in the back than the front, which only covered her chest. She led a dog that looked a lot like a mastiff on a thread-like leash, and she carried a loaf of bread very like a baguette.

It was Frank who recovered his wits first. "Ma'am," he said, politely removing his hat. "If you are the great lady called Nehallenia, then yes, I would be." He held out his hand. "I hope you don't mind me not bowing nor going to my knees. I'm an American, and we don't do that."

She laughed, a beautiful sound like a babbling stream, and put the loaf in his outstretched hand. "And I don't require it. I am pleased to accept such a good and polite gentleman as one of my own. Please have a bite of that bread, then tear the rest in four pieces and throw it into the sea."

Frank did as he was told, never taking his eyes off her. She smiled benignly the entire time. She looked like one of the statues of goddesses that Annie had seen in Rome, except that she was dressed in a modern dress that Annie would rather have liked for herself, and had all her limbs and her nose, which could not be said of those statues.

"Now we are friends," she said, in the sweetest of voices. "And it is time for me to introduce the lady to another friend."

She gestured, and another figure . . . gradually faded into view, starting from a vague, faint human shape, then slowly growing more distinct, until a tall, blond-haired man stood beside the Water Elemental.

Like her, he was dressed in modern clothing, a suit even Bill would have been proud to wear. But one of the arms of that suit was pinned up against his chest, and it was clear that he had no right hand.

"Mister Telwaz, I presume," said Frank, who had *clearly* been paying more attention to De Witt than she had. Or maybe he had just recovered his senses before her.

The man nodded. "Indeed I am, Master Butler. And Master I acknowledge you to be, as has the lady Nehallenia."

"But you're here for my Annie," Frank said, and pushed her forward a little.

"So I am. No loaf for you, dear one, for that is not my way. I have two things for you. First, the kiss of peace." And he leaned forward and kissed her chastely on each cheek, as the French did. "And with this, I accept you as one of my own. And the second is a gift from your friend, who forgot to give it to you at parting. And a message goes with it. Please hold out your hand."

Annie obeyed and the Elemental placed in her outstretched hand—of all unexpected things—a Remington Derringer in what she recognized to be a shoulder holster meant to be worn under a jacket or coat. Then he placed a leather pouch loaded with what felt like cartridges beside it.

"Is this from Frida?" she managed to ask—because so far as her universe went, things had gone askew again. Since when were magic creatures supposed to be handing out modern pistols?

"It is," said Telwaz. "Obviously, too heavy for a sylph to carry, and I asked to be able to give it to you in token that we are now friends. The message that comes with it is this: *Keep this on you and keep it loaded. Silver and Telwaz's blessing keep you safe.*"

"That is a mighty fine set of gifts," Frank said with admiration. "I think the blessing's the more valuable of the two."

Nehallenia laughed. "Oh, truly you have a silver

tongue, Frank Butler! I like you! I have no material gift, but you may have my blessing too!"

They might have said something more, but a shout of "Hey!" from behind them caused the two Elementals to glance at each other—then wink out, as if they had never been there at all.

A sailor hurried up to them. "You all right?" he said in good English. "Not sick or nothin'?"

"Just enjoying the night air," Frank said, as Annie hid her gifts in her coat pocket.

"Ah, good." He fidgeted. "Ah, I don't suppose you'd go back to your cabin where it's nice and safe?"

He seemed terribly nervous and Annie could not imagine why. "It's a lovely night—" she began, but Frank suddenly burst out laughing, and slapped the young man on the back hard enough to make him stagger.

"Don't you worry, lad, I'm not about to heave my wife over the tail! Don't you recognize her? This is Annie Oakley!"

"Annie—Oakley?" She could almost hear his mouth dropping open. "Oh—gosh—ma'am—I mean—I'm sorry—I didn't mean anything—"

"I think we can both agree that the star of the Wild West is in no danger of assassination," Frank said, still chuckling.

"No, sir! I mean, yes, sir! I mean—it's an honor to meet you, Mrs. Oakley!" Now the poor boy clearly was so bedazzled that he couldn't tell his head from his heels. Annie didn't correct him, but did take his hand and shake it vigorously. When she released it, he stared at it, as if he couldn't believe he'd just touched hers.

"But it's getting late, and we show folk need all the sleep we can get," Frank continued. "So we'll take your advice and go back to our cabin. Good night and calm seas to you!"

"Uh—likewise!" the sailor managed, and Frank took Annie's hand, tucked it into his arm, and the two strolled back to their deck and their cabin before the poor boy exploded.

Once there, Annie sat abruptly down on the lower bunk and looked up at Frank. "Did that just happen?" she asked, incredulously.

"Check your pocket," Frank suggested. She did. The derringer and the pouch of what were, indeed, rimfire cartridges with silver bullets were still there.

"I . . . expected lightning and thunder," she said weakly. "I expected great echoing voices from the sky. I expected swirling winds and storms. I *did not* expect a couple that looked as if they strolled in off an Antwerp boulevard!"

"Hmm," Frank agreed. "Very good bread, though. I expect throwing it overboard represented a sacrifice of some sort."

"Should I have—" she began, now worried that she had made some mistake, and that Telwaz would be angry with her.

"If you should have, he would have told you," Frank assured her. "Don't worry. Remember what De Witt said about him. He represents justice. It wouldn't be just if he expected a sacrifice, knew you wouldn't know what to do, and didn't tell you what he wanted—"

But then Annie remembered something. One of the things every single female member of the company had gotten when the show was in Cologne was a bottle of the justifiably famous light scent *Eau de Cologne*. In fact, she had gotten several, for herself and as gifts for those at home, and one of the smallest bottles was with her now on the (unlikely) chance that she got seasick, because smelling it was said to ward off nausea. She opened the overnight bag at the foot of the bunk and rummaged through it, taking out the bottle and one of her handkerchiefs. She soaked the fabric in scent, then stood up to touch the little sylph on the wing to awaken her.

The sylph woke up slowly with a stretch and a yawn— then suddenly perked up as the scent reached her nose.

She shot off the bunk into the air to hover in front of the scent-laden handkerchief. Annie held it out to her.

"Can you take this to Telwaz as my sacrifice?" she asked.

The sylph nodded so hard that she bobbed in midair.

Annie applied her finger to the top of the bottle, got another drop, and dabbed it on the top of the sylph's head. The sylph looked as if she was going to swoon with delight. Then Annie gave her the handkerchief and opened the window, and the sylph zipped out into the darkness.

But before Annie could close the window, a breath of ocean air puffed in and touched her, just on the cheek, like a kiss.

She closed it and sighed. "Well."

"Well," Frank echoed. "Reckon we're due for some sleep."

17

LEEDS in Yorkshire was one of the worst cities they had ever played.

Not because of the crowd—the audience was appreciative and all eight thousand seats were sold out for both shows—which, now that it was actually summer, had reverted to "early evening" and "late evening."

No, it was the city itself, which extended its noisome nature as far as the encampment at a place called Cardigan Fields, next to the Aire River. The air was horrid; Annie had a headache as soon as the trains pulled into the unloading siding and felt as if she was inhaling soot with every breath. Well, actually she was, and worse. Leeds was a coal-mining city. Mines were everywhere, sending the noxious dust to all parts of the place, and coke ovens worked round the clock, filling the air with bitter haze. The Aire was hopelessly polluted; Fred Gibbs pronounced the water "not fit to drink" and the cooks voted it "not fit to clean with," which meant they had to get water from pumps.

Evidently Mr. Burke, whose job it was to assess the

fitness of a venue for camping, had not bothered to look at the water.

This did, however, make the job of the grooms and latrine-emptiers easier: they just dumped the sewage straight into the river.

Frank was as horrified by the state of the water as Annie was by the condition of the air, but what were they to do? At least they would be gone in fifteen days. What Annie looked forward to back in Antwerp as a nice long stay in one place had turned into something to endure.

"I can't imagine how bad this would be for an Earth Magician," Annie said sotto voce to Frank as they turned their horses over to the wrangler at the end of the second show on their first day. "They're much more sensitive to these things than we are."

"You ain't the only one feeling this, sweetheart," Frank said with a sigh. "Doc's run clean out of headache powder." The show had its own doctor—long ago, Bill had learned better than to depend on the varying abilities of local physicians.

"Bother." They headed straight for their tent, in no mood to linger around a campfire. At least inside the tent Annie could work some magic to clear the air and make it possible to sleep. "Do we *really* have tomorrow off? I cannot remember the last time we had a Sunday off."

"We do," Frank replied. "I don't know why, but we do." They got inside the tent as quickly as they could, with both of them coughing into their hands, and shut the entrance flaps. Finally with some privacy, Frank lit the oil lamps while Annie performed the magic that Frida had taught her that cleared away bad air. There was already another version of that spell on the canvas of the tent, which would now act as a filter, keeping the air inside clean and sweet.

Annie's headache vanished immediately, and she stopped having that urge to cough. Frank's face cleared,

showing that the cleaner air had had the same effect on
him. "Do you think there is any chance an apothecary
might be open on a Sunday?" she asked him, as he settled into a chair with a newspaper someone had left for
them.

"It's England. They don't got the same sorta blue
laws we got back home," Frank reminded her. "Apothecary'll be open. They're sensible here. People get sick
sudden on Sunday too."

"Then that's what I'll do tomorrow, first thing after
breakfast. Go to the apothecary and get more headache
powders. Heaven only knows how soon Doc will be able
to get into town to get them himself."

"Don't forget your derringer," Frank replied. "Silver
bullets will take care of a thug just as good as lead ones."

Although there were no shows today, the camps were
still open to tour, and idlers were already turning up to
be led around as Annie fought her way upstream
through them. Dressed not in one of her Western costumes, but an ordinary summer frock, with her hair up
and a rather nice straw hat she had gotten in France
pinned atop it, no one gave her even a second glance,
much less recognized her as Annie Oakley. They might
have, if she'd had the derringer in the shoulder holster it
had come in, but she'd rigged it on a belt between her
dress and petticoat, where she could reach it through a
slit in the pocket. The men might not think twice about
parading into any town at all fully armed, but she was
not at all interested in garnering the gawking of strangers, much less having to explain herself to constables.

The gown and hat she had chosen were a dark dove
gray, and she was very glad that she had them, because
the air was just as filthy as it had been yesterday. Evidently no law forbade working on a Sunday, and the

smoke and smuts rising from kiln chimneys in the distance told silently that work was going full force.

Special omnibuses had been put on to take people to the Fields for the Wild West, and she spotted one just letting off its last passenger. The conductor seemed a little surprised to see someone leaving so soon. "Tired of the Wild West already!" he exclaimed, as she offered him the fare.

"I should think so, since I'm in it," she replied. And before he could respond with some attempt at wit, like *Oh, and I suppose you're Annie Oakley?* she added, "And I would be forever in your debt if it's possible to put me down at an apothecary. Our doctor is running out of everything, and I am perishing of headache."

His demeanor turned from surprised and then skeptical to completely sympathetic. "Get a seat and let me go talk to the driver for you. It will be no trouble at all. We pass at least three on the way back, and we'll set you down at the best one."

All this was spoken in such a thick Yorkie accent that if she did not have an ear for such things, she'd never have understood him. With a nod and a sweet "Thank you," she took a seat inside, just behind the driver, and discreetly performed the little spell that cleaned up the air. It wouldn't be as effective in a moving 'bus with all the windows open as it would have been in a more closed environment, but it would at least make things a bit better.

The conductor spoke to the driver; the driver turned and gave her a little hat tug and a smile, started the engine of his beast with a grinding noise, and started down the street.

Traffic was light—it was Sunday, after all—and mixed, about two thirds horse-drawn and one third motorized vehicles. Annie took the time to examine the motorcars carefully as they passed. Frank had talked about getting one, but while they were with the show, it seemed like a foolish expense that could not be justified. There was no problem with riding their horses into a city, or taking trams, cabs, or 'buses from the camp, and the car would just be one more thing to unload and re-load, with a chance that every time that happened, something would be broken. But if they did settle in New Jersey . . . it might be nice to have a motorcar. *Frank would certainly enjoy it, since he's the one that brought it up in the first place.*

"Almost there, miss!" the driver shouted over his shoulder, the words coming out as "A'mos' t'ere, muss!" She smiled and nodded her thanks, knowing he couldn't hear her over the sound of the motor anyway.

He managed to maneuver the unwieldy thing right up to the curb, where, as promised, there was an apothe-cary shop; most promising, the display windows were large, very clean plate glass, and displayed an assort-ment of goods that were sparkling clean. She wondered how they did it. Did they clean and dust every hour?

No matter. "Thank you, ever so," she said—or rather shouted—at the driver as she got down.

The conductor hurried over to intercept her before she went in, and handed her a "special 'bus" schedule, show-ing where the Wild West 'buses picked up passengers along the route. Armed with that, she entered the empo-rium with the firm intention of buying headache powders. *Just* headache powders.

She left the apothecary with rather more than that; the sales lady had successfully talked her into getting what amounted to a miniature version of Doc's stock-pile of nostrums. Normally it would have been impossi-ble to talk her into any such thing, but it was a nuisance to run to Doc for every little thing, and to have such a kit at their tent would be very handy. She consulted her "special schedule" and determined that it would be faster to walk to the main loading zone than to wait at one of the special stops. And since the street was mo-mentarily deserted, she stopped for a moment at the entrance of a side passage to read the instructions on the box of headache powder packets.

And that was when something fast, dark, and strong hit her, driving her into the passage and knocking the breath out of her.

And a moment later, she had just time enough to register that she'd been struck in the head when all went black.

Her head hurt so much it did not bear thinking about.

Not just from the headache the terrible air gave her, but from the blow that—someone—had struck her. Nausea washed over her when she tried to move, and it was with incredible difficulty that she opened her eyes.

And horror struck her a blow as terrible as the one to her head when the first thing that she saw was the He-Wolf.

"'Bout time you woke up," said the He-Wolf.

All she could do was stare at him in terror and disbelief. In that moment, she went from woman to terrified child again. Her insides knotted with fear, she began shaking, and tears leaked from the corners of her eyes. She was literally frozen; she felt as if she had been dropped into ice water. She couldn't move. She could scarcely breathe. All she could do was stare.

The He-Wolf smirked, but said nothing.

She licked lips gone dry, and forced herself to look beyond the He-Wolf, but what she saw didn't tell her anything much. She was in a room, windowless, with a stone floor and stone walls. A basement room? Impossible to tell—

But the He-Wolf had noticed the movement of her eyes. "Well, Annie Moses, don't you go thinking you can holler and scream and get help. No one's going to hear you through these walls. And your little butterfly-gals aren't coming in here. I got this place sealed up tighter than a new jar of jam."

She wanted to try anyway, but all she could manage was a whimper.

The He-Wolf grinned. "And don't go thinking your husband is going to come save you. I got me some help too." He raised his voice. "Come on in, boys! She's awake!"

The sound of a door behind him, followed by the sound of feet shuffling in, was all the warning that she got. Within minutes the room was full of fifteen to twenty men, most of them dressed like shabby laborers, all of them with that same look in their eyes of the beast that dwelled within them.

"These are my kin!" he said, spreading his arms wide, as the men all stared at her. "Didn't know I have kin in Germany, now, did you? Oh, you got away from me for a while, sure, but once I put my mind to tracking you down, it wasn't so hard to find out where you'd gone, and what you were calling yourself." He snorted. "Annie *Oakley*. Like plain old Annie Moses wasn't good enough for you. Like you deserted all of *your* kin and wouldn't even share their name."

That's not what I did! she wanted to scream. But nothing would come out of her mouth.

"I wasn't worried when you ran off," he said, while the rest of the men continued to stare, silently. "I knew I could get you back anytime I wanted. And I didn't need you for a while, 'cause I was still building my pack, and it was going to take a while before you were old enough to turn and breed. I forgot about you for a while too." He sneered. "Not like you were worth remembering, being no use to me till you were older." He shook his head. "Time flies when you're a busy man, a big man, like I am. Pack to create. Pack to *feed*. Enemies to tear apart. And magic to master. And I woke up one day thinking, *Damn, I need to find a power source for all my doings*, and then I remembered you." He leered.

"For gott, Ernst," one of the men finally said. "Mit

der talking stop. Claim bitch and turn her. Bring her to heel. I am wanting to go home."

"Keep your lederhosen on," the He-Wolf said lazily. "I want the bitch to know just how completely I have her. I want her broken when I claim her. If that takes some talking, that's none of your business."

But that tiny interlude had brought Annie a moment of clarity. A moment when fear didn't completely paralyze her. A single moment that was enough to let her claw back more and more of herself, as "Ernst" continued his monologue, taking vicious pleasure in describing, in detail, exactly what he was going to do *to* her and *with* her and how she was going to be helpless to stop any of it.

It was when he had gotten to the part about how he was going to take away every bit of her will, and force her to come with him on his arm to the show, and parade her past Frank and all her friends—how he was going to make it impossible for her to speak or even acknowledge them—that her fear suddenly turned to pure, white-hot rage.

And suddenly she knew she could move again.

But she didn't. Instead—

Instead, she stole the breath from his lungs. From *all* their lungs.

Slowly, at first, and he didn't immediately notice. Not until he found himself gasping around words. Not until, one by one, his "kin" put their hands up to their throats, or found themselves abruptly having to sit down. Not until he exhaled, and could not inhale again, stared at her, and made a clawing motion toward her.

But by then, it was too late. He didn't have enough breath to get to his feet, and with every passing moment, he had less.

One by one, his kinfolk succumbed and dropped to the stone floor unconscious. She left him until last, until he slid out of his chair to his knees, making wheezing sounds. Then she got up and stood over him as he stared up at her with horror-filled eyes.

"God tells us to be merciful to our fellow men," she said into a room that was filled with the gasping and gurgling of men desperately trying to get air. "And if you'd shown a shred of humanity, I might have given you mercy. I could right now. I could release your kinfolk, one by one, and tell them to run. And they would. They'd desert you in a heartbeat. Wouldn't they, *Ernst?*"

The sick look in his eyes told her that she was right.

"And then, when you were alone. I could let you go. If you promised to break this thing that you did to me. . . ."

The beginning of that statement caused hope to dawn in his eyes.

The end of it made them bulge with panic.

". . . but you can't, can you?" She gazed down at him dispassionately. "You can't, because you're not *really* trained. You found or inherited a mess of a spellbook. You 'learned' higgledy-piggledy out of it. You just gather power by killing things, then blindly spew out whatever drivel you memorized. And it works, so you think you are a great and powerful magician. How many helpless people have you killed? Ten? Twenty? A hundred?"

The jerk he gave told her that the number was probably a lot more than a hundred.

"God tells us to be merciful to our fellow man," she repeated, and drew the derringer out from underneath her skirts. "But you're not a man anymore, if you ever were. You're a monster."

She aimed the gun for the point between his eyes. His face blazed with terror.

"And I have no problem with killing a monster."

Little Sure Shot, adopted daughter of Sitting Bull, the girl who never missed, pulled the trigger, sending the silver bullet into the He-Wolf's brain.

And with the sound of the gunshot still echoing in the room, the door slammed open, and Frank, Jack, and

Frida burst through it, to find Annie standing over the dead He-Wolf, surrounded by the unconscious bodies of two dozen *werwolfen*.

Part of Annie would have liked to throw herself into Frank's arms and weep until she couldn't stand. The rest of her kept her on her feet—though she did run to him and hold him as tightly as she could. "It's the He-Wolf—" she said tightly. "I killed him. He said these are his kin—what are we going to do with them?" She felt herself just on the edge of hysteria. But what *were* they going to do? Surely they couldn't leave these . . . things . . . here, to wake up later, and then flee to Germany to destroy other decent people's lives!

"Go outside, Annie," Jack said, slowly and carefully, enunciating each word clearly. "You did what you had to do. Now we'll do what *we* have to do."

"Come on, sweetheart," Frank said, taking the gun from her hand, putting his arm around her shoulders, and pulling at her gently. "Jack's right. You got no stomach for slaughter, and that's nothing to be ashamed of."

So she let Frank pull her out the door and shut it behind him.

And the muffled sounds of gunfire began.

The underground room had turned out to belong to a vacant workshop of some sort. Frank got her to sit on a barrel while she stared in a kind of daze, trying to figure out what she should be feeling. Finally she looked up at him, and blurted out just that.

"I—don't know what to feel!" she told him.

"Are you glad?" he prompted gently, beginning to talk her through this, as he talked her through her nightmares.

"That he's dead? Yes! That *I* killed him?" She shook her head. "I don't—I don't think so. I don't—I don't feel anything about that."

"So you got rid of a monster. That's good. And you're not dancing in the street because it was you that done it. That's *better*." He took both her hands in his and patted them. "That means you're a good person, Annie Butler. You don't get happy because you killed something, even if it was a monster. Right?"

"I—suppose?" As ever, things were starting to sort themselves out under Frank's logic. "I suppose it was like killing game. I did it because it was that or starve and I was proud of my marksmanship, but that didn't mean I was happy that something was dead."

"There, now you see?" He gave her back her derringer and she put it in the holster under her skirt again. "That's how you should feel."

Now tears started to fall, but now she knew why. "He couldn't take this curse off me, Frank! Not wouldn't, *couldn't.* He was just an ignoramus who got himself some kind of book or something, maybe inherited it or found it, and he didn't know any more what he was actually doing than a monkey." She sobbed softly. "That means . . . that means we can't have children. *I* can't have children—"

"Whoa, there, whoa there," he said, cutting her off. "Remember when you found out about this? And I told you it didn't matter? It still don't. You don't love me any less. I don't love you any less. All right?"

And before she could object, he kissed her. And it was the kind of kiss that was as if none of this had ever happened, none of this mattered, because he loved her better than anything in the world, and she felt the same about him.

And it was all going to be all right.

The little private room they took in the tea room a few blocks from the deserted workshop had probably never witnessed a conversation like this one, and Annie was just as glad that there was no one to overhear it.

". . . and we decided back about Cologne that when we got to Antwerp, we'd pretend to go through with leaving you, but we'd follow you for a while just in case." Frida picked up her cup of tea, sipped it, frowned, and put it back down. "All those *werwolfen* being reported made us all think your He-Wolf had allies over here, and they were working on his behalf. We never guessed he'd come up with the means to travel here himself! Gah, how can the English drink this? It's nothing but colored water!"

"Next time we'll pick a better tea room," Annie said, trying to make a weak joke. She still felt very shaken, very unsteady, and she was grateful beyond words that there were no shows today.

"Anyway, De Witt has a friend with a racing yacht, and we beat you to the port. Then Lord Kelson loaded us on the express train to Leeds and we set up to wait. I scryed you to keep an eye on you, while Jack went to the Wild West to keep a physical eye on Frank—just in case your He-Wolf tried to get to him first."

"And it all came apart when the He-Wolf moved afore we was ready," Jack admitted.

"I think he had one of his kin following you once you left the camp," Frank said thoughtfully.

"I think you are right," Frida agreed. "But the good thing was that I was scrying you in the first place, because I saw what happened, and where they took you, and sent a sylph to tell Jack what had happened. He and I got to Frank, we all armed up, and the rest you know."

"What are you going to do with the bodies?" Frank asked dispassionately.

Frida snorted. "Jack is going to burn them later tonight. No one's been in that workshop for months, maybe years. Jack and I locked the door to that storeroom, and the way it smells around here—" she made a face "—it's very likely no one will smell the smoke, and no one will know they were in there, unless someone finally buys or rents the place and breaks down the door." She tried a sip of the tea, and grimaced again. "In the meantime, before that can happen, I'll get in contact with whatever poor unfortunate Hunt Master is in charge up here, let him know what happened, and they'll take care of disposing of the evidence. It's not as if I haven't done the same in the past."

"And we just go on our way?" asked Annie. "Like it never happened?"

"If that's what you want." Frida shrugged. "In fact, if you want, you'll never hear from Elemental Masters again for as long as you live. Well, except for our Sunday scrying. I am not allowing you to get away with never speaking to me again, Phoebe Ann Oakley Butler."

Annie smiled tremulously. "Mama never calls me Phoebe Ann unless she is being *the most* serious."

"Well, I am being the most serious." Frida pushed the tea away. "I think this is that awful river water they've just boiled and are pretending it's tea."

"But . . . what if . . . what if that's not what I want?" she asked. Then looked at Frank, who nodded. "What if that's not what *we* want?"

Frida smiled broadly. "Well . . . in that case . . . we'll make sure you get all the proper introductions to all the Lodges here in England, Scotland, Cornwall, and Wales. No one will ask you to help directly if you are too busy with the show, but there is a very great deal that can be done indirectly. If there is a Hunting Party out, for instance, you can scry them and get help if they run into difficulties. There are almost as many layers of history and nasty things on this island as there are in Europe. And of course, there are renegade magicians, like your He-Wolf." She stopped, and her face took on an expression of sadness and sympathy. "I am so sorry about what—"

Annie shook her head. "It's—not quite all right now.

But it will be. And it doesn't change anything between *us*." And she reached over the table to squeeze Frank's hand.

"Well . . . that's the thing about renegade or would-be self-taught magicians like that idiot. They create a trail of unwitting destruction behind them. That's why we try and shut them down before they get a chance to do much harm." Frida looked down at the table, where her hands were sitting, clenched. She relaxed them. "If there had been someone in America who could have done that—he'd never have gotten his hands on you in the first place. But there are not nearly enough mages, much less Masters, to keep up with the need."

Annie nodded. "I think—we should do that. Don't you?" She looked to Frank, who also nodded, soberly. "I think it's important that we do that. And even if we leave the show eventually, the way we plan to travel about, we can cover a *lot* of ground."

"More'n us, minding our little territory in Schwandorf," Jack observed. "That might could be how magicians in America are a-gonna *have* to be, like circuit-ridin' judges. Cain't jest sit in one place. Gotta keep movin'."

Annie felt a sort of peace and certainty settle over her, as if Jack had just outlined what she had only vaguely sensed was the right course. "Then that's what we'll be. Circuit riders. We won't wait to find bad things, we'll flush them out!"

Frank grinned. "That sounds fine!" he proclaimed. "That sounds fine to me! And anything, magician or monster, that wants to hurt people is going to find he has to deal with the silver bullets of Annie Oakley!"

Patrick Rothfuss

THE NAME OF THE WIND
The Kingkiller Chronicle: Day One

"It is a rare and great pleasure to come on somebody
writing not only with the kind of accuracy of language
that seems to me absolutely essential to fantasy-making,
but with real music in the words as well.... Oh, joy!"
—Ursula K. Le Guin

"Patrick Rothfuss has real talent, and his tale of Kvothe
is deep and intricate and wondrous." —Terry Brooks

"[Rothfuss is] the great new fantasy writer we've been
waiting for, and this is an astonishing book."
—Orson Scott Card

Hardcover (978-0-7564-0407-9)
Trade Paperback (978-0-7564-0589-2)
Mass Market Papeback (978-0-7564-0474-1)

10th Anniversary Special Edition Hardcover
978-0-7564-0474-1

www.dawbooks.com

Tad Williams

The Dirty Streets of Heaven

"A dark and thrilling story.... Bad-ass smart-mouth Bobby Dollar, an Earth-bound angel advocate for newly departed souls caught between Heaven and Hell, is appalled when a soul goes missing on his watch. Bobby quickly realizes this is 'an actual, honest-to-front-office crisis,' and he sets out to fix it, sparking a chain of hellish events.... Exhilarating action, fascinating characters, and high stakes will leave the reader both satisfied and eager for the next installment." —*Publishers Weekly* (starred review)

"Williams does a brilliant job.... Made me laugh. Made me curious. Impressed me with its cleverness. Made me hungry for the next book. Kept me up late at night when I should have been sleeping."
—Patrick Rothfuss

The Dirty Streets of Heaven: 978-0-7564-0790-2
Happy Hour in Hell: 978-0-7564-0948-7
Sleeping Late on Judgement Day: 978-0-7564-0987-6

www.dawbooks.com

DAW 207

Nnedi Okorafor

Winner of the World Fantasy Award

WHO FEARS DEATH

978-0-7564-0728-5

"A fantastical, magical blend of grand storytelling."
—*Publishers Weekly* (starred review)

"Both wondrously magical and terribly realistic."
—*The Washington Post*

"Dystopian fantasy at its very best."
—*Library Journal* (starred review)

and don't miss the stunning prequel,
The Book of Phoenix (ISBN: 978-0-7564-1079-7)

www.dawbooks.com

DAW 188